CANTO BIGHT

STAR WARS™

CANTO BIGHT

Saladin Ahmed
Rae Carson
Mira Grant
John Jackson Miller

DEL REY
NEW YORK

Published in the United States by Del Rey, an imprint of
Random House, a division of Penguin Random House LLC, New York.

Del Rey and the House colophon are registered
trademarks of Penguin Random House LLC.

Hardback ISBN 978-1-5247-9953-3
International edition ISBN 978-0-525-48036-5
Ebook ISBN 978-1-5247-9954-0

Printed in the United States of America on acid-free paper

randomhousebooks.com

2 4 6 8 9 7 5 3 1

First Edition

Book design by Elizabeth A. D. Eno

THE DEL REY

STAR WARS™

TIMELINE

THE DEL REY STAR WARS™ TIMELINE

A long time ago in a galaxy far, far away. . . .

CONTENTS

War is returning to the galaxy. As the First Order prepares to unleash their power on an unsuspecting New Republic, the only true opposition is the Resistance. Safe places are growing scarce, except on Cantonica.

Emerging from the endless sands is Canto Bight, a city of excess and indulgence. In this luxurious escape for the wealthy and unscrupulous, dreams are made reality and the prospect of war brings only the opportunity for profit.

Even as the darkness grows, visitors chase their fortunes enthralled by the glamour and thrill of the casino city. The fate of the galaxy matters little amid the glittering brilliance of Canto Bight. For whatever happens, Canto Bight prospers. . . .

RULES OF THE GAME

By SALADIN AHMED

CHAPTER 1

AS THE *CANTONICAN DREAM* DROPPED OUT OF HYPERSPACE, KEDPIN Shoklop sneezed loudly and blew his nose-slits, then smiled apologetically, blinking his big single eye in what he hoped his seatmate would understand was a placating gesture.

His seatmate, a well-dressed, broad-shouldered specimen of some fanged-and-horned species Kedpin didn't recognize, growled. But Kedpin had plenty of experience dealing with grumpy customers. The key, he always told his co-workers, was a cheerful attitude.

"So! Canto Bight!" Kedpin said to his seatmate, filling his voice with fellow-feeling. "Playground of the most glamorous beings in the galaxy! Big-money card games and high-stakes fathier races! The galaxy's biggest artificial ocean! And the fanciest food this side of Coruscant. I can't believe I won this trip!" Against all odds, Kedpin had been named VaporTech's Salesbeing of the Year and received an all-expenses-paid two-standard-week getaway to Canto Bight! Everyone had been so shocked! When the admin-droid had read his name out loud, Kedpin had hardly believed it himself, though he'd imagined the moment ten thousand times over the decades. He'd won. He'd doubted the competition for years, wondered whether he was getting a fair shake. But Kedpin kept on following the rules and doing his best, like he'd always been taught. Like he'd done for a hundred years.

And now he was on his way to claim his reward. The voyage had already been more luxurious than anything Kedpin had ever experienced. Such snacks they had! But that was nothing compared with what was coming. He would finally get to see the legendary Canto Casino, get a zero-g massage at Zord's Spa and Bathhouse, and, most exciting of all, watch a live fathier race!

"I can't believe I'm really here!" Kedpin said again. His seatmate simply ignored him now, turning away rudely to stare out the viewport. But Kedpin was on his first vacation in a hundred years, and he wasn't going to let anything bring him down.

The captain of the *Cantonican Dream* announced that they were now in orbit around Cantonica. Kedpin's seatmate had brusquely claimed the viewport seat when the trip began, but by twisting and craning Kedpin could get a decent view. What he saw made all three of his hearts race.

Pink, blue, and green nebulae shimmered against the jet-black space-scape, which went on forever. Every bit of it was studded with sparkling stars. Closer—so close Kedpin felt he could reach out and touch them—Cantonica's moons hung glowing in the darkness. Kedpin had been offworld a few times to meet with VaporTech clients or to attend conferences, but the company had always booked him in cramped, viewportless personnel transports. He'd never seen space like this. It was *beautiful*.

Cantonica itself was a dull yellow-brown orb swirling with sand-colored clouds. As they began to descend, the bright lights of a massive city—Canto Bight itself, Kedpin realized!—formed a glowing patch on the planetscape. But one feature dominated the view: a great turquoise spot, unnaturally precise in its borders. The Sea of Cantonica.

The viewport shutters lowered and Kedpin was instructed to sit back as the ship came in to land. A short while later, after a brief struggle with his luggage floater, Kedpin was herded into the line for Cantonican Planetary Controls. He was called to a booth staffed by a uniformed human male with a neat beard and an irritated expression.

"Good morning and welcome to Cantonica," the man said, though he didn't at all sound as if he meant it. He took Kedpin's datapad. "Name?"

"Kedpin Shoklop." *Turn their growl into a grin,* Kedpin repeated to himself silently. He smiled at the annoyed-looking officer and added, putting extra nectar into his words, "But call me Ked! All my friends do!"

"No," the man in the uniform said. "Species?"

"Wermal."

"Homeworld?"

"Werma Lesser."

"Sponsoring agent?"

"VaporTech! I won this trip, you see. I'm the VaporTech Vaporator Salesbeing of the Year!"

For the first time the man really looked up from his terminal, and Kedpin wished he hadn't. "Yeah, that sounds about right." He looked as if Kedpin were a pest he wanted to squash! "Is it your intent to act as an active agent of any political, parapolitical, military, or paramilitary organization while on Cantonica?" he asked finally.

Kedpin blinked his eye. He didn't quite know what he was being asked. He blinked again.

"He wants to know if you're a spy for the First Order or the Resistance," someone in the line behind Kedpin said.

"Ha! *Ha!*" Kedpin laughed. "A spy?" There was no fighting on his homeworld—not yet. But Kedpin had heard unbelievable stories from VaporTech salesbeings who'd been caught in the battles. It all sounded perfectly terrible, and Kedpin wanted nothing to do with any of it. "No, no of course not!"

The man looked at his datapad. "You work for VaporTech, huh?"

"Yes, sir! One hundred and two years selling vaporators! Cut me and I bleed VaporTech processed moisture!" Kedpin laughed a small laugh. "That's just a little joke I make."

"Uh-huh," the officer said. "Well, you're missing your sponsorship chip."

"My what?"

The man ran his thick hand through his thick beard and sighed, even more annoyed for some reason Kedpin didn't understand. "Come with me, sir."

Kedpin was taken out of one line and moved to another. The beings in this line didn't look like tourists. They looked different. Scarier. They looked to Kedpin like the sort that caused *trouble*. Kedpin didn't know why he was being placed in this line, but he knew there had to be a reason. Canto Bight was a classy operation. There were rules.

Kedpin was placed in line behind a tall, gaunt, silver-skinned being covered in sharp, bony spurs. It looked like an angry woman made out of knives. When the guard walked away, the creature began to rattle its "knives" at Kedpin, who yelped.

A friendly tale is half the sale was another of Kedpin's favorite Salesbeing's Sayings. "So! How was everyone's flight over? Are you folks tourists, too?" he said to no one in particular. No one in particular answered him.

"Sharpie don't like the way yuh smell," said the knife-woman suddenly in a high-pitched voice. "Sharpie might have to *cut* the smell outta yuh." She began to rattle her blades again. *She's some sort of miscreant trying to frighten me,* Kedpin told himself. *The authorities won't let her harm me. There are rules!*

Sure enough, at that moment another human in a different uniform—an old woman with a cybernetic arm—approached, taking Kedpin's data card and scanning it in a reader. Something on her device made an unpleasant pinging noise. "Ah, Karabast," she muttered. *"Hey, Ohlos!"* she shouted across the big hall to the bearded man who'd first seen Kedpin. "Why didn't you *say* this guy was on a sponsored visa? Do you know he's missing his sponsorship chip?"

"Of course I know he's missing his chip, Lorala!" the bearded human shouted back, even though he was now walking over. "That's why he's in the police line instead of in my line! He's your problem now."

The old woman shook her head at Kedpin's datapad. "Yeah, well if we file this, the datawork is gonna take *both* of us all day," she said to the bearded man. She looked around and lowered her voice. "What do you say we let him go, Ohlos? He's clearly just an idiot tourist. And I want to get home sometime this cycle."

Idiot? Kedpin blinked his eye rapidly. Had he heard correctly? This woman was a duly appointed officer representing one of the most sophisticated planets in the galaxy. But she was nothing like the smiling officials who greeted visitors in the holovids Kedpin had seen. *I'm sure she's just tired,* Kedpin told himself. *Humans can be very grumpy when they're tired.*

The man with the beard shrugged. "I don't know nothin' about this. You get caught skipping forms by the brass, you're the one who's bantha fodder." He walked away muttering.

The old woman handed Kedpin his datapad and pointed to the hall's huge exit doors. "All right, sir. You're free to get your bags and go. Don't cause any trouble and there won't be any trouble. Enjoy yourself, but remember: Canto Bight PD is watching."

Minutes later Kedpin found himself standing outside the massive main building of the Canto Bight spaceport, his luggage floater beside him. For a few long moments he could only stare. He couldn't help himself. The fancifully landscaped greenery, the musical fountains, the soothing scent-clouds that roiled around—it was all so much more vivid than it had been in the holovid! But the crowd was what really made Kedpin stare. There were at least a dozen species represented, many of which Kedpin had never seen before. All of them looked immaculate and were luxuriously dressed, with no sign of having traveled half the galaxy to get here. And it was as if their outfits were in some competition with one another for grace and elegance. Walking among them, Kedpin felt clumsy and out of place.

Kedpin pushed his luggage floater along down a tree-lined walkway, following the signs for transit. The broad path passed under a huge arch of red stone that glinted in the midmorning sun. He remembered seeing this landmark in the holovids—the Great Arch was a remnant of Old City, preserved to teach visitors about the history of Canto Bight. As Kedpin passed under the arch, a being with a datapad and some sort of indistinguishable badge approached him.

"Luggage pass, sir?" The blue, tentacled being, obviously an official of some sort, was another species Kedpin had never seen. But they had a friendly face. The sort of potential customer who came as a blessing after a string of hard sales.

"Luggage pass?" Kedpin repeated.

The being scanned Kedpin with their datapad then looked at Kedpin's face, their blue tentacle-fingers twitching. "Kedpin Shoklop?" they asked in a kindly voice.

"My friends call me Ked!" Kedpin said, smiling widely.

"Well, I'm the acting gate agent here, Ked." They flashed their badge quickly, though Kedpin still had no idea what the badge said. "Where's your luggage pass, my friend?"

"Luggage pass?" Kedpin asked. No one had said anything about this to him. He hadn't seen anyone *else* get a luggage pass. Others seemed to be passing through the arch without one.

The gate agent's eight yellow eyes widened in unison. "You mean they didn't sell you a luggage pass?" they said, outraged.

"Do I need one?" Kedpin asked.

All eight of the gate agent's eyes expressed regret. "Yes, Ked. As a first-time visitor, you can't bring your bags into Canto Bight proper without a luggage pass. The standard fee is one hundred credits or equivalent assessed currency."

"B-but I was told this was an all-expenses-paid trip!" He blew his nose-slits. The air here was irritating his breath-cavities.

The gate agent wrung their blue tentacles. "I'm not sure about that, Ked. You'd have to file a claim with the awarding agent. In the meantime, though, we'd have to hold your bags at the spaceport."

"But . . . but I *need* my things!" Kedpin insisted. Wermals like Kedpin needed moisture. There was no way he would be able to enjoy his vacation without his collection of personal vaporators, humidifiers, and moisturizers. Not to mention his eye wipes!

The gate agent looked around. "Well, Ked, this seems like an honest mistake on your part. I *could* file an exemption claim for you. If you're able to settle the fee with me now, I can even include the luggage transit fee. That way you don't need to push that floater halfway across town."

Make the buy as easy as you can, and soon they'll put money in your hand. It was one of Kedpin's sayings, and he could see it at work here. This gate agent clearly made a nice business of charging an outsized "fee" to tourists. But it seemed that was how things were done here.

The fee took him way past his budget for the day, but it didn't seem like he had much choice. There were rules, after all. And his bags would be waiting at the hotel when he got there!

A few minutes later, with the help of his new friend the gate agent, Kedpin's belongings were loaded onto a cargo speeder headed for the Canto Casino Hotel. And Kedpin himself was scooting along in a shiny limospeeder, as excited as he could possibly be to begin the vacation of his dreams.

CHAPTER 2

ANGLANG LEHET STOOD AT THE NORTHWEST CORNER OF PIAZZA CANTO Bight, towering over most other beings around him and soaking in the heat of Cantonica's late sun through the leathery crest of his oblong head. Unlike the furred and feathered beings of the galaxy, Caskadags like Anglang needed *heat.* Anglang had been a company man for a century. He had learned to adapt when, over his 102 years of grim work for the Syndicate, professional requirements had called for him to travel to some near-sunless world or some ice-sheathed moon to steal or kill. But Anglang had been born on a desert world, and, whatever the planet, few things made him happier than basking in the desert sun.

The delicious sunlight aside, however, credit-grubbing despoilers had mostly ruined *this* desert. Over the decades, Cantonica had been warped and twisted. Once it had been a quiet, dusty world dotted with ancient, half-buried cities. A world of sand mynocks and smugglers' hideouts. A desert with desperate people living among the ruins of some civilization no one remembered. Once Cantonica had been the sort of place the Right Kind of People could use to lie low or ply a quiet side hustle—a place where the hard and the clever survived. Now the planet had become home to Canto Bight, the most glamorous casino city in the galaxy. Quiet crooks' bars gave way to luxury stim-mist parlors. Impossibly expensive yachts full of the galaxy's most important people sailed an ocean that had appeared out of nowhere. Cantonica had become an embroidered pillow beneath which the wealthy hid from conflict as they got even richer off it. A playground for spoiled beings whose crimes were above even the Syndicate's scale. So the Syndicate had moved on to other worlds.

But none of that was Anglang's problem. He no longer worked for the Syndicate. New operatives, of course, were told *Once you're in, you're in for life.* But as with everything involving the Syndicate, it was just a matter of money and turf and seniority. There were rules to this thing, and Anglang followed them. After 102 years of work, he paid the appropriate fee to the appropriate people and bought his freedom. The agreement was simple, unstated, and sacred: Anglang would stay out of his former employers' way, and they wouldn't kill him. He just needed a score big enough to hit the stars with and live on for a while. Open war between the First Order and the Resistance was coming, even if few had seen it so far. Anglang had decades of life before him, and he intended to live it out as far as possible from guerrillas and stormtroopers shooting at each other. But for that he needed money. And that meant doing a job, freelance.

Anglang found that job on Cantonica. A good old-fashioned send-a-message hit job courtesy of Canto Bight's once notorious Old City Boys. The gang had been there before the Syndicate and remained after the Syndicate had moved on, plying petty crimes away from the lights of the casinos, and dodging the cops. Recently they'd lost one too many members to the notorious brutalities of the Canto Bight Police Department's Officer Brawg, a notoriously corrupt and vicious beast who ran the night desk at CBPD. Anglang had dealt with a lot of different cops on a lot of different worlds. In general the CBPD was better than most. Not savages bent on breaking limbs, but agents of the orderly spending of money. Nonlethal force was the order of the day on Cantonica. Cooperative policing, they called it. Hospitality training. There were still a few old-school head-crackers in the CBPD. But nowadays the cops here mostly ferried belligerent drunks off the

strip to sober up, then turned them around so they could start spending money again.

At least that's how it was for the visitors with money. The scam-
mers and hustlers who made their livings off visitors got different
treatment. And, the Old City Boys had told Anglang, they got the
worst treatment from Officer Brawg. Two and a half meters tall and
covered in purple fur, Brawg was the dirty cop who specialized in
brutalizing Canto Bight's out-of-view and rarely discussed street
criminals. A torturer, extortioner, and bully. He was hated enough by
the Canto Bight underworld that they wanted him dead, and hated
enough by his fellow CBPD officers that they probably wouldn't put
too much effort into avenging him. Anglang had never met Brawg,
but he knew the type of cop intimately. He'd had his bones broken
more than once by said type. Anglang had killed dozens of beings
over the decades. He rarely took pleasure in it. In some cases taking
out a target had even made him feel bad. But none of that mattered.
Contracts weren't about his feelings. They were *work*. Still, Anglang
couldn't help but make an exception and take pleasure in the thought
of killing a bully cop like this Brawg.

Sunlight hit the Alderaanian chinar trees that lined the piazza, and
they exploded with their distinctive scent of spice and fire. Anglang
had smelled sun-sensitive chinar trees like this once before—
fifty-odd years ago, as a young miscreant pursuing the Syndicate's
interests among the irksomely incorruptible citizens of Alderaan.
The trees before him now had been grown exclusively for Canto
Bight from a private, incalculably valuable, seed bank. The last green
remnant of a dead world, in turn bringing life to a dead desert. It was
a gesture intended to inspire, but something about it made Anglang
uneasy. Things had their place, and these trees' place was not here. It
all came at a cost, Anglang knew. He thought of his old friend Stinky
Qal, the crooked contractor who had drowned all these years ago.
How many beings died building their artificial ocean?

Pedestrians stepped respectfully around him as they passed. Anglang was taller than nearly all the other species here, and he knew he
cut an imposing figure in his severe black cloak. He paid the tourists

and the rich idiots little mind as they peered up at him then looked hurriedly away, seeing something dangerous in his eyes. He set his mind back on the job.

The Old City Boys' contract had very specific requirements—this was no simple home ambush, and the money reflected that. It had to be done at the isolated night desk that Brawg worked from—the detox chamber far away from the rest of the station where Brawg was allowed free rein on the natives and the visitors who fell too far below Canto Bight's Standards for Quality of Life. It had to be tonight—Anglang didn't know why, but they were paying extra for the tight time window. And it had to be an explosion. Vicious and flashy, but contained enough that Brawg would be the only cop hit.

Anglang had settled on an ingested remote-operated nano detonator, complete with audio monitor, as the tool for the job. Expensive and hard to acquire, but perfect for the task. To be effective, though, the device would have to be implanted in someone who could get into CBPD and next to Brawg without warranting a Level 2 internal organ scan. That meant someone with no criminal record and no connection to Canto Bight's underworld elements.

Anglang needed a mark. Someone new to Canto Bight, stupid enough to be turned into a living bomb and hoodwinked into jail for the night. Someone fresh-faced enough not to warrant the sort of attention from Brawg that would reveal the device. Fortunately, his contacts had just delivered.

Anglang had a name and a description: a little pink one-eyed Wermal named Kedpin Shoklop was headed his way in a gold limospeeder. An offplanet rube, the winner of some sort of ridiculous sweepstakes, vacationing above his pay grade. He sounded perfect. Now Anglang just needed to find him.

Elegant beings from dozens of different systems milled about the Canto Bight city center. Wealthy younglings, bloated politicians, career gamblers, feted artists. Most were species Anglang had encountered before. Some were species he had killed before.

At last a gold limospeeder—the gaudy kind the transit guild used to make clueless tourists feel important—slid to a halt not ten meters away. Filled with sudden anticipation, Anglang watched the door of the vehicle hiss slowly open. A pink, soft little alien with a big single eye wide with dopey wonder emerged, fumbling with his currency and fretting about his luggage. *Kedpin Shoklop*. A mark if Anglang had ever seen one.

The job was a go.

CHAPTER 3

"SIR, I'M SORRY, BUT I HAVE TO DROP YOU HERE. DRIVERS NEED A SPECIAL license to enter the actual casino zone, and I'm afraid mine has expired. It's only a few blocks from here, though." Kedpin's driver—an actual living humanoid, not a droid, Kedpin marveled, feeling important—looked mortified to be disappointing him.

"It's no problem!" Kedpin said, determined to stay cheerful. "I can see more of the city this way!" He clambered slowly out of the gleaming golden limospeeder. He handed the driver another of the thin little bars of precious white metal he'd received at the spaceport in exchange for his VaporTech-issued voucher card. Kedpin had few of them left.

Kedpin thought about his luggage again. He worried that perhaps he might have been taken advantage of. During the ride to the Canto Bight city center he'd had time to wonder whether there really was such a thing as a luggage stamp. And try as he might, he couldn't find any receipt from the helpful gate agent on his datapad. In fact he had no record whatsoever that his luggage existed! He could only hope that it had arrived at the Canto Casino Hotel safely.

The limospeeder scooted off and Kedpin took a long look around him. Humanoids of several sorts milled about a city square paved with pearly stones and dotted with the Alderaanian chinar trees he'd seen so many times in holovids. At the square's center was a great white marble fountain that played soothing music as it flowed. Kedpin's mood improved immediately. *"Canto Bight Piazza! I'm really here!"* he blurted. A tall being in white arched an irritated eyebrow at him as she passed, but Kedpin didn't care. His vacation had officially begun. Now he just needed to find the Canto Casino Hotel.

Kedpin found he couldn't make heads or tails of his datapad's directions, so he looked around, hoping to ask someone for assistance. He had settled on an extremely tall being with an angled head and a severe black cloak when a sparkling silver protocol droid on treads whirred up to him and addressed Kedpin in a matronly, cultured accent.

"Good sir, forgive me my presumption, but are you having difficulty navigating our beautiful city?" the droid asked, her eye-lights flashing green in unison with her words.

"Oh! Why yes, as a matter of fact," Kedpin replied, happy for help. "I'm trying to find the Canto Casino Hotel."

"Ah, an excellent choice, sir," the droid whirred. "As classic as they come. Spectacular accommodations and exemplary service. I'd be happy to show you the way. But first let me ask you: Have you been properly welcomed to Canto Bight?"

Kedpin didn't know how to answer that. "I . . ."

"What I am asking, sir, is whether you have been welcomed in the spirit of luxury, of indulgent pleasure, that truly *defines* our city?"

"I . . . don't know?" Kedpin answered honestly, blinking his eye self-consciously.

The droid made a low whistling noise and fluttered her eye-lights. "Oh you would *know*, sir. You *should* know! You *could* know. If you wish to."

Kedpin blinked again. He was confused. "I'm not sure what . . ."

"Sir," the droid asked, a note of reproach entering her voice, "do you want to go home having seen only the surface of Canto Bight? Or do you want to see *all* we have to offer here?"

"Oh, I definitely want the full experience!" Kedpin said, excited again. "I'm going to see a real fathier race! Live!"

"Sir, I have something much more exciting than fathiers to show you. Something for the truly discriminating. Will you put yourself in my capable hands?"

Again, Kedpin didn't quite know what the right answer was. But he certainly didn't want to be rude. *Yes opens more doors than no,* he recited to himself. "Um, okay?"

"Follow me, sir," the droid said, and Kedpin followed her fifty meters down the street, to an ornately decorated storefront of shimmering pink metal. The doors whooshed open and a wave of delicately perfumed air wafted out, irritating Kedpin's nose-slits. He sneezed loudly.

"This way," the droid murmured pleasantly, leading Kedpin inside.

It was darker inside, dim enough that Kedpin felt his pupil dilate. They were alone in the building's large front room, which was lit by smoky half lamps and decorated with strange sculptures. Kedpin didn't know anything about art, but they looked expensive. The droid led Kedpin down a long hallway, her delicate treads whispering across the room's plush purple floor. They came to a door of golden wood, decorated from top to bottom with engravings of various beings kissing and touching one another.

"Behind this door, sir, is one of the galaxy's truly unique pleasures. I have no doubt you are bold enough to take a taste of it. Do you consent?"

Not once in his century and a half of life had Kedpin been called bold. He liked it. And after all, he didn't want to insult the droid he was counting on to guide him to his hotel. "Um, yes?" he managed to get out.

The droid knocked three times on the golden door, and it slid open slowly, almost teasingly. The droid ushered Kedpin into the room, then withdrew, closing the door behind her. The room was smaller than the front room had been, but it had high ceilings. It was completely bare, save for a large bathing vessel filled with what looked like mud. Opposite the door Kedpin had entered through was a set of unadorned double doors four meters high. Kedpin had only been standing there a moment when they swung open.

A massive, rocky alien, like a three-meter-tall boulder with arms and legs, lumbered out. It wore makeup and ribbons and an incongruously tiny outfit that Kedpin realized was intended to make it look like a child's toy. It took a big, booming step toward Kedpin, grabbed him by the shoulders, and hoisted him up with its huge, hard hands.

"You such a pretty boy! But you such a bad boy!" the creature shouted in Kedpin's face, its voice like a landslide. A third rocky hand sprouted from the alien's chest, and it began to gently pet Kedpin's head. Kedpin felt a hundred strange things at once.

"Pretty! But bad!" the creature repeated, stopping its not-unpleasant petting. It suddenly lifted Kedpin above its head. *"Such a bad boy!"* it said again, and slammed Kedpin bodily into the tub of mud.

"Ow!" Kedpin shouted. The mud was warm and smelled like flowers. For a moment he just sat there, stunned, as the alien withdrew and the silvery droid reentered.

"That hurt," Kedpin told her as he climbed out of the tub. Every drop of the mud—not normal mud at all, Kedpin realized, but some inorganic substance—slid off his body and rolled along the floor to re-pool in the tub. He was completely clean now! "I think there's been some mistake. Can I ask you now to *please* point me to the Canto Casino Hotel?" Kedpin asked.

The droid's eye-lights blinked pleasantly. "Of course, sir, I'd be happy to! And I do hope you have enjoyed yourself. You are one of a select few beings in the galaxy to have experienced Sweetheart's irreproducible ministrations, after all. I trust you were pleased?"

Kedpin blinked rapidly, unsure how to answer. "Every dish tastes great to someone!" he said at last, reciting one of his Salesbeing's Sayings. He'd learned long ago that he sold more vaporators when he pretended to like things his clients liked.

The droid made a sort of purring noise. "Now. There is just the small matter of the fee for Sweetheart's exquisite services." Rather than presenting Kedpin with a simple data card, the droid produced a small, thin plaque of wood, burned a number and a fanciful calligraphic pattern into it with a laser, and handed it to him.

Kedpin didn't understand. Was he being charged *money* for being thrown into a pile of mud? The fee was a month's pay for Kedpin. He'd have almost none of his saved-up spending money left. But rules were rules, and even if Kedpin hadn't meant to, he had hired . . . whatever that rocky alien was to . . . do whatever it had done to him. Feeling as though it physically pained him, Kedpin passed the droid most of his little slivers of precious metal.

The droid gave Kedpin a blue thank-you flower, a piece of candy, and directions to the Canto Casino Hotel, which was only two blocks away. He stepped out onto the street and could feel his pupil contract immediately from the sun, so much brighter than the sun at home.

Kedpin sneezed in the sandy air and blew his nose-slits. He resolved to be a bit more cautious in dealing with this sometimes surprising city. Then he headed for the Canto Casino Hotel, still determined to have the vacation of a lifetime.

CHAPTER 4

ANGLANG SAT AT THE OUTDOOR TABLES OF THE CAFÉ RADULI, SIPPING the blue honeycup that some called the best in the galaxy, and waiting for Kedpin Shoklop to emerge from the shimmering pink façade of V-333's Silken Parlor. Blue honeycup was one of Anglang's very few indulgences. He relished the piquant sweetness, knowing he wouldn't have time to finish the whole cup. Anglang had watched the soft little fool stumble out of his limospeeder, apparently already having been conned out of his luggage, and bumble around the city center, wondering which way to go, until he'd been roped in by V-333 and her treat shop for depraved richlings. The idiot probably had no idea he was about to spend half his vacation budget on thirty seconds of "pleasure."

A clueless buffoon, like all of those who visited Cantonica these days, though most of the fools in Canto Bight were rich enough to disguise their foolishness more effectively. Caskadags lived longer than many species, and he knew this meant he was slower to recognize change than some. But even he knew it now—Cantonica had been permanently ruined. Anglang sighed. He would miss the perfect, luxurious heat that warmed his crest now as he sat in the sun. But he would be happy to be done with this job and away from the various sorts of fools that had overrun this planet and given rise to the new city.

First, though, there was a job to do. The device would need to be implanted in the mark by means of ingestion. Anglang figured a spiked drink was his best bet. Then he had to get the mark into Canto Bight PD, at the start of the detox desk night shift. Which meant getting the one-eyed idiot arrested for the right crime. Brawg would be in the detox tank alone, conducting the sorts of "investigations" the other cops put up with but conveniently disappeared for. The blast radius on ingested nano-detonators was tiny. Anglang just needed to get his mark right next to Brawg, then *bam!*

If he was being honest with himself—and Anglang Lehet tried always to be honest with himself—he didn't feel great about this job. It wasn't the target. This Officer Brawg character was clearly the sort of head-cracking scum who deserved death. There was no problem there except the problem of logistics. And the plan involving the ingested detonator was logistically beautiful, the sort that had made Anglang's pulse race with the rush of creativity as he'd come up with it. But having gotten a good look at that stupid surprised-by-everything face, and imagining it being blown up—well, it sat a bit wrong with Anglang. Kedpin Shoklop, huge worried eye constantly agape, was clearly a chump, but he'd done Anglang no wrong. Anglang had hit prestigious targets for the Syndicate for years. He was a professional. Ending his career by using such an utterly clueless civilian as his bomb—well, it wasn't ideal.

Still, this plan was the best plan. The one most likely to end with Anglang alive and paid. And it was one guy. A fool. Hardly Anglang's first unlucky bystander. A fee was a fee, a job was a job. Same as it ever was. Except that this one could be his last for a long time if he played it right. Anglang took another sip of tea.

A door-hole opened in the façade of the Silken Parlor, and Anglang shook himself out of his musings. *Shoklop.* The little pink man emerged and, shocked by the brightness of the sun, yelped loudly enough that Anglang could hear him across the street. Anglang set down his tea and stood slowly, in a manner that wouldn't draw attention.

His mark was on the move.

CHAPTER 5

BY MIDDAY KEDPIN SHOKLOP STOOD STARING, EYE WIDE, AT A BEAUTI-
fully orchestrated splay of coral-and-sand-colored buildings studded
with gleaming black glass and shining white tile. Jewel-hued land-
speeders and speeder bikes of makes and models Kedpin had only
ever seen in holovids hovered in front of the complex, and Kedpin
saw famous faces among the impossibly well-dressed beings min-
gling near the main entrance: Krin Kallibin, the celebrated fathier
jockey! And—

"Oh my! Is that . . . is that *Orisha Okum*!? She must be the most
famous card player in the galaxy!" Kedpin tugged excitedly on the
sleeve of a passerby, who huffed irritably and kept walking.

"The Canto Casino Hotel! *I made it!*" Kedpin shouted, ignoring
the well-dressed beings who frowned at him. *Sometimes you have to
be your own booster rocket:* Kedpin recited the Salesbeing's Saying to
himself silently.

The hotel grounds were dotted with gardens that held not only
Alderaanian chinar trees, but also beautifully radiant plants that his
data card told him were Dagobean brightmoss bushes and tall, luxu-
riant Kashyyyk orchidferns. Their combined scent was subtle and
overpowering all at once. Kedpin's nose-slits quivered on the crest of
a sneeze, but no sneeze came. It was as if his sense of smell were being

pleasantly teased. Nothing in the holovids could have possibly prepared him for this.

Kedpin made his way toward the main entrance, marveling at the variety of species around him. Tall creatures with elongated faces, tiny hovering beings, hulking things on plinths. He had only just stepped inside the palatial double doors when a green-faced, scaly little being even shorter than himself and dressed in black and white approached him as if he were a lord.

"Welcome, my good sir, to the Canto Casino Hotel. My name is Altovan and I exist only to serve. What can I do, sir, to make your experience here one of a lifetime?"

Kedpin had never in his life had a living being address him with such deference. Droids, sure, but that was about it. For a moment he just stood there.

"I . . . oh! My name is Kedpin Shoklop, and I've won a two-week all-expenses-paid trip. I'm the VaporTech Vaporator Salesbeing of the Year!"

The little alien's face scales shimmered happily and he beamed with pleasure at Kedpin's accomplishment. "Why, that's wonderful, sir! Warmest congratulations on your accomplishment and welcome to Canto Bight. Please just give me a moment, and I will check on your arrangements, Master . . . Shoklop, was it?"

"That's me—but you don't need to call me Master!"

The green-faced alien smiled as if Kedpin had told a joke, then bowed his head, and led Kedpin to a computer terminal. His scaly little fingers danced over the keys as he spoke to Kedpin. "Your room is ready for you, sir. It looks like the Hero's Suite has been reserved on your behalf! An excellent choice. If you'd just be so kind as to point out your luggage, I'll happily have it sent to your room."

Kedpin felt his hearts sink. "My luggage!" He'd completely forgotten about the business at the Great Arch. "I gave it to someone who said they'd bring it to the hotel, but . . . well, I think they might have been lying. My . . . my luggage hasn't shown up here, has it? Under my name? Kedpin Shoklop?"

The little alien spread his hands apologetically. "I'm afraid not, sir."

Kedpin moaned. What was he going to do? "I can't believe I gave my luggage to a stranger. I'm an idiot!"

The alien made a soothing noise. "No, no, sir. You are the trusting sort. There's nothing wrong with that, sir. The galaxy could use a few more kindhearted, trusting beings."

Kedpin's breath caught. The opulent lobby was full of guests and casino-goers from a dozen different species coming and going, but Kedpin felt as if he were alone with the little green alien. He smiled. Aside from his mothers, this was the nicest anyone had ever been to him in his life. "Well, thanks. But I still need my personal vaporators. And humidifiers and . . ." He felt himself growing tense again.

The alien cut him off gently. "Well, with those matters at least, sir, we can perhaps help. While we know of course that no things are quite as satisfactory as one's own things, we can easily have an array of personal vaporators, humidifiers, and dermal moisturization packages sent to your room."

It felt like the first real good news Kedpin had been given since arriving in Canto Bight. "You . . . you can?"

"Of course, sir!" the little alien said, clasping his hands. "Why, we wouldn't deserve our—if you will forgive me—unparalleled reputation if we didn't attend to trifles such as this efficiently."

Kedpin almost couldn't believe it. "But . . . Well, I haven't traveled much, you see, but I've stayed at VaporTech Travel Housing several times for business and they *never* do that."

The alien smiled at him. "Sir, if you'll again forgive me a moment of pride, and meaning no insult: This is not VaporTech Travel Housing. This is the Canto Casino Hotel! And speaking of which, where are my manners? This is the midmeal hour—would you care for a bite or two before you retire to your room?"

"That sounds great!" Kedpin said. He hadn't eaten since his very early morningmeal on the *Cantonican Dream.*

Midmeal at the Canto Casino Hotel was unlike anything Kedpin had ever experienced. The holovids didn't do it justice. How could they? Kedpin hadn't seen this many different dishes in his long lifetime, and here they were all together in one meal. Delectables for every palate in the galaxy. He walked through room after room filled with jellies, meats, eating-papers, plants, insects, chew-blubbers, cakes, marrow-bags, pies, carni chips with glaze sauce, hydrosoy sprays, cheeses, kamtro grassticks, and a thousand other foods. In each room Kedpin had only to point to a thing, and it would be brought to his table. The yeast-worm jelly was the most delicious thing Kedpin had ever tasted. It was so good it nearly made him cry.

By the time he was done, he was so full he felt barely able to walk to his hotel room. The room itself was bright and beautiful. The walls were tastefully draped with glimmering tapestries, and the floor was covered in plush rugs that tickled Kedpin's feet as he walked. The huge, perfectly soft sleeping pod fit Kedpin's body as if it were made for him. Within moments of crawling into it he fell into a deep, restful sleep, dreaming of all the new things he'd seen and smelled and tasted.

An hour or so later, Kedpin was woken by a gentle rippling noise at his door. It took him a few moments to realize it was a sort of signal, alerting him to press the intercom button on his sleeping pod. Kedpin rolled over and pressed the flashing blue diamond.

"Master Shoklop, this is Altovan, your hospitality liaison. I am terribly sorry to disturb you, sir, but in your itinerary module you did indicate an interest in visiting Zord's Spa and Bathhouse. Are you still interested in a session?"

With some effort, Kedpin sat up in the squishy sleeping pod. "Oh, yes, please! Very much so!"

"Excellent, sir!" Altovan's voice over the intercom was so full of cheer, Kedpin could almost see the little alien's green scales shimmering. "I'll have an attendant escort you. They will be by your room in precisely thirty minutes."

An olive-skinned human in understated livery—again, Kedpin marveled, not a droid—arrived soon after and guided him on the walk from the Canto Casino Hotel to Zord's Spa and Bathhouse. The man left Kedpin standing in front of the facility's huge façade of sculpted stone. "The hotel is just a short way back the way we came, Master Shoklop. But I've programmed the route into your data card as well, just in case. If you require anything else at all, please don't hesitate to have a Zord's employee contact the hotel's front desk."

As he entered Zord's, scents of soap and seawater steam filled Kedpin's nose-slits. He stared in awe at the sandstone and marble façades and watched beings of all sizes and shapes come and go, each clutching a small white towel. Armed with information from his datapad, Kedpin asked after the services of the renowned masseur Lexo Sooger, whom Kedpin had researched during the voyage, but was told that Zord's most famous employee had left for the day.

The massage itself was nothing short of astonishing. On a few occasions over his more-than-a-century working for VaporTech, Kedpin had displayed what the company termed a "productivity-impacting proclivity for panic." On these occasions VaporTech had required that Kedpin, at his own expense, retain a company-sponsored tension macerator droid. The experience was never pleasant.

But Zord's Spa and Bathhouse was completely different. Kedpin was ushered into an elegantly cobblestoned room and invited to lie on a towel that was draped across the smooth little stones. A vault door was sealed shut behind him. Then a tiny blue masseur roughly the size of one of Kedpin's feet briskly introduced himself as Gven, climbed onto Kedpin's back, and began kneading his flesh with a strength beyond his tiny stature. The sensation was so painfully pleasant that it took Kedpin a few minutes to realize that the gravity in the room was slowly being reduced to zero.

Once aloft, with the tiny, now silent masseur climbing all over him and doing things to his flesh that no one had ever done, Kedpin's mind began to wander. How many times in his life had he been able to do this, Kedpin wondered—to just lie there and think? About something other than vaporator models or client lists or productivity models? At first it was exhilarating. But then it began to terrify him even as it thrilled him. The oddest memories and feelings floated up. Embarrassment from Kedpin's first failed sale, a century past. Resentments against his co-workers that Kedpin thought he had buried decades ago. Shame about good customers with whom he'd been less than honest. Guilt. But eventually even these melted away beneath Gven's pseudopods.

When Kedpin emerged from Zord's the sun was low in the sky, smudging the horizon with hearts-racing oranges and purples that Kedpin's eye had never beheld. The air had cooled enough to be more tolerable, and the sand that had been irritating his nose-slits seemed to have settled. Gentle music and pleasant spices wafted from the cheery cantina next door. He decided to walk back to the Canto Casino Hotel.

Kedpin felt wonderful. His body felt better than it had in years, thanks to his visit to Zord's. But it was more than that. Kedpin felt wonderful *inside,* in a way that felt new to him. He was living his holovids! He had flown through hyperspace on a private cruiser, eaten yeast-worm jelly at the Canto Casino Hotel, had a zero-g massage at Zord's Spa and Bathhouse. And soon he would fulfill his decades-long dream of seeing a real live fathier race. He felt not only as if his fortunes on Canto Bight had turned a corner, but as if his very life had. Everything he had done to get here had been worth it.

Kedpin's data card told him he was just two blocks from the hotel when he was approached by two lanky orange humanoids. Kedpin could not tell them apart except that one wore blue and one wore red. Kedpin thought they looked like they had bad news.

"Pardon us, sir, but are you—" one began.

"—Master Kedpin Shoklop?" the other finished.

"I . . . I am," Kedpin said.

The alien in red said, "We're terribly sorry, sir, but there's—"

The alien in blue stepped in. "—been a problem with your hotel room."

CHAPTER 6

ANGLANG LEHET WATCHED HIS MARK EMERGE FROM ONE OF THE OLD stone archways that fronted Zord's Spa and Bathhouse. Then he took a deep breath and silently counted to twenty.

Zord's, housed in one of the most beautiful Old City–style buildings left on this side of Canto Bight, was a true institution. It wasn't just hype for the tourists: Zord's attendants could make a being of any species feel cleaner and more relaxed than that being had ever felt in its life. Once, many years ago, one of Anglang's Syndicate bosses had insisted Anglang accept a heating wax soak at Zord's as a bonus when he'd taken out a particularly hard target. Anglang had hated the idea, but if one wanted to live long one didn't refuse gifts from one's boss in the Syndicate. Truth be told, those hundred minutes in Zord's wax vat had been some of the most pleasant in Anglang's life. For decades afterward, when he found himself cold and cranky on some hit job or other, the memory of his heating wax soak at Zord's Spa and Bath-house would come to Anglang unbidden.

Anglang reached twenty and shook himself out of his memories. He'd given Shoklop enough distance; time to follow now. Anglang tailed the little man for two blocks, finalizing his approach tactic, when he saw two thin orange beings approach his mark. They were identical as far as Anglang could tell, except that one of them wore red and one wore blue.

Anglang had been away from Cantonica's underworld for years. He didn't know these punks. But he knew their type. And the con they were running was an old and low-rent one, rare on Cantonica: scan someone's data card remotely, pretend to be hotel staff transporting their "guest" somewhere based on some nonsense story, drive the mark out to the desert, and rob him blind. Not the sort of thing they would ever try on the beautiful and important people of Canto Bight. The sort of brutal hustle that only the occasional middling idiot ended up on the receiving end of.

Anglang watched the exchange for a moment, then stood and strode into action, his black cape swirling as he moved. This was *his* mark! He couldn't let these amateurs screw this up. It could take him days to find another chump so perfect for his purposes, and he didn't have that kind of time. He would have to turn this around and make it work somehow.

In the seven strides it took him to reach Shoklop, Anglang improvised a plan to do just that. He had already started cooking up both a story about being a Cantonica Tourist Bureau official and a series of events to gain Shoklop's trust. But this might actually work better.

He walked over to the beings in a way that was meant get their attention, and it worked. The group all looked up—*way* up—as Anglang approached. "Gentlemen," he said in his deepest, most threatening voice as he towered over the twins, cutting off their spiel. "I think you two need to leave this nice man alone."

"Huh? Who're you?" the one in blue asked, startled enough to drop his affected obsequious tone.

Anglang fixed his stare on the twin in blue. Anglang had killed beings. Many beings. Not a few of them with his bare hands. When he wanted to, he could wear this fact in his eyes. And when he did that, not many could meet his gaze.

"I'm someone you don't want to anger," Anglang said, giving a taste of his death stare to the twin in red as well.

They were basic street punks, still children, really. But they weren't stupid. They saw what was in Anglang's eyes, and they mumbled a few words and walked away as quickly as they could without running.

"I must confess, I am *very* confused right now," Shoklop squeaked out. "Did you just chase away my hotel guides? And what's the problem with my hotel room? Nothing serious, I hope!" The little man breathed deeply, as if trying to hold on to some tranquil thought.

Anglang managed to keep from screaming out loud at the fool's naïveté. "There is no problem with your hotel room. Those two were criminals. They were about to convince you that they worked for the hotel, then take you out somewhere and rob you."

The little man's breath grew rapid and shallow. "R-rob me? But this is Canto Bight! City of glitz and glamour!"

Anglang barked a half laugh, but smothered it when he realized the fool was serious. "Well, even a city as elegant as ours has its criminal element, I'm afraid. Pleased to meet you, by the way. I am called Anglang Lehet. I work for the Canto Bight Tourism Commission." Anglang bowed slightly, and Kedpin Shoklop bowed back. It was a thin cover, but it would be enough. Anglang almost never bothered with fake names and long stories—they were a lot of work to maintain, and rarely worth it.

The little man was holding a handkerchief he'd produced from . . . somewhere, and blowing his hideous little nose-slits. The sound made both Anglang's stomachs curdle.

"Well, thank the stars you showed up to stop them, sir! I've already had my luggage stolen or lost or, oh, I don't know, *and* I was thrown into a pile of synthmud by a living boulder," Shoklop blurted. Then he slowed just a bit. "Robbers, you say? Well, I suppose there *are* always those who refuse to work hard and follow the rules."

Anglang grunted. He could almost smell Shoklop's sad sense of reassurance at his commanding "official" presence. A sniveling little creature of order and law. *Pathetic.* But perfect for Anglang's purposes.

"Sounds like you've had a hard first day in Canto Bight, Master . . ."

The little man smiled. "Shoklop! Kedpin Shoklop! But you can call me Ked—all my friends do!"

"Well, Master Shoklop, I'm off duty. Let me buy you a drink to welcome you to our city more properly." Anglang tried as hard as he could to sound pleasant.

The little idiot's face lit up like a laser array. He actually clapped his fleshy little hands together in joy. "That sounds *wonderful*! A real official native host! It seems my luck is turning yet again!"

Anglang sighed quietly and tried to keep his contempt from reaching his face.

Twenty minutes later they were ensconced at a floating table at Klang's Place, drinking crystalmead. It was a cheap bar, the kind Anglang's sort of people gathered at. The sort that was nearly gone from Cantonica. The antigrav on the seats was rickety, but the table at least didn't spill their drinks.

Dropping the tiny, ingestible detonator into Shoklop's drink was simplicity itself. The little alien had a massive eye, but he wasn't particularly observant. Anglang talked to distract Shoklop, but it hardly even seemed necessary.

"So, Master Shoklop, you were saying you won this trip to Canto Bight?"

That big eye beamed and Shoklop pointed to himself with a pink, stubby finger. "That's right! You, sir, are looking at the VaporTech Vaporator Salesbeing of the Year!"

"Well, that certainly sounds like a big deal," Anglang said, almost managing to sound like he meant it.

"You bet it is!" Shoklop said with an enthusiasm that almost frightened Anglang. "Every year, in a big announcement broadcast over the entire company network, one salesbeing is chosen as VaporTech's Vaporator Salesbeing of the Year and awarded a two-standard-week all-expenses-paid vacation. I've been working there long enough to remember when the vacation was to Coruscant. But for the past several decades, it's been to Canto Bight."

Without wanting to, Anglang realized he and Shoklop were roughly of an age.

"A hundred times over a hundred years, I entered my name into the competition. I worked harder than anyone. Followed the rules day in and day out. But every year, someone else won."

Shoklop wobbled in his antigrav seat then steadied himself. The little man was so boring it was almost engrossing. It should have made Anglang want to kill him more, but it just made Anglang tired.

"Every year, you see," Shoklop went on, "the winner is, let's see, how does the announcement go? *Selected by a completely objective algorithm that incorporates original sales, reorders, satisfaction reports, attendance, and other factors.* I never won. I had the most sales, the best customer reports, the most hours logged, but I never won. I started to think it was all fixed. That I'd put in all those years of service to the company for nothing."

"I know what that's like," Anglang said before he realized it.

"But this year, I won! I actually won!" Shoklop beamed, and if Anglang was honest with himself it was hard not to feel happy for the little man. And to feel a bit bad about what he was about to do.

But there was work to do. Anglang smothered the guilty gnawing in his guts and raised his glass.

"A toast, then," he said. "To the big winner, Kedpin Shoklop!" They both drained their drinks. Anglang watched carefully to make certain the detonator had been swallowed.

When he was sure it had been, Anglang moved on to part two of his plan—the contraband that would get his mark detained. From within his sleeve he produced a naturally adherent dermal patch the size of a human thumbnail. He discreetly slid it into the palm of his hand.

"Salesbeing of the *Year!*" Anglang bellowed good-naturedly. Then he bent down and clapped Shoklop on the back. The little alien's clammy skin felt repulsive to Anglang.

The tiny dermal patch attached perfectly, though, and Shoklop didn't seem to notice. Six vacced packets of raw condensed spice. They were only the size of sand grains, but they were a big enough score—and, from what Anglang's inquiries had turned up, precisely the right kind of merchandise—to get Shoklop hand-delivered to Brawg. The spice was fake, of course—Anglang didn't have money like that to burn on props. But it was a good fake, and Brawg would be dead before he could test it.

Anglang let the little fool finish his drink. Then, under pretense of relieving himself, he sneaked off and contacted the back desk of CBPD with an anonymous tip about an easy bust: an offworld spice slinger having a drink at Klang's before trying to unload product in Canto Bight *without* having paid Brawg his mandated, if unofficial, "licensing" fee. Anglang returned and bought Shoklop another crystalmead. *Why not.* They had perhaps ten minutes until CBPD arrived.

"Master Shoklop," Anglang said, handing the little alien the drink and trying to look obsequious, "I'm afraid I have to attend to a brief business matter, but please have another drink on me while I handle this. I'll be back in five minutes."

That huge ugly eye blinked three times. "Oh! Well, I'll be right here! And I keep telling you: Call me Ked!"

Anglang grunted and left the bar. He moved swiftly to a discreet rooftop two blocks away, lay flat, and found the entrance of Klang's through his binocs.

Within moments two sleek CBPD lawspeeders pulled up, each with two big officers inside. They piled out and filed quietly into Klang's, no blasterfire, no stun sticks. *So neat and so polite until they are* certain *it's okay for them to be monsters.* It was a con, as sure as the one those twin orange aliens ran.

Brawg wasn't among the cops there, but it was still late afternoon. According to Anglang's sources, he was probably still sleeping off last night's stim-mist binge. Brawg's cronies would probably stick Shoklop in a cell, maybe rough him up a bit, before Brawg came to deal with him. *Poor idiot.* The thought came to Anglang from nowhere, and he shoved it away.

The entrance to Klang's burst into activity. It took Anglang's binocs a moment to refocus. When they did, he saw Kedpin Shoklop being dragged out of the bar.

Anglang didn't feel good about getting this rube locked up. He didn't feel good about killing the fool, either. But he felt good about the money. He felt good about getting out of the life. This was still the best plan.

CHAPTER 7

THIS CAN'T BE HAPPENING, KEDPIN SHOKLOP THOUGHT TO HIMSELF AS A human officer and a security droid led him from the barred back door of a police lawspeeder through the back entrance of the Canto Bight Police Department. *This can't be happening!*

But it *was* happening. How? Why? Kedpin had been sitting at a floating table sipping his second glass of crystalmead and waiting for Anglang Lehet to return as he'd said he would. The bar's entrance had burst into activity, with uniformed officers shouting orders. Before Kedpin had had time to wonder what was going on, he was slammed onto the none-too-clean floor of Klang's Place, and an officer removed some sort of sticker from his back. The floor had smelled of old liquids that came from bottles and beings' bodies, and Kedpin recalled it with a shudder.

After he'd been loaded into a lawspeeder and they were racing from the bar to police headquarters, Kedpin had tried his usual friendly approach on the officers. But he'd been told promptly and forcefully to shut up. They never even explained to him what crime he was accused of.

Now Kedpin sat locked alone in an isolated cell under the guard of a sole human officer, a kind-faced older man. Kedpin's throat, his eye, his entire epidermis was uncomfortably dry. He'd not had any water or

vaporations since being dragged out of the bar. He had managed not to
cry so far on this trip. But in the still and quiet, as the weight of everything that had happened today crashed down on him, Kedpin Shoklop
was confused. He was upset. He was afraid. This was not at all how his
vacation was supposed to be going. He felt a wail rise from his throat,
and despite his dehydration thin tears began to spill from his eye.

"Hey. *Hey, shut up!*" the kind-faced officer shouted. "You want me
to zap you? You got busted with six grains, pal. I don't know how they
do things where you're from, but in Canto Bight you don't just walk
away from that." He gave Kedpin a nasty smile that burned away his
kind features. "Officer Brawg is gonna wanna talk to you."

"*Spice?*" Kedpin could hardly believe his earholes. "Oh, dear, that's
impossible! There must be some sort of mistake!"

"Yeah. Big mistake," a new voice broke in from the doorway. It
sounded like a garbage crusher. Kedpin turned and saw the most
frightening being he'd ever beheld.

More than twice Kedpin's height and impossibly muscled, Officer
Brawg was covered in coarse purple fur. Thick horns jutted from his
temples, and his eyes looked permanently angry.

Those eyes reminded Kedpin of his Level 3 managerial overseer,
Laz Lazzaz. Laz was Kedpin's least favorite thing about being a VaporTech vaporator salesbeing. He was cruel and lazy and had taken
credit for Kedpin's work more than once. Laz was also the Level 1
managerial overseer's cousin, and Kedpin knew that he received special treatment because of it, despite the company's rules about nepo-
tism. Laz was a human, of course, not near as threatening-looking as
this Officer Brawg. But they had the same eyes.

To make matters worse, Brawg was dragging in another prisoner.
One who looked like she was made out of knives. *Oh, dear.* It was the
same blade-skinned alien Kedpin had seen being detained at the
spaceport. She began taunting Kedpin as soon as she saw him.

"Stinky boy! Sharpie remember yuh! Hooo this Sharpie's best day!
Sharpie gonna cuuuuut yuh!" Kedpin tried not show his fear, and he
hoped desperately that he would not be left alone in a cell with this
creature.

"*Shut up!*" Officer Brawg bellowed at Sharpie, casually bringing a huge fist down on the smooth top of her head. The knife-edged alien collapsed in a whimpering pile, her blades flattened in what Kedpin took to be a show of docility.

"Alabash!" Brawg shouted at the human officer who'd been watching Kedpin. "Get Sharpie here processed and booked. I'm done *talking* to her."

The human officer lifted Sharpie from the floor with surprising gentleness, then turned her toward the hall she and Brawg had come from. "How long you want me gone, boss?"

"Come back in an hour," Brawg said, turning to smile menacingly at Kedpin. "This little creep and me, we're gonna have a *talk.*"

Alabash left, pushing Sharpie ahead of him. Kedpin was alone with Brawg now. In all Kedpin's long life, it had never once occurred to him that one might need to fear the police more than one feared criminals. It occurred to him now, looking into Officer Brawg's eyes.

"Officer," Kedpin began, "there's been some sort of mistake! If you'll just let me—"

Brawg didn't answer. He kept his eyes locked on Kedpin's and slowly began opening the cell door. Kedpin didn't realize he was backing away from the entrance until his back bumped against the wall.

Officer Brawg put one massive fist around each of Kedpin's biceps and lifted Kedpin into the air. Kedpin felt like a doll. He tried not to release his waste fluids, for he knew instinctively that this would make Officer Brawg hit him.

Officer Brawg put his fanged face next to Kedpin's. His breath was hot and dry and it burned Kedpin's face.

"You know what I spend most of my time doing?" Officer Brawg asked, pressing his face even closer to Kedpin's. Kedpin was not the smartest being in the galaxy, but he was smart enough not to answer. "Protecting *special* people," Officer Brawg continued. "Making sure they get to do whatever weirdo escapades they want to do, without them getting hurt. That's what we do at CBPD! Make sure the *special* people and the *beautiful* people stay safe and happy and spending money."

Kedpin tried to stay quiet, but it just wasn't in his nature. *Win them with warm words.* "Well, that sounds nice!" he said.

Brawg threw him to the cell floor. It was hard plasteel, and it hurt a lot more than landing in the synthmud had this morning. Had that only been this morning? It felt like he'd been in Canto Bight for a week already.

"You?" Officer Brawg continued. "You ain't nobody special. Maybe you're a big-dung spice slinger back home. Here you don't even rate. And you sure as hell ain't beautiful. You're just *mine*."

He kicked Kedpin in the stomach. It hurt badly, and he began to cry. "W-why—" he began, but Brawg cut him off.

The huge alien paced back and forth over Kedpin's prone form. "You listen to me now, ugly-meat. Listen good because if I have to say it again I'm gonna be annoyed: You're going down. No way outta that. Question is, how hard are you gonna go down? You ain't gotta take all the pain yourself. Who are you working with? You got a partner? No way you're slingin' all that spice by yourself. Who is it? Another little creep posing as a tourist? Or a local?"

"Officer," Kedpin said, getting to his feet and getting his tears under control, "I told you, there's been a mistake. I would never—"

Officer Brawg's huge fist knocked Kedpin back to the ground. It hurt, but it wasn't as bad as the kick. To his amazement Kedpin found he was growing used to pain. "Stay down there till I say you can get up, creep," Brawg said. "Now let's try again. You had six grains of spice skinned to your shoulder. That don't exactly happen by accident. Who are you working with?"

Kedpin didn't understand crime. He barely understood what he was being accused of. But Kedpin was beginning to realize that someone had set him up. And he was beginning to suspect that it was Anglang Lehet. That friendly moment when he'd clapped Kedpin on the back had felt so wonderful. But now Kedpin wondered how friendly it had been. *He could have planted something on me then,* Kedpin realized.

Should he name the tall alien in black to this Brawg, then? Perhaps that would straighten everything out. There were rules, after all. Criminals were punished and innocent people weren't.

But . . . what if it hadn't been Anglang? The tall alien had been so kind to Kedpin, and he tried to think the best of beings. And Kedpin had been in close contact with plenty of others since arriving in Canto Bight—what if Kedpin's tiny masseur, or the friendly-seeming being who'd stolen his luggage, had been the one to plant contraband on him? Kedpin was sure that anyone he named would be subjected to worse brutalities than he had been, their pleas of innocence similarly ignored. That was wrong.

Criminals were punished and innocent people weren't. But Kedpin was innocent and *he* was in jail. Well, perhaps not *innocent*, exactly. How many vaporators had he sold by exaggerating claims? How many service contracts had he established by being perhaps less than completely honest about the terms? But these things were just part of the vaporator business, and Kedpin certainly wasn't a criminal!

There were rules, but if he was being honest with himself—and *Never lie to yourself about a sale!* was one of his Salesbeing's Sayings— Kedpin knew that sometimes—sometimes—the rules were bent. Maybe, he managed to admit to himself, even twisted. This Officer Brawg was a policeman. Kedpin was supposed to listen to him. To tell him everything. That was what the rules said . . .

"Give me a name, little creep." Kedpin looked into this Officer Brawg's eyes and saw the cruelty of his Level 3 managerial overseer Laz, amplified by a hundred. He knew then that naming another wouldn't save him; it would only condemn a second poor soul to this pain. Just as Laz was never reprimanded, the rules would not punish this monster.

Anglang Lehet had bought Kedpin a drink and toasted his success. When was the last time something like that had happened? He couldn't damn the man to Brawg's clutches. What if he was wrong?

Brawg twisted Kedpin's arm behind his body. Kedpin yelped in pain. He had to tell the officer something. He smacked his lips together, working up enough saliva to speak.

Anglang's room near the CBPD wasn't much, but it was cheap and inconspicuous, rare qualities for lodging in Canto Bight. A good place for him to monitor Shoklop's audio signal and to trigger the thermal detonator when the time was right. Shoklop should be at the back desk alone with Brawg by now. Anglang's research had found that Brawg always questioned low-rent offworld detainees with contraband personally. It was about confiscating their goods, but it was more than that—it was practically a compulsion. Anglang knew Brawg's mentality, had seen it in cops on other resort worlds: furious at having to babysit their vacationing social betters, they took out their fury on the few offworlders low-ranking enough to be vulnerable to their predations.

Anglang turned on the detonator's audio monitor and set the detonator remote before him on the table.

"Yeah. Big mistake." Brawg's voice through the detonator's audio monitor was crackling and muffled, but his words were still clear.

Anglang listened to an exchange between Brawg and another officer, waiting for Brawg to be alone with Shoklop. Beneath the talk he heard a strange metallic scraping sound and what sounded like Brawg roughing up another prisoner.

Mostly he heard Kedpin Shoklop fretting and whining. But beneath it all, as a soft background pattering, Anglang could hear Kedpin Shoklop's hearts beating in terror. It was more upsetting than it should have been. Anglang had heard plenty of men beg for their lives over the course of his career. He'd killed most of them without a second thought. This shouldn't have bothered him so much. *I'm getting old,* he decided. *Long past time to get out of the life.*

Anglang listened for a few minutes while Brawg roughed up Shoklop, wanting to be absolutely certain that the big cop and the little alien were the only ones left near the back desk when he pressed the button. He was raising his hand to press it when Brawg's voice broke in again.

"Give me a name, little creep." Anglang was astonished that Shoklop hadn't mentioned him yet. Why hadn't he? Did he not get that

Anglang had been the one to set him up? Had the crystalmead and the shock done things to the little man's memory?

"I don't know what you're talking about," Shoklop's voice said, sharper and crisper than before. "But I'm not going to help you hurt anyone else."

Anglang moved his hand away from the detonator. *This,* he was not ready for. The rube was showing some backbone! Refusing to snitch. Amazing. Anglang would've put the odds at ten thousand to one.

Anglang wished he hadn't heard that bit. He wished he'd pressed the button a few moments earlier.

It was time to do his job. He'd been paid an advance. There were rules. Brawg wouldn't be alone much longer. If he didn't do this now, he would be botching the job. Anglang looked at the detonator.

A hundred years of work. Clean work. First-class targets. One of the Syndicate's best. This is how it's going to end? Snuffing some rube who refused to snitch on you?

It couldn't be. He couldn't let it be. Anglang had done a lot of things he wasn't proud of over the years, but this just couldn't be the note he ended his career on. Rules or no.

Cursing himself for a fool, Anglang disarmed the nano-detonator.

Anglang dug through his belongings and pulled out his old Syndicate sigil patch and the little lockbox that held his advance from the Old City Boys. The Syndicate wouldn't be happy about him invoking their name now that he was freelance, but Anglang had earned a few indulgences.

He shut off the monitor, headed out the door of his rented room, and prepared to break the rules.

CHAPTER 8

KEDPIN SHOKLOP WOKE FEELING WORSE THAN HE EVER HAD BEFORE TO see Anglang Lehet speaking to Officer Brawg across the back desk of the Canto Bight Police Department.

Kedpin remembered saying, *I'm not going to help you hurt anyone else.* He didn't know where the words had come from, but they'd felt right. Then he remembered a flurry of blows from Officer Brawg. Kedpin realized he must have blacked out in the cell.

"Even if you are . . . affiliated, and this guy is one of yours," Brawg was saying to Anglang, who was flashing some sort of badge, "you got a lot of nerve coming in here trying to get your merchandise back. Most of the cops here would lock you up for flashing that thing. You boys ain't got much clout these days."

Anglang's voice was quiet and placating. It was the voice Kedpin used on an angry customer complaining about a defect. "Oh, this isn't about merchandise, Officer. My employers have already written off any such loss as tribute to the tireless law enforcement officers of Canto Bight. My employers are not interested in recovering merchandise, but in . . . downsizing inefficient operatives." Kedpin didn't know what they were talking about, but the look Anglang flashed him was frightening.

Officer Brawg smiled a nasty smile, and he spoke about Kedpin as if Kedpin weren't sitting right there. "Oh, I get it," he said. "You want your boy back to spank him."

Anglang Lehet just shrugged. "We are, of course, willing to provide appropriate recompense."

"You know, my old man was a cop here in Canto Bight, too," Officer Brawg said, heading toward Kedpin's cell. *What is happening here?* Kedpin was afraid, but he tried not to show it.

"That right?" Anglang said.

With Anglang beside him, Brawg opened the cell. "Eighty years. The old man used to talk about how different it was when the Syndicate was here. How we took care of one another. How there was a pecking order."

"Rules," Anglang Lehet said, handing Officer Brawg a small velvet bag that clinked. Kedpin had the terrible sensation that he was being bought for slaughter.

"Exactly!" Brawg said, grabbing Kedpin roughly and shoving him toward Anglang Lehet. "Anyway, I only bopped him a few times. Little wimp passed right out. I didn't even get ta break nuthin'."

Anglang Lehet took hold of Kedpin ungently and guided him forcefully toward the CBPD exit.

Kedpin knew he wasn't the fastest thinker in the galaxy, but even he was beginning to put together the pieces. "You . . . you're a criminal, aren't you, Anglang?"

The tall alien shrugged, his heavy black cloak shifting like a shadow. As they exited the building, he leaned down to speak into Kedpin's earhole. "If you want to be technical about it, I'm a criminal who's been planning all day to kill you," he said quietly. At first Kedpin thought it was a joke. But he saw no mirth in Anglang's jet-black eyes. "K-Kill me?" he heard himself say stupidly. Kedpin felt sick to his stomach. He stood there for a moment, suddenly overwhelmed by a horrible sense that there was no such thing as paradise and that everyone in the galaxy was a liar.

Then Anglang Lehet pushed him forward and together, they walked out of the jail into the warm Canto Bight night.

CHAPTER 9

ANGLANG LEHET SHOULD HAVE BEEN RIDING IN A SHINY LAND-speeder. But his money was almost gone and he couldn't afford to waste it on indulgences anymore, since there was no money coming from this botched job. In a fit of madness he'd spent his advance on springing some rube he barely knew. So he was walking from CBPD central booking on foot to a less savory corner of the city where he could find a medical droid to remove the detonator from Kedpin Shoklop. The tiny weapon was harmless now, but it was still worth a little something. Not much, but more than nothing, which is what Anglang had now.

He pushed Shoklop ahead of him with a little shove. The little man yelped and it was all Anglang could do not to pound him. This job was supposed to have paid a small fortune. Something damn near retirement money. Instead Anglang was stuck herding this idiot ahead of him and watching his back to make sure no dirty cops were following. All because Anglang's brain had decided to go soft.

"Move!" he barked again at Shoklop. The sun was a mere sliver on the horizon now, and Canto Bight was lit by that painted purpling sky that lasted for only a few minutes each evening. They were nearly alone on the street among the dusty old half ruins. They'd been walking for half an hour and were finally nearing the chop shop Anglang was leading them to.

"Why are you so angry at me?" the little idiot asked, sniffling like a child. He had produced another handkerchief, from where Anglang didn't know and didn't want to. "What did I ever do to you?"

It was so pathetic Anglang almost felt bad. He reminded himself that this sniffling little fool had just stood strong for him against an alien cop five times his size. They turned down a long narrow alley. "It's not you, little man. It's what you're part of. You're just chump change. Nerf-herding lowball tourists like you are just a by-product of this city. It's the rich scumbags and their overpriced drinks. It's—"

"Lehet! Nice night fer a walk!" a coarse voice broke in.

Damn. Anglang *was* getting soft. Old. He'd been so distracted by being pissed off that he hadn't noticed them.

Klatooinians. Maybe five of them who'd just poured out of an alley intersection, wearing Old City Boys colors. Here to break his limbs for botching their job. Maybe even here to kill him. *How did they get word this fast?* Each of them was wielding a thick, stout club or a set of spiked knuckles. Their leader—the one who had spoken—was a notorious brawler named Uk. She wore an eye patch and had a stun stick. Anglang was unarmed. It didn't look good.

"Listen—" Anglang began, when Shoklop broke in, *stepping between Anglang and his assailants!*

"Nice? Why it's a positively *beautiful* night! Are you friends of Anglang's? I'm Kedpin Shoklop, but you can call me Ked!" All the wounded confusion of a moment ago was gone, and the little man was all extroverted good cheer.

Shoklop knew damn well the Klatooinians were there to hurt them, Anglang realized. He was trying to soothe them. In his own strangely brave little salesman's way, he was trying to handle the situation. In answer, one of the Klatooinians slapped Shoklop and the big-eyed man began to whimper, hurt and shocked.

Anglang spoke to Shoklop but kept his eyes on the Old City Boys. "These beings aren't my friends, little man. They are going to try to kill me and they are weighing whether it is worth killing you, a tourist, too. Get out of here and keep your mouth shut about what you've seen. Go. Now!"

Shoklop gave Anglang a long, pained look. Then he ran back up the alley the way they'd come. The little man just would have been in Anglang's way anyway.

The Klatooinians snorted and chortled watching Shoklop shuffle away. Then Uk turned back to Anglang. "'Fore we get started, bosses wanted me ta ask ya: Why's Brawg still alive, Lehet? You get scared? You don't seem the type ta turn coward."

The Old City Boys moved into position to surround him, their fists and weapons up.

Anglang turned his head slowly, trying to keep his eyes on all his enemies. Were there five? Six? Too many, regardless. If it'd been humans maybe, but Klatooinians . . . "Not scared," he said, buying time.

Uk peered down her stun stick with her one good eye as if examining it for straightness. "Then what? Bosses really wanna know. Ya can't just bail on a job like that, Lehet. There are *rules* to this thing."

The stun stick! If he could get his hands on it, he could disable the field restraint safety and knock *all* these idiots out. *If.* Ah, well. Anglang tensed. "Screw the rules," he said, without quite knowing why.

Everything exploded into movement.

Anglang hated Klatooinians. One punch from Anglang could floor most humanoids, but his assailants weighed one hundred kilos each and fought like rabid beasts.

Still, with a series of sweep kicks and a few throat punches he managed to take two of the dog-faced aliens out of the fight. The remaining four surrounded him, closing the circle tighter.

"You always were a tough guy," Uk said. The stun stick sparked menacingly. If Anglang could just get his hands on it!

But Uk saw his plans in his eyes. "You want this?" she asked. "Here." She jabbed Anglang.

Anglang tried to wrest the stun stick from Uk as she jabbed him, but the pain of the electricity coursed through his veins like white fire. He screamed. Another jolt like that and he'd be out cold. Two more and he'd be dead.

It would have been nice to have had Cantonican cactus liqueur one last time, Anglang Lehet thought. He prepared to die.

CHAPTER 10

KEDPIN SCUTTLED OUT OF THE ALLEY, THANKING THE STARS THAT HE had escaped with his life. Then he heard the sounds of fighting behind him, and his relief was eclipsed by sudden, overwhelming shame. It didn't make any sense. Anglang Lehet was an admitted criminal. A criminal who had framed him and planned to kill him. And besides, Kedpin was no fighter. Kedpin did everything he could to avoid ever being hit. And he cried when people hit him.

Kedpin wasn't a fighter and this wasn't his fight. Why should he feel shame? It was ridiculous. He kept walking, ignoring the guilty gnawing in his guts.

He was almost out of the long, narrow alley when he heard the violent crackling of electricity and Anglang Lehet's scream.

Kedpin froze in his tracks. Whatever the big alien had been planning, when it had come down to it, Anglang Lehet had not let him die. How could Kedpin leave him like this?

Be bold in the sale and you'll surely prevail; Kedpin had written that one decades ago, but he didn't think he'd ever quite lived it.

Summoning something within himself that he couldn't quite name, Kedpin Shoklop turned around and raced back into the alley.

Anglang Lehet was preparing to die when a bright pink ball of flesh came hurtling at the Old City Boys from behind, screaming something about payback and vaporator sales. *Shoklop!*

Shoklop's soft little form was no match for the Klatooinians, of course—he merely crashed off them, having managed only to knock himself down. But it was all the help Anglang needed. While the Old City Boys were distracted, Anglang grabbed onto the stun stick that had just been used on him and bodychecked Uk as hard as he could. It normally would have been a fool's move, but she was surprised enough that it worked. He wrested the stun stick from her grasp and backed up three steps.

Anglang smashed the capacity safety module on the end of the stun stick, pointed it toward the Klatooinians, and pressed the activator button.

The stunfield pulse shot out in a fan shape, a visible wave of energy hitting all three remaining Klatooinians and instantly knocking them flat. The weapon sparked and grew hot, and Anglang dropped it. The smell of burnt ozone filled the air.

For a moment Anglang just stood there in shock, as immobile as the comatose Klatooinians. Then Kedpin Shoklop's cries roused him. The little pink alien was trapped under one of the Old City Boys, who'd apparently staggered back from the stun stick blast and collapsed on top of him.

Anglang rolled the dog-faced creature off his unlikely rescuer. Anglang was impressed in spite of himself. Shoklop couldn't fight worth a damn, of course, but he'd come back and *tried to,* which showed more grit than Anglang had thought the little pink fool capable of. And he just might have saved Anglang's life. "Not bad, little man," he said. "Not bad."

"Well, when I started out, VaporTech used to send me to sell vaporators door-to-door in the Grime Quarter. I guess I learned a thing or two about fighting!"

Anglang bent over Uk and her henchbeings, rifling through their pockets. All told, enough to get by for a week or so. Not much. But not much was always better than nothing.

Shoklop's too-loud voice broke in on his thoughts. "Are you *stealing* from these beings?"

Anglang shrugged. "It's not stealing. They tried to kill us. It's how this works. Rules."

Anglang looked at Shoklop. "As a matter of fact, put out your hand, little man." He put a few slivers of precious metal into Shoklop's pink, soft palm. "It's not much, but you helped knock heads, so some of it's yours. Maybe enough to replace some of the things you lost in your luggage."

Anglang noted with surprise that Shoklop didn't protest or refuse. He simply closed his hand around the money. "Forget my luggage," the little man said. "Let's go to the races."

CHAPTER 11

KEDPIN SHOKLOP STOOD IN THE STANDARD CLASS STANDS OF THE Canto Bight racetrack, taking in the scents and sounds of a lifelong dream fulfilled. He was about to watch a live fathier race on Canto Bight! Unlike the spacious, well-appointed Prestige Class viewing boxes that Anglang Lehet had pointed out resentfully, the Standard Class stands were crowded and less than pristine. Beings pressed in on every side, shouting out numbers and fathier names. But as they'd moved through the city together, Kedpin had noticed that other beings tended to make way for Anglang Lehet. The racetrack had been no exception. They had a splendid view of the track.

Kedpin had seen fathiers on the holovids, of course, but being this close to them was something different entirely. The power and grace with which they moved, the noise they made, the stinky-spicy *smell* of them as they sauntered past and lined up for the start of the race—the holovids couldn't capture any of this, Kedpin realized. He could almost reach out and touch one of the beasts. Perhaps he'd get a chance to. This was no holovid; he was *here*. After years and years of dreaming, after the strangest and hardest and maybe best day of his long life, Kedpin Shoklop was here, about to watch a real live fathier race in Canto Bight.

At Anglang's advice, Kedpin's money was on a veteran fathier a little past his prime. The beast's name was Kessel Runner.

The starting signal fired, and the fathiers launched into beautiful motion. Kedpin felt his pulses pounding uncontrollably as he watched the fathiers run. Though Anglang Lehet hadn't bet on the race himself, he was cheering loudly—shouting in that booming baritone—for Kessel Runner, Kedpin's fathier. Kedpin thought himself as happy in this moment as he'd ever been in his life.

The announcer's voice rang out over the speaker system, almost too fast for Kedpin to follow.

"AND THEY'RE INTO THE HOMESTRETCH! KESSEL RUNNER IN THIRD, MYNOCK MINUTE JUST AHEAD IN SECOND, AND LEADING THE PACK IS SHIFTING SANDS!"

"Come on! Come onnnnnn you stinker! Put on the juice!" Kedpin heard himself shouting. Anglang Lehet turned briefly from the race to look at Kedpin, and Kedpin saw that the big man was smiling.

"SHIFTING SANDS LEADS, BUT KESSEL RUNNER HAS JUST PASSED MYNOCK MINUTE AND IS COMING UP FAST! BY THE STARS, FOLKS, KESSEL RUNNER AND SHIFTING SANDS ARE NOW NECK-AND-NECK! THIS IS GOING TO BE A CLOSE ONE . . ."

Kedpin Shoklop held his breath until it felt as if he'd forgotten how to breathe.

"AND IIIIIIIIT'S . . . KESSEL RUNNER BY A NOSE, FOLKS! WHAT A RACE!"

Kedpin Shoklop slowly released the breath he'd been holding. His three hearts hammered in his chest. He felt dazed and thought he might fall over, until Anglang Lehet bent down, grabbed him by his shoulders, and bellowed in his face.

"You won, little man! You won!"

"W-won?" Kedpin repeated stupidly. Then it washed over him. It was the mini jackpot! A year of earnings! "I won! I won! I won!" Kedpin was not much of a dancer, but he began to do a little dance.

"Well blast me, you little son of a Jawa, you sure did. Talk about beginner's luck!" Anglang clapped him on the back, then laughed, a sound like low thunder.

"Don't worry, no implants this time!"

Kedpin laughed. *This must be what it's like to have a friend.* The thought came unbidden, out of nowhere, and it nearly stopped Kedpin's hearts. Could a being Kedpin had only known for hours, a being who had planned to kill him, be a friend? Kedpin realized he didn't know much about friends. Work had always mattered more.

"Oh! I have to celebrate! That's what you're supposed to do, right? Anglang, will you join me? Please?"

Anglang Lehet looked at him for a long moment. Kedpin recognized the look. It was the same one many of his clients wore when deciding on whether to buy a vaporator. "Why not?" Anglang Lehet said finally. "A block away from here, there's a bar where the rich idiots go to celebrate. Not my usual type of place, but then this hasn't been a usual type of night."

Anglang Lehet led Kedpin down the avenue toward a tall building with pristine and exotic vegetation imported from all over the galaxy. Normally, this façade of Ubialla Gheal's nightclub was lit with tall beacons that extended high into the night sky. Instead, the club was dark, quiet, and the swinging doors stood closed and unattended. "Odd," Anglang remarked.

"Something wrong?" asked Kedpin. The little man craned his neck trying to see the top of the darkened nightclub.

"Ubialla must be hosting a private affair."

Anglang considered knocking, then paused. Turning, he gestured for Kedpin to follow him. "The nice thing about Canto Bight," Anglang said with a smile, "there's always another place to get a drink."

The façade of the Blue Wall was not brick or metal or plasteel but simply a screenfield of pale-blue energy. Kedpin realized it kept insects out and cool air in. As Kedpin stepped through, he felt . . . cleaner. A dermal exfoliation field! The sensation was one of the most pleasant things Kedpin had ever experienced.

"Wow, is this place ever fancy!" he said to Anglang after taking a deep breath. "Is it very expensive?"

"It is obscenely expensive. And you're buying," Anglang Lehet said in that impossibly deep voice. Kedpin supposed he didn't mind buying a drink for a . . . friend? A *friend.*

Kedpin looked around at the other patrons. They looked like the sorts who'd been lounging in the Most Eminent Class stands at the racetrack. Ever since he'd arrived in Canto Bight, Kedpin had felt as if he were being stared at and disapproved of, but as he and Anglang entered the Blue Wall, he felt more truly out of place than he had since landing. "I thought you said you hated these overpriced bars," Kedpin said.

The towering alien shrugged. "They have a drink here made from Cantonican cactus that you can't get anywhere else in the galaxy," Anglang said. "This might be my last chance to taste it." Kedpin didn't know what Anglang meant by that, but it sounded sad and he felt bad for his new friend.

Still, as a human woman in a rippling iridescent gown led Kedpin and Anglang Lehet to a comfortable little table and filled two glittering glasses with Cantonican cactus liqueur, it was hard to feel *too* bad. Kedpin removed the tiny black velvet bag he'd been given at the racetrack from around his neck. He opened it gingerly and carefully poured out the dozen or so shards of precious metal that were his winnings onto the table. A year's worth of his salary. A year's worth of his salary sparkling there beside a little bowl of fried seeds. Kedpin had sold vaporators that cost many times that amount, of course, but that was credit wands and computer accounts. This much money-metal in one place just *looked* so different.

"Put that away, you idiot!" Anglang Lehet said, but Kedpin knew he just was being protective.

"I'll put it away," Kedpin said. "As soon as you take your half."

Kedpin had the great satisfaction of finally seeing Anglang Lehet look shocked. "My . . . what? This is your money, little man."

Kedpin shrugged. "I figure we earned it together. So you take half. I won't take no for an answer."

Anglang Lehet didn't protest further. He counted out half the winnings and scooped the sparkling slivers of metal into a some sort of hidden pocket. "You know what? You're all right, lit—*Ked*. You're all right, Ked."

Kedpin felt his hearts swell with happiness and he knew he'd made the right decision about the money. Despite his bruises, despite everything, he thought that this might just have been the best day of his life.

"I still can't believe my fathier won!" he said. "I've never won anything in my life!"

"What about Vaporator Salesbeing of the Year?" Anglang asked.

Kedpin's guts began to clench painfully. He had buried the truth about the contest so deep it never surfaced anymore except in dreams. But . . . it was time to come clean, Kedpin decided. Anglang Lehet was a criminal, a professional liar, yet he was more honest than Kedpin, Kedpin realized with a shudder of shame. Kedpin didn't know much about friends, but he knew they were supposed to be honest with each other.

"Ummm . . . Yes, that," Kedpin began. "Well, I did win Vaporator Salesbeing of the Year, but . . . well, maybe not exactly by the rules."

"Oh, really?" Anglang Lehet said, sipping his drink. Kedpin thought the tall alien might be holding back a smile. "Do tell."

"The contest was rigged, Anglang. It took me decades to realize it, but the facilitators of VaporTech's contest for Vaporator Salesbeing of the Year rigged things so that the computer that spits out the name of the winner always spat out Laz Lazzaz or some other managerial overseer who hates me. When I realized that, it was like getting punched in the face. One hundred and one years, Anglang. One hundred and one times I filled out my data card to apply for VaporTech's Vaporator Salesbeing of the Year. I sold the most units. I signed up the most clients. I worked the most days. One hundred and one years and I never had a chance. So . . . I *made* a chance."

"*Made* a chance, huh?" Anglang took another sip. He was looking at Kedpin differently now.

Kedpin sipped his own drink. It made his eye water pleasantly, and he had to blink a few times before going on. "The computer was old and clunky, and the program they used to cheat was pretty easy to reroute with my name attached. The way I won in front of everyone on the company network, they would have had to reveal their own cheating to expose mine."

"Your bosses didn't come stomp you down?"

Kedpin took another sip. The flavor was strange and strong. "You know what's funny, Anglang? They never mentioned it. But when I was sent off by my Level Three managerial overseer—Laz is his name—he kind of smiled like he knew. Like he was *proud* of me for cheating. Or relieved. Like it *proved* something to him, Anglang. Oh . . . I didn't like that smile he gave me at *all*." Shoklop looked down with shame at his repulsive feet, too large for his little body. "And I don't like being a cheater. But it wasn't *fair*."

"Beings talk about rules. Beings talk about fair. None of it ever seems to work out, little man," Anglang observed. "But you're here, tonight. Here in Canto Bight. Sipping . . . or in your case *slurping* Cantonican cactus liqueur. So what will you do now?"

Kedpin had to think about that for a moment. He closed his eye and took a deep breath. "Now?" he said at last, "Now I'm going to enjoy my vacation, darn it."

Anglang Lehet watched as Kedpin Shoklop noisily finished his drink and spilled a thin trickle of it down his rubbery pink body. Shoklop slid determinedly off his barstool and toddled toward the exit of the Blue Wall. Anglang had serious doubts that the squishy little man knew how to get back to the hotel himself, but Shoklop apparently wasn't going to let that stop him. As he *pardon-me*'d and *oh-excuse-me*'d his way out through the crowd, Shoklop teetered, clearly unused to strong drink. But the salesbeing also had now, beneath the oafishness, a boldness in his step. He should have looked comical. And yet, to Anglang at least, he didn't.

Shoklop had nearly made it to the door when he collided with a Palandag whose exolung made what was supposed to be an exquisite natural music. Anglang had never heard it. There was a weird, beautiful noise now, though, when Shoklop, uttering apologies all the while, somehow managed to press *harder* against the alien in an awkward effort to squeeze past it. It was like watching a musician apologetically wrestling his instrument.

Well, perhaps he looked a *bit* comical, Anglang admitted.

Shoklop turned and waved at Anglang one last time before stepping through the Blue Wall's blue energy field and out onto the street. Anglang waved back at the tougher-than-he-looked little fool, and he couldn't help but smile. It had been years since Anglang had been reminded how much people could change, and how quickly.

It had happened tonight, and for that he was thankful.

Anglang took a long last sip of Cantonican cactus liqueur. It really was one of the most satisfying things he'd ever tasted. His people's homeworld was light-years away but this stuff tasted like home.

He wouldn't be retiring after this job after all. It would take every bit of the winnings Shoklop had shared with him to appease the Old City Boys. Even then, even if he lived, Anglang would be working this botched job off for years. He'd made a stupid, soft-headed mistake, and now he was stuck in Canto Bight. Stuck in the game. But for now, Anglang Lehet would remember this one night when he'd managed to change the rules.

THE WINE
IN DREAMS

By **MIRA GRANT**

CHAPTER 1

THE GREATEST JOY OF HYPERSPACE IS THE BRILLIANCE OF ITS LIGHT. There is a radiance that can never be matched, or even truly described to those who have never seen it. Derla Pidys closes her lower eyes as her ship drops from the glory of hyperspace into orbit above Cantonica. The stars flash into being, dazzling bright in their own right, if not the impossible glory of their hyperspace shadows.

The planet below her is dark, the sky a dizzying web of ships being pulled into place around the curve of the horizon. She presses the trigger for her prearranged docking, and feels the ship shudder around her as the autopilot engages with the beacon. Relaxing into her seat, she adjusts the folds of her sommelier's robes and allows herself to anticipate the glory that is to come.

Hyperspace cannot be matched, but it can be challenged. And the architects who set the sky above Canto Bight ablaze will never cease their efforts. The legend of the city grows, its seeds planted by moments such as this—and perhaps, to someone with more limited vision than her own, the challenge is a closer one.

Her ship sails smoothly along the beacon's route. The world curves below her, dark, purposeless Cantonica, and then, in the time it takes for a millitile to vanish into its hidey-hole, the horizon catches fire.

It is the burn of uncounted lights, of beams slashing high into the atmosphere, as if they would sever the stars and take them for their own. It is the rainbow radiance of Canto Bight, the only reason any sensible creature would travel to this otherwise pointless planet. Canto Bight, the city of dreams, the destination of uncounted sentients, all of them following one legend or another, most chasing a lie. Derla smiles, wishing she were not on her way to work, so she might toast the brilliance of the story unfolding in front of her.

She is not the only sommelier working this sector, but she is, without question, the best. Any wine merchant and liquor trader can claim her title as their own, if they like; she's not the one to stop them. What they can't claim is her peerless skill, her ability to assess the quality of any alcoholic beverage from a single sip. Nor can they claim her track record. Despite peddling her wares to representatives from dozens of species, she has never been the source of an accidental poisoning. It is a point of pride, and part of what has grown her reputation—her legend—to its current heights. She is a sommelier. She is *the* sommelier, the one to call when everything must be *perfect*.

Arriving on the dark side of the world merely for the sake of this moment is a small indulgence. It wastes time, which is the only resource more limited than wine itself. But the time is hers to waste. Time that is never spent in any frivolous way will turn to vinegar even as wine does, as wasted as too much time spent heedlessly. Balance in all things.

She could never live here—the costs, in every sense, are simply too high—but there is a sweetness to the lie of Canto Bight that sings to her sommelier's soul. It began, as most beautiful things do, with money, with ambition, and with deceit. "Come to Canto Bight, the greatest city of pleasures the galaxy has ever known," they cried, and if they lied in the beginning, the ones who carry the cry now are telling the complete and utter truth. They crafted reality out of story.

Derla respects that. She has carried wines that her more sophisticated customers would consider little better than vinegar to backward farming planets where the names on their labels and the scent of distance clinging to their corks rendered them the finest vintages anyone had ever seen. She has taken the wines of those same worlds—

common, ordinary things to the gawping farmers who press the grapes in their basements, who bottle their own harvests simply for the sake of having something to wash the dust away—and sold them for profits that would stun their vintners into silence. It is the *story* that moves the bottle, as much as the taste of what's within.

This came from a city so far away and famous that its name would burn your uncultured tongue if you tried to speak it, she says, and hands reach out to grasp the glass, currency spilling from their palms.

This was crafted by simple farmers, aged on a world untouched by modern notions, as pure as the Force itself, she says, and people who would never step foot on that world's soil stumble over themselves to claim it first.

Everything is the legend. Everything is the lie. She sells good wine, yes, sweet wine from the frozen vineyards of Orto Plutonia, bitter, astringent, cleansing wine from the drowned fields of Naboo. She sells vintages worth drinking. But more than that, she sells the sour, virtually undrinkable wine that comes from Naboo's native fruits, bottled in the air by human vintners who say that Gungan wine will never compare. She sells the faintly poisonous wine of Alaspin and the overly potent wine brewed by the Yuzzum of the forest moon of Endor, which can be safely consumed only when mixed with the simpler, sweeter wine of their Ewok neighbors. She sells *dreams,* the idea of the galaxy in a single cellar, ready to be sipped and savored. She gives them what they ask for, nothing more and nothing less. Never mind that most of her customers will never crack a single seal on their purchases.

She is lovely, by the standards of her own kind, which makes her hideous to so many others: trading on personal beauty is not something to be done lightly. Her head is bulbous and heavy, with no visible nose. Instead, a single wide mouth sits at its center, anchored by two pairs of eyes, one above and one below. Her body is much like a human woman's, a small piece of convergent evolution that has always amused and delighted her. Their faces are so flat and hideous, their eyes so small, and yet she looks so like them! What a fabulous galaxy this is. What a delightful story.

Canto Bight spreads out beneath her, and her prepaid docking port opens its doors to welcome her. Derla closes her upper eyes and hums softly. There is so much good work yet to be done, and so many good stories yet to be bought and sold. Tonight, in Canto Bight, she may acquire the best one ever.

CHAPTER 2

"HELLO, YES, HELLO," SAYS ONE OF THE SOLEMN-EYED SISTERS, STARING raptly at the woman unlucky enough to be stationed at the front desk of their hotel. The other sister is brushing her fingertips against the petals of the decorative bromeliad that grows along the wall, watching raptly as its petals curl and bend away from her.

They are identical save for the cut of their clothes, with features as white as bleached coral, smooth, hairless skulls as white as bone, and frilled sensory organs that lend credence to the idea that their race may have arisen in some strange sea, very far from Cantonica. Both wear black, covering everything below their faces.

The clerk—who is human, brown haired and brown skinned, and as ordinary as the sands of Tatooine—forces a smile and says, "Yes, Miss Grammus? How can we improve your experience today?"

The solemn-eyed sister shakes her head and says, sadly, "You don't know who I *am*. Three days we've been here, and all the walls know me, but you still don't know who I *am*." Her voice is soft, filled with shame and sadness.

The clerk's smile stiffens, freezes, pulls upon her face. She took this job when she lost her life savings in the casinos and realized she had no way offplanet and no real reason to go. Here she's part of the faceless mass that keeps Canto Bight alive, the beating heart of the city that the tourists constantly see but barely remember. The sweet powder she mixes in her food at night keeps her tapped into that heart, keeps her working for the dream of somehow making her fortune there. It's the powder—the memory of it, the longing for it—that keeps her rooted in her place, allows her to say, as carefully as she can, "I'm sorry, Miss Grammus, I didn't mean to offend. Of course I know who you are. You and your sister are among our most honored guests."

All guests are among the most honored, at least as long as the credits keep flowing, as long as they can pay. When the money runs out, that's when they join her and the others like her on the subservient side of the counter. A quick, bitter thought crosses her mind: She very much looks forward to the day the Grammus twins are forced to don some cheaply made, objectifying uniform and force a smile for someone clever enough not to lose everything they have to the great greedy beast that is Canto Bight, city of dreams, city of schemes, city of nightmares.

"Do you?" The sister tilts her head in an unrecognizable gesture, part of a strange biology from a stranger land. "Tell me, then, and I will buy the remains of your indenture to this hotel and have you on the first ship out of this place, returning to your world of origin with full pockets and a head full of stories that will make you sound like the hero of the ages. Tell me. Who am I?"

The clerk's heart stutters in her chest.

Canto Bight is not *only* a destination for gamblers. There are a thousand pleasures to be had here, a million opportunities for decadence or deprivation. But it cannot be denied that *most* who come seeking the shining city do so because they yearn for the roll of the dice, for the turn of the cards. They follow the lady across the stars, and when she opens her arms to pick their pockets, they laugh from the sheer delight of her presence.

"What if—and I ask only for curiosity's sake, because of course I know each and every one of our honored guests like my own family— what if I cannot answer your question?" she asks, with the utmost of care.

The sister looks briefly, achingly sad, like the very concept of sorrow has been distilled into a single bipedal form. "I am afraid I will have to request your immediate termination from this position, for you will have offended me so gravely that the very sight of your face will cause my heart to bleed. If there is any mercy in this world, it is that you are so shamefully singular in nature that you need fear no repercussions striking your sister, whose face you should, in all propriety, share."

Not *only* is Canto Bight a destination for gamblers, but they hold the greatest share of the city's heart. The clerk calculates her odds, reviews every encounter she has had with the strange pair over the past three days, every glance and gesture, every tiny thing that might allow her to tell one from the other. Finally, serenely, she smiles.

"You are Parallela Grammus," she says confidently.

"Ah," says the sister. Her sorrow, if anything, has deepened. She turns.

One of the hotel managers is suddenly there, his nictitating membranes drawn politely tight across his eyes, reducing his vision to a subservient level. "You are distressed?" he asks, voice fluting and groveling.

The clerk realizes two things in the same breath: that she was wrong, and that once again she has gambled everything . . . only to lose.

"Yes," says the sister, glancing back to the clerk. Her expression softens but becomes no less sad. "We have been treated poorly by this establishment. We will be removing ourselves from this place and traveling to one that better suits our needs. We desire a . . . keepsake . . . of our time here."

The manager's eyes widen, nictitating membranes briefly pulling back to reveal the bright magenta of his irises. Showing them so plainly is a shameful display that would normally cause him to grovel and apologize before two such highly regarded clients. In this moment, faced with the reality of losing them, it seems doubtful that he even notices.

"But how— We have met your every request! Fulfilled your every desire!"

The second sister, who must actually be Parallela, if only through the process of elimination, turns away from her bromeliad, one hand still caressing its petals.

"You have only met the requests we *made*," she says, and her tone is gentle, as if she were speaking to a child. "A truly fine establishment would meet the requests we uttered only in the space behind our souls. We have been insulted by your carelessness. If you would appease us . . ."

"Yes, yes, anything," says the manager.

"You will give us the woman," says Parallela, and indicates the clerk with a lazy wave of one hand. Her face, like her sister's, gives away only what she wants it to: It is impossible to look at her and know the reasons for her demand.

The clerk feels her stomach turn to water, and wonders if this is the day she finally admits that she is never going home, save in death. Sweet, distant Naboo, which seemed so common once, when the stars of Canto Bight came calling . . .

The manager blusters. "We are not—you must understand—Cantonica does not condone slavery. Canto Bight is subject to the rules of the planetary governing body."

The planetary government is controlled by the city, which represents most of the world's population, and even more of its wealth. To claim that it acts independently of the interests of Canto Bight is to indulge in a fantasy even wilder than the rumor the clerk has heard whispered behind the backs of the Grammus sisters. She's heard people say the sisters come not from another world—everyone comes from another world; save for the street urchins and stable children, no one is *born* in Canto Bight—but from another dimension, something on the far side of hyperspace, as impossible and untrue as the Force of the old Jedi Order. Some even say that they come from the dimension where the Force retreated after the fall of the Jedi, that they have crossed impossible distances to see what happened to their gifts.

It would only make sense for them to wind up in Canto Bight, if all those lies were true. Everything comes here sooner or later, to shrivel and forget itself beneath the bright and shining sky.

"We don't want to *keep* her," says Parallela patiently. "She could never survive the journey back to our . . . home . . . and she would never be accepted if she did. All things come in two, the right and the wrong, the action and the consequence. Your resort has performed an action. You have wronged us. You must lose one of your finest jewels in consequence, else how will you learn to do better?"

"You *must* do better," agrees Rhomby. "This is as great an opportunity for change as you will ever receive. We do not desire a slave, merely someone to carry our bags from this resort to our new one, which we hope will take both the lesson and the gift we offer them to heart."

"Gift?" asks the manager blankly.

"Yes," says Parallela. "We are bringing them the rare advantage of a woman who has already tended to our needs, and can thus explain what must be done to please us."

The clerk stiffens. She took the bet when she placed her guess: By being willing to consider the positive outcome, she also allowed for the possibility of the negative.

The manager protests. The Grammus sisters are firm, and remain so through the process of acquiring the severance forms for their new "souvenir," collecting her things from her place in the employee quarters—theirs are already packed and ready to move—and ostentatiously resigning their claim to their rooms. In a matter of time that seems too short to be believed, the three of them are standing outside, Rhomby summoning a chauffeur-driven speeder with an airy wave of her hand as Parallela attempts to conceal a large cutting from the lobby bromeliad in her valise.

The clerk—clerk no longer; she doesn't know *what* she is anymore, has defined herself by her job for so long that all of this seems impossible—shifts her weight from foot to foot, uneasy. Finally, she blurts, "What happens to me now?"

Parallela blinks, seemingly nonplussed. "You take care of our needs on this world," she says. "You smooth our way."

"And when you go . . ." The clerk pauses. Nothing she can say feels right. "When you leave, what happens to me then?"

"Ah." Rhomby steps back, picks up two of the bags, contorts her face in what would, on a human, be considered a smile. "That is when your story starts. Come now. We have an appointment to keep tonight. We must hurry."

The speeder's doors are open, and all objection is swept away in the face of the sisters' calm, implacable insistence that this is how things must be.

CHAPTER 3

DERLA HAS RENTED HER CUSTOMARY ROOM AT ONE OF THE SMALLER, less fashionable casinos: palatial enough to allow her to bring clients to sample her wares without shaming herself, small and spartan enough to stretch her budget over several days. It is a delicate balancing act, which is why she has not chosen to make any changes, not even knowing she will—all things being equal—be on her way by morning. She has brought no sample cases, nor has she reached out to any of her usual contacts.

This, too, is intentional. The elite of Canto Bight are unaccustomed to being denied whatever pleases them, and most will only hear that she was onplanet long after she has gone. They will writhe to think that they somehow missed her, their palates growing dry with longing for wines they have not tasted. They will *ache* for her good regard. And on her next visit, their thirst will be all the greater, and their generosity will be increased to match. Anything to keep her from spurning them again.

Now, however, she has a different role to play, that of the eager subordinate. She lifts a bottle as black as the heart of a dead sun from its case, holding it up until the light catches stardust hints of gold and purple from the liquid within. It is lovely. It is *perfect*. Nothing else will do.

There are clients who can be sold a legend independent of a bottle's quality, who will eagerly buy the last bottle of wine from Alderaan even knowing that Derla has sold a hundred "last bottles" discovered in smuggler's caches and concealed cellars the galaxy over. They care more for the story than the substance. Not this client. Not this night.

Ubialla Gheal would not, on first glance, strike most as a threat. She is long, she is elegant and lithe, as comfortable draped across a golden bench as standing at her own bar, a cocktail in her hand and an inviting smile upon her lips. Where Ubialla is, the party is sure to follow—and if the party somehow gets lost along the way, another will spring spontaneously into being, all for the privilege of pleasing her. She is beauty, grace, and charm personified.

She is, naturally, corrupt. Most in Canto Bight are. Derla finds Ubialla's corruption almost charming: Few who rule this city bother with such petty concerns as concealing what they are. Ubialla still pretends to respectability. As such, Derla has always felt reasonably safe in her company. After all, respectable businesswomen don't harm highly valued assets, such as the galaxy's finest sommelier.

The hotel stairway unwinds beneath Derla's feet as she descends, a cunning thing of repulsorlift fields and delicate thrusters that exists only as it is being used. It dismantles itself behind her, racing forward to catch her feet again, so that it looks as if she walks along a trailing stream of flower petals or of frost, something natural, something *real*. It is as artificial as everything else about this place, a small and un-necessary luxury supplied by her hotel, and she revels in it. These are the things that draw people back to Canto Bight again and again, even once they understand the city lurking beneath the shimmer and sparkle, ready to rise up and devour. There is magic, to choose a quaint and outdated term, to the workings of the city.

Speeders zip by as she passes from the tower height of her room and into the traffic lanes. Here, too, her stairway guides her, sliding itself into the space between the beacons, threading the needle of the organic-operated vehicles. No one licensed to drive in Canto Bight would be foolish enough to strike a tourist—not here. On the artifi-cial inland sea, yes; there, her body could vanish beneath the waves, never to be seen again, and she could become but one more set of bones sleeping in the great breast of the city. Here . . .

If she were to be struck, she would fall. How she would fall, until she shattered almost artistically against the pavement. The lights of Canto Bight would shine off the fragments of her carapace, off the broken bits of the bottle now tucked safely into her valise, and it would not be covered up, and it would not be concealed. Her death would damage tourism, if only for a day, if only in this district.

If there is a religion in Canto Bight, it is tourism. Tourism, which fills coffers and replenishes staffing pools, which spreads the legend of the city across the stars. Even the wealthiest and most arrogant of the city's elite have no desire to damage tourism. Without it, where would they be? In some other criminal enterprise, no doubt, but one without style, without grace. Without tourism, they might as well be Hutts—a fate the controllers of Canto Bight would die to escape.

The staircase allows her the illusion of a leisurely descent while actually moving her at a speed well above what she might have managed on her own. In what seems to be no time at all, Derla steps onto the pavement, the staircase fluttering away into the air. She will take a speeder home when her business is done. A beautiful entrance, a quiet exit: these are respected things here in Canto Bight.

Adjusting the drape of her gown with her free hand, Derla strolls down the avenue, chin high, allowing herself to be seen. She recognizes the house staffers of many of her past patrons as they hurry about their errands; some spare a look in her direction, careful not to stare, and she can almost hear them noting her presence, preparing themselves for a night of wine tasting and drunken orders from their masters. How surprised they'll be when she never appears. How surprised, and then how concerned, as they wonder whether their households have fallen from favor. There is status, too, among the serving class of Canto Bight, and to serve a master or mistress who can no longer arrange for something as simple as a delivery of wine is to serve nothing good.

Derla smirks as she walks. Oh, she will be in *high* demand when next she comes this way. Her own legend grows, and all she has to do is keep moving, her hand clutching the handle of her valise, the scent of mystery trailing in her wake.

Her destination would be impossible to miss even for someone who had never been here before, whose eyes were dazzled and whose heart was struck by the beauty of the place. For Derla, who has walked these streets more often than perhaps she should have, it is a simple star to steer by.

The shell of Ubialla's nightclub extends high into the air, peppered with beacons that steer the traffic around it, allowing the speeders to zoom startlingly close, so the wind from their passage becomes a part of the façade, rippling the vegetation her gardeners have so carefully cultivated. The club has other faces, Derla knows, entrances styled to suit the streets they face onto. This approach is one of the more "civilized," intended to appeal to casual tourists.

The bouncers on the door straighten at the sight of Derla, offering her the tightest and most proper of nods, unable to conceal the confusion in their eyes. They have never been faced with her unscheduled appearance before. Always her visits have been things of pomp and circumstance, her own hired help following her with a hoverunit piled high with crates and boxes, each containing its own wonders. Ubialla has been an excellent customer over the years, and she has been rewarded for her patronage with alcoholic delights from every corner of the sky.

Derla inclines her head politely and walks on, through the gracefully swinging doors, into a palace of wonders and delights.

She has never bothered to learn the décor of Ubialla's place, which changes so often as to be ephemeral, now rustic, now sleek and clean. She entered once to find every wall covered in a veil of living insects, delicate winged creatures from a thousand worlds. Their incubation and transport must have cost a fortune, but when she had returned the very next day to look upon them again, they had disappeared, leaving not even a single trace behind. The walls had been layers upon layers of netting that day, and some of the customers had climbed them, cocooning themselves above the floor as they sipped their drinks and dreamed of cleaner stars.

Looking for commonalities within Ubialla's territory is a fool's game, and Derla Pidys is no fool. She steps lightly and nimbly, marking the location of the walls—those, at least, rarely change—and noting with relief that this layout sports the private booths of which she is so enamored. She has done much business in those booths, pulling their curtains fast and blocking out the world while she and her customers deal with the less delicate aspects of commerce.

There is more privacy in her rented room, or in their palatial estates and apartments and speeders, but a surprising number of her clients would prefer to come here, to be seen in public making their purchases from one of the best-regarded sommeliers in the galaxy. No one thrives in Canto Bight without learning to cultivate their own legend, to shape it as their heart desires.

No matter how often Ubialla changes the appearance of her club, the layout remains essentially the same. It grinds on her, Derla knows, to be bound to any static thing—but drunks will be drunks the galaxy over, and someone who has dived too deep into their cups moves mostly on the dim traceries of memory rather than what stands before their eyes. If Ubialla were to move the walls, she might gain in short-term customers looking for true novelty, but she would lose her regular clientele, and upon such backs are fortunes made. So the walls remain where they have been for years, and the club bends around them, shaped and reshaped upon a whim.

Derla follows the patterns this club has held since she first entered it, and her eyes merely skim the new fripperies, noting them for later consideration. In any other establishment, she might worry that the bare walls with their crystal racks of wine and liquor spoke to some shortage of resources: that Ubialla had finally managed to offend one or other of her many patrons and was on the verge of losing everything. Here she has no such concerns, nor does she feel she needs them. Ubialla is mercurial. If the place is bare now, it is simply because it was palatial yesterday, or because it will be a forest of singing bells tomorrow.

The day is young, as yet, and the crowd is sparse, only a few serious drinkers tucked away in booths or perched at tables, their glasses in front of them, their eyes far away. Derla passes a table of giggling girls in resort uniforms, their indenture chips flashing a calm green—off duty, not available for hire or requisition, not currently affiliated with their employers or their etiquette standards. They have ordered a bottle of what she knows to be overly sweet Socorro mescal, splitting it among themselves with the air of celebrants.

She signals one of the servers to approach her, indicating the girls' table with a blink of her lower left eye.

"What do they celebrate?" she asks.

"One of them is buying her wife's indenture contract to enable her to pursue work in the medcenter system," the server replies. "It is a brash move. It could end them. But it could elevate them as well, far above their current status. The coin is worth the chance."

"Ah," says Derla approvingly. This is Canto Bight at its best and brightest—hopeful, chasing fortune as a child might chase a falling star. She discreetly slips a few slivers of metal into the server's hand. He takes it without looking, as if he has been expecting the gesture— and indeed, perhaps he has. Generosity, too, is part of her legend.

"Bring them a bottle of dry Socorro white. A good vintage, if you would be so kind. Bravery should be rewarded in the present, as it may not be treated so kindly by the future."

The server nods and scurries away. He will, she knows, bring the table the best bottle of wine he can justify, pocketing the remainder of the currency she has given him as a service fee. It does not bother her. He will not attempt to defraud her, to pass off something cheap and common as the bottle she has paid for. In another place, perhaps, where she was less known, that might be a concern. Here, where she has established herself as expert, patron, and benefactor, she will be treated fairly, if only to keep her returning. Someone like Ubialla does not burn such connections lightly.

Derla continues on her way, and there is Ubialla, tall and grand and shining like a star. That, too, is intentional: has always been so. Ubialla Gheal is a woman who knows her angles. She, like Derla, is dressed in white, but where Derla wears the color as a way of bowing her head to the spectrums of other eyes, Ubialla wears it like a challenge, bright and blazing and impossibly present. Something in the fabric catches the light, not enough to glitter—that would be crass, and so far below Ubialla as to be unthinkable—but enough to make her shine against the dark backdrop she has created for herself. Her skin is flawless, dark enough that the white gown contrasts like the space above Cantonica, beautiful, untouchable, rare. The high dome of her head is similarly adorned and similarly glorious.

Derla has wondered, at times, whether Ubialla chose to become a nightclub owner because she understood that she was no legendary beauty, no myth waiting to unfold, but that with the right lighting and the right lies, she could easily elevate herself to the position. Here Ubialla controls everything, and everything is designed to two parallel but complementary goals: to make a profit, and to flatter its creator.

The thought of parallels is enough to make her upper eyes blink in quick amusement. Steeling her expression and its inappropriate expansiveness away, Derla approaches the woman in white with her shoulders back and her chin high.

"Derla," says Ubialla, with precisely the correct amount of surprise to make it clear that this is no surprise at all: She has known of the other woman's arrival since Derla docked her ship. She approaches quickly, grips Derla by the shoulders, and kisses the air next to the other woman's cheeks, first the right and then the left, before letting go. "What a delightful treat it is to have a visit from you! And so mysterious! I had no idea you were coming before I received the notification that your room had been reserved."

A polite but pleasant fiction. Derla allows it to stand. Blinking her upper eyes in quiet subservience, she reaches into her valise and withdraws the wine she has brought for Ubialla. Offering it without comment, she says, "I am afraid this is a very brief stop on my part. I am here to acquire, not to sell, and have only this single evening on which to make my acquisition. My client is similarly pressed for time, and very much wished to come here and sample your delights. I was hoping you might have a booth available for me to reserve. Something quiet, out of the way, where I can conduct my business."

Ubialla takes the bottle, looks at it, and smiles a small and secretive smile. "Coruscant Black. Really, Derla, you spoil me."

"Only the finest for my best customer."

Ubialla is not her best customer. But then, Derla has never once said she was.

"I *might* have a booth available—oh, Derla, if only you had contacted me sooner, I might have been able to arrange something so much nicer." Ubialla waves her hand. A server is suddenly there. She hands him the bottle of wine, and it is gone, whisked away to Ubialla's private stores, where it will sit until she has some wealthy or renowned personage to flatter. Everything is a tool in this place, even Derla.

Even Ubialla herself.

"There wasn't time," says Derla, and now she *is* lying, the lies small and civil enough that she can hope they won't be heard, that she will get away with them. The planning of this moment has been the work of many long hours, chasing lies and they are used to anchor, looking for the place where truth and fiction collide.

The Grammus sisters seem to come out of nowhere, leaving nothing—not even a hyperspace trail—behind. They claim to be from another dimension, and maybe they are; stranger things have happened in this galaxy, where rich sapients can craft themselves a private sea, where the stars of hyperspace dazzle even in dreams. They claim a lot of things. None of them *matter*, not really, because here is the most beautiful part of all:

People *believe* them.

They look at these sisters, and they see possibility. They see potential. They see the clever tilt of a head, the strange cadence of a sentence sometimes in a language known only to the sisters, and they dream of a world where those things are commonplace and unremarkable. They want to believe there could be something more than the skies they know, and the Grammus sisters, in all their oddity, are that belief given flesh.

None of that would have been enough to catch Derla's interest had the sisters not, on their second such appearance, casually traded a bottle of an unknown vintage for dinner at a seaside restaurant that served several species of local crustacean and did not maintain a liquor list. The bottle had passed from the owner's hands into the hands of a local tax collector, and from there to a senator, and from *there* to the dinner party of a queen.

Derla had not been present at that celebration, but she has spoken to several people who were, and all have informed her, in tones of wistful wonder, that it had tasted like the wine they drank in dreams, crisp and light and sweet. No two had ascribed the same notes to the flavor, but each of them has insisted they would pay anything, *anything,* for another such bottle.

Derla doesn't believe the sisters come from somewhere outside the normal flow of space and time. The galaxy is not infinite, but it is near enough as to make no difference, and there are worlds where she has never been, where no one who was not born there has ever been. The simplest answer is often the truest one, and it is so much simpler for these sisters to have come from some unknown world, perhaps hidden by its own desire, and claim themselves to be something stranger than they are, if only to deflect attention. But.

The legend. The *lie.* That is what matters, when people are dying for the chance to taste the wine they drink only in their dreams. Derla needs a bottle. She needs a bottle more than she can say. Not only for the cachet of having it—although that cannot be overstated—but for the chance to put it through the proper paces. She must analyze it, catalog each molecule, identify each delicate, dancing sugar, to be sure of its compatibility with her customers. The difference between a renowned sommelier—courted by the wealthy of a hundred worlds, welcomed wherever she appears—and a wanted poisoner is an updated catalog. Killing one's clients is not a good way to remain in business for any length of time.

"I see," says Ubialla, and it's impossible to tell, from her sweet expression, from the way she holds her arms, so poised, so relaxed, whether she knows she's being lied to. That's the trouble with dishonesty. One cannot simply ask whether it happens to be working. "Well, of course I have a place for you, especially after such a kind and generous gift. May I ask who you happen to be meeting?"

"My client for this evening would like to remain anonymous for the time being, to prevent attracting undue attention," says Derla formally. She's fairly sure she's wrong about that. The sisters thrive on notoriety and visibility, and make as much of a fuss as possible whenever entering a new city. Too much of a fuss, in fact: There's no way they don't know what they're doing. They want to be looked at. They want to be *seen*.

Derla would rather avoid fulfilling that particular desire, if possible. Some of the eyes watching from the shadows are less friendly than she prefers, and many of them might have their own ideas about the dispensation of something radiant and rare. Let her get what she came for, pay their asking price, and make the vital connections that will allow her to acquire more of this "wine of dreams," assuming it can live even halfway up to its legend.

For a moment, it appears that Ubialla's eyes narrow; for a moment, it seems that she is looking at Derla as a predator looks at prey. The moment passes, a trick of light and shadow swept away by the motion of one of the servers in the background, and Ubialla is all smiles again, ever the perfect hostess, ever without fault or flaw.

"Everything will be as you desire tonight," she says sweetly. "For you, my dearest friend, everything will be *perfect*."

CHAPTER 4

THE NEW RESORT IS IN EVERY POSSIBLE RESPECT DIFFERENT FROM THE old resort, and is simultaneously in every possible respect the same. Where the previous resort towered high into the air, this one plunges deep into an artificial flooded cavern, the water lapping against the crystal windows, the distant shadows filled with the motion of imported fish and aquatic mammals. Instead of being staffed primarily by indentured organics, it boasts a fleet of droids, each of them programmed to a specific need.

They were able to tell the sisters apart within seconds of their arrival. The clerk, whose name the pair still have not asked, feels more than faintly uncomfortable as she considers this fact. None of them would ever have been caught as she has been.

The similarities between this resort and the last are even more striking than the differences. The rooms follow almost the same layout, which saves on programming costs for the cleaning droids that sweep through every resort save for a few that charge a premium for organic cleaning—not as prestigious as being driven by an organic, as so many resort guests have things in their room they would rather not be touched by another's hands. The toiletries in the bathroom are relabeled and rethemed to smell of ocean and air rather than flowers and soil, but they come from the same manufacturer, the same basic set of options.

This is the same resort, remade into something new by a simple change of the superficial, still perpetually and utterly itself.

One of the sisters drapes herself across a bed, eyes on the window to the water, and waves a lazy hand. "Souvenir, go to the desk and tell them we will need a speeder called for us precisely at sunset. Not a second later, nor a second before."

The clerk is unsure that sunset can be measured with that sort of precision. She says nothing, only bobs her head and asks, "Will there be anything else?"

The second sister emerges from the bathroom with the bromeliad in her hands. She has managed to find a vase for the thing, and it spills out on all sides, vines like tendriled roots reaching for the ground.

"There must be a manager," she says. "Tell them we will wish to speak to the manager come morning. The manager must be an organic. If they do not have an organic manager, they will need to find one before the sun comes up. That gives them all of a night and some small sliver of a day. Quite reasonable, don't you think?"

The clerk blanches. "I don't—"

"When we came to Canto Bight, they told us this was the city of dreams," says the sister on the bed dreamily. The clerk decides she must be Rhomby, as Parallela was the one enamored of the lobby bromeliad. "They said whatever we could see when we dreamed of hyperspace would be found here, walking the avenues, shining in the sky."

"We dream of an organic manager," says Parallela. "This resort dreams of our money. Let us hope that tonight both of our dreams come true." She places her bromeliad, vase and all, lovingly on the room's second bed.

There is no third bed. The clerk has yet to ask where she is intended to sleep. She is afraid that none of the available answers would be pleasant ones.

"I also dream of food," says Rhomby. "Of sweet food and savory food and something to tear with the fingers and something to tear with the teeth. You should go, Souvenir, and find us these things. We want them."

The clerk considers objecting. Considers shouting. Instead, she says in a small voice, "My name is Calla," and exits the room, leaving the door to slide shut again behind her.

Silence reigns. Rhomby looks at Parallela. Parallela looks at Rhomby. Rhomby is the first to sigh.

"A *person*?" she asks. "When I said you should acquire something charming to make the resort remember our stay, I meant—"

"The lobby décor? Small. Provincial. I'm sure they have people wandering off with their centerpieces and shiny objects all the time. A desk clerk, now. *That* makes an impression." Parallela sits daintily on the bed's edge, stroking one of the bromeliad's leaves with a thoughtful hand. "It will ease things tonight to have someone native to the city as our guide."

"As native as any of them get."

"As native as any of them get," Parallela agrees. "I have never seen any place so eager to pretend itself entirely rootless. No one comes from here. They all speak of away as if it were a dream, and this the place they found themselves on waking. It is a glorious showpiece of a city. I think I will want to return here, when we go."

"Then we should not be seen to be acquiring too many *people*," says Rhomby. "People make poor collectibles. They always ask after one another, and I've no stomach for keeping them."

"We will resettle her. Find her a position here, or at another resort. One that will view her as a rare commodity for knowing our ways, for how many on this world can boast such an intimate association?"

Rhomby heaves another sigh, louder this time. "How many on *any* world can boast such an intimate association?"

"Sister. We are here for business as much as pleasure."

"Yet it pleases me to remind you that we are in the business of creating a certain amount of confusion about our pleasures. She will see too much."

"She will see what we choose to show her. Let them think us this kind of capricious, that we would acquire and then discard a sentient. Let her carry stories of us out into the world." Parallela strokes her bromeliad again. "Nothing convinces the ear like a story from a source who was there."

Rhomby is silent for a moment before she asks, "Is everything prepared for this night?"

"Oh, yes," says Parallela. "The stage begins to set itself; the pieces fall into place."

Rhomby smiles.

CHAPTER 5

UBIALLA GHEAL DID NOT, AS SO MANY ASSUME, REACH HER CURRENT position of comfort and connection by playing the fool, nor by allowing others to exploit her. She is lovely, yes: She knows the value of loveliness, and so she has worked tirelessly to maintain it, never elevating herself to the type of beauty that disturbs, never allowing her appearance to falter or to fail her. She is cultured in cultured company and inappropriately vulgar when the moment is right, allowing the stories of her quick tongue and matchless wit to spread across Canto Bight. Her patrons are many. Her debts are even deeper, and that affords her a measure of security. The people she owes know that she is worth more to them alive and working than she could ever be sinking to the bottom of the sea.

Perhaps one day, she knows, she will acquire the wrong debt or offend the wrong person, and all of this will come tumbling down. But this is not that day.

"Well?" she asks of the street urchin—filthy thing—standing in the doorway of the club's kitchen. None of them are allowed *inside.* That would be an insult not worth bearing.

"Took the parameters you gave to the port, ran them through," says the urchin, gills working desperately. "Got the list. Food now?"

It's amazing, how base and animal these children can be. Ubialla holds her hand imperiously out. "The names."

Reluctantly, the child hands over a thin copper card with the names embossed in governmental font. Ubialla makes it disappear and turns to the nearest cook.

"Enough for this belly and two more, before you head back to the stables," she says. She can afford to be seen as generous, as long as she is never seen as soft. Generous keeps them coming back.

The child makes a squealing sound of delight. Ubialla ignores it. So far as she is concerned, this is already over, and she is ready to move on.

The club is preparing to open fully at sunset, when it will blossom into the jewel of Canto Bight, when everyone who is anyone will be clamoring at the doors to be admitted. Clearing a booth for Derla required canceling a standing reservation by a mid-range jockey who will no doubt be terribly offended. Let him be. Maintaining a reputation for exclusivity requires work, at times. Perhaps it will inspire him to race better, win more, improve his station. He will forever link her with his good fortune, even if he can't quite find his way to "why."

The question is who Derla intends to meet in that booth when she returns from her afternoon in the city. Ubialla knows Derla wouldn't reserve a booth to meet with someone who lives in Canto Bight. The sommelier would meet with them in their homes, or in her rented room, or in a temporary accommodation arranged by one or another of the resorts. Only tourists do their business in public. Tourists, and people who desire to be seen. Ubialla does not care for secrets that do not include her. She slides into her own private booth, which is never canceled nor offered to any other, and produces the card, running her fingers across the text. Every name is someone whose travel plans have corresponded with Derla's, on a delay, as if they had been chasing each other across the sky.

Most are minor dignitaries, functionaries whose work would never have brought them into contact with the sommelier. A few she recognizes—a celebrity, some sporting professionals, a senator—but the rest are so much meaningless noise, inconsequential.

Then she pauses, fingers still pressing against the list, breath catching in her throat, until the room spins and the veins along her long, smooth forehead pulse with excitement and dismay. The Grammus sisters are in Canto Bight. That is no surprise: She heard of their arrival when it happened, as did all the other movers and shakers of her level. She has been hoping their wanderings would bring them to her door sooner rather than later so she might charm them without seeming inappropriately eager to do so. They are something new, and novelty sells very, very well in certain circles. If she could convince them to become regular fixtures at her club, she could increase patronage by some glorious amount.

And they have traveled the same long, looping elliptical as Derla, touched on the same worlds, breathed the same air. They have been luring the sommelier here, always one step ahead of her, whether intentionally or through fortuitous accident, and now she is here, and they are here, and there is no one else who fits the bill of Derla's mysterious client.

One does not achieve a position in Canto Bight's underworld without knowing all the angles of profit and risk, all the ways and places the world can either benefit or betray. Ubialla knows as much as it's possible for anyone to know about the chaotic, capricious sisters. She knows their world has never been identified, and that they claim to have come from a reality on the other side of hyperspace, a place they are absolutely firm about existing, but about which they will disclose no details.

She knows that sometimes the sisters bring things from their home, wherever or whatever it is, to sell to the interested. Trinkets, toys, little things that betray nothing of their true origins—almost like they're trying to guarantee that they'll be remembered after they've moved on.

And sometimes they sell wine.

It would be impossible to move in the circles she moves in and *not* have heard of the Grammus sisters' wine. She has asked Derla to acquire a bottle for her three times, only to be politely but firmly rebuffed as the sommelier claimed that the vintage was impossible to acquire, and would need to be fully analyzed before it could be sold. Ubialla has promised one of her . . . benefactors . . . that she will, someday, be able to fulfill his desire to taste this supposed "wine of dreams." At the thought, her skin goes cold and the veins in her forehead pulse again, this time with fear.

If this exchange goes off as Derla has no doubt planned—the sisters handing over their wine, the sommelier slipping away to decant and catalog it, as if anyone would, upon acquiring a single bottle of the stuff, ever be so foolish as to *drink* it—then Ubialla will be left in the cold. When her benefactor hears that the wine was not only on-world but in her *club*, in her *grasp*, without her being able to secure it for him . . .

She swallows, hard. She has spent a very long time dancing away from his wrath, and she has no intention of stopping now. Derla has been an excellent customer, and a source of many delicious and valuable prizes. None of that matters as much as Ubialla's own skin. None of it ever could.

The wine will be hers. There is no other option.

CHAPTER 6

NIGHT COMES TO CANTONICA AS IT COMES TO ANY OTHER WORLD: THE
planet rotates, the sun slips over the horizon and is gone, and darkness descends, riding a rainbow of sunset light, carrying a cascade of
stars. Some say the best stargazing in the system is in the vast deserts
of Cantonica, far from the blinding lights of Canto Bight, where
nothing pollutes or diminishes their brilliance.

Night comes to Canto Bight merely as a change of backdrop. The
buildings blaze in the new-fallen dark. Some glow, either artificially
or through cultured bioluminescence. Others turn on a hundred
lights, a thousand, becoming shifting auroras of controlled glory. The
sky is a river of colors, reflecting off the casinos, the resorts, the race-
tracks.

The streets transform when the sun goes down. Fashions shift, becoming more eye catching, more esoteric, until it becomes clear why
this is *the* destination for the fashionable elite. Giggling model-
celebutantes cluster in the tourist areas, letting themselves be posed
with tourists for a few credits, letting themselves be seen as more
important than they are. Speeders fill the air, their running lights
adding a shifting quality to everything below. The walkways and
moving stairs are packed with a shimmering selection of who's who
and who wants to be, all of them moving with casual lack of purpose,

as if none of them have any reason to do anything so common as *hurry.*

The ones who needed to hurry have already long since passed, the beautiful, impoverished faces that will smile from host stands and from behind bars, the less intentionally attractive ones who will conceal themselves behind the scenes, preparing meals, cleaning floors, keeping the vast, complicated mechanism of the city operational. Each of them has a story, a secret, a dream they hope to one day render real. Most of them will fail, but this is the city for dreaming, and so they endure.

They endure.

"There is a call for you, Miss Gheal."

"Is there?" Ubialla allows herself a moment of quiet before she rises, moving smoothly through the gathering crowd to the privacy of her office. From the windows, she can see the entire room. She shuts the door before she positions herself in front of the holoscreen.

The face that flashes into visibility is familiar, as familiar as her own. She meets his eyes, straight backed and unflinching. She's proud of herself for that. There are so few who can look the councilor in the eye.

How she ever thought she could walk these streets unscathed, she no longer understands. She has not been so young, nor so innocent, in a very long time. She was a fool to have ever been that young in the first place.

"Ubialla," he says, "I understand my property is set to enter your establishment."

She doesn't bother asking how he knows. It would insult them both, and he does not care to be insulted. "I will do my best to obtain it."

"You will obtain it, for me, or we will have words. I have a gathering coming up. My guests require the best. Provide it."

The holo winks out: She has been dismissed.

Her chest aches with the stirrings of panic as she looks around the office. Subtlety is no longer an option. There is a blaster in the desk drawer. She grabs it. If she cannot be subtle, she will be direct: There is elegance, at times, in directness. Most of all, she will not lose.

She can't.

Derla Pidys moves through the crowd with head high, valise, as ever, by her side. She grips the handle like a woman who would sooner die than release her burden. It is a clever pose; she carries nothing of value. The valise contains a small device built to her specifications, capable of modifying its density within a narrow range. There will be no change to her mass or gait when she returns to her room; no thieves watching her come will find anything unusual about her when she goes. It is a small protection. It is enough to lend her an additional layer of security.

She does not look around herself; she does not need to. Creatures with binocular vision often forget that those with additional eyes can see more than they can; they plan their approaches and attacks as if everyone shared the same field of vision. She knows precisely where her followers are located, can see the way they measure her steps and study her valise. This, too, is a natural consequence of her legend. They know her presence means, or can mean, profit. She carries wonders.

"Not tonight, my friends," she murmurs, and watches with amusement as the nearest of them fade back into the crowd, trying to look like they were completely unaware of her presence. "I carry nothing worth stealing, and I will not place myself where you can have me. Go about your business."

Some of them do. Others, too far back to hear her, do not. It matters little, for there is the entrance to Ubialla's palace of wonders, and she will be safe there. It would have been safer, she knows, to have taken a speeder from her room and never dangled herself in front of these street toughs like a prize to be won or stolen, but there is—always—the legend to be considered. Derla Pidys is humble, they say, because she walks when she can, keeps her feet on the ground. She is simple, they say, because she does not ornament herself, allowing her wines to speak for themselves. She can be trusted. She will not lie to you.

It is pleasing when a lie takes on such weight that it begins to outmass the truth, which must be sipped in small and careful doses, like the poison it is. With back straight and chin high, she approaches Ubialla's place. The bouncers step aside to let her pass. One of them, a Wookiee she has known for many years, shoots her what she might read as a sympathetic look.

There isn't time to wonder about it, not without stopping where she is, which would attract more attention than she wants to risk, and which might make her late for her appointment. She continues onward, past the threshold, into the cool air of Ubialla's domain, where the only law is that of the owner's whim. She takes another step.

The muzzle of a blaster digs into her spine, just below her ribs, where a single shot would be enough to kill her before a medic could reach them.

"Ah," says Derla, disappointed all out of proportion with the likelihood of this moment. "You have decided to interfere with my business."

"All business in this place is *my* business," Ubialla replies. She leans close, her breath warm against Derla's skin. "You were holding out on me. You know I don't care to be left in the dark."

"I have conducted private business here in the past."

"Not involving people who have something I want. Or were you planning to turn around and hand your prize to me? Was this all an elaborate attempt at granting me a present? Tell me it was. Make me believe you, and I'll allow you to broker this deal between the twins and myself. I'll let you walk away. We may even do business again, you and I, and have no bad blood between us."

Derla closes her upper eyes, a sign of true regret, scanning the club for signs of the sisters with her lower pair. They have not arrived, or have not chosen to show themselves. She might yet be able to salvage something from this dire mistake.

She should have pressed them harder to meet her in private, to come to her rooms and not to this dangerous feeding ground. She does not blame Ubialla for her betrayal. There is no point in blaming a sarlacc for its hunger. All it knows is wanting. Ubialla is the same. All she knows is wanting, and when she is not satisfied, she could devour the world in her eagerness and greed. Derla blames herself. She should have found a way to move the meeting.

"I apologize for misleading you, although I provided exactly as much information as I have on earlier occasions, and you did not draw a weapon on me then," says Derla. "I am meeting with the Grammus sisters, yes. They tell me they have a bottle of wine available for purchase, and I am keen to acquire it. I did not come to yield my prize to you, nor do I have any intention of doing so. The wine needs to be tested. It needs to be analyzed, so we can determine who may drink it without harm. If I were to give it to you, and it were to prove incompatible with your biology—"

"Liar," says Ubialla fondly. "You wouldn't be here merely to test the stuff. You have a buyer in mind. Who is it?"

This time Derla closes her lower set of eyes as well. Only for a moment. Only long enough to feel the depth of her regret. "He is offworld. Very far offworld. He has had the wine before, and he craves it, dreams of it. He has agreed to my decanting a measure for my own purposes, if I will bring him the remainder. It is a fair exchange, given the price he is willing to pay for even a partial bottle, and I will reach him in plenty of time to guarantee its potency. Nothing will sour in my hands."

"Nothing will *enter* your hands," says Ubialla. "This is my place. These are my walls. Any treasures to be found in this night will belong to me, only me, and entirely me. Do you understand?"

"I understand that your greed will be your undoing," says Derla, opening all four of her eyes. "Do you have a buyer chosen already? No . . . not a buyer. You love a profit, but so do we all. You have someone who *craves* this wine, even as my client does, but who is less inclined to sharing. What pots have you placed your fingers in this time? A torn web catches no flies."

The muzzle of the blaster digs in deeper. Derla does not cry out. To cry out would be to reward Ubialla, and to shame her family line.

Even if none of them ever heard of what happened here, they would know, somewhere deep and aching, that she had died without dignity.

"When are they meeting you?" Ubialla spits.

"Please, milady, but they are here already." The voice is female, human, unfamiliar. Ubialla and Derla both turn toward it, the one furious, the other relieved. Anything that breaks the moment is worthwhile.

The woman is dressed plainly in one of the interchangeable resort uniforms, her hair styled in the polite fashion. Such a terrible, bestial thing, hair. Derla finds it difficult to understand how the humans can bear it.

The human woman raises her chin in defiance and says, "My mistresses have sent me to inform you they have seated themselves in the booth prepared for their use, and that while it is perfectly pleasing, you should have reserved a second as well, for symmetry. They would each like a glass of water and a glass of your finest candied ice wine. They understand they will not be billed for this evening's libations, as you are currently engaged in a fight for their favor, and look forward to the both of you joining them." She pauses, clearly all too aware of the blaster Ubialla holds, and swallows before she adds, "If either of you chooses not to come, they will leave immediately, and no business will be conducted tonight."

"Why?" asks Derla. "They were originally meeting only with me."

"That's why they brought me," says the woman. "Their culture requires that all important conversations be balanced on each side. Had you not brought a second for your side, I would have filled the role."

"I'm not her *second*," snarls Ubialla.

The woman looks at her anxiously. "I am only relaying what my mistresses have requested. If you will excuse me, I have to tell them that their message has been given, and then I'm to return to our resort to prepare their room for the night."

She turns then, and walks away. The look on Ubialla's face—horrified disbelief, as if she has never in her life borne such an insult—would almost be enough to make the moment worthwhile, if not for the blaster still digging into Derla's back.

"I have a suggestion," the sommelier says politely.

"I shoot you here and now, and let the stones fall as they will?" says Ubialla, in a voice like ice.

"While that might be very satisfying for you, I doubt it would be enjoyable for me," says Derla. "As the sisters have seen fit to indicate that we are both expected at the bargaining table, perhaps we should do as they have requested. Let them decide how the wine is to be portioned. I will promise to abide by their decision if you will."

"Or I could shoot all three of you," says Ubialla.

"Then there will be no more wine, ever," says Derla. She pauses before she adds, with careful venom in her voice, "Although perhaps it will not matter, if their home dimension takes umbrage at your arrogance."

"That's a lie," says Ubialla.

"You sound uncertain."

After a moment of silence, Ubialla gives the blaster a twist. "You will let me have the wine."

"I believe the sisters will decide that. Should we really keep them waiting?"

Ubialla pulls the gun away with a snarl. Derla does not smile. That would be taunting a woman near the edge of her endurance, and she is smarter, by far, than that mistake.

Perhaps she can survive this after all.

CHAPTER 7

"CALLA HAS DELIVERED OUR MESSAGE," SAYS RHOMBY, CARESSING THE leather of the booth's seat with one hand. "She's scampering home as I speak, to take her little drugs and dream her little dreams. Do you think she'll sleep in my bed while I'm away? Will I return to the room to find it smelling of dismay?"

"She'll sleep on the floor if she sleeps at all," says Parallela. "We terrify her."

Rhomby gives her a chiding look. "You're the one who chose to keep her."

"Yes," says Parallela. She folds one hand across the top of the valise that sits on the seat between them, latched and sealed and waiting. "It's good to keep frightened things. It makes them calmer in the long run. You'll see."

"I will not."

"You will not," agrees Parallela. "Here they come."

Rhomby turns to watch, gravely, as the two women in white approach. To an outside observer, it must look as if they planned their attire to complement the twins' sense of symmetry: Ubialla and Derla will never pass as sisters, are too clearly the evolutionary outcomes of two different worlds, circling two different suns, but their dresses are similar enough in cut, style, and color to seem an intentional choice.

Sometimes the galaxy is generous with its coincidences. Rhomby sits a little straighter, and sees out of the corner of her eye as Parallela does the same, both of them settling into the solemn silence that has served them so well, on so many worlds.

People do enjoy the opportunity to fill a silence. It is an art, quieting, calming, allowing others to betray themselves with their inability to hold their tongues. The sisters have been the speakers, on more than one occasion, but when they babble, they do so from a careful script, playing the flighty fool, playing the part set for them by their unwitting hosts.

Tonight that part is superseded by something far greater and more exciting. A true piece of art. Something this world has never seen before. They trade a glance, dipping their chins downward in place of the smile they dare not sport. Mystery thrives in shadow and all too often dies in the light.

Derla is the first to reach the booth. She does smile, closing her lower eyes in greeting, and it is a credit to her professionalism that the strain only shows around the corners of her mouth and in the tightness of her lids. Her life has been endangered once already, and still she spreads her hands on the table's edge, fingers splayed to show their emptiness.

"What a mercy and delight to finally be in your presence direct," she says, voice formal and carefully cadenced, so that each word is clear and ready for inspection. "Was the journey difficult?"

"Hyperspace is a veil through which only the most beautiful fish may swim," says Rhomby, her voice serious, as if she were imparting the deepest secrets of the universe. "Their fins weep rainbows as they pass. It is no small thing, to cross a veil. To cross it twice is something only fools aspire to do, and yet here we are, beautiful still, with all our rainbows bled away."

"We asked our souvenir to find us libations," says Parallela, her voice pitched to be identical to her sister's. "We told her our desires, made them clear and plain and perfectly balanced, and we released her into the world to fulfill them. Has she failed us, or has she succeeded? Shall she be coated in glory or smothered in shame?"

"Your drinks are coming," says Ubialla, her years of social grace coming to the front before they fade again before the reality of the moment. "On the house, of course. Under the circumstances, it seems the least I can do."

"What circumstances?" asks Rhomby. She tilts her head very slightly to the side. "Do you mean your forcing your way into our negotiation, which was intended to be private, in order to demand that we give to you what we brought with the intention of giving to her?"

Ubialla's smile is slow and languid, the expression of a predator preparing to close its jaws. "Yes. That is precisely what I mean. My name is Ubialla Gheal, and I—"

"This is your place: You own it, and you have built it, not brick by brick, but rumor by rumor, until it seems unassailable," says Parallela. "It is a fine palace of artifice. You should be very proud. We are Rhomby. We are Parallela."

"You can't both be both," says Ubialla.

"Perhaps not here, but where we come from, all things come in duplicate, so that if one is destroyed, the other may endure, and continue. Lessened, yes, and sorrowing until the end of all things, but alive. So we are Rhomby, and we are Parallela, and we mourn for you, that you should be singular and alone from the beginning of your days, never to know the security of a shadow who will live on in your absence." Rhomby folds her hands in her lap. "We did not come here to give you our wine, Ubialla Gheal, but as you are to stand as Derla Pidys's second in this discussion, we will allow the chance that it will be you who walks away with it. Please. Sit. Both of you. We must all be present, or no business can be done."

Derla folds herself onto a seat while Ubialla is still gaping. Derla has bargained for wines that are never meant to leave their home-worlds, for liquors considered to be religious relics and politically unwise brews. She can follow the discussion where it takes her. "It is a pleasure to finally meet you, even under these circumstances. I have been following your journeys for some time."

"Have you?" Parallela is the one to tilt her head this time, becom-

ing her sister's mirror image once again. "And what have you con-
cluded?"

"That if your wine is as good as people claim, I don't care where
you come from. Be from another dimension. Be from the bottom of
the Cantonican sea. I want what you have to offer me, and as there is
no one else to make that offer, I would be a fool to question you.
Whether you speak truth or lies is of absolutely no consequence. All
that matters is the wine."

Ubialla finally sits, concealing the blaster in her lap as she watches
the others with wary eyes.

"We have tasted so many marvelous things since arriving on your
side of space," says Rhomby. "Why do you call what we offer *wine*?"

This is familiar ground. Derla's shoulders relax slightly, some of
the stress of the moment slipping away. "Wine is made by fermenting
fruit or other vegetation with a rising agent, usually yeast, although I
have tasted some truly remarkable fungal wines. Grains are used for
beer or ale, biological sugars for mead, and other pressed, fermented,
and blended ingredients for liquors. Our definition of what is or is
not *wine* has to expand every time a new world joins our understanding of the galaxy, but all good sommeliers will tell you that wine is
something they know when they taste it. Or in my case, when I hear
it described. The alcohol you have sold before could be nothing other
than wine, and as you have promised me more of the same, I feel
comfortable using the name."

"Sapience likes similarity," says Parallela. "It is easier than too
much difference. In that your people and ours are united. We are very
fond of knowing that things we find in one place can also be found in
another."

"All by twos, and two at a time, we will see all there is to know,"
agrees Rhomby.

Derla places her valise on the corner of the table, undoing the
clasp with a flick of her fingers. "Is that why you have invited Ubialla
to join us? Because all things must come by twos?"

"That, and we were not particularly interested in anyone being
shot because of us," says Parallela. "She was prepared to do it, you

know, and all over a single bottle of wine. Your dimension is not a peaceful place. It's a wonder you've discovered horticulture, with as much time as you spend stabbing one another in the back. Do you ever make wine from blood?"

"Technically, that would be a mead, as it would be fermented from a biological sugar," says Derla.

Ubialla, as all of them have in some degree expected, snaps. Slapping her hands flat against the table, she demands, "Where is the wine?"

Rhomby and Parallela look at her in silent, reproachful unison. Ubialla slowly lifts her hands, tucks them back into her lap.

"My apologies," she says. "My excitement got the better of me."

"Indeed," says Rhomby. "There is a time and a place for excitement, and who are we to dictate the forms it takes? The sky is excited every morning, and none dares bid it stop. Sister?"

"I am ready," says Parallela, and opens her valise, reaching inside to draw a bottle carefully—not reverently; for her, this is something precious but common—into the light.

Ubialla leans forward, suddenly every bit the predator. Derla remains perfectly still, if no less predatory, eyes fixed on the bottle.

It is a beautiful thing. The glass is smooth and clear, polished until it glimmers in the dim nightclub light. There is a label, but the script is no language either of them has ever seen. Derla shivers in approval. A mysterious label for a mysterious libation. It doesn't matter if what it says is "do not drink" or "cooking only." People will still drink the contents, and feel themselves blessed for the opportunity.

"Whatever she's offering you, I'm prepared to double it," says Ubialla sharply.

Derla leans back a little, pleased. She has expected Ubialla to overplay her hand, and she has not been disappointed. Everything she knows about the sisters tells her that they dislike being pressured, which is why it has taken her so long to arrange this meeting in the first place. She could win simply by being the less offensive of the potential buyers.

"No figures have been discussed as yet; double of nothing is still nothing." A server appears, putting down the drinks that were previously requested. Rhomby favors him with a smile. "Two clean, empty glasses, please."

He nods, and vanishes back into the crowd. Derla, who understands the ritual of sale, nods understanding. Ubialla looks outraged.

"We're here to make a *sale,* not to have a drink," she snaps. "Stop this foolishness at once."

"This isn't foolishness," says Parallela.

"The waters are for you," says Rhomby, and pushes the tumblers toward Derla and Ubialla. Patiently, she explains, "It will clear your palates, wash away the dust of this world. It is better to drink what we bring with nothing to change the flavor. You have such distinctively sour dust."

Ubialla, who has never noticed anything sour about the dust of her world, scowls. "I don't see the point in clearing our palates. There's no reason to drink."

Parallela cocks her head, the precious bottle still cradled in her hands. "But how will you know that what we offer is real, if you do not take the opportunity to taste it? The agreement we made with the lady of trade was for a partial bottle, following decanting for tasting and verification."

"We are willing to allow you to participate, if only for the sake of balance, and by allowing you to participate, we have allowed you the opportunity to win," says Rhomby. "That does not mean we have extended you the authority to change the rules. That would be . . . foolish of us."

Ubialla pulls her blaster from beneath the table. Derla, moving with surprising speed, grasps her wrist and holds it tight.

The look Ubialla gives her then is as sweet as Coruscant brandy, and twice as precious. Derla half-lids her upper eyes in satisfaction.

"That," she says patiently, "is a glass bottle. If dropped, it will shatter. If the bottle is shattered, the wine will be lost. You might be able to sop it off the floor and wring it into a bucket, but would your client, powerful man as he must be to make you come to heel as he's done, really desire a draught that has been painted across the floor? Shoot and lose."

"She is correct," says Parallela.

"She is wise," says Rhomby.

"We will open the bottle; you will see what we offer, and see that it is good, and then conversation will continue," says Parallela. "Remember that there are two paths through every city, two ends to every tale, and two prizes in every race. Sister?"

"Sister," agrees Rhomby, and produces a small, overly complicated device from inside her robes. She waves it above the bottle of wine. The stopper dissolves into a line of beads that wind their way down the outside of the bottle, wrapping tight around it in an intricate design.

It is not new technology: Derla makes note of it as one more piece of evidence that the sisters come from this world, this reality, and not from someplace farther or stranger. It is still impressive. Ubialla is staring. She, surely, must have seen the trick before; she deals in too much high-end liquor to be fooled by a parlor trick.

"I regret interrupting at this most elegant and essential of moments, but my reputation for preserving the safety of my clients and my desire to continue drawing breath combine to require me to ask this question," says Derla. "How are we to know that we can drink this delicacy and live? Allergic reactions and incompatible sugars must be taken into account, which is why I desire the wine. Proper analysis and cataloging would allow me to determine—"

"We knew you were clever," says Parallela approvingly.

"I am still not assured that we can safely drink," says Derla.

Parallela reaches into the valise again, extracting a bioreader. She extends it toward Derla. "We took the liberty of running a basic analysis between your biology and the chemical makeup of our wine. It is not, perhaps, the thorough breakdown you would need before brokering a sale, but it will prove that you can drink safely."

Derla takes the reader, slides her finger down the screen, and frowns. "You have a record here for Ubialla as well."

"Yes," says Rhomby.

"She wasn't exactly . . . invited." Derla shoots a dark glance at the other woman. "How did you know to prepare an analysis for her?"

"Her inquiries had reached us in our travels," says Parallela. "It seemed likely she would want to be included in the negotiations. We acquired our souvenir as a backup plan, in case Ubialla did not decide to involve herself in your private business."

Parallela smiles at Ubialla. Ubialla, for her part, does not look chastened in the slightest.

"This is my club," she says. "There is no private business here, only business I haven't become a part of yet. Derla should feel honored that it took me this long to decide that I wanted my cut. Really, she owes me. She should relinquish her claim immediately."

"I think not," says Derla.

Rhomby picks up her glass and takes a sip of ice wine, nose crinkling briefly in pleasure. "You are so fascinating, you mismatches," she says. "To find a proper two in this dimension, we must build it ourselves, one plus another to form a whole. You never quite synchronize as you should. How wonderful. How lonely."

The second server returns, carrying two empty glasses, which he places in front of Parallela. She nods to him and he vanishes again, back into the dim recesses of the club, where the rest of Canto Bight—or so it seems—has come to play, laughing and drinking and plotting and weeping, all unaware of this small and terrible drama.

Most dramas are like that. They are small, and petty, and inconsequential to everyone who stands outside them, while mattering more than anything else in the galaxy to those who are fully committed, who are fully involved. They fill their jaws with moments, and they do not release them until they have been shaken lifeless, dead things to be thrown at the feet of the next drama to come along.

Carefully, Parallela tips the bottle to first one glass and then the other, filling them halfway with a liquid that seems to hold every color of the setting sun, somehow dividing them as it settles, so that the bottom of the wine is clear as crystal, and the top is the deep, bruised purple of night. Between those states stretch yellow, orange, pink, a dazzling array of shades swirled and twisted and impossible. Derla frowns.

"Are you satisfied that you may drink safely?" asks Parallela.

"I am satisfied that we can drink the wine," says Derla. "I am not satisfied that we can safely drink a blended liquor. Can you provide an analysis?"

"Oh," says Rhomby. "This *is* the wine."

Derla's breath catches in her throat, and everything is understood, and everything is different. She sips her water to clear her head. Out of the corner of her eye she sees Ubialla do the same, possibly for the same reasons.

When people spoke of the wine—the wine of dreams they called it, over and over again; the wine of dreams—they never seemed to give the same color twice. They would call it dark, and she has, until this moment, believed they referred to a red wine. They would call it light, and she has, until this moment, believed they referred to a *different* wine, a white wine from the same vineyard, perhaps, something meant to be carried and presented in tandem. She has not understood—did not, *could* not understand—that they meant the same wine, a single beverage that did too many impossible things to comprehend without seeing them.

"I . . . see," she says, voice squeaking under its burden of eager avarice. "Do you know, perhaps, how the effect is achieved?"

"We're tourists, not winemakers," says Parallela. "Are you prepared to try what we offer you?"

Ubialla greedily grabs the first glass before the sentence is finished, bringing it to her lips and drinking her first mouthful in a gulp better suited to something much more common, some rum or brandy or bitterfruit liquor. Derla takes her glass but does not raise it to her lips until she sees Ubialla take another gulp. Then, finally, she allows all four of her eyes to close, and smells what is before her.

Sweetness, yes, but sourness, too, and notes of soil and rock and green growing things. This single glass of wine smells like an entire field of potential. She sniffs again. The fruit, as expected, is unfamiliar, likely native to the world that birthed the Grammus sisters. The rest of the notes are familiar enough to reaffirm her belief that they have come from a world she has yet to see, and not from the other side of hyperspace. However amazing and impossible their wine appears, it smells too much like every other wine she has had the good fortune to know for it to really be from another dimension.

Her first sip, in contrast with Ubialla, is taken with the utmost precision and care. She rolls it gently on her tongue, teasing out all of its secrets. The sweetness is dominant here; the wine is deep and rich and blankets her mouth in a gentle veil of mysteries yet to be solved. She swallows, taking another sip, and then another, and marvels at the way the flavor shifts with the color, sweetness being slowly replaced by something much sharper and less cloying, until the glass finishes, far too soon, on a crisp, astringent note.

There will be no need for hosts to buy a dozen different bottles for their parties: a single vintage will supply every flavor profile, cleansing the palate and allowing the drinker to begin again, refreshed, never tiring of the wine presented. The other vineyards will revolt when she brings even a single glass of this to the market. She will be able to ask any price she likes, and people will pay, oh, yes, they'll pay in full, they'll pay in plenty. The other vintners, once they realize that she's done the impossible—oh, no one loves a challenge like an artist. She expects they'll bring competing brews to market inside a standard decade. Long enough for her to make a hefty profit, quickly enough to be a true innovation.

She's going to change her own world, and she's going to delight in doing it, and all she needs to do is walk away from here with the wine in her possession. All she needs to do is *win*.

"As advertised," she says simply, and puts her glass down on the table. Parallela moves as if to refill it.

"No!" Ubialla does not go so far as to put her hand over Derla's glass. She flinches as if nothing would please her more. Composing herself, she says, "We were promised—*I* was promised—a bottle for sale. The more we drink here, in the process of supposed negotiation, the less will remain for me."

"You were promised nothing, Ubialla Gheal," says Rhomby. For the first time, her voice is truly cold, truly unforgiving. "You came to this table as one uninvited, but essential, part of a negotiation begun without you, planned without you, *promised* without you. That you are here at all is upon our sufferance and because we must have balance. We control how this is to be done. If you do not approve, you are welcome to break the negotiation and go."

"Wait." Derla looks between Rhomby and Ubialla before asking, with exquisite care, "What happens to the negotiation if she leaves us?"

"Balance will be gone," says Parallela. "Without balance, there can be no auspicious result, and we will go as well, hoping that we may have the chance to meet with you again in some better time, under some better circumstance. We will sorrow greatly, Derla Pidys, for we have hoped for this meeting for a very long time, but when balance has been lost, there is nothing to be done but walk away as quickly as feet can carry."

"So you need me," purrs Ubialla.

"Apparently so." Derla holds her glass toward Parallela. "I would adore another sample to consider as we discuss."

"So be it," says Rhomby as Parallela fills the glass again.

Derla brings it to her lips.

It has barely reached them when the lights go out.

The lights of an establishment such as Ubialla's are not an inconsequential thing to extinguish: They are not, as they might be in a shop or a university, all the same, nor are they run off a single circuit. Stopping the lights of the individual booths, the overheads, the floor lights, even the lights behind the bar, all with the flip of a switch or the press of a remote, should be quite impossible. But off they all go, casting the room into brief and absolute darkness. Someone screams—several someones, their voices joining in strange, bone-tingling harmony. Someone else laughs, the high, delighted tones of a person whose species sees perfectly in the dark.

"Do *not* move," spits Ubialla.

Derla, closest to her, does not. As for the sisters, who could say? They are only a meter or two away. They might as well be on another planet, in another system entirely. The darkness is too deep.

Something falls over at another table. Something shatters. It is only the fear of hearing that sound again, much closer, that stops Derla from grabbing for the bottle with the remaining wine. She is still sitting, paralyzed by fear, when the lights come back up and the nightclub is revealed.

Nervous laughter spreads from all the tables around them as people reassure themselves that nothing has changed, there was no robbery or attack or invasion. They are still the people of Canto Bight, still in one of the most beloved and luxurious settings in the world, and nothing can harm them here. Let the rest of the galaxy go as it will, it can neither find nor reclaim them.

There is no laughter at the table shared by Ubialla, Derla, and the Grammus sisters. Silence falls over them, weighted around the edges, driving them down. Finally, Ubialla finds her voice.

"Where," she asks darkly, "is the *wine*?"

A sister spreads her hands. "Not here."

Ubialla lunges for Derla's valise, snatching it up and spreading it open. Wisely, Derla does not object, merely watches as the other woman's search turns quickly frantic. There is nothing she can say. The wine, precious and irreplaceable thing that it is . . .

The wine is gone.

CHAPTER 8

CALLA TOUCHES HER PALM TO THE ROOM DOOR, WHICH READS HER prints, verifies them against the list of authorized residents, and slides smoothly open, allowing her to step inside. Everything is as they left it, even down to the ridiculous bromeliad on Parallela's bed. It seems to be regenerating portions of its broken root system; they are beginning to quest across the duvet, looking for something to bury themselves inside.

This particular species is large, ornamental, and considered a terrible, invasive pest on all worlds with more arable land and available water. So far as Calla is aware, only Canto Bight is cocky enough to consider it a candidate for use as an ornamental. She wonders whether Parallela is aware of the origins of her new "pet," and whether the sisters will be trying to take it back with them to their homeworld, or home dimension, as the case may be. She spares a moment to consider an entire planet choked under a veil of bromeliads. Then she gets to work.

Her dismissal from the nightclub was not a dismissal from service. She has much to do before she returns to her temporary keepers. She knows, by this point, that they intend to release her, and this resort is certainly an excellent place to be let go; she thinks she can be happy here, can make herself useful and increase the level of her credit.

Maybe, after a few cycles here, she could even go home. The idea is more appealing now than it was before the sisters came. After all, she has gambled so many times on Canto Bight, and she has lost every attempt. It is time to try something new.

It's time to try getting out.

She opens the datapad Rhomby handed her before she left to gather Derla and Ubialla. She reads its contents silently before looking at the bromeliad again.

She smiles.

"Well?" says Ubialla. "Have you lost understanding of language in your shock? Have you become unable to speak?" The blaster is in her hand again, barrel terrifyingly large as it swings from one person at the table to the next. With her free hand she reaches out and snatches Derla's wine away. "Where is it?"

"We do not know," says Parallela.

"We are as shocked by this violation of our persons as you are," says Rhomby.

"Do your customers risk robbery often?" asks Parallela.

"Perhaps we have chosen poorly," says Rhomby.

"I'll say you have," snarls Ubialla. She stands, blaster still aimed at the others. "Security!"

They appear out of the shadows as if they have been waiting for this call all night—and perhaps they have been. This is Ubialla's place, after all, and she has shown interest in a specific table. Such things are all too often signs of danger.

Derla recognizes half of the bulky forms now towering over her as the bouncers from before. She looks regretfully at the Wookiee. He turns his eyes away, not making a sound.

"My *colleagues* seem to have misplaced an extremely valuable bottle of wine," says Ubialla, ice in every syllable. "You will be locking the doors and keeping everyone inside until it is retrieved and brought to me. Do I make myself clear?"

"The clientele—" begins a guard.

"Do. I. Make. Myself. Clear." Ubialla swings her blaster around to aim at the center of his chest.

He nods quickly. "Perfectly," he says.

The guards disperse. Ubialla swings her blaster back to the table.

"Now," she says. "You will find what I want. You will bring it back here. And you will give it to me. The negotiation is over. Your compensation will be your lives. I trust that is sufficient to put me at the head of the current offerings. I find the dead have little need for material goods, and rarely can they spend what they have earned. Do we have a deal?"

"Your world is very violent," says Parallela. She stands as gracefully as a reed bending with the wind. "I would consider that a failing were it not so clearly beneficial to your survival. A pity."

"You are not the sort of person we will choose to do business with more than once," says Rhomby. She follows her sister to her feet. "We hope you have considered the ramifications of your actions."

"I don't care about the ramifications of my actions," says Ubialla. "I care about the *wine.*"

Before Derla can stand, Ubialla brings her blaster around, muzzle aimed directly at the sommelier's chest. Elsewhere in the club, people are beginning to complain loudly, the reality of their confinement sinking in.

"She stays," says Ubialla. "I want my bottle. Understand?"

"Of course," say the sisters in eerie unison, and ghost away into the crowd.

Derla spreads her empty hands in supplication. "Please, Ubialla," she says. "We've known each other for so long. You know you don't have to do this. You know I won't run—and they have no reason to care one way or the other. They could slip away while you're focused on me."

"You tried to set this up under my nose," snaps Ubialla. "You *knew* I needed this wine. What do you think happens to me if I let a prize like this escape from the planet? What do you think happens when *he* learns that it was sold right here in my club, and I didn't bother to acquire it for him? Do you think I get forgiven for being outwitted by an offworld merchant? Or do you think I pay for my failures?"

"I think it is unfair to expect you to know everything that happens in Canto Bight," says Derla calmly. This is not the first time she's been held at blasterpoint: It will not, luck willing, be the last. Her line of work brings her into contact with people from all ways of life. It's the money that matters. And the super-rich, or their hired help, do not take well to being told no.

She has refused to sell senators wines that would set off allergic cascades guaranteed to kill them, has refused to trade intoxicants with mercenaries and bounty hunters whose reputations painted them as somewhat more vicious than her reputation can afford. Her legend says that she can get anything, that she will do business with anyone who trades in good faith, but a part of good faith is protecting herself from having too many dealings with the truly dangerous, the truly foolish, and the truly corrupt. A few threats are a natural consequence of conducting business as she does. If the threats stop, it is a sign that she has lost her edge, and everything else will soon stop as well.

Ubialla laughs, thin and bitter. "Listen to you, talking about *fair* and *unfair* like they mean something. This is Canto Bight. We make our own reality, and there's no room in it for fairness. It would get in the way of the dice."

"Be that as it may. I don't think I can be blamed for putting my business ahead of your ambition."

"And look where it's got you," says Ubialla. "If they don't find that wine, you're dead. You know that, don't you?"

"I knew when the first glass was poured," says Derla, and settles back to wait.

CHAPTER 9

RHOMBY AND PARALLELA MOVE DEEPER INTO THE BAR, SIDE BY SIDE, AS they almost always are. It's important to make the best possible first impression, and being seen as a matching pair helps with that, it genuinely does. Alone, they are faces in a crowd, plain, dismissible. Together, they are rare and strange in this largely singular place.

They lie so often that sometimes even they lose track of where the truth is waiting—and this, too, is to their benefit; a lie told as the absolute truth is far more powerful than a lie told to deceive—but in this they are always honest: It is still so *strange* to walk in places where most require a mirror to see their own face. They have encountered twins, even triplets, as they traveled through the galaxy, but they are so rare that they are almost an aberration, and none of them have chosen the polite unity of matching, or even complementary, attire. To stand so distinct from one's twin . . . the thought is abhorrent.

Ubialla's security is fanning out through the bar. Rhomby watches as one of the men grabs the handbag of a human dressed for some sort of sporting event, short skirt and attractive but supportive top. The woman objects loudly, demanding to speak to the manager. Her words go unheeded. Parallela watches as the Wookiee more deferentially approaches a table of off-duty jockeys, their shoulders slumped with exhaustion, their eyes glittering with the memory of stimulants and the roaring crowd. They object to his presence, snapping and shooing him away. One even throws the decorative garnish from his drink at the Wookiee's chest, where it sticks in the heavy fur like some sort of badge of shame. The Wookiee snarls. The table quiets, allowing him to search their bags.

Neither security guard finds anything worth reporting to Ubialla. A few illegal drugs; a few even more illegal weapons. Nothing of sufficient interest to involve confiscation, much less the authorities, although one bouncer does get a lead on a new supplier for his own extracurricular interests. They move on. The sisters exchange a glance and do the same.

"Sorry, so very sorry," says Rhomby, approaching the table with the qianball player. She slips her hand inside her dress momentarily as she walks, pulling it out with a thin, caustic slime on her fingertips. "Did they bother you? Oh, I am so very sorry. These are people with no manners, none at all."

The qianball player sniffs, plainly offended. "What do you expect from this sort of two-bit tourist attraction? I can't believe I ever thought this place was worth my time. As soon as those doors open, Ubialla can find herself someone else to fill my table."

"Of course, of course," says Rhomby soothingly. She brushes her fingers across the label of the wine bottle sitting unguarded on the table. The label comes away with the motion, sticking to the translucent slime. She moves her hand behind her back before the qianball player can see. "I heard—forgive me if I am incorrect, but—I heard the southern door had been left unlocked for the truly important patrons."

The woman's eyes widen. She is on her feet like a shot, disappearing deeper into the club without so much as a word. A cry of "Out of my way!" drifts back, accompanied by irritated shouts and objections. Rhomby does not smile, but anyone who knew her would be able to see the satisfaction in her stride.

Parallela drifts toward the table of jockeys and asks them, in a dreamy voice, "Is it true? Have we been locked in here because there's to be some sort of raid? I heard they were planning to do drug tests on the spot. Any of us who have a legal substance with restricted uses in our bloodstream could face penalties, depending on the nature of our professions. Can they do that? Is it legal?"

Her fingertips, when she pulls them from behind her back, are coated in the same gleaming substance. As the jockeys exchange horrified looks she moves, brushing her fingers across two of their wide collection of bottles, and whisks the chemically loosened labels away behind her back.

"There's a secret door at the back of one of the closets, from back when they had raids all the time," says one of the jockeys. "Come on." They vanish with remarkable speed, these agile athletes, and Parallela is left alone with her prizes dangling from her fingertips. Serene as always—there is power in serenity, in the ability to step back and let the scene unfold around her, its participants unaware that without that seed of calm, the chaos would be unable to bloom—she walks toward the bar.

The bartenders who should be seeing to this stretch are elsewhere, distracted by a shouting qianball pro, a group of jockeys trying to sneak into a janitor's closet, a model having a fit of claustrophobia, and a dozen other problems and complications. The bar is, for the moment, unattended. Parallela slips behind it, doing her best to seem innocent and lost even as she begins to move her hands across the bottles. Labels come away like leaves falling from a tree, only to re-adhere when she presses them into their new homes. Brandies become rums become wines of a dozen different kinds. When she steps away, moving back into the public area, she leaves a jumble of mislabeled bottles behind her, and her hands are empty.

Rhomby is on her way to another stretch of bar when a hand grabs her shoulder and whips her around. She stares into the face of the unfamiliar human behind her, a man in gray-and-white clothing tailored to look shabby—but not shabby at all, not really. It is a clever illusion, which makes this man a liar before he has even said a word. Fascinating.

"Did you do this?" he demands.

Slowly, she blinks at him, putting every shred of confusion she can muster into the expression. "What do you mean, sir?" she asks. "I don't know you. I can't possibly have done anything to you. Whatever has been done to you, you must have done it yourself."

"The doors," he says. "They're locked."

"I believe security did that, sir. I do not have access to the keys."

"Ubialla has never locked the doors before."

A regular, then, someone who comes here often enough to understand the place and its rhythms. Rhomby looks at him more carefully, as behind her something smashes and another voice screeches anger and disapproval. Oh, the chaos here is winding up nicely, twisting and turning and becoming a delightful sculpture that this city will gaze upon for years and years to come. They may not be able to return to Canto Bight for a while after this night's work, and won't that be lovely? A world that doesn't want you back is a world that has been well and truly *enjoyed*.

"You're a thief," she says, with pleased wonder in her tone. "An actual thief, inside the bar. Oh, you're in a great deal of trouble, sir, should Ubialla realize who and what and where you are. Something she wants very badly has gone missing, you see, and you'll make a splendid target for her anger. I would run, if I were you. I would run so far and so fast and so hard that there was no chance of my ever being found again. I might even go so far as to quit this world altogether. There are so many other stars in the sky. Go and orbit one of them for a time, and see whether the long hands of the wronged come reaching for you there."

The thief stares at her, releasing her shoulder and taking a step back. "What are you saying? I'm no thief. I'm an honest dealer for a local casino. My tables are clean."

"Your clothing is expensive. Good fabric, careful tailoring. The sort of thing one wears when the goal is never needing to do repairs on the run. But you've chosen a style that looks cheap, that came into your hands already tattered and stained in ways that have nothing to do with wear. You have too many pockets. Your hands are too strong, and your fingers move like a hummer's wings, almost faster than my eyes can follow—and my eyes are very good. There's no shame in thievery. It's a profession like any other, and you're not to be blamed if the world disapproves. It's simply that Ubialla has lost something that, as I said before, she wants very badly. The doors are locked because there has been a theft. You are a thief. You are inside. Can you see the connections as I draw them? You'll be held as proof that no fault attaches to her, and I doubt you'll survive it, or enjoy it if you do." Rhomby shakes her head in apparent sorrow. "There are those who say there is no justice on Canto Bight. I say there is. It's simply justice with teeth, which is the most terrible kind of all."

The man—the thief—takes a step backward. "What are you?"

"A friend. An artist. A sister most of all, which is why I do each and every thing I do. Run. I'll tell no one that I saw you, nor which way you've gone, and you'll be clear of this place before anyone knows you were here." Rhomby tilts her head slightly to the side, that impossible angle that is neither mammal nor bird, but something awful and in-between. "I doubt Ubialla will make such a generous offer."

"So why do you?" he asks warily.

"It suits me to have the mystery stand a little longer. Run away while you can."

The thief hesitates. Finally, he turns on his heel and is gone, racing into the dark of the bar. Rhomby waits where she is for several seconds before drifting after him, trying to look unconcerned.

Parallela is better at this part of the game than she is, always has been: Her sister has amazingly clever hands, and an air of controlled helplessness that can buy her access to the most restricted of areas. As long as she continues to work quickly, she can pull off the confusion entirely on her own, if necessary. Soon the people trapped inside will begin queuing up at the bar, demanding recompense for their lost evening. Ubialla doesn't know it yet, but she'll be pouring a great many free drinks tonight—first to keep her patrons calm and happy, and then to replace the drinks they receive but did not order. It would be a fascinating exercise to calculate how much money the woman is going to lose.

This part of the plan was optional, one more way of increasing chaos and keeping the club off balance. Had Ubialla not decided to enter the negotiations in the most hostile way possible, they might have spared her profits somewhat. Then again, they might not have. They have found her to be oily and somewhat cruel, unnecessarily so. There is value to kindness, even when it is a deceitful thing.

The thief heads for a small door in the wall, and past it, pressing his hands against what appears to be a flat section. After glancing around to see if he is being watched—an ineffective precaution; he does not see Rhomby, hanging back unobtrusively and pretending to study the ceiling—he pushes inward, and the wall slides away, making a hole he can pass through. He does, and he is gone.

"Interesting," says Rhomby. She glides to the nearest rack of bottles, swapping several labels in quick succession. When she looks up, a table full of ruffled, displeased-looking models is watching her. She raises a finger to her lips, signaling that they should be silent. They exchange glances with one another before nodding, accepting her offer of conspiracy.

Yes. Ubialla should really have learned to be kinder. But then, this plan would never work if she had.

The Wookiee returns, hands empty and expression downcast. He makes an apologetic statement in his own language, guttural and lovely, like the song of a bright, beautiful bird. Derla regrets that she has never learned Shyriiwook. It is such a gorgeous method of communication.

Ubialla stares at him for a moment, her blaster wavering, before she snaps, "Keep her here. If she moves, rip her arms off."

She strides away into the club, leaving Derla and the Wookiee alone. Silence falls between them, broken by the occasional shouts, screams, and other exclamations from the rest of the club.

Finally, Derla speaks. "I would like to stand, if you don't mind," she says. "My back is stiff from sitting here too long. I was not expecting our negotiations to last more than a short time. Please?"

The Wookiee hesitates, clearly torn between his desire to be kind to a woman who has never been cruel to him and his desire to follow the instructions of his employer. Finally, he makes a resigned growling sound and gestures for Derla to rise.

She stands smoothly, wiping the wrinkles from her dress with the heels of her hands before she lifts her head and closes her upper eyes in polite acknowledgment. "Thank you. I appreciate this act of kindness. I am so very sorry that we cannot converse more easily; your language, while lovely, does not come easily to my tongue, and I have never been one who could understand languages I cannot also practice. A sincere pity. The wines of Kashyyyk have always struck me as among the most interesting in the galaxy. Their density of flavor is unmatched by virtually all other worlds."

The Wookiee makes a noise she interprets, loosely, as embarrassed pleasure.

"If you are ever looking for a taste of home, and know me to be onworld, please feel free to call upon me. I would be delighted to help you."

The Wookiee makes a noise somewhere between a warble and a growl. Derla sighs, half laughing at herself.

"Yes, I suppose I *have* fallen prey to the first danger of Canto Bight: I forgot that the house will always emerge victorious. I apologize for making another request of you so soon after the first, knowing that both or either could cause you trouble, but would it be possible for you to escort me to the facilities? We had time to begin our sampling before the lights went out, and I need to make use of them rather badly." Derla looks at him hopefully. She's pushing her luck, and she knows it, but she still needs to see what's going on. It's important. Important enough, in this moment, to take the risk.

The Wookiee hesitates long enough that she's fairly sure her gamble has failed: Then he nods and growls, and grasps her upper arm in one surprisingly gentle hand, all but engulfing it. He holds her, not as he might hold a prisoner, but as he would hold someone he was instructed to escort. He looks like a bodyguard, and she is relieved and honored in the same measure.

"If you're ever looking for more than wine—another employer, perhaps—please feel free to seek me out," she murmurs.

He purrs acknowledgment, and they begin making their way across the floor.

The other security guards and bouncers are still moving table-to-table, and from the looks of the chaos in their wake, they have yet to learn subtlety. They question; they accuse. They leave people angrier than they were before—and since no one is remaining stationary, some of these people must have been questioned two and even three times. Tension within the club is growing. Derla can easily believe that it might erupt into violence before too much longer, and can't see any easy way to make it better.

Ubialla will not stop, will not open the doors, until the wine is in her possession. If she's willing to push things this far and risk this much damage to her reputation, she can't be overstating the danger she faces if she fails to recover that bottle. Derla fights to keep the realization from showing on her face.

If she wins the negotiation, she will not leave here alive. If she withdraws, the sisters may declare it to be over, with no winner, and *none* of them will leave here alive. And if the wine is somehow gone forever . . .

It is too dismaying to consider, and so she considers, instead, what she believes to be the most likely situation. She continues walking, continues scanning the club, until she sees one of the sisters wandering, seemingly aimless, through the crowd. It's all an act. There is purpose in every step, every move of her hands and turn of her head. The crowd seems calmer after the sister passes, as if whatever nonsense she speaks is somehow soothing to them. They turn, almost as one, to head for the nearest bar, and the sister, briefly without a crowd for cover, sees Derla.

Derla nods to her, minutely, and jerks her chin toward the restroom door. The sister nods, and turns her path in that direction.

The Wookiee, who has not been instructed to keep them apart, nonetheless looks faintly nonplussed when he reaches the restroom door, Derla in tow, at the same time as the sister. He looks to Derla and makes an inquisitive sound.

She closes her lower eyes and says, solemnly, "I promise you we are not doing anything that would hurt Miss Gheal in any way. I would like to resolve this as quickly and painlessly as possible. Wouldn't you like the same?"

The Wookiee makes a sad sound and lets go of her arm. Derla touches his hand.

"Please consider my offer," she says.

She slips through the door. The sister, whichever it may be, is close behind.

Like everything else about Ubialla's club, the facilities are normally in exquisite condition, with organic attendants prepared to direct patrons to the stalls and private rooms designed to serve their needs. Once the door is closed, Derla reaches out and grasps the sister's elbow. The other woman looks at her.

"I don't know which you are, and I find I do not particularly care," says Derla. "I know the wine wasn't stolen."

The sister blinks. "How?" she asks.

Derla has to fight not to laugh out loud. It had been a guess more than a certainty. It seems like she's a better gambler than she ever thought. "You were too calm," she says. "Had a treasure of such importance been stolen from me, I would have been the first to lose my composure. You and your sister both, you have remained so calm. We don't know much about your world—"

"Hyperspace is a rainbow," says the sister.

Derla does not quite suppress the urge to snort. "Your *world*," she repeats. "I have tasted your wine. I know every flavor this galaxy has to offer. Yours is exotic, yes, and exciting, but it's not from another dimension. It comes from a place that can be found. That will be found, one day. You'll want friends when that happens, not only enemies. Ubialla is not going to be a friend. Any chance of that died when you contacted me instead of her. Right now all you can do is try to minimize the damage already done."

"What do you suggest?" asks the sister.

"Appease her. Flatter her, favor her, grant her the wine in our negotiation, whatever is necessary to see that all of us walk out of here tonight alive. You carry a treasure. There's no question of that. Should you ever wish to sell more than a single bottle, I would be honored to be your agent in the wider galaxy. Discretion comes very easily to me, and you would never need to tell me how to find your world. My only request is that we do no further business on Cantonica. I believe the city of Canto Bight will be a bad place for the three of us to be seen in tandem for quite some time to come." Derla shakes her head decisively. "You have played an excellent game, and I applaud you for your audacity, but there is no victory here. There is only the hope of walking away more or less unscathed."

The sister is silent for a moment, considering Derla's words, before she says, with no small trace of amusement in her voice, "And your desire to be the sole agent of our wine has nothing to do with this warning."

"It has *everything* to do with this warning," says Derla. "Everything. If we all die here tonight because you've backed Ubialla into a corner from which she sees no escape, well. You certainly won't be in any position to provide me with more wine, and I won't be in any position to move it. If I believed in a deity, I would be suggesting you appeal to its mercies now, and hope that it could guide you to some favorable if unlikely outcome. I want your wine. You want, one presumes, to make a profit. Neither of us gets what we want if we don't walk away."

"I will tell my sister what you have said," says the sister. "We will consider your words. We will come to an accord."

"I suggest you consider quickly," says Derla. "I don't believe Ubialla's patience is going to last for much longer, and it's going to end badly for someone. I would rather it not be me."

The sister nods and slips away, leaving Derla alone in the cavernous room. She still doesn't know which sister she just spoke to.

She doesn't know whether either sister is going to listen.

The water from the taps is cool and pleasant on her fingers. Real water, not sonic waves: one more luxury for one of the most luxurious places in the sector. Derla lets it run over her fingers for a moment, savoring the sensation of it, before she splashes some over her face, turns off the tap, and walks back to the door. The Wookiee is waiting just outside. He growl-grumbles relief at the sight of her.

"It is all right, my friend," she says, touching his arm lightly. "I would not escape and leave you to face the wrath of Ubialla alone. Come now. Return me to my chair before she comes and finds us gone."

He folds his hand over hers, like some strange parody of a queen's attendants seeing her to her throne, and leads her back toward the booth where everything went wrong.

CHAPTER 10

CALLA WALKS CALMLY TOWARD THE CLOSED NIGHTCLUB DOORS. IT'S strange to see the place shut down when every other business on the street is open and enjoying increased business—not only from the sudden lack of competition, but from the mystery of it all. What could possibly lead Ubialla to close down at mid-cycle, when there's drinking to be done and the casinos and racetrack are churning out their endless stream of newly minted rich, each of them dying to drink to their success at the fabled Ubialla's? Every minute those doors are closed costs her more than simply credits. She's losing reputation, losing cachet, and while no one doubts her ability to win it back, it seems beyond strange for her to take the risk at all.

The walkways are well lit and reasonably safe, especially here, with merchants hawking their wares and criers for the various clubs waving discount slips and shouting promises to try to entice this sudden windfall of free custom their way. If she were to tread into the shadows, she would quickly find herself in substantially more danger, and so she will not do that.

She wears a long silver cloak over her resort uniform. She carries a bottle in one hand. She knows she should be afraid, but everything that has happened since she made—and lost—her unwise bet with the Grammus sisters has happened so fast that there hasn't been time for fear. She's been so busy reacting to everything that there simply hasn't been an opportunity to stop and really *think* about what she's been doing.

That's good. As far as she's concerned, this specific brand of thoughtlessness can last all the way to the moment when she gets either released or carted off to some alien dimension where she won't know anyone and won't have any way of escaping. Right now she has a job to do, and she needs to be as calm and clearheaded as possible if she's hoping to achieve it.

There are no guards outside the door. That's fine. If anything, that makes what comes next slightly easier. She steps up into the sheltered alcove that protects Ubialla's guests from the ruffians on the street, and pauses to adjust her cloak and knock the dust from her shoes. She must look better than she is if she's to play this part. She must look like she *belongs* here and not behind a resort counter.

It's hard to suppress the small thrill that runs through her as she finally raises her hand to knock. Ubialla Gheal and people like her are the reason that the honest citizens of Canto Bight—the ones who came for a weekend and found themselves staying for a lifetime, whether intentionally or not—can never break even, much less get ahead. Their grift and graft is small-time, designed for survival, not for counting coup. They are small predators in a dangerous jungle, and Ubialla and her kind are so much higher up the food chain that even the thought of getting one over on her is deliciously intoxicating, sweeter than any wine.

Calla knocks. There is no answer, so she knocks again, and again, until it becomes almost a game, until she's hammering out the tempo of a song she heard once, played by a strange little band in a strange little bar that she's never been able to find again, no matter how hard she's looked. Canto Bight is like that. It gives and it takes, and it never slows down enough to let you figure out whether the books balance after all. She's fairly sure they don't. For the books to balance, the city would have to occasionally lose.

Sometimes she feels like she's standing in the belly of a great machine designed to grind people up and spit them out, over and over again, with loaded dice and marked cards and poisoned drinks and honeyed lies. She loves it here, she honestly does. She wants to be a creature born to this environment, capable of breathing this air without feeling it stinging the bottom of her lungs—a feeling born of failure to thrive, not any toxin or pollutant. There has never been a city as clean and as filthy at the same time as Canto Bight, where everything is planned, everything is controlled, and nothing is free.

She keeps knocking until the side of her hand goes numb, and then she keeps knocking after that, hit after hit after hit, and every strike is another wrong that Canto Bight has done to her, another hand that didn't play her way, another customer who didn't tip, another manager who thought she needed to learn humility, or at least learn to play the game of flesh and favors. Every time she knocks, she sees another reason the city set her up for this, another card played toward this eventual outcome. She never had a choice. She never had a chance.

She keeps knocking.

The door opens.

At first she's so surprised that she raises her hand to knock again anyway, ready to slap flesh against open air and see what happens. Then she catches herself, lowering hand and head in the same instant, and says, "I apologize for disturbing you, but my mistresses instructed me to come meet them here, and I would have to do far more than apologize if I failed to meet their expectations. I know you're closed for the night, but please, may I come in?"

The sound of shouting, shrill laughter, and loud protests drifts out from behind the weary, wary guard. He looks her up and down, expression barely shy of a scowl, and asks, "Who are your mistresses?"

"Rhomby and Parallela Grammus."

The change in the guard is gratifying. He straightens, weariness replaced by shock, wariness replaced by something that looks very much like greed. "The sisters," he says. "You belong to the sisters."

Calla wants to bristle at the idea that she belongs to anyone apart from herself. She does no such thing, bowing shallowly instead as she replies, "They are my mistresses, and they have bid me to meet them here."

"Why?"

Her instructions have prepared her for this possibility. She draws her cloak aside, revealing the bottle she clutches by the neck. The glass is dark, concealing the contents, but it is a wine bottle connected, if only tenuously, to the Grammus sisters; it is as good as any bribe, as valuable as any promissory note.

"I am to deliver this," she says.

"Come with me," says the guard, and grabs her by the wrist, hauling her into the club. The door slams as soon as she's inside the dimly lit antechamber. More guards are present, holding back agitated patrons who have just been teased with freedom.

"Ubialla will want to see you immediately," snaps the guard.

"Please," says Calla, summoning every scrap of humility she's learned from working at the resorts. There's a surprising amount of it, coupled with a less surprising amount of scorn. They think they know her so well. They don't know her at all. "My mistresses are expecting me. I'll be in trouble if I don't come. You have to let me go to them."

"I don't have to do anything but take you to Ubialla," says the guard. "She'll decide when you see your mistresses. *If* you see them."

Calla allows herself to stumble, as if shocked by his blatant implication that she'll never see the sisters again, as if pulled off balance by his hand. His response to the motion is, predictably, to yank her back onto her feet, keeping her from breaking free. That's what she was hoping for. Using the momentum of the guard's pull for cover, she lets her hand come open.

She lets the bottle fall.

It strikes the marble floor of the club and shatters into a million shards, too broken to ever be pieced back together. Dark-purple liquid splashes outward like a bruise, staining everything it touches. Patrons close enough to be in range step back, crying out in disgust and dismay.

Calla starts to cry, small, hitching sobs, and feels the sympathy of the crowd shift. Yes, she dropped the bottle, but only because that brute of a guard pulled on her. The guard who has, in tandem with his fellows, been keeping them locked in all night, refusing to let them leave as they deserve. He's the one to blame here, not her.

The mutters swell to grumbles to open-voiced complaints. The guard, still struck silent and motionless by the destruction of the greatest treasure his employer has ever pursued, finds himself surrounded in an instant, hemmed in by a wall of angry bodies. He tries to take a step. They're making motion—making flight—impossible.

He raises his hands to ward them off, releasing Calla in the process. Her tears stop immediately. She ducks low, making herself a smaller target, and pushes through the crowd, finding the natural holes among their bodies as they move in and she moves out.

The smell of the spilled liquid fills the air, sweet and cloying and passably believable as an unfamiliar vintage of wine. It's not wine, of course, was never fermented, never aged, never put through any process more elaborate than a single woman in a resort bathroom crushing flower petals into a funnel, but it can pass for the stuff in the right light, under the right circumstances.

There is a screech of fury behind her. Calla turns. Ubialla stands at the edge of the antechamber, staring at the spill with horror. Ubialla's eyes flick upward, and widen as she sees Calla.

"You," she says, voice trembling, and raises her hand to point. "What was . . . was this . . . ?"

"My mistresses contacted me and asked me to bring it after the bottle they carried with them was stolen," says Calla. She doesn't have to work to make her voice shake. Part of her is still pleased by the chaos she's helped to create, by the understanding that the strange women who plucked her from her safe resort job are well on their way to beating the house for once. They're going to win. For Ubialla to be this angry, for the club to be this restless . . .

They're going to win. But there's a blaster in Ubialla's hand, and Calla has been on Canto Bight too long to believe that any victory comes without a cost. Someone has to pay when the cards are marked and the dice are loaded, when the edges of the tiles are dusted with pheromone pollen. Someone has to pay. Always, it's been people like her. Why should tonight be any different?

"You *dropped* the wine?" Ubialla's voice is low and dangerous.

Calla takes a step back, prepared to run. A hand closes on her shoulder, stopping her where she is. She glances back, sure she'll see the face of another one of Ubialla's goons, some hulking bruiser with the strength to pull her head off her shoulders for her offenses against the house—

—and finds herself looking at the calm, even solemn face of one of the Grammus sisters. She still can't tell them apart, may never be able to tell them apart, and that doesn't matter, because in this moment she loves them both with a bright, fierce devotion that will never fade away. No one has ever taken the time to save her before, no matter how much she's needed it.

"This is ours," says the sister. Her tone is calm, patient, the sort of voice best used for addressing a child. "You should not threaten what is ours, not when you still hope to benefit from us. Is this how business is done on this world? Perhaps this is not a good world for us to visit, if this is the way of things here. We are accustomed to more civilized spaces."

The crowd grumbles. Ubialla glances around, sees her guard still hemmed in by angry bodies, sees the looks of loathing and disdain on the faces surrounding their little tableau. The top of her head pulses as the magnitude of the situation sinks in. She lowers the blaster, a smile painting her face. The night has taken its toll on her: The strain is visible around the edges of her lips, rendering the smile artificial and cloying. Repairing the damage already done will be the work of weeks—and in Canto Bight that might as well mean "years." Time works differently here. It moves faster, both in destruction and creation.

"I didn't threaten her," says Ubialla. The blaster vanishes into her dress, somehow failing to break the lines of it at all. "I was merely concerned by all the noise, and wanted to be sure she found her way safely back to you. That's all. Nothing more."

"Then it is good that we have been found," says the sister. She removes her hand from Calla's shoulder, looking sadly at the mess on the floor. "A pity. It was a fine vintage."

Laughter claws at the inside of Calla's throat, threatening to break loose and overwhelm her. A "fine vintage" indeed. Squashed flower juice and mouthwash from the bathroom toiletries have been called many things, she's sure, but this may be the first time anyone has tried to use that particular term.

Ubialla looks at the spill again, this time calculating, and Calla can't help but wonder how long it will be before the cleaning droids are instructed to suction up every drop, filter out the glass, and serve the stuff as something too rare, too impossible to obtain to be sold for anything less than everything. And these people, these rich, glittering, terrible people, will pay. Oh, they'll pay, and pay, and pay until there's nothing left in their pockets, and then they'll tell anyone who'll listen about the time they sipped the rarest wine in the galaxy while sitting at Ubialla Gheal's left hand, elevated by her very presence.

Even those who hold the power in Canto Bight aren't immune to losing. Maybe it's time to start trying in earnest to get out after all.

"The night is almost finished," says the sister calmly. "If you will return with me to the place where this began, my sister and I are prepared to conclude negotiations. Unless you would prefer to remain here, guarding the exit from honest customers who may wish to return home and freshen themselves before a new day begins. It is important that it be said, however, that if you choose that path of the two available to you, the negotiation will be declared in the sommelier's favor, and you will receive nothing more from us than you already have. Regardless of tonight's outcome, we will not be returning to this place for a very long time. We do not care for your . . . hospitality. And if either of us is harmed, you will never see another of our kind." The threat—not obtain their wine—does not need to be spoken to be heard.

"I will come with you," says Ubialla.

The sister nods. "We suspected that you might," she says, and turns, and walks away.

Derla looks away from her Wookiee guard—who is charming, in his way, for all that they have no language in common—at the sound of footsteps moving toward her booth. It is somehow unsurprising to see one of the Grammus sisters approaching, with Derla's own valise in her hands. She thinks it may be the sister from the restroom. She has genuinely no idea how to be sure. That's an art in and of itself. She has met identical twins before, has even met identical *species,* worlds where distinction between individuals has never been visual. Usually something will come to the surface following even a brief interaction, some quirk or twitch or otherwise distinctive attribute. Here . . .

There's nothing. Either the two are so alike as to forget what it means to be individuals, or they are playing a role designed to obfuscate them for reasons of their own. Derla cannot say which might be true. She isn't sure it matters. She's here, and they're here, and Ubialla, unfortunately enough, is here, and what happens is going to happen regardless of who wears which name.

"Where did you get that?" asks Derla.

"If enough confusion is created, almost any object can be moved," says the sister, sliding into a seat and holding the valise out toward the Wookiee. "It might be best if you held this, for now. Your employer is likely to be quite angry when she realizes it has been moved."

The Wookiee looks at Derla, uncertain. She decides to learn Shyriiwook at her first opportunity. It will come in useful when her new employee comes to find her.

"It would be a great favor to me," she says. "If you feel the risk is worth taking."

Slowly, he picks up the valise, making an inquiring noise.

The Grammus sister nods. "Precisely," she says. "You may go, if you like. We are reaching the conclusion of our business. I expect it will be short, sharp, and potentially very violent. You did not enter these negotiations as a participant. We cannot require you to stay."

The Wookiee looks at Derla again. She finds the strength to smile.

"I am pleased by your company, but I understand you work for Ubialla," she says. "Don't endanger yourself on my behalf."

The Wookiee nods and moves the valise behind his broad back. It's such a simple ruse that it may well work; after all, the cons here are so much more complicated. Derla turns her attention to the Grammus sister.

"Have you made your decisions, then?" she asks.

"We have," says the sister.

"Will you share them with me?"

"In good time." The sister looks thoughtfully at Derla. "We expected more concern from you."

"Calmness serves me better, in my profession."

"Indeed." The sister's gaze flicks to a point beyond Derla. The final act is beginning.

The second Grammus sister appears with a human woman by her side, Ubialla trailing angrily after them. The Wookiee makes an inquisitive growling sound. Ubialla barely even glances at him.

"Tell them to open the doors and release the trash," she snaps. "I'm saving my life right now. I don't have time to deal with *you*."

Derla believes she sees sympathy in his eyes as he looks at her. Then he's gone, and Ubialla is sliding into the booth by her side, as if none of the events of the night have changed anything. As if they, and the sisters, are still conducting a simple business deal.

"Calla, you are excused again," says Parallela. "We thank you for your service—every part of it."

"But . . ." Calla glances over her shoulder toward the door. "What about . . ."

"Think and you will understand," says Rhomby.

"You have done well," says Parallela. "Return to the resort."

Calla bows quickly before she turns and goes. She does not look back. Her part in this show—and show it has absolutely been; Derla has no doubt of that—is done.

"Where is my wine?" Ubialla's voice is low, calm, with an underlying layer of dangerous warning. She is a predator backed into a corner and pushed too far past where it is safe. Soon, she will strike.

Please, let them have listened, thinks Derla.

"It is not your wine until the deal is done," says Rhomby chidingly. She reaches below the table and lifts a valise. Not Derla's, which is safely away from here, nor the one the first bottle came from, which has been searched thoroughly: a new valise, distinguished by the reversed orientation of the latch. She opens it.

Her sister reaches inside and withdraws a bottle of wine identical to the first. Ubialla gasps, hunger apparent in the sound. The Grammus sisters exchange a glance.

"Where there is one of something, there must be two of the thing, or balance is not upheld," Parallela says. "The exception lies with things that have been marked disposable. A bottle of wine whose twin has been consumed, for example, might be used as a tester, to allow potential clients to taste what we have to offer and see that it is good."

Rhomby reaches into the sister's valise and pulls out a second—no, a *third*—bottle of wine. It is in all ways identical to the two that have come before it. It is beautiful.

There has been some question in Derla's mind, before this, as to the nature of the game the Grammus sisters play. This moment confirms her suspicions. They entered the club intending everything that has happened, from Ubialla's involvement to the theft and the unfolding chaos that followed. This has all been an intricate performance, and she wants to laugh in delight. What a way to build a legend. What a terribly beautiful, terribly dangerous way.

"This is our decision," says Rhomby. "One of you came in good faith and one of you came in poor faith, and these are such beautiful oppositions that you both should be rewarded. Here." She extends her bottle toward Derla.

Parallela does the same with her bottle, holding it toward Ubialla. Ubialla snatches it from her hands.

"Fools," she snarls. "Petty, thieving, conniving *fools*. I'd be within my rights to have you banished from the planet." The blaster, once safely tucked away, is in her hand again, aimed squarely at the bottle Rhomby holds toward Derla.

Quick as a wink, Derla jerks her reaching hands away. Rhomby lets the bottle go. Before it can strike the table, where it might not break, Ubialla fires, and glass shatters, and the air is filled with the sweet, unique scent of the wine of dreams.

"*One* bottle," says Ubialla. She stands, the blaster vanishing into her dress once more. Somehow, not a drop of wine has touched her. The veins on her cheeks pulse with pleasure as she says, "You brought *one* bottle. I secured *one* bottle. My patron will be pleased, and all of you will leave here alive. I trust that will be sufficient payment?"

She doesn't wait for their reply, only turns and walks away. Derla looks at the shattered remains of the bottle with no small measure of regret.

"It was a pleasure doing business with you," she says, rising. The sisters do not speak. They simply watch her go.

CHAPTER 11

CALLA PACES IN THE ROOM, GLANCING EVERY SO OFTEN AT THE DOOR. IT
has been hours. The sisters have yet to return. She is surprised to realize that she's worried about them. Ubialla is not a forgiving person:
She is unlikely to be happy with them, especially given the mess they
commanded Calla to make in Ubialla's club. And for what reason?
People will still drink it.

People will be people. Someone will, inevitably, steal a sample of
this fine, rare, exclusive thing from Ubialla's menu. Someone will
analyze it. Someone will realize that Ubialla has been selling flower
juice and mouthwash, and everything else she has to offer will be
called into question. It is a small but terrible sabotage, and one for
which the club owner will be paying for quite some time.

It's difficult not to see it as elegant and terribly well-deserved. Calla
smiles to herself as she begins making a bed out of spare sheets beneath the window. Perhaps she's going to enjoy her time with these
new employers more than she expected.

The door slides open. Calla turns, expecting to see Rhomby and
Parallela. Instead she finds the owner of the resort, a tall, orange-
skinned Twi'lek in a uniform very much like her own, if made of
finer fabric and cut to the specifics of his anatomy in a way that her
work clothing had never achieved.

"You are the human Calla," he says. "Temporarily indentured to the Grammus sisters. Is this correct?"

"Yes," she says, straightening, tensing, waiting to hear him say that Rhomby and Parallela have died deaths as interchangeable as they were, waiting to be evicted.

"They have asked me to inform you that, regretfully, they will not be returning to this room, as their business has taken them away from Canto Bight. They have paid in full for their week's stay, and have requested that you be allowed to use their room until the payment expires. They have also requested that I extend to you the offer of employment." The manager looks at her gravely. "It is quite impressive for someone to connect with clients so completely that such a request seems reasonable. I would very much appreciate the opportunity to discuss your terms for employment."

Slowly, Calla smiles.

Derla settles into her ship's chair like she is coming home—and in a very real way, she is. Canto Bight was only, is only, ever a port in the storm. Preparing to engage the engine, she sets her valise—recovered from the Wookiee after Ubialla had dismissed her—by her feet.

It clanks.

Pausing, she leans down and opens the valise. The density engines have been deactivated: The weight she felt on her trip back to her room, and then to the port, was a reflection of reality. Carefully, she pulls the bottle out into the light, noting the conflict between its label and its contents. According to the label, this is a fine vintage of dry Tatooine white—the same wine she ordered for the celebrants at their table. A wine whose purchase would be in the club's records, under her name.

But the wine is dark as nebulas and glitters when she moves the bottle. This is the wine of dreams, so sweet, so fine. The cork is back in place; the bottle is more than half full. There is a note. She flicks it open.

D. Pidys:

   We apologize for misleading you. We would be delighted to discuss further sales in person. Say, on Naboo,
in three cycles' time? Your proposal was quite engaging.
   We believe we can work well together.

   It is not signed. It does not need to be.
   Laughing, Derla sets the bottle back into its cradle and engages her
engine. She will toast her good fortune, and her escape, later, when
she is far, far away from the schemes of a woman who got everything
she thought she wanted, from the poisonously lovely, legendary
streets of Canto Bight.

HEAR NOTHING, SEE NOTHING, SAY NOTHING

By **RAE CARSON**

CHAPTER 1

LEXO SOOGER HAD FORTY-ONE BONES IN EACH OF HIS HANDS—
fourteen more than his human daughter Lula had in each of hers—
and every one of them burned like fire. He loved to work with his
hands, he truly did. He was the star masseur at Zord's Spa and Bathhouse, with a loyal clientele and a two-month-long waiting list. He
could work out any knot, relax even the most anxious customer. But
decades of twelve-hour shifts would age anyone, even a Dor Namethian at the top of his game, and Lexo knew his massaging days were
nearing their end.

He didn't know what would happen to him and his daughter then.

"Papa," said a small, clear voice. "Let me help you with your
hands?"

"Please," Lexo said. He laid them flat on the rickety wooden table
that served as the centerpiece for the tiny apartment they shared.
Their room was small, low-ceilinged, and windowless, with adobe
walls, two built-in beds, and a single small hearth. The table, along
with two chairs and a sagging shelf, made up the only furniture.

Lexo contemplated his human daughter as she gathered the necessary ingredients from the shelf. Lula was slight, even for thirteen
years old, with bright brown eyes, dark skin, and hair like a cloud of
charcoal.

He used to consider humans revolting, with their smooth epidermis and excessive fingers and necks that stood straight up like fur-long markers. But on that day thirteen years ago when he'd found Lula abandoned in an empty cargo box, staring up at him with big, trusting eyes, he'd decided humans weren't so bad.

Lula dropped a pinch of corwindyl herbs into a mortar, added a little oil, and mashed away with the pestle. The oil released the corwindyl's odor and color, turning the mixture bright blue, filling their tiny apartment with its tangy-sweet aroma. Lexo felt his shoulders begin to relax at the scent, because it signaled that real relief was coming.

Gently, Lula rubbed a bit of the corwindyl paste against his knuckles, along his tendons. Warmth seeped into his muscles, loosening his joints. "Thank you, my azure sea," he said.

Something snagged against his thumb, startling him.

"Sorry," Lula said. "Just a callus."

Lexo grabbed her hand and turned it over, examining the offending bit of excess skin. Not a callus. A scab, barely covering a fresh injury on the fleshy part of her palm. "What happened?" he demanded.

Lula wrenched her hand away. "It's nothing. My glove split is all."

"And Bargwill Tomder refused to provide a new one." Lula worked at the fathier racing stables, and Tomder, the stable keeper, was the cheapest, meanest fellow he'd ever met. It gave Lexo a shiver to send Lula off to work with him every day.

"It's fine, Papa. I can handle it." She smiled. "I guess I inherited some toughness from you."

Lexo regarded her gravely. He reached a pleading hand toward her and announced in a solemn voice, "Lula. I am *not* your father."

She feigned shock. "But we look so much alike!"

It was a constant joke between them, almost a family ritual. She bent to kiss the top of his head. "Ready for the injections?"

His Lula missed nothing. "You can tell I need them."

"I always know," she said with a shrug.

Lexo glanced down at his hands. Bright-blue corwindyl paste outlined every line and crease, warming his fingers, allowing them to bend. But it wouldn't be enough. Not today, anyway. His worst client was on the schedule.

"Do it," he ordered.

"I promise I'll make it quick," she said, reaching for the injector probe on the shelf.

"I know."

"You'll be so relieved in just a few minutes."

"I know."

The probe was scrap, salvaged from an old interrogator droid. Lexo forced himself to watch, to not flinch away, as his tiny daughter leveled the probe's tip at the base of his metacarpals, just above his wrist. Lula had to manually depress the injector button.

The initial puncture was never too bad, just a tiny pinch. But the liquid flowing into his blood burned like fire, and he half expected flames to start shooting from his fingertips. The injection cocktail—corticosteroids, enzyme blockers, numbing agent—made it hard to draw breath, made his scent glands fill with liquid. He was glad none of his clients could see him like this. Only Lula knew how hard it was.

The pain, though exquisite, only lasted a minute. It was always followed by delightful warmth, increased flexibility, even a little surge of energy.

There were better ways to get relief, of course. But a derelict injector probe was the best they could afford, and besides, he could handle it. He was tough, just like Lula said.

"Better?" Lula asked.

"Better," he agreed, flexing his fingers.

They repeated the process with the other hand—stabbing pinch, incredible pain, slow but sure relief. Lexo rose from his chair.

"Papa," Lula said, "I have a favor to ask."

Lexo grabbed his robe from the peg by the door and started to swing it on. "Oh?"

"Would it be all right if I took some corwindyl to the stables today?"

He nearly dropped his robe. "My azure sea . . ."

"I know it's expensive. I know how hard it is to acquire. It's just . . ." Tears welled in her eyes, and she blurted, "Hard Luck got hurt!"

"Your favorite fathier." The long-legged, wide-eared fathiers were built for speed, and their races drew thousands of guests to the track every night.

She explained, "Pinrado Jozo was riding Casual Retort last night—you know what a cheat that jockey is. He pushed Hard Luck into the rail so he could pull Retort ahead. Luck's got a nasty rail burn now, but only because his hock joint is giving out. He was too weak to push back, see, and maybe the corwindyl will help? I mean, he's gelded, so they won't retire him if he's lame. They'll just take a blaster and . . . but he's so sweet, Papa. The best fathier in the whole stable. He loves treats, and every time he sees me he dances in place, his ears flopping, and—"

"Yes, you can take some corwindyl."

She wilted with relief. "Thanks."

"Are you going to make a paste?"

"No. Too hard to smuggle into the stables. I'll just rub the herbs directly onto his hock joint."

Lexo watched silently as she stashed some of the herbs in her pocket, then grabbed her ruined gloves, her pitchfork, and her leather bag from their place by the door. Like all the indentured children at the stable, she was responsible for maintaining her own equipment. She worked hard, long hours in the hope that she'd pay off her indenture debt one day. If she never missed work, if her equipment didn't break down too often, Lula could be a free woman by the time she was nineteen.

After that, her dream, the thing she wanted more than anything in the galaxy, was to ride in the fathier races. She yearned to be a jockey, to feel the wind in her hair, to hear the screams of the crowd, as she urged her mount toward the finish line. She felt connected to the fathiers. She insisted to Lexo all the time that they were more intelligent than people gave them credit for, that she understood them better than anyone. And she knew, she *just knew*, that if she got her chance to ride she'd be the greatest jockey Canto Bight had ever known.

Lexo was the only person she'd ever told about her dream, and Lexo couldn't bear to give her the dose of reality she probably needed. A tiny human girl, an indenture and orphan besides, was about as likely to become a fathier jockey as a droid was to become a Jedi.

Lula was heading for the door when she whirled back around. "Papa, what's wrong? If you're mad about the corwindyl, I won't—"

"You've done nothing wrong, my sea."

"Then . . . ?"

He decided to tell her *some* of what was bothering him. "I have Big Sturg Ganna on my schedule today."

Her mouth formed a little o.

"I was hoping he'd given up on me," Lexo admitted.

Lula frowned. "Don't do it, Papa. One of the stable kids agreed to inform for that gangster. He was dead inside a month."

"I have no intention of giving him what he wants. I left that life behind decades ago."

"Good," she said fiercely. "He's horrible."

"He's also horrible to massage. So many hard-to-reach places."

She swung the strap of her bag over her shoulder and hefted her pitchfork. "Good thing you're the best in the galaxy," she said. "Just . . . please be careful tonight." They both worked a swing shift, which inevitably dragged into a night shift, and the sun would be rising before they would be reunited.

They stared at each other a moment. Maybe Lula had a bad feeling, same as him.

But as her papa, it was his job to be encouraging. "I hope Hard Luck feels better," Lexo said.

Lula gave him a final wave as she exited their apartment. He watched the bag bounce against her back as she hurried down the corridor toward the long stairway that would take her up to the surface, to the shining, beautiful city of Canto Bight.

CHAPTER 2

LEXO TOOK A CROWDED PUBLIC HOVERSHUTTLE TO ZORD'S SPA AND Bathhouse.

His place of employment was a wonder of false sandstone, false marble, and false terra-cotta. The bathhouse had to survive multiple environmental shifts throughout the day, so every wall and bed and floor tile was made of artificial material that not only was hypoallergenic to over two hundred sentient species, but could flex and breathe in any temperature and humidity.

Lexo ducked into the hot, tight servants' closet to exchange his threadbare robe for a flowing white gown. It was sleeveless, with a high chest band and a long skirt whose elegant gathers drifted like feathers to the floor. He was not allowed to set foot inside the common areas of the spa without it. *True relaxation starts with luxury and beauty,* Zord always said.

Next, Lexo donned his translator necklace, then a series of golden bracelets, which the spa advertised as being magnetic and therefore "able to detect biorhythms." The bracelets were useless, of course, but many of Zord's clientele were soothed by having a technological explanation for how wonderful they felt after one of Lexo's massages.

He disciplined his features and rolled his shoulders. Lexo was now "on," and the next twelve hours would be a flawless performance. He exited the servants' closet and descended the stair with quiet grace, gown flowing at his ankles. In anticipation of Big Sturg Ganna's visit, the bathhouse was playing the councilor's favorite music, which Lexo loathed. "Serenity Starscapes" was predictable and twee, composed for creatures with limited frequency range. But he would never say so aloud.

Lexo's first client was already lying facedown on the table, waiting for him. Joris was a tall bipedal creature who always kept her beautiful silver hair in perfect order. Lexo always felt you could tell a lot about a personality by the hair.

Joris had no business being here. She couldn't possibly afford Zord's high-end services. She worked in currency exchange in the casino but fancied herself a player, betting the fathier races whenever she wasn't working in the hopes that she could give up her day job. And maybe she would be able to; Lexo hoped so. But instead she seemed to spend whatever she won with him, a fate that seemed to satisfy her.

Lexo had a lot of clients like her.

"It's nice to see you again, Joris," Lexo said.

"My shoulders need extra attention today," Joris said.

"Of course."

"It's going to be my big night, Sooger; some good prospects on the track. I want to be ready."

"I can't wait to hear all about it at your next appointment."

Lexo let his hands drift up the being's spine, toward the base of her head. Thanks to the corwindyl and the injections, his fingers were nimble, his chemical receptors as sensitive as ever. Sure enough, he detected a large knot of lactic acid buildup in the left trapezius and set to work coaxing it out. It was stubborn, but Lexo was an artist.

As he worked, Joris blathered freely about her recent decision to designate a new favorite viewing spot at the tracks and her picks for tonight's fathier races. Lexo didn't mind the talking. He just made affirming noises at appropriate intervals and occasionally said things like "Good point" or "You are very wise."

Lexo always ignored what he heard, what he saw, and never got involved, not for any reason. He'd seen plenty of others get involved in order to improve their lot in life. And sure, they would make connections, earn some side money, maybe even maneuver themselves into better working conditions. But there was always a cost. Always. So Lexo had decided to remain neutral and nonthreatening in a city like Canto Bight. Ever since leaving the slave pits of Askkto-Fen IV, his personal motto had been *Hear nothing, see nothing, say nothing.* It had kept him safe for decades. Now it kept his daughter safe, too.

The knot was proving unusually tenacious, and stress pheromones assaulted Lexo's sensitive nose; Joris harbored more anxiety than she let on. Lexo began oscillating the floating distal bones of his long fingers, creating a soothing vibration that could penetrate the toughest muscle fibers. He would be too old for this soon; his tendons were giving out. But not today. Today's knot would be soundly defeated.

"Oh . . . my," Joris breathed. "That's amazing. How did you do that?"

"My bracelets are able to detect biorhythms," Lexo said.

"Oh, that makes sense," Joris said.

"I'm just glad you feel better."

"I do! I feel much better! Hey, Sooger, do you ever bet on the fathier races?"

"Never."

"Well, you should. Tonight. I'm going to give you a tip, because I'm the type who always repays her favors. So listen close."

"I'm listening," Lexo said, immediately tuning her out.

He sensed tension in Joris's lower back; instinct led his fingers toward the problem. Less lactic acid here, but still plenty of work to be done. Joris nattered about a great tip she'd gotten from a reliable source, mentioned the name DeFancio Storsilt, blah, blah, blah. Lexo didn't care one whit but he said "Yes, certainly" and "Oh, I see."

"—especially that gelding, Hard Luck," Joris said.

Lexo drew in a breath, and his fingers paused over the lumbar vertebrae.

"An unfortunately named fathier, if you ask me," Joris continued. "He's had some hard luck lately, but tonight will be his hardest."

Lula's favorite fathier. The one she felt deserved their precious cor-windyl herbs.

Lexo kept his voice even with some effort. "What, *exactly*, do you mean, Joris?"

"Haven't you been listening?"

"Of course."

Lexo decided to use a trick he saved for special occasions. Very few knew about this ability, and he wanted to keep it that way. First he glanced around the spa, looking for species with superior olfactory senses, but he didn't see anyone who might figure out what he was up to.

Then he pressed firmly against Joris's lower back, just above her hip joint, and excreted a pheromone that was absorbed quickly into the skin. It should warm the muscle, increase blood flow, produce a slight feeling of euphoria. On the right being, sometimes the calming effect reduced inhibitions enough to loosen tongues. Joris was exactly the right being.

Lexo waited a few seconds for it to take effect. Finally, as he felt the muscle relaxing beneath his fingertips, he gently asked, "But why Hard Luck in particular?"

"Hard Luck is . . . Oh, that's nice, real nice. How did you . . . Er . . . Hard Luck is one of Storsilt's best sprinters, right? Never wins, but often places second or third. He's been underperforming lately though. Everyone's noticed it."

"I hear he got pushed into the rail last night," Lexo said.

"He'll do even worse tonight, along with Storsilt's whole fathier fleet. So you'd better bet against them, Sooger. Trust me on this, all right? Pick one or two with long odds instead, like Shifting Sands, maybe. You're bound to make a fortune. I'd do it myself, but between you and me, I can only afford to bet on the red-eye races at the end of the night."

Lexo wasn't sure how long he was frowning before he caught himself and fixed his features into what Lula called his "spa face." Blandly pleasant, worry-free.

But he was deeply disturbed. Sure, race fixing happened all the time at the Canto Bight track. He suspected that Lula's boss, Bargwill Tomder, would help or hurt any steed for the right price. But Lexo had never heard of anyone sabotaging a whole herd before.

He shouldn't press the matter. *Hear nothing, see nothing, say nothing.* But this was happening at Lula's stable. What if she got dragged into a huge mess? He had to know more.

"You are even more well connected than I realized," Lexo said, his voice carefully tinged with wonder and respect. "To be given such powerful information. Most impressive."

The flattery worked. Joris's voice dropped to a whisper. "She wouldn't say how it was being done," she admitted. "I suspect some kind of poison."

Her source was a *she*. "It's a reliable source?"

"The reliablest! A pity, though. Hard Luck's a magnificent critter. Loves to run. Given the chance, he'd run right off that track, wild and free."

Lula would agree with her on that count.

Lexo was about to press for more information on Joris's mysterious source, but a slight hum reverberated through the spa's artificial limestone walls. The air changed, becoming thicker, colder, wetter.

Only the wealthiest, most powerful clients could buy an environmental shift for the entire spa. It meant that Big Sturg Ganna was getting prepped for his massage.

Lexo's shoulders began to ache. His large humpback was the center of his limbic and endocrine systems, and he felt everything there—tension, happiness, love, dread. As he finished Joris's massage, he willed his shoulders to relax, breathing deeply of the spa's humidified air.

He told himself to ignore the rumble of wheels as a giant stone plinth rolled in behind him, replacing the regular massage table. He closed his nose to the scent of rotting swamp that filled the air—a prized perfume, purportedly, from Ganna's home planet. Instead, he made Joris his whole world, giving her a final lumbar stretch and covering her with a warm towel.

Joris tipped him with two casino chips, which Lexo stuffed down the chest band of his gown. He took his time thanking Joris and giving her up to the assistant masseurs, bathing his hands in ultraviolet light to disinfect them, because Lexo needed the extra seconds to make sure he was calm. Serene. Implacable.

He turned to greet his new client. "It's a pleasure to see you, Councilor Ganna," he lied. "How can I help you today?"

The councilor was a massive amphibious creature with a gray leathery hide stretched over a thick layer of blubber, all of which made it nearly impossible to massage the muscles beneath. His round, slitted eyes were the size of Lexo's fists, and his wide salamander mouth did a poor job of hiding his prehensile tongue. He weighed eight hundred kilograms at least, and his body ended in a stubby, ticklish tail, which was totally off-limits.

Ganna's body was made for swimming in cold water, and Lexo supposed that he was graceful in his element. But on land he was a lumbering beast who needed special accommodations to travel any great distance. Lexo had no idea why he'd chosen to settle on the desert planet of Cantonica. But settle here he had, and despite his physical limitations he was one of Canto Bight's richest, most powerful citizens.

"Lexo, my friend!" Ganna said, in a deep voice that rumbled like rocks falling down a cliffside. "I need your very *special* attention today."

"I will do all I can for you, of course." Lexo said. But when someone like Ganna called a lowly servant "friend," it meant trouble was ahead.

Ganna chuckled, and Lexo felt the sound in the deepest part of his shoulders. "Heard anything interesting today?" Ganna asked.

"No, Honorable Councilor. It's been very quiet." Lexo's fingers traveled up Ganna's massive neck to his head. The gangster had several jagged scars across his face, which he needed massaged to keep supple and pain-free. Lexo wasn't the only one whose life before Canto Bight had been very, very different.

"What about yesterday? Or the day before?"

"Those days were quiet, too," Lexo said.

"Oh, come on, Sooger. Surely you've heard something interesting? A juicy tidbit for your old pal Ganna?"

Lexo massaged circles at Ganna's temples, and the gangster's eyes grew heavy and lidded. "I'm just a lowly masseur," Lexo said. "No one tells me anything interesting."

Ganna's eyes opened wide, and his slitted pupils flared. "I don't believe that for one moment. All of Canto Bight's wealthiest, most powerful citizens frequent this fine establishment, and they all come to see you. You, Lexo Sooger. You've attended DeFancio Storsilt, Baron Attsmun, Ubialla Gheal, even the countess herself."

"I'm very fortunate to have so many wonderful clients," Lexo said.

Ganna shifted on the stone plinth, a massive, heaving effort that tilted his whole body upward to the side—just so he could look Lexo in the eyes. "Give me something. Even something small. Show me you're worth having around."

Lexo's fingers stilled. Was that a threat? It was oblique, as threats from Ganna went. The gangster wasn't known for subtlety.

"Of course I'm worth having around," Lexo said with the most relentlessly serene smile he'd ever mustered. "It is my honor and privilege to bring joy, pleasure, and relief to Canto Bight's finest residents and visitors."

Ganna frowned, allowing himself to flop back down onto the massage table.

A familiar scent tickled Lexo's nose, seemingly from the air Ganna's massive body had just displaced. Spicy sweet.

Corwindyl.

Lexo's shoulders tightened mercilessly, and his heart began to pound like a drum.

He forced himself to dig deep into Ganna's massive shoulders, to pretend that nothing was amiss, but his mind churned. Ganna's impenetrable hide and thick blubber made corwindyl impractical for him. There was no reason for him to use it.

Maybe the scent had come from Lexo's own fingers. Yes, that must be it. Though the paste Lula made had been completely absorbed by now, the scent of it was somehow lingering. Maybe it had something to do with the increased humidity in the spa.

It took a tremendous amount of strength to access the muscles of Ganna's shoulder, so Lexo was bearing down hard, concentrating, and he almost missed the movement on the balcony above them.

He glanced up. Looming over the faux-stone railing was Contessa Alissyndrex delga Cantonica Provincion. She was dressed in a black gown, the Onyx Bands of Cato Neimoidia draping from epaulets at her shoulders—all in sharp contrast with the halo of thick, white epidermis around her head and neck. As always, the stem of a crystal wineglass was pinched between her delicate fingers.

Lexo caught her eye, and she nodded to him once, slowly.

He returned his attention to Big Sturg Ganna's massive deltoid, but the heat and stress in his shoulders was becoming unbearable. The countess. Here, unannounced.

She was one of the spa's partners. Lexo didn't know the proportion of her stake, only that she was provided free services whenever she wanted them. He also knew that she loved wine and preferred zero-g massages, that she tipped well and rarely spoke. As far as Lexo could remember, she'd never before paid the spa a visit without an appointment.

"You could get whatever information you wanted," Big Sturg Ganna said, blithely unaware that the countess was watching them. "You have a way about you, Lexo Sooger, you and your bracelets and your unnervingly strong fingers. You could convince people to tell you anything."

"I couldn't possibly," Lexo replied. "Even if I could, the Zord's experience is guaranteed to be elegant, relaxing, and safe. Discretion is the larger part of safety, yes? I see nothing but the sore muscles of my clients, and hear nothing but their sighs of satisfaction."

"For some of us, *knowledge* is the larger part of safety." He paused. Then: "Lexo, my friend, I shall be frank."

Here it comes, Lexo thought.

"I need you," Ganna said. "You are perfectly positioned. A war is looming in Canto Bight, you see. It will be a silent, invisible war to most, but make no mistake, blood will be shed."

"That sounds very serious."

"I'm going to win this war, Lexo. And don't you want to be on the winning side of a war? Of course you do. Everyone does."

Lexo said nothing. Feeling the countess's eyes on them, he glanced upward. She took a sip of wine, her stare resolute.

"Be my eyes and ears," Ganna coaxed. "I pay very well. Ask anyone. And I'm loyal to those loyal to me. Someone of your positioning, your abilities, could go very far in a city like this. I'm just the one to help you do it."

The councilor didn't know the half of Lexo's abilities, and Lexo planned to keep it that way. To stall, to give himself time to think, Lexo asked, "That's it? You just want me to gather information?"

"And sometimes *give* information," Ganna said. "There may be occasions when I want specific tidbits planted in specific ears."

"I see," Lexo said. He had to be more careful than he'd ever been right now. "I can't imagine Zord would approve of information brokering in his flagship spa."

"It will be our secret," Ganna said.

"Neither would the countess approve," Lexo plunged on. "She's here, by the way. Watching us right now."

Ganna's body tensed. "She is? Well, that's interesting. Very interesting. Anyway, there's no need to bother either her or Zord with such trifling matters. Besides, you needn't worry about the countess at all. I'm buying her out."

"Oh?"

"I'll be part owner of this spa very soon, and when I am, I plan to make some personnel changes."

"Oh."

"Depending on how things go, someone could find himself with a raise and a promotion. Or, you know, without a job at all."

Lexo was massaging along the councilor's spine now. Every creature had a vulnerable point. An artery, a nerve cluster, a *weakness*. Ganna's vulnerable point was near his neck, where blood traveled from heart to head, just as in Lexo's human daughter, Lula. He would have to press very hard through hide and blubber to reach it.

Not that he would, of course. But the very fact that it crossed his

mind startled him. He hadn't had thoughts like these in years. Decades. That life was long gone, as dead to him as the fighting slaves
he'd tended on Askkto-Fen IV.

"Surely you've sold information before?" Ganna continued. "All
you service types do. I'm a man of the people, Lexo. I provide a way
for the poor and downtrodden to improve their lot in life. Lucky for
you, you're in the perfect position to take advantage of my charity."

"Indeed," Lexo said, thinking of the stable hand Lula had known,
the one who died in Ganna's service. "Your generosity is well known."

"I won't take no for an answer."

"Of course I shall have to think about it."

Ganna made a noise that was something between a snort and a
rumble. "You won't think about it too long," he said, and the smug-
ness in his voice gave Lexo a shiver.

It was time to turn Ganna over and massage his monstrous chest,
and Lexo gestured for the assistant masseurs. Maby Sagedo and Oble
Rumb hurried over. They were well known for climbing all over their
clients, using heels, toes, and knees to compensate for their lack of
size.

"It's time for your turning," Lexo warned. Ganna grunted acknowledgment, and Lexo flipped a switch on the base of the stone plinth.

A soft mechanical hum reverberated, and Ganna seemed to expand on the table as his blubber became buoyant in the artificially
lightened gravity. With Sagedo's and Rumb's help—and careful to
avoid Ganna's highly ticklish tail—Lexo heaved and scooted and
nudged until Ganna was lying on his back, his whitish chest and belly
exposed.

Then Lexo froze.

This time, as the scent of corwindyl filled the air, Lexo couldn't
pretend it came from his own hands. Ganna was definitely using the
stuff. Or someone else had placed it on him.

"Get on with it, Sooger," Ganna said.

"Yes, of course." Lexo placed his fingers against the councilor's left
pectorals and began to knead. He watched as Ganna made eye contact with the countess, who was still standing on the balcony above,

her wineglass nearly empty. After a moment the countess turned and fled, gown swishing at her feet.

Big Sturg Ganna chuckled.

Lexo's shoulders were almost quivering now, with the physical exertion of massaging this creature, and with the sure knowledge that something was deeply, deeply wrong.

To calm himself and stave off panic, he thought of Lula. She was probably mucking crowded stalls now, dodging fathier hooves, giving pats and kind words whenever her boss wasn't looking, trying to make the poor creatures' plight a little less awful. He hoped she'd gotten a chance to rub the corwindyl into Hard Luck's hock joint. Maybe her favorite fathier was feeling better already.

Councilor Ganna opened his mouth, but Lexo interrupted him. "Do you ever use corwindyl, Councilor?" he asked.

"Huh? Cor-what? Never heard of it."

"It's an herb that—"

"Don't know, don't care. Look, Sooger, you're going to work for me whether you want to or not. I'm doing you a favor. You'll realize it soon enough, and you'll thank me."

"I don't think—"

"I don't care what you think. I'm hiring you to broker information for me, not think." Ganna's voice had become low and dangerous. "You have to ally yourself with the winner. And that's me. If you don't, no one is safe. Not you." He paused for a long moment. "And not your human daughter."

Lexo's breath hitched. "You know I have a daughter," he said flatly.

"Of course. I never bring someone into my employ without vetting them thoroughly. She seems like a nice kid. A bit on the small side, though. Too fragile for working in the stables. It's a wonder she hasn't been kicked in the head already."

Lexo couldn't seem to fill his chest with enough air.

"You see," Ganna said, "I had a feeling you'd resist my generous offer. So I took some precautions. I feel confident that you'll come around very shortly."

"I told you I would think about it," Lexo said in a small, tight voice.

"Take as much time as you want," Ganna replied. "But I suspect you'll not want to take much time at all."

Lexo was desperate. He didn't want Ganna to know the extent of what he could do, but he had to take a risk. He had to know more.

Pheromone flooded his fingertips. As he pressed into Ganna's chest, osmosis allowed it to secrete through his porous epidermis, onto Ganna's hide. He massaged it in, making little circles, then wider circles, pressing hard, hard, harder.

"You're really outdoing yourself today," the councilor observed. "I may have to increase my sessions to once per week."

Lexo would rather massage a rathtar. He said, "It would be a delight to see you more often."

"I mean, I'll practically own the place soon. Stopping by regularly is just good management."

"You are very wise."

Ganna wasn't relaxing. He was talking, sure, but he wasn't saying anything useful. Lexo's pheromone wasn't working.

Lexo tried again, secreting a small amount at the base of the councilor's neck. Many species were especially sensitive there, where their skin was a little thinner.

"Do you smell something?" Ganna said.

"Just an enchanting, swampy perfume imported from your very own homeworld."

"No, it's something else."

"Your olfactory senses must be superior to mine."

"Maybe. Just give my face another once-over, will you? We're running out of time."

"Of course."

Not only was Ganna immune to his secretions, he could smell them as well. Lexo would have to find another way to get the information he needed.

They chatted a while longer about nothing in particular, Lexo responding with things like "Yes, I expect you'll do a lot of winning," and "No, he was a fool for doubting you," but all the while his mind was screaming, *What have you done with Lula?*

When their session finally, *finally* drew to a close, Ganna insisted that they would talk again very soon, and Lexo said he was looking forward to it, and the moment the giant plinth rolled away, Lexo was sprinting up the stairs to the servants' closet to change into his regular clothes.

On the way out, he grabbed Oble Rumb and said something he hadn't said since that day thirteen years ago when he found a cargo crate containing a tiny human baby: "Cancel all my appointments. I'm taking the rest of the day off. Zord can dock my pay."

Lexo fled into the streets of Old City and hailed a speeder cab.

CHAPTER 3

OLD WAS A RELATIVE TERM. THE NEIGHBORHOODS SURROUNDING THE Canto Casino were certainly older than the casino itself, and their age showed in the occasional cobbled street or stone archway or crumbling façade. But for the most part everything was shiny and new, with luxury shops and restaurants housed in domed towers made to blend seamlessly with the original architecture. Tourists never saw the truly old parts of the city, because those parts were poor, dank, cramped, and mostly underground, like the tiny apartment he shared with Lula.

Lexo considered going there first, but he had last seen Lula heading up the stairs to the surface, toward the stables. He had to know if she'd arrived at her destination. Lexo fished out the chips he'd received from Joris as a tip and inserted them into the cab's payment slot. He directed the cab toward the stables.

Evening was quickly becoming dusk, and the city was springing to life. Speeders whizzed by his passenger window, faster, shinier, and sleeker than the one he had hired. Many of them, he knew, were chauffeured by organics. Big Sturg Ganna himself always eschewed automatic and droid-driven speeders. He considered it a point of pride and a symbol of his status that he could afford a living driver.

To Lexo's right the horizon glowed dark purple with the setting sun, a strange phenomenon that had manifested with the creation of Canto Bight's artificial sea. Lights from various yachts and pleasure barges twinkled against the vast water. He had to admit, it was beautiful, albeit a colossal waste. On the hot desert planet of Cantonica, water evaporated at a rate of several tons per day, which meant that the cost of maintaining the false sea was astronomical.

The cab turned toward the casino and was forced to slow down to accommodate traffic. Everyone was arriving for the night, checking into the hotel, trying to make a grand entrance. Lexo didn't care about any of that. He leaned forward in his seat, as if he could will the speeder to go faster.

It took a frustratingly long time to pass beyond the sleek, brightly lit entrance to the casino and its rows of rare Alderaanian chinar trees. Maybe the trees were real, maybe they weren't; last Lexo had heard, the planet Alderaan wasn't doing so well. But that was Canto Bight for you. In this city it was almost impossible to tell the real from the fake.

Ahead, a glow loomed on the horizon, indicating that they were nearing the racetrack. The beautiful show stables were just ahead, and tourists crowded around to pet well-groomed fathiers, enjoy refreshments, and, of course, buy souvenirs.

But the real stables were behind them, their unseemly smells and tight quarters and filthy workers kept mostly out of sight of the city's wealthy visitors. The cab curved around the show stables, ducked into an alley, and finally came to a stop.

Lexo practically leapt from the vehicle and headed straight for the main stable where Lula's boss, Bargwill Tomder, was most likely to be lingering. The air was musty with fathier dung and unwashed bodies. Children were everywhere, hefting pitchforks and feedbags, running messages, even mending stall doors. Lexo scanned the area, hoping against hope to spot Lula. Maybe he'd misread Ganna's threat. Maybe she was right here after all, safe and sound.

The stables were made of brick and stone, with stalls that were more like jail cells—small and dark, with barred gates that opened electronically. Fathier heads peered over the gates as if dreaming of air and light, their broad ears nearly touching the tight walls, their silky coats often scarred or caked with dirt. Looking at their sad, soft eyes, Lexo couldn't help but wonder if Lula was right. Maybe the fathiers were more intelligent than everyone realized.

Lula was nowhere to be seen.

But he found the stable keeper easily; Lexo simply followed the stench of rot and disease until he discovered him leaning against a fathier stall, his dressage whip held at the ready.

Bargwill Tomder was a four-armed Cloddogran with rotting teeth, oozing skin, and a perpetual scowl. His plague-ridden nose tendrils were slowly but inexorably forming a mass of infection that would someday overtake the whole creature's face, and possibly, Lexo considered, the entire star system. He wore a utility vest that hadn't been washed in several years, where he stashed all manner of rusty tools—a wrench, a hoof pick, a collapsible glow rod. Lexo was willing to bet that the last time those tools had been used was probably around the same time that the vest had been washed. According to Lula, Bargwill Tomder hadn't worked a day in his life. He just liked to use that whip.

"Who're you?" Tomder barked at Lexo as he approached.

They'd met several times, but Lexo was unsurprised that Tomder did not recognize him. His eyesight was poor, and failing rapidly.

"I'm looking for Lula Sooger," Lexo said.

Tomder squinted, peering closer. Stench rolled off him in waves. "Are you that Dor Namethian fellow? The masseur?"

"Have you seen her?"

"You've come to beg for her job back, haven't you. Well, it won't work. That lazy pile of rotting dung is done here. You hear me? Done."

Lexo was just about out of patience with dissembling and making nice. He unrolled his shoulders and stretched his spine to full height, gaining another meter—a trick he pulled only when he wanted to intimidate someone. In a dangerous, precise voice, he said, "What, exactly, do you mean by 'done here'?"

Tomder flinched away, his fingers tightening around his whip. "Girl didn't show up to work. So she's fired. That's just the rules."

The air left him in a rush, and Lexo's shoulders deflated. His worst fear realized. Lula was missing. Ganna had taken her hostage.

"By the way," Tomder said, "when you see her next, tell her she owes me her indenture debt. If it's not paid by month's end, there'll be hell to pay."

Lexo's fingers twitched. He could reach for Tomder's carotid. The disgusting creature could be dead in seconds.

It was the second time today he'd considered killing. He shook the thought away with some difficulty. Now was the time for clearheadedness. Rage would make him careless and sloppy.

He took a calming breath and said in a voice full of sympathy, "It must be hard to take care of all these urchins only to have some of them turn on you."

Tomder's rheumy eyes bugged out and he nodded vigorously. "No one understands!" he said. "I work hard all day long, giving these kids a better life. And how do they repay me? By ditching work and leaving me destitute."

"You're to be commended for soldiering on," Lexo said. "In your position, I'd have to find other avenues for generating income. So I could take care of the children, of course."

Tomder shrugged. "I find ways to make it work."

Lexo steeled himself. He knew what he needed to do, but Bargwill Tomder was the most revolting creature he'd ever encountered. It would take days to get the stench off himself. Only for Lula.

He reached out and placed a companionable hand on Tomder's shoulder, making sure his fingers brushed the boil-ridden skin of his neck. "I've heard some compelling rumors," he said. Chemicals seeped from his fingertips. Tomder's infected skin gave them easy access to his bloodstream, and Lexo felt the stable keeper's shoulder muscles soften almost immediately.

"Oh?" Tomder said. "I do enjoy a good rumor."

"I've heard that something's going down with DeFancio Storsilt's fleet of fathiers." Maybe the race fixing was related to Lula's disappearance; maybe it wasn't. Lexo wasn't going to chance not knowing about it.

"Oh," Tomder said, his gaze darting around the paddock as if worried they might be overheard. "Of course I don't know what you mean."

Lexo excreted another dose of pheromone, and a wave of dizziness hit him. Using his abilities so often in a single day was exacting a cost. He blinked to clear his vision and said, "Let's say a fellow wanted to repay his daughter's indenture debt to the local stable keeper—along with some extra for his trouble—but just needed a little help getting the money. How should a fellow like that bet tonight?"

"Ooh," Tomder said. "I think I could help a fellow out."

"I'm so glad to hear it."

"I'd tell a fellow like that to bet against any fathiers owned by Storsilt, which as most people know is almost all of them. That leaves only a few left to earn the laurels, right?"

"Right." Lexo smiled winningly. "Naturally, a fellow would want to know how this information had been received. To ascertain its validity. A fellow really wants to make good on his debts, you see."

Tomder glanced around again. Lexo gave him one last helping of pheromone. The ground swayed beneath him.

"Look," Tomder said after a moment. "I got a holo. It was no one I recognized. Tall, bipedal, cloaked, with an altered voice. Maybe even a droid. They asked me to switch the feed of certain fathiers."

"And you did."

"Of course I did. The offer was too good to pass up. I had to do it. For the children, right?"

"Of course. And you were paid as agreed?"

Tomder nodded. "Along with a new shipment of special feed came a special package. Mostly aurodium dust. A few rubies. A handful of casino chips. I'll be able to buy new gloves for the kids, finally."

Lexo startled at this, peering closer. Tomder was fully in his control now. He'd answer any question Lexo asked. There was no need for him to be coy about helping children. Which meant that even though he was a lazy, slave-driving sadist, part of him actually cared a little.

Lexo had one last question. "Do you have any idea why Lula didn't show up to work today?"

"Not a clue. She's one of those peculiar kids who actually *likes* the fathiers. Don't ask me why; they're stupid, filthy, reeking creatures."

Lexo chose not to point out the obvious hypocrisy.

"I admit," Tomder added, "I was surprised when she didn't show."

"You've been very helpful," Lexo said, finally, *finally* removing his hand from Tomder's shoulder. "I'll return later to take care of Lula's debt."

"Be sure that you do!"

Lexo didn't bother with parting niceties; he turned on his heel and strode away, wiping his hands on his robe. At his soonest opportunity, he would have to disinfect them.

He didn't feel any closer to rescuing his daughter, but he wasn't out of options yet. He'd been on Cantonica a long time, and he had a friend or two. Besides, Ganna wasn't his only rich and powerful client. If all else failed, maybe he would break his code and get involved—in exchange for a little help. Just this once.

And Lula, his sweet, smart, strong Lula, had left him a trail of corwindyl to follow. She had undoubtedly planted it on Ganna when she was taken, knowing Lexo's olfactory senses would pick it up right away. He just had to follow his nose.

Big Sturg Ganna didn't know it yet, but he had messed with the wrong masseur.

CHAPTER 4

LEXO SPENT MONEY HE COULDN'T AFFORD TO HIRE A CAB AGAIN. THIS time he directed it to a high-rent part of Old City, an office he knew about but had never visited. A sign above the door said NEEPERS PAN-PICK, PRIVATE INVESTIGATOR.

He pushed the door open and found Panpick himself sitting at a desk, a datapad in hand. Above him a ceiling fan creaked as it went round and round. To his left a holo played a live feed of the casino entrance; the investigator probably had a deal worked out with the Canto Bight Police Department to access their surveillance.

Panpick was a short biped with a round bald head and huge black eyes that made him seem perpetually surprised. He wasn't wealthy like most of Canto Bight's residents. But his job required him to rub noses with the elite, so he always dressed to impress in a black velvet suit, a long, quilted vest, and shoes in a perfect state of shine.

When he saw Lexo, he smiled. "For once!" he said. "A face I'm actually glad to see." Panpick's voice came out high and thin, like that of a squeaking bird, but Lexo's translator necklace made easy work of it.

They shook hands. "Nice to see you too, Neepers," Lexo said, and he meant it. The private investigator was one of the few beings whose company he genuinely enjoyed. They'd met at the spa, of course, and though Panpick couldn't afford Zord's luxuries often, he occasionally went to celebrate closing a big case. And he always requested Lexo.

"Though I must observe," Panpick said, his face suddenly troubled, "that my friends never visit my office unless something terrible has happened."

Real concern, coming from a real friend, was almost Lexo's undoing, and he found it hard to keep his voice steady. "Lula is missing," he said.

"Oh, sands, I'm so sorry to hear. Sit down, sit down. Tell me all about it." He gestured toward a chair facing his desk.

The chair was a little small for a Dor Namethian, but Lexo sat anyway, hunching over so that his knees nearly reached his ears. "Thank you."

"Do you have any idea at all what might have happened?"

Panpick deserved total honesty, so Lexo said, "I think Councilor Ganna took her as leverage, to force me to turn informant."

Panpick recoiled in his chair. "Oh, *sands*. That's . . . that's . . ."

"I don't expect you to get involved," Lexo said. "In fact, I forbid it."

The private investigator seemed visibly relieved. Then guilty. Then suspicious. "So why are you here?"

Lexo folded his hands carefully into his lap. He stared at them a moment, remembering how Lula had helped him. A tiny puncture at the base of one wrist still hadn't quite closed up. "I just need a direction," Lexo said. "Once I know where to start, I have a . . . a trail of sorts that I can follow. I just need that start. I guess it's hard to expl—"

"The casino hotel," Panpick said.

"What?"

"Everyone knows Councilor Ganna has a big estate on the outskirts of town. But only a few people know that he also keeps a private apartment at the casino. One of the hotel suites, I'm told, retrofitted to accommodate his particular environmental requirements."

It was the most tenuous of leads, but it filled Lexo with hope. "And you think he might have taken Lula there? Do you know where in the hotel? Which room?"

Panpick shook his head. "I'm sorry, I don't know any of that. Ganna has kept very quiet about the place."

Lexo deflated a little.

"But if I were a betting man—and I most certainly am not—I'd lay odds that his suite is located belowground and has multiple access points."

"Why belowground . . ." he started to ask, but then the answer came to him. Because Ganna's retrofitted suite would certainly be located where it was cooler and wetter. Since the advent of the artificial sea, the lower levels of Canto Bight had become damp and dank, with occasional moisture seepage. Nearest the coast, sump pumps worked full time to keep the water at bay. "He needs the humidity."

"I suspect so," Panpick said.

"And having a secondary residence at the casino means he can retire quickly, if the desert is getting to him. It's a safety measure."

"Exactly."

"So what would you do if you were me?" Lexo asked.

Panpick gave Lexo a long, frank look. "My friend, you are *not* me. You never get involved, right?"

Lexo opened his mouth. Closed it.

"'Hear nothing, see nothing, say nothing,' am I right? Well, I'm afraid that's not going to work for you right now. You have to go into this with eyes and ears wide open. There are things you can do. If you're willing."

For Lula, Lexo just might be willing.

"Any suggestions?" Lexo asked, feeling a little sick. He wasn't sure whether it was from using too much pheromone today or from the decisions he felt himself about to make.

"Start small. Case the casino posing as a guest. Keep an eye out for people you know are in Ganna's employ. A few chips in the right hands might give you a good start. Servers, bartenders, drivers . . . they hear and see everything."

And unlike Lexo, they were likely to sell that information at the soonest opportunity. He would have to be very convincing and very discreet.

Panpick added: "Ganna has spies everywhere. Watch yourself."

He was right about that. Lexo stood to go. "Thank you so much, Panpick. I'll find a way to repay you for this, I swear it."

"But you were never here, right?"

"Never. We hardly know each other."

Panpick grinned.

A *creak, creak* sound drew Lexo's attention upward. "Nice fan, by the way," he said.

"Sands, that thing is fantastic!" he agreed. "Now I don't have to turn on the environmental controls at night. It's saving me a fortune. Last week, some rich heiress lost her pet—an overgrown rat with three tails, all dyed different colors. I found the poor thing hiding out near the countess's estate. My client was so overjoyed that she doubled my fee. Paid for that fan and a new suit. Speaking of . . ." Panpick fished inside his jacket pocket and pulled out three casino chips. "Take this."

Lexo put up his hands. "I couldn't."

"Please, Lexo. Assuage my guilty conscience. You know I can't openly cross Ganna, not for anyone. But this might help with expenses. Think of it as a loan. An advance against your future tips."

Lexo took the chips. He stared at them a moment. "Thank you, friend."

When he stepped outside the office, night had fully descended on Canto Bight. The street lanterns glowed, store windows were rimmed in light, and a few blocks away the blinding nimbus of the Canto Casino washed away any chance of seeing the stars.

CHAPTER 5

YOU CAN GET ANYTHING IN CANTO BIGHT, OR SO THE SAYING WENT. STILL, it wasn't until his third try that Lexo finally found a shop that carried traditional Dor Namethian robes. He didn't think he could enter the casino in his ragged everyday wear; he'd be kicked out before he could utter a word. He briefly considered stealing the white working gown he wore at the spa, but too many people would notice and recognize him on sight. He decided to emulate his friend Panpick and buy clothes to fit the part, even if they were ridiculously overpriced, and even if the blue embroidery on the silken black sleeves was a clumsy appropriation of Dor Namethian culture and nothing at all as beautiful and intricate as the real thing.

The robe was reversible, lined in bright-blue silk. Lexo considered it a moment, then opted to wear it black-side out. Wouldn't do to be so bright.

Next, Lexo found a postal center, which Canto Bight visitors used to ship purchases home and send long-distance communications. He bought a disposable comlink. The clerk assured him that all their comlinks were untraceable, but Lexo was mostly interested in the fact that they were cheap.

Armored with the traditional garb of his homeworld, and armed with a new comlink, Lexo found a solitary bench beside a tinkling fountain and placed a call to Councilor Sturg Ganna.

As expected, the communication was answered by one of Ganna's personal assistants. "How can I help you," said a bored, flat voice. It was not a question.

"My name is Lexo Sooger, and I wish to speak—"

"Yeah whatever the councilor is unavailable but he is jubilant to receive so many messages from his constituents please leave your name and the reason for your call His Greatness will read your message with humble trembling and incandescent joy begin recording in three, two—"

"Wait! The councilor is expecting my call. Just give him my name."

"Oh why didn't you say so one moment please hold to enjoy the award-winning musical composition 'Serenity Starscapes' from His Greatness's home planet."

Lexo groaned audibly as all four chords of the song played over and over in an endless, mindless loop. It was almost a relief to hear Ganna's deep, rumbling voice.

"Lexo, my friend!" he bellowed. "I assume you've called to say you've made the very wise decision to work for me."

"Return my daughter to me," Lexo said, "and I will do whatever you want, whenever you want, no questions asked."

Ganna laughed, and the deep, awful sound shuddered through Lexo's shoulders. "You must think me a fool," he said. "What's to stop you from fleeing the planet if I let her go? No, it's best you do a few jobs for me first. Prove your worth and your loyalty. Then we'll discuss the *possibility* of you seeing your daughter again."

Lexo hadn't expected anything different from Ganna, and it had been worth a try. Still, he gripped the comlink so hard his fingers hurt. "At least assure me she is safe," he pleaded, in a shamefully small voice.

"Of course she's safe. I'm not a monster! Naturally, I can't guarantee that she won't accidentally injure herself. She's so tiny and delicate, after all."

Lexo almost choked. If at all possible, he was going to destroy Ganna. *Destroy* him.

"But so long as you work for me," Ganna continued, "she'll be well cared for. A meal per day. A suitable cot, labor that fills her life with meaning and purpose, a roof over her head. I realize many children do not have it so well, but I can't help being softhearted."

"So you'll keep her safe and healthy," Lexo said.

"As much as I am able," Ganna assured him. "And so long as she earns her keep."

Poor Lula. To go from indenture to outright slavery. Well, it wouldn't last long. He would figure out a way to free her and then extricate them both from Ganna's manipulations. Either that or escape the planet Cantonica completely. There had to be a way.

"Then I suppose there is nothing more but to await my first assignment," Lexo said.

"Indeed. Will I be able to reach you at this comlink?"

"It's disposable."

"Pity. I'll set you up with a better one. You should be able to pay me back for it with just a few jobs."

"How generous."

"And Lexo?"

"Yes, Councilor?"

"Behave."

"Yes, Councilor."

But Ganna had already clicked away.

Lexo wasted precious moments sitting on the bench, staring at the fountain. Lights from beneath made the water glow blue and then green and then blue again. He used it as a meditation, forcing calm into his shoulders, into his thoughts.

The call had been a good idea. Now that Ganna believed he would cooperate, the gangster was less likely to harm Lula. Lexo had bought them some time.

But not much time. Like Panpick said, Ganna had spies everywhere, and he hadn't become one of the most entrenched and powerful beings in Canto Bight by being stupid. Whatever Lexo did, he had to do it tonight.

He rose from the bench. Black robes swirled at his ankles, the silky fabric sheening with reflected light, as he strode toward the Canto Casino.

———

The casino complex was massive, housing a luxury hotel, intergalactic shopping options, and several fine restaurants catering to a huge variety of species. Lexo was only interested in the gaming areas that abutted the hotel. There he hoped to discover exactly which part housed Big Sturg Ganna's secondary residence.

A river of beings poured into and out of the casino's main entrance. Everyone was dressed immaculately in the richest fabrics, the rarest jewels, the highest-end accessories. Formal black and white dominated, but flashes of color could be seen on silken stoles and dripping necklaces and—in one instance—the flowers adorning the hair of a human woman.

Lexo had to blend in, and the only way to do it was to act like a rich jerk. So he kept his eyes focused ahead and strode forward with confidence he didn't feel, not deigning to notice the lowly casino guards or the scurrying janitor droids. He had been acting his whole life. Pretending to listen to his clients. Pretending he didn't hear anything interesting or useful. Pretending he belonged among the elegant and the elite. He could do this.

The gaming rooms were vast and sweeping, with curved walls and domed roofs, surrounded by stained-glass windows depicting fathier racing scenes. The windows were lit from outside, so that even at night the stained glass cast a warming glow onto the gaming tables. Everything was painted in desert colors—ocher and yellow and soft cream and tan dominating. The cumulative effect was one of luxurious calm. Of peaceful elegance. It was all designed to put patrons in the perfect mindset for spending money freely.

Lexo moved through the crowd quickly. He spotted another Dor Namethian near the bar and indulged in a small moment of relief. He was less likely to be noticed tonight, less likely to seem unusual. But he turned away before the other fellow could spot him and wave him over. He wasn't here to make friends.

Slot machines clanged and croupiers called out to draw patrons to their tables. To Lexo's left, a cheer went up—someone had hit a streak with Hazard Toss. To his right was a small stage where a trio of Pa-landags played wind instruments. Lexo would have liked to stay and listen to the Palandags, who, unlike the musicians of Ganna's home planet, actually played *real* music.

But he ignored it all, focusing instead on scents. And there were a lot of scents. Perfumes, stress pheromones, disinfectant, attraction pheromones, flowering plants, even a hint of vomit. For a species with superior olfactory senses, it was almost too much.

The sharp, smoky aroma of one of his favorite beverages alerted him to the fact that an SE-8 was approaching. He turned and, sure enough, a waiter droid bleeped at him, flashing his lights. Lexo de-clined.

What he didn't smell, no matter how hard he concentrated, was corwindyl.

Lexo moved deeper into the casino. He had to find someone who spent a lot of time here, someone in a position to see everything. But Panpick's words rang in his head: *Ganna has spies everywhere.* The type of person Lexo needed to talk to was exactly the type of person Ganna would press into his own service. He would have to be very careful and very lucky.

One wall of the casino opened up into a lofty hallway, which Lexo assumed led to the hotel. Beside the opening was another bar, so hotel guests could order drinks first thing before heading into the gaming area. Lexo drifted closer. Maybe he would order a drink him-self. Sip it slowly. Stall for time and think, think, think about how to proceed.

As he approached, he hit pay dirt.

An odor assaulted his nose. Not corwindyl, alas, but the bar reeked like a place where beautiful growing things went to die. Like a rotting swamp.

The bartender was a light-skinned human with a full beard and a patch over one eye. He was wiping down the long, night-black bar surface until it shimmered. He spotted Lexo and stashed his rag out of sight. "How can I help you?"

"What is that delightful smell?" Lexo said. "It reminds me of home—the wafting aroma of the famous . . . er . . . Peat Bog of Benevolence . . .” There was no Peat Bog of Benevolence on his homeworld, or peat bogs in general, but humans were notoriously ignorant of other species. “It almost brings a tear to the eye,” he finished gamely.

“Huh,” said the bartender. “I only get complaints about this stuff.”

“What stuff?”

“It’s a drink, custom-made for a very special class of customer. Don’t fancy the smell myself.”

“It’s magnificent.”

“If you say so. Can I get you something? Not *that* drink, mind you.”

Lexo gasped with mock affront. “Whyever not?”

“Those ingredients are hard to come by. They’re reserved. As I said, for a very special class of customer.”

“But I want one.”

“Not going to happen. Look, can I get you something else or not?”

Poor fellow. Lexo almost apologized for taking up his time, but he was supposed to be blending in. He gave the bartender his best condescending glare and said imperiously, “Are you always so rude to casino guests?”

“I wasn’t being—”

“Who do you work for?”

“Gheal, of course. She owns this bar, and a few others besides.”

“Ah, yes. I’m well acquainted with Ubialla Gheal.” That, at least, was not a lie. The nightclub owner came in at least twice a month for a massage. “She’ll be keen to know what kind of service I received here. She’s been considering replacing all her employees with droids.” Also not a lie.

The bartender’s jaw twitched. Lexo stared.

Lexo allowed the pause to grow huge and menacing before saying, “I believe you were about to tell me more about that drink.”

The bartender slumped a little. “It’s called storga. It’s filled with active microbes that . . . never mind. Just please either buy it or don’t buy it and then leave. Sounds like I’m screwed either way.” Stress pheromones oozed from his pores, making Lexo wrinkle his nose.

Lula would be so ashamed of him, to see him bullying this poor man. Lexo clenched his teeth for a moment and thought hard. How far would he go to save his daughter? How far would she *want* him to go?

Sighing, he fished out the chips he'd received from his friend Panpick and laid them on the bar. "I won't buy the storga," he said. "And if I see Ubialla, I'll let her know what a tremendous asset you are to her business."

The bartender's good eye narrowed. "What's the catch?"

"Just tell me where that drink goes. Whose room will you send it to?"

The bartender rubbed his beard, considering. "All right. Here's the honest truth, so listen close. I have no idea where it goes. I receive an order maybe once per day, about this time. I make the drink. Soon after, a waiter droid swings by to pick it up and leaves me a small tip That's all I know."

"I see. How long has this been going on? The last few weeks?"

"The last few *years*. Since the first day I started working here."

So the drink belonged to someone in residence. Someone who liked the smell and taste of a festering swamp. It had to be Councilor Ganna.

"And you expect this droid to roll around any moment?"

"I do. You can . . ." He leaned closer and whispered, "You could probably follow it, if you wanted to. But please don't tell anyone I said so."

"Of course not. Those chips are yours. Thank you."

As Lexo stepped away, the bartender swept the chips out of sight with a smooth, well-practiced gesture.

Lexo headed toward the nearest carousel of slot machines, in plain sight of both the bar and the corridor leading to the hotel. He had no more chips, so he pretended to contemplate the machines, as if deciding which one would bring him the most luck. Really, he was watching that bar. The bartender helped a customer, then another. He wiped the bar down. He reached beneath the counter and grabbed a small metal tube from under the bar—was it a comlink? Maybe the bartender was a Ganna informant after all. Lexo was poised to flee.

But no, it was just an ingredient cylinder. The bartender tipped it over a glass, and something like liquid gold poured from it. Lexo's shoulders slumped with relief.

Finally an SE-8 waiter droid shuffled into view and bleeped at the bartender, who settled a glass full of mud-brown sludge onto the droid's round tray table. As it shuffled away, Lexo hurried to follow.

If there was a talent for following without becoming noticed, Lexo was certain he didn't have it. He felt clumsy and obtrusive as he hurried down the corridor after the droid, dodging guests, keeping an eye out for cams and security personnel.

The droid led him through a beautiful atrium with a fountain and a massive skylight, then down another corridor into a separate tower of the hotel. The droid stopped at the entrance to a lift and programmed it to head downward.

As soon as the door opened, Lexo took a chance and swept inside to stand beside the droid. Surely the SE-8 had noticed him following by now? He kept his eyes firmly ahead, did not look down once, even when the droid's head swiveled to look at him, swiveled back, and then looked at him again. It was definitely growing suspicious.

The lift clunked to a halt, and the doors opened into a well-lit hallway of sandstone. Even here, deep in the ground, luxury was everywhere—in the carpet runners lining the corridor, the fine paintings along the wall, the chandeliers dripping with crystal above his head. The air was cooler, though. Wetter. And as Lexo continued to follow the waiter droid, he noticed two pipes running along their path, tucked in where the wall met the floor. They were painted to blend in with the sandstone, but they couldn't possibly be part of the original architecture. Any unseemly infrastructure would have been hidden away in the walls and floors, out of sight of the hotel's discerning guests. These pipes were a late addition.

The corridor—and the pipes—curved left and ended abruptly at a set of double doors, blocked by two brutish, tusked Gamorrean guards in studded armor. The droid scooted forward, but Lexo froze.

Gamorreans were one of the few species he couldn't affect with his abilities. He couldn't even interpret their pheromones. Lexo flexed his fingers, wondering if he was still young and strong enough to take care of the guards the old-fashioned way. Probably not. Stiffness and pain were already returning to his joints. Only a few more hours until he wouldn't be able to move them at all.

The guards grunted, hefting their battle-axes.

Lexo wasn't sure what to do next. Run for his life? Insult their mothers? Pretend he was drunk?

Drunkenness won out. He careened sloppily into the wall. "You seen a Twi'lek girl?" he asked the guards brazenly. "Said she would meet me here. She promised. One floor down, she said. Or was it one floor up?" He hiccuped. "Prettiest blue skin I ever saw. All I had to do was buy her a drink, yanno? But I think maybe . . ." He swayed on his feet. "Maybe she was lying. Ditched me. Probably back at the bar flirting with another . . . oh, dear. I think I might throw up."

One of the guards deftly rescued the foul drink from the droid's serving table. The droid gave one indignant bleep and fled back the way it had come.

The other guard moved forward to block Lexo's path. "Go ahead and deliver the drink," he ordered his companion. "I'll take care of this fool." His mean-looking tusks made speaking Galactic Basic impossible, but Lexo still had his translator necklace, and he understood just fine.

His companion punched a code into a console, but Lexo's view was blocked. The double doors slid open, then shut decisively behind him.

"Whatwasat you say?" Lexo said. "Can't understand."

The remaining guard thrust the battle-ax against Lexo's chest and shoved him backward with it. Lexo didn't have to fake drunkenness as he staggered violently. "Get lost," the Gamorrean said.

"I'm sorry I'm sorry so sorry," Lexo said, hands up. "I don't know what you just said, but I'm leaving. I promise. Just . . . had too much to drink. Gimme a sec. Have to get my bearings." He placed a hand on the wall and made as if to take some deep breaths.

The gleaming wet porcine nose of the guard began to twitch. He was *sniffing* Lexo.

Drunken Lexo was not to be outdone, so he sniffed right back. "I bet you're a good smeller," he said, still sniffing. "A great smeller. The best smeller."

And Lexo almost lost his footing again, because the scent came to him, spicy yet sweet, faint but unmistakable. Corwindyl.

"This fool does not reek of someone who's been drinking," the guard muttered to himself. His eyes narrowed, and he cocked his head.

Lexo had mere seconds before he had to flee. He probably should have fled already. Cams were undoubtedly hidden everywhere. Ganna could be watching him right this moment. But he had to know more.

"Hey, whatkinda gentlebeing has a big fancy suite like this?" Lexo said. "With such dangerous guards? I mean, thatsa really fancy door. Lookit that carving. Flowers, isit?"

He didn't really expect a response, so he was both thrilled and terrified when the guard pulled a comlink from a pocket and spoke into it, saying, "Tell the councilor that someone is outside asking questions. But don't worry; I'm taking care of him."

The guard stashed his comlink, and then he advanced, ax held high.

Lexo turned and fled. His Dor Namethian robes allowed for his enormous stride, and he was around the corner and at the lift in seconds. But the lift itself lowered too slowly. Footsteps pounded behind him.

Finally the door opened, and he thrust himself inside. The Gamorrean popped into view just as the doors closed. Lexo backed into the corner and huddled there, gasping for breath, as he rode up to the ground floor.

Lula was somewhere inside that suite, he was certain of it. But the corwindyl scent had been so faint! Which meant she hadn't arrived that way. The suite had another entrance.

He considered those pipes he'd seen. There hadn't been time for a close look, but one seemed like it might camouflage power lines. And the other . . . Water, maybe? It made sense that Big Sturg Ganna would build extra environmental controls to survive in such a hot, dry place. Based on the size of the pipes, Lexo wouldn't be surprised if Ganna had a whole aquarium hidden down there, all to himself.

Not for the first time, Lexo wondered why Ganna would come to Cantonica at all. Why settle on a planet where one or two careless days of exposure could kill him? Ganna was hiding, or fleeing, or planning something.

Something that was worth the risk.

Lexo had to figure a way past those guards. Once inside, he was sure to encounter even more security precautions. Someone as wealthy as Ganna could afford environmental poison, or even illegal battle droids.

Now that he knew where Lula was, he needed help. Councilor Ganna had said that a war was coming to Canto Bight. Maybe Lexo should figure out who the gangster's greatest enemy was, who stood to gain the most from inconveniencing him. It would have to be someone powerful, with insider knowledge of the city and its casino.

His heart sunk, because all of a sudden, he knew exactly who to ask for help. Of course.

Lexo's friend Panpick had been exactly right. Tonight, he needed to have eyes and ears wide open. For once, he would allow himself to hear everything, see everything.

The door opened onto the ground floor and Lexo strode out like he had as much right to be there as anyone else.

CHAPTER 6

CONTESSA ALISSYNDREX DELGA CANTONICA PROVINCION MAINTAINED A government office adjacent to the racetrack, in a beautiful domed tower with a patina glaze of greening copper. She did not frequent the casino often, but she loved the races, and she was known to observe them from her tower balcony whenever her duties kept her away from the track itself.

As Lexo approached the reception area, he checked the chrono. Less than an hour remaining until the first post time. If he was lucky, the countess would still be here. If he was very lucky, he'd win an audience with her.

He considered three different introductions that might get him past the door to see the countess. He settled on "a representative of Zord's, on an emergency business matter." To his surprise he only got as far as his name before the receptionist buzzed him through, and he was allowed to ascend the tower straightaway. Four sentry droids guarded the entrance; they followed him inside, blasters hefted menacingly.

The countess stood beside her desk, still wearing her sleeveless black evening gown. Her thick epidermis had been expertly styled into a mass of waves around her face. Behind her, floor-to-ceiling windows displayed the whole city in all its lighted glory. He could even glimpse the massive reclamation waterfall that tumbled into the sea.

"You've been running around my city quite a lot tonight," she said without preamble.

There was no reason to lie. "Yes, Your Grace," he answered.

"I wasn't aware that Zord allowed his employees so much free time."

"He doesn't, Your Grace."

She took a sip of her wine, swirled it around in her mouth, swallowed. "I don't imagine you've come here to kill me," she said. "You could have done that a dozen times at the bathhouse."

Lexo blinked. Why would she say such a thing? "I came because I need your help," he said.

The countess gave him a bored look, steeped in disappointment.

"It's about Big Sturg Ganna," he added quickly.

The countess sat, crossing her legs. She swung one ankle back and forth, taking another sip of wine. To all appearances, she didn't have a worry in the world, but Lexo knew better. The moment he'd mentioned the councilor's name, tension began oozing out of her, filling the air.

Finally, she said, "Tell me about it."

Lexo told her everything about Lula, about Ganna wanting to hire him as an informant. When he finished, he took a deep breath and prepared for the worst.

The countess said, "You are guessing that Ganna and I are at odds. That I might help you in order to hurt him."

Lexo remembered the way she watched them from the spa balcony. Surely he hadn't misread the tension between them? He said nothing.

"Ganna is my greatest ally and a dear friend, of course."

Lexo opened his mouth. Closed it. How could he have read the situation so poorly? How could— But, no. She was lying. The pheromones leaking from her skin screamed her lie to him.

So he replied, "Did you know that Councilor Ganna intends to buy out your share of the spa?"

"Yes. We have discussed it."

"I can't imagine why you'd want to sell."

"I grow bored of the bathhouse business."

Again, she was lying. Which meant either the councilor had something on her, or she needed the money.

Once again, Lexo decided on the honest approach. "I'm sorry for whatever is wrong, whatever he's doing to you. He's doing the same or worse to my daughter and me."

"He's doing nothing to me. As I said, he is my greatest ally."

"Of course, Your Grace," Lexo said, bowing his head. "Apologies for my presumption."

"Naturally, though, the fate of any Canto Bight citizen, a child no less, is of the utmost importance to me."

It was hard to stay calm. "Of course," he said again.

"So I will help you, Lexo Sooger. I know exactly how to get you inside that hotel suite. But first, you must do something for me. A tiny favor."

In Canto Bight, there was no such thing as a tiny favor. Everything inside him screamed to decline, to flee, but he thought of Lula and said, "Anything."

She smiled, and Lexo knew she was springing her trap. "I need you to kill someone for me."

His heart pounded in his shoulders.

"I know about you, Sooger," she said. "Born into poverty. Raised in the slave pits of Askkto-Fen IV. You were made to serve in the steam baths, catering to fighting slaves, until you were plucked from that horrible life by a traveling merchant, who saw your potential as a masseur."

Lexo's shoulders felt like they were about to explode. He had told no one this. No one but Lula.

"Tell me, Sooger," the countess continued relentlessly. "Did that merchant ever know? What you really did? Who you really are?"

Lexo felt a little dizzy. Maybe he should sit down.

"You sabotaged matches by sabotaging the fighters—or healing them, depending on who paid the most. There were so many species represented in the fighting pits, and you learned about them all. You learned their strengths, their weaknesses. My reports say you could kill with a single touch."

He sat. "Your Grace," he choked out. "I left that life behind. I'm a father now."

"Ah, yes. Your daughter." She swirled the wine in her glass, staring at it as though it contained all the mysteries of the universe. "Your human daughter. Tell me, how did you come to possess such a creature?"

He blinked at her. "I came to care for her, not possess her."

She waved a hand. "Same difference. How?"

"I found her in the stairwell. In an empty cargo box. Someone had just left her there."

The countess raised one eyebrow. "Did you ever try to locate her parents?"

"Of course I did. But children are so quickly and easily abandoned here. It was like trying to find a flea on a fathier. Those first few days were hard. I knew all about human anatomy, but it turns out I didn't know anything else. I didn't know what to feed her or how often, whether she was a species that needed or loathed physical touch, or what it meant when she made those awful wailing sounds."

"But you figured it all out."

"I did. And I almost went broke hiring someone to care for her while I was at work. Humans aren't independent until they're many seasons old."

The countess was leaning forward, eyes wide, hanging on his every word.

Lexo resisted the urge to flinch away. "Why are you asking me all this?"

"Would you be interested in finding her real parents?"

Lexo stared. He didn't know such a thing was possible. Thousands arrived and departed Canto Bight via the spaceport every single day. Lula's parents could be anywhere in the galaxy. "You can do that?" he said.

"I might. Let's see . . . it was about thirteen years ago, and she is a dark-skinned variety of human, yes?"

Lexo nodded, still dumbfounded.

"That's enough information to begin making inquiries at least. I'll tell you what. You do this tiny favor for me, and I'll help you get inside Ganna's suite *and* make inquiries about your daughter's parentage."

"Only if Lula wants to know."

"So you'll do it?"

"I . . ." He hadn't killed in decades, and he was rusty. Killing required finesse, strength, young tendons, a willingness to bear the burden of conscience. He wasn't sure he could do it. He certainly didn't want to, maybe not even for Lula.

"Do you have a better plan for reaching your daughter?"

His silence was all the answer she needed.

She smiled. "If *I* know you've been running around town all night, then it's only a matter of time before Ganna knows it, too. He will hurt your daughter. Maybe even kill her. You must act tonight or lose her forever."

The countess was right, and Lexo didn't know what else to do. His gut churned and his shoulders grew tight, tight, tighter as he said, "All right then. Tell me about the mark."

The countess set down her wine as relief pheromones filled the air. "It's a human male, middle-aged, light-toned skin, blue eyes, black facial hair. Very tall for a human; the top of his head would probably reach your shoulder. His name is Jerdon Bly, and he'll be entertained tonight by Baron Yasto Attsmun on his yacht, the *Undisputed Victor*. The yacht is scheduled to sail within the hour, so you must hurry."

A human. Lexo knew all about humans now. Hard to raise, easy to kill.

"Jerdon Bly is a buffoon," she said. "Easy to manipulate, very full of himself. He's an easy mark if you can just get him alone. I'll arrange for you to be on that yacht in a serving capacity." She gave him the berth number and a passcode.

He memorized the information and asked, "Why do you want him dead?"

"That's above your pay grade."

"It most certainly is not."

The countess seemed astonished that he would contradict her. "I will tell you only what you need to kn—"

"A good assassin wields knowledge as much as any physical weapon. You know this to be true, or you wouldn't have been tracking me with spies. Councilor Ganna also understands this, or he wouldn't be going to such lengths to recruit me. So you will tell me *exactly* why you want him dead, because my success may hinge on that knowledge."

She pressed her lips together, considering. Then: "He's an arms dealer. A dangerous one. He's playing both sides, you see. Selling to both the First Order and the Resistance."

Lexo gave her a withering look. "Everyone in Canto Bight plays both sides."

"Yes, but he is gauche about it."

"Gauche? In Canto Bight? I can't imagine."

She swept up her glass and brought it to her smiling lips. "Dangerously gauche. This city survives on open secrets. Yet Jerdon Bly boasts to anyone who will listen about the major deal he has arranged, something going down very soon. He's going to bring trouble on my city, mark my words."

Lexo could smell the lie, but it wasn't a strong one. A partial lie, perhaps. The intended mark was almost certainly a weapons dealer, just as the countess claimed. But Lexo would bet his floating distal bones that the real reason the countess wanted him gone was to eliminate her competition. She was the one who wanted to play both sides.

Lexo stood, and the countess grabbed her wineglass and stood with him. If she were a head taller, they'd be nose to nose. On impulse, he reached for her arm. Her epidermis was thick and protective, but porous enough, allowing the chemicals from his fingertips to penetrate.

He squeezed gently and said, "Ganna must have considerable leverage on you, for you to be willing to help a lowly masseur, assassin or not. As I said, I'm sorry for whatever he is doing to you."

To his surprise, tears filled her eyes. "I don't want to sell my share of the spa. But I need resources . . . my husband . . ."

Her husband the count was rarely seen in public. In fact, Lexo couldn't remember the last time he'd made an official appearance. "Is he all right?" Lexo asked, his voice full of sympathy.

"He . . ." The countess's eyes widened, and she swung her arm, throwing off his hand. Wine sloshed in an arc across the wall, onto the rug. Anger pheromones filled the air. "Never touch me again," she spat out.

Lexo bowed, backing away. "Apologies, Your Grace. I'll return when the job is done."

She turned her back to him and stared across the balcony toward the racetrack. "You do that," she said.

Lexo stopped at the door to get his bearings. He was using his ability too often. He needed food and rest. Not getting them soon might cost years off his massaging career.

"Why are you still here?" the countess said, still gazing into the Cantonica night.

Lexo said to her back, "I don't know if this will help or not, but I've heard that it would be wise to bet against DeFancio Storsilt's stable tonight. Maybe place a small wager on a long shot instead."

"I *always* bet on Hard Luck."

Lexo sighed. "Me too, Countess. Me too."

CHAPTER 7

LEXO SOOGER DID NOT KNOW HOW TO SWIM, A FACT THAT BECAME suddenly and terrifyingly forefront in his mind as he entered the monolithic boathouse and felt the deck sway beneath his feet.

The *Undisputed Victor* was berthed exactly where the countess said it would be, and it was sleek, beautiful, and enormous. It stretched at least twenty-five meters from stem to stern, and boasted several levels culminating in a massive viewing deck with a shiny rail. Most impressive of all, it was equipped with repulsorlift technology, which could allow its lustrous hull to barely skim the water.

A long line of impeccably attired guests waited to board. Lexo pulled up the cowl of his robe—being recognized now would ruin everything—and scanned the crowd. No one matched Jerdon Bly's description. Maybe the arms dealer was already aboard.

Lexo reached the front of the line, where an electronic voice said, "Invitation or passcode, please."

A protocol droid stood sentry at the bottom of the gangplank, flanked by two Trandoshan guards. He was an older model, refurbished but in good condition, and painted pure, reflective white—a smart precaution under the Cantonica skies. He held a datapad and was checking off guests as they embarked.

Lexo gave him the countess's passcode.

"Most excellent," said the droid. "You're expected down in the galley. Up the ramp and to your right, inside the first door, and down the stairs. Please proceed with all haste and decorum."

Lexo did as he was told, climbing the ramp quickly. He was much relieved to discover that the repulsorlift retrofit made the yacht feel as solid as the ground itself. If not for the sound of tiny waves lapping against the dock, he could almost forget he was on a boat at all.

He wasn't able to get a good look at his surroundings—much less the observation deck where his mark would probably be—before he found the aforementioned doorway and had no choice but to proceed down the steep, narrow stair into the belly of the yacht.

The galley was in chaos, as cooks and servers and dishwashers—both organic and droid—scurried to fill trays with hors d'oeuvres, only to have them swept away, then replaced by newly washed, empty ones. Cauldrons boiled at one end, ovens baked beside them, and an automatic dispenser looked like a tentacled monster as it squirted, mixed, and arranged drinks using a variety of tubes and attachments.

A rock of dread settled in his shoulders. The baron was expecting an enormous crowd. Based on all this flurry, it would be the party of the millennium. At least until the next party. In spite of the crowd, Lexo would have to single out one guest, assassinate him, and get away unseen.

"You there!" hollered a droid's voice. A refreshment tray was thrust into Lexo's hands. On it were tiny glass cups, each filled with a bright-purple gelatinous mass. "You're dressed well enough to serve. Head up to the observation deck and circulate. Do not speak unless spoken to. When the tray is empty, pick up any refuse and return. Now go, go, go!" Metal appendages shoved him away, and the purple gunk inside the tiny cups wobbled dangerously.

Well, at least he now had reason to cruise the observation deck. Lexo headed back up the stairs as fast as his quivering cargo would allow.

He took a few wrong turns before finding the center staircase leading to the top. Just as his head was breaching the deck, the mammoth doors of the boathouse swung wide, letting in the Cantonica night.

The floor rumbled as the engines purred, and the yacht began a smooth, gliding journey into the open sea.

Almost immediately someone swept by and grabbed one of the tiny glasses from his tray. She tossed it back into her throat, swallowed it with a single gulp, then returned the empty glass—all without acknowledging Lexo at all. That suited him just fine. It was best to be invisible.

Guests were everywhere, some of them already inebriated. A few danced to a live band. Others gathered around tiny refreshment tables. Still more posed against the railing, displaying themselves to their best advantage. Lights reflected in the water from other pleasure barges, from the city itself, and from spaceships skimming the sky on their way to the port. A pleasant breeze ruffled the waves, sending only the slightest, most elegant spray against the skin of Lexo's face.

It was a beautiful, glorious sight, on a beautiful, glorious night, and Lexo wished with all the feeling in his shoulders that Lula could be there to share it with him.

He resumed his search for Jerdon Bly, moving across the observation deck with perfect composure. Really, he thought, it wasn't so different from being a masseur. Glasses disappeared from his tray table, only to reappear empty moments later. On the starboard side, partygoers crowded around a holo of the racetrack; a loud cheer went up when the first horn sounded and the fathiers burst free of their gates.

Lexo looked everywhere, weaving in and out of dresses and stoles and robes and even the occasional personal hoverchair. He was beginning to despair when he spotted a tall humanoid creature with dark hair, speaking to Baron Attsmun near the stern.

He hesitated, shoulders tightening. The baron was one of his clients. It's possible he would be recognized, even cowled as he was. Then again, his clients so often remained facedown on the massage table, eyes closed. Many of them—like the baron—never deigned to acknowledge a servile being, much less really look at them. Maybe it would be fine.

Gradually, carefully, Lexo approached.

The dark-haired fellow laughed at something the baron said, shifting slightly . . . Yes! Definitely human, with black facial hair and light eyes. Lexo just needed to get close enough to confirm his mark, then figure out a way to separate him from the throng.

"Do I know you?" asked a feminine voice.

He nearly dropped the tray.

Sidling up to him was a woman, a beautiful biped in an iridescent gown, with a cone-shaped head and the softest, smoothest skin he'd ever seen. He couldn't remember her name, only that she had been a client once or twice, and had name-dropped the countess during her massage.

"I doubt it, my lady," Lexo said, bowing to hide his face. "I'm new to Canto Bight."

Her lovely eyes narrowed, and she cocked her head as if to see him better. "You Dor Namethians do look very much alike."

"Yes, my lady. So I've heard."

"Huh. Well, have a pleasant night."

"You, too, my lady."

He spent a dangerous moment marveling that someone like her would remember him, much less speak to a lowly server where she could be seen by everyone around. Maybe not everyone here was so bad.

She headed away without sparing him another glance, but his shoulders did not ease in the slightest. If she could recognize him, someone he'd served twice at most, anyone could.

Lexo returned his attention to the man who might be Jerdon Bly. In fact, the woman who'd just recognized him was heading Bly's way. She caught the man's eye. He paused whatever he was saying to the baron and stared at her. A lascivious grin spread across his face.

Another glass disappeared from Lexo's tray. He was running low and would have to return to the galley soon, but he didn't dare take his eyes off his mark. He crept closer. Suddenly their conversation broke through the din of engines and party chatter, and Lexo could understand what they were saying.

"Tomorrow, is it?" the baron was asking.

"By this time tomorrow night, I'll be the richest man in Canto Bight," Bly crowed. But his eyes were still on the woman. What was her name? It was on the tip of Lexo's tongue.

"And you're selling the same blasters to the First Order that you already sold to the Resistance?"

"Yes, of course. Once the First Order knew the Resistance carried them, they had to have some, too. Wouldn't do to be outgunned."

Contempt oozed from the baron, but he clapped Bly on the back. "Brilliant!" he said. "Simply brilliant. Oh, hello, Centada. I'm so glad you could join us tonight."

Centada. That was it. The woman's name was Centada Ressad. Lexo crept closer still.

"Introduce me," Bly demanded. The sharp musk of attraction made Lexo's nostrils twitch.

The baron completed introductions, and Lexo was relieved, because even though he'd been almost certain of his mark, it was still good to hear the name Jerdon Bly spoken aloud.

"May I steal Lady Ressad away for a while?" Bly asked.

"By all means," the baron said, and Lexo sensed a sudden excretion of fear. Centada Ressad did not fancy being alone with Bly.

The baron strode away to greet a different cluster of guests, while Bly indicated that Ressad should follow him toward the railing. She did, but Lexo noted how she glanced around furtively, perhaps looking for allies.

Two more glasses on his tray were emptied as Lexo followed the pair. He could kill Bly easily—he needed exactly seven seconds. But he had to get him alone. How? Maybe a distraction would be best. Something to draw everyone's attention away while he did the deed.

Bly grabbed for Ressad's waist, but she slipped away. She was so graceful about it that it almost looked like a coincidence. She laughed at something he said, but fear continued to radiate from her skin. Bly tried again, and this time he was successful. He pulled Ressad close, whispering something. She tried to squirm free. He held on tighter. Panic filled her eyes.

Lexo dreaded killing again. Not the act itself so much as the burden of conscience that followed. But Bly being a scum would ease that burden a little. If Lula were here, she would describe him as "horrible." Maybe she would even understand what Lexo had to do.

Ressad continued to protest. Bly brought his face toward hers. She lifted her knee and sent her foot crashing down on his instep.

Bly squealed in pain.

Ressad glided away as Bly doubled over. Others in the crowd flocked to him, offering comfort, drinks, sympathy. Everyone wanted to get close to the man who would soon be the richest in Canto Bight.

Lexo had an idea.

His final glass was emptied, and Lexo returned to the galley.

He dropped his empty tray full of empty glasses with the dishwasher and swept up a new one. This time, though, he did not head up to the observation deck. He found another staircase and went down instead, toward the engine room.

He kept an eye out for likely places as he went . . . there! An alcove, with a door hatch that probably led to a supply closet.

"Hey! What are you doing here?"

Sands.

An alien approached. Small horns jutted from each of his temples. He carried a blaster. Security, no doubt.

Think, Lexo.

"You are approaching an off-limits area," the alien said, fingering something on his blaster.

"Sir, the baron just won big in the first race of the night. To celebrate, he ordered that I bring refreshments belowdecks for you and your colleagues."

The security guard's eyes narrowed.

"I was surprised," Lexo soldiered on. "He's not a man known for generosity. I'm really not sure what came over him. I can assure you, though, that this particular refreshment does not have any inebriating qualities. The baron wants you to celebrate with him, but that is not an invitation to abandon your duties."

The guard holstered his blaster. "In that case, I'll just take that tray off your hands."

Lexo smiled, handing the tray over. "Please give the baron's regards to everyone working hard tonight."

"Yeah, sure. Now go back the way you came."

"At once."

Lexo turned to go, but he listened carefully as the guard's footsteps retreated in the opposite direction. When he was sure the way was clear, he turned back around and darted into the alcove.

He had to move fast now. That refreshment tray wouldn't occupy the guard for long.

Lexo noted the deck number on the wall. He needed to contact Jerdon Bly. But how? Maybe Panpick could help. No, the countess was a better option. She knew everyone.

He pulled out his disposable comlink and called the countess's office, and without any questions asked, his request to connect with Jerdon Bly was approved.

"Bly here. This is not a good time to—"

"Good evening, sir," Lexo said. "I'm the personal assistant to Lady Centada Ressad."

"Oh?"

And just in case their connection was traceable, Lexo added, "Her great friend the countess was so kind as to connect me to you."

"Oh."

"Sir, my mistress regrets that she was unable to return your . . . kind attention in public. A matter of protocol, you see."

"I . . . uh . . . appearances matter, I suppose."

"You are wise. In any case, my mistress finds you . . . intriguing, and would very much like to continue the scintillating conversation begun on the observation deck."

"She would, would she?" Lexo could almost hear him preening.

"Indeed. If you are still available, she has arranged a private space for you both."

"Where?"

"Deck two, just below the galley. She is there now, with a one-hundred-fifty-year-old vintage of Gorvinian red, and she does not care to drink it alone."

"I'll be right there."

Their communication clicked off.

Lexo began warming up his fingers, using a grip-and-flex technique that would loosen the tendons and increase blood flow. The pain had returned in full force, and every motion was agony. At his peak, he could kill a human in seven seconds. Tonight he might need eight or nine.

It seemed as though he waited forever before footsteps echoed on the nearby stairs. It could be wait staff approaching, or the security guard on his rounds again. Lexo didn't know what excuse he'd use a second time. He peeked out from the alcove.

It was Jerdon Bly, striding down the narrow corridor as if he owned the whole yacht.

"This way," Lexo said, gesturing. "Quickly."

"I've seen you before," Bly said.

"I'm certain you have not." Lexo indicated the door to the supply closet. "My mistress is inside."

Bly hesitated.

"I'm to stay outside and make certain you both are not disturbed. She wants you all to herself for a while."

That decided him. Bly stepped beyond Lexo, raised his hand to the access hatch. It was locked.

"Here, let me help you with that." Lexo made as if to reach down over Bly's shoulder.

He touched the man's neck. A gentle touch only, right on top of the carotid artery. Chemicals seeped from his fingertips.

Human skin was so porous. It only took one second for the chemical to reach Bly's heart, another second to flood his entire bloodstream.

Bly swayed on his feet. "I feel funny."

Three seconds.

"You'll be able to sit down soon," Lexo said. "I will steady you."

Four seconds.

Lexo leveraged Bly against the wall, then pressed down on both sides of his neck, digging deep, deep, deeper, cutting off all blood flow to his brain. The chemicals had done their work. Bly was too relaxed, too confident, too stupid.

Five. Six.

Bly's eyes widened. He had finally realized something was wrong.

Seven.

Jerdon Bly dropped to the floor.

Lexo felt the ligament in his right forefinger tear.

Lexo knew he should flee, but he couldn't risk an assassination gone wrong, so he squatted beside Bly's body, continuing to press down a few seconds more—and *oh*, it hurt—just to make sure he was well and truly dead.

Now to stash him somewhere and escape. No, that wouldn't do. It was essential that Bly's body be discovered. The countess had to know that the job was done in order to fulfill her end of the bargain.

More footsteps.

The closet was locked. He had no place to hide.

Lexo dashed from the alcove toward the stairs. But he was dizzy and weak from using his ability, and his shoulder crashed into the wall.

"What are you doing?" came the familiar voice at his back. The security guard had returned. "Stop, or I'll . . . *Sands*. Hey, are you all right? Sir?"

Bly's body had been discovered. Lexo regained his footing. He was almost up the stairs.

Blasterfire erupted near his shoulder. The scent of burning fabric filled the air. The blaster had grazed his robe.

He reached the galley level, and slammed the hatch shut behind him. He sprinted for the next stairway, too slowly. If he made it to the main deck, maybe he could figure out a way to escape. A yacht this size surely had safety measures in place. Floating devices, hovercraft, some kind of emergency egress. He just had to find one.

A cheer went up as he was gaining the main deck. The yacht hit a wave, sending him into the railing, as spray drenched his face. *Keep moving, Lexo.*

The baron's guests would know where to go. He hosted parties on the *Undisputed Victor* constantly, and many of his guests came night after night.

He jogged toward the stern, figuring it was the most likely location for an emergency craft, keeping an eye out for any stray partier. In the distance, fireworks lit up the horizon, painting the silhouette of the now distant city in rainbow colors. The first group of fathier races was at an end, and the guests had an intermission to buy more drinks and place more bets.

"Why aren't you at your assigned post? You should be on the observation deck."

Lexo whirled. It was the supervisor droid from the galley.

He yelled the first thing that came to mind. "The yacht is on fire!"

"What?"

Lexo twisted to show him the blaster mark on his robe. "See? Get everyone to safety!" Lexo sprinted away, yelling over his shoulder, "And sound the alarm!"

The railing curved around toward the stern and Lexo followed it. His back itched with the expectation of feeling a blaster bolt any moment. Every door he passed was sure to contain a horde of security personnel. Every alcove a Trandoshan guard.

He reached the stern. Shapes huddled on couches, watching the horizon, surrounded by faint candles. It was darker here than on the observation deck, quieter, more private. Quickly, Lexo pulled his black, Dor Namethian robe over his head, turned it inside out so that the blue silk side showed, then re-donned it.

Lexo strode forward, hands clasped. "Excuse me, gentlebeings," he said.

Several heads turned his direction. He could barely make out their features in the candlelight.

He announced: "There is no reason to panic, but I've received word of a minor conflagration in the engine room."

Everyone jumped to their feet. And to Lexo's very great relief and delight, the yacht's alarm siren began to wail.

Over the sound of the alarm, he yelled, "Please proceed in an orderly fashion to the life craft."

People started running.

"The baron apologizes for the inconvenience, but he is concerned for your . . ."

No one was left to lie to anymore. Lexo took off after the last straggler, knowing he would lead Lexo home.

CHAPTER 8

THE COUNTESS WAS STANDING ON HER BALCONY, WAITING FOR HIM. Makeup smeared her face, and a wine stain marred the front of her gown.

She opened with, "You look terrible."

He declined to note that the observation was mutual. "It's been a long night," he said. "You see, my patron for this assignation did not provide me with an egress, and I had to improvise."

"How did you get away?"

She seemed disappointed. Maybe she had counted on him being caught. "I convinced a droid to sound a fire alarm, then followed several of the baron's guests to an emergency life craft. Once we reached the mainland, I dashed away before I could be recognized. So I'm somewhat in disarray. By the way, Jerdon Bly is dead."

"Yes, I heard." She leaned out over the railing. A glass was in her hand again. Full, again. "The news broke right away. The baron will stop at nothing to find the person who was uncouth enough to commit murder on his yacht. He has the Canto Bight police speeding everywhere, looking for a Dor Namethian in black robes."

"It's a good thing these are bright blue."

She smiled slightly. "Indeed. You should be careful, though. There are only a few Dor Namethians in Canto Bight at any given time. You're sure to be questioned."

"You wouldn't allow that. And I can't imagine that this tiny incident will hold their attention long."

"It's true. Sooger, you did me a great favor tonight. I'll do what I can to protect you."

"Thank you. About our bargain . . ."

Fireworks flooded the sky again. The main fathier races were officially over for the night, though some gamblers would linger for the after-hours races. Lexo thought of Joris, who was probably on her way to the track now to bet on the red-eye runs.

"I did as you suggested," the countess said. "I broke from my usual tradition and bet on a long shot. A creature named Shifting Sands. He placed second."

Was that good or bad? Lexo knew little about racing. "I'm . . . glad for you?"

"I won enough money that I no longer need to sell my share of the spa."

"That's wonderful news. How did Hard Luck do?"

"He placed sixth in his race."

"Impressive."

"It is?"

Lexo smiled. Lula would be so glad to hear her favorite fathier was all right. "He had some extra obstacles to overcome tonight. In any case, our bargain—"

"I've told you how Big Sturg Ganna is a great friend and close ally, yes?"

"Yes, Countess," he said, warily.

"Well, as a gesture of friendship between us, and to show what a good sport I am about selling my share of Zord's Spa to him—"

"I thought you had decided not to s—"

She raised a hand to silence him. "Ganna has been struggling with the climate lately. As a gesture of friendship, I've arranged for you to attend Ganna tonight in his own suite at my expense. I've promised him the very best massage, using a technique reserved only for the most elite guests. For royalty, like me."

"I won't kill him for you," Lexo said. "I can't. His is one of the few species I have no effect on." The truth was he didn't know if he had the strength. Not without food, rest, a splint for his injured finger, and another series of injections.

"Has this city made you so obtuse? So cynical? I'm not asking you to kill him, Sooger. I'm fulfilling my end of the bargain."

He stared at her. The Onyx Bands glittered at her chest, reminding him how far above him she was in station. "Apologies, Countess," he managed. "Please go on."

"He doesn't know it's you. He thinks I'm sending one of the other masseurs. I was concerned that if he knew you were coming, he'd remove your daughter to another location. So the moment you're inside, I've arranged for the hotel to cut all utilities to Ganna's suite—even his emergency generators will go down. Routine maintenance, of course."

"Of course."

"A fan will come on, pushing hot dry air into the suite. Ganna will be forced to shelter in his regen aquarium for safety until the issue is resolved. You will have a very short period of time to find your daughter and escape."

Lexo breathed relief, his shoulders swelling with hope. "A short period of time is all I need."

"I've arranged a speeder to transport you there."

"Thank you, Countess." He turned to go.

"One last thing."

Lexo stopped. "Yes, Countess?"

"You did me a favor with that racing tip, so I have a tip for you, too. When you are at Ganna's, if you have a spare moment, even the sliver of an opportunity, it would be worth the risk to investigate his personal library."

"Oh? What will I find there?"

"Nothing, of course. If you do not find it, I certainly did not know about it. And if you are caught, you won't be able to say what you're looking for."

Lexo's eyes narrowed. "But it's something you can't retrieve yourself."

"Ganna is my great friend and closest ally, after all. Now go. I don't want to see you in my office ever again."

CHAPTER 9

AFTER SNEAKING AROUND THE CITY ALL NIGHT WITH HARDLY ANY resources, it felt strange to arrive at someone's front door in style. The luxury speeder the countess provided had a fully equipped bar, vidscreens, and a temperature and humidity perfectly adjusted for Dor Namethian physiology. Two of the countess's sentry droids accompanied him into the hotel and down the lift to the front door of Ganna's suite.

One of the sentry droids said, "The masseur from Zord's Spa and Bathhouse is here, as expected."

The Gamorrean guards looked at Lexo, then at each other.

"Isn't that the drunk we chased off a few hours ago?" said one.

The second guard wrinkled his nose. "Sure smells like him."

Lexo touched his translator necklace. "How do you feel when people say that all Gamorreans look alike or smell the same? I've been employed by Zord's Spa for years, and I never drink. Please do call to check my credentials. And then explain to the councilor why you delayed his massage."

They let him pass.

Ganna's suite seemed like a lush cave. Potted ferns lined the entry, vines crept up the walls, fountains boasted flowering lilies and bioluminescent algae that cast a bluish glow over everything. The sound of tinkling water filled the cold, damp air. A few pale lights hung from the ceiling; Lexo guessed they were the same spectrum as the sun of Ganna's homeworld.

He would have found the place beautiful, were it not for the fact that it smelled of rotting vegetables. In fact, the scent was so strong, he'd be lucky to detect Lula's trail of corwindyl. It had been hours since he was here, when he'd caught that barest whiff. The scent had since faded, possibly to nothing.

He reached a vestibule with a low, domed ceiling. Doorways branched off in all directions; each doorway was enormous to accommodate Ganna's large form. One of the Gamorrean guards grunted, indicating that Lexo should turn to the right.

Lexo hesitated. The environmental controls would go out any moment, so he glanced around, breathing deep through his nose on the off chance that some corwindyl scent lingered.

There! To his left. Faint but sure. Lula was that way.

The guard grunted again. Lexo took a very slow, very small step in the indicated direction. He just needed to stall until—

A loud whine. A thump. All the nearby doors slammed open— a safety precaution in times of mechanical failure.

Something began to whir loudly—an environmental fan deep in the hotel ductwork. A breeze caressed Lexo's face, bringing dryness and unbearable heat.

"What is the meaning of this?" said one of the countess's sentry droids.

Lexo stepped quietly to the left. Only a few paces to get to the door.

The Gamorrean guards began to argue. They were too far away for his translator necklace to work, but it was clear they would be charging into the room at any moment. He took another soft step.

"Is this how the councilor treats his guests?" the droid continued. "My mistress will hear about this, mark my words."

Lexo's toe thumped the wall. He had misjudged the direction of the door.

He inhaled through his nose. The corwindyl was just a little to his right . . . there. He felt around until he encountered the empty door-frame.

He ducked inside. It was another hallway, long and low-ceilinged, with dim light and lush plants. A plush carpet runner woven with vines and flowers ran its entire length. The corridor was too long, too wreathed in shadow, for Lexo to see where it led.

The countess's sentry droids would keep the guards busy for as long as they could, but Lexo had little time. He moved forward as quickly as he dared, following the scent of corwindyl. The thick rug softened his footsteps.

Abruptly, the scent of corwindyl disappeared. He stopped, sniffed the air.

It was behind him now.

But that made no sense. He hadn't encountered another room, not even a bit of furniture. The only thing he'd found so far was a rug.

He squatted, reached around for the edge of the rug, pulled it back. The scent became stronger.

Lexo's fingertips brushed cool metal, a sharp, surprising contrast with the stone floor. The colored lights of an access panel blinked up at him. It was a trapdoor.

With the controls out, the panel wouldn't work, so he rooted around until he found a manual lever. Wary of his throbbing finger, he yanked up with all his strength. The hinges creaked. He glanced around nervously.

He propped the trapdoor open and probed the space with his feet until he discovered the lip of a stair. Lexo descended carefully, feeling out each step before settling his weight on it. He considered closing the trapdoor, but decided against it. Lula and he might need a quick egress.

He reached the ground floor. Another dim room filled with plants, and Lexo vaguely noted shelves full of knickknacks on display. But he had more important things to focus on because the scent of corwindyl was stronger now. Much stronger. He dared to whisper: "Lula?"

No response. It was dead silent down here. Even the *wop-wop-wop* of the hotel's environmental fan was muted.

Which was odd. There's no way Ganna wouldn't have some kind of security personnel down here, or at least a janitor droid. Lula was sure to be guarded.

Unless Ganna had moved her to another location.

Lexo's hopes were sinking fast, but he pressed on. The scent of corwindyl was so strong. She had to be here. She *had* to be.

He heard a scuffling sound. Footsteps maybe? Like someone had tripped over something.

A weapon would come in very handy about now. Lexo did not doubt his ability to kill most species, acting by feel and instinct. But if he encountered a droid or another Gamorrean, he'd need a different plan.

The scuffling sounded again, and Lexo moved toward it. Might as well face whatever was ahead.

Something plunged against him. He put up his hands in defense and encountered smooth skin, a pulsing wrist.

"Let me go!" said a high, familiar voice. The wrist slipped from his grasp, and small hands attacked him fiercely, mindlessly. "I won't go back there! I won't—"

"Lula!" he said, finding her shoulders, pulling her close, ignoring the beating she was giving him. "It's me, azure sea."

Her tiny form stilled in his arms. "Papa?" Her voice was shivery with terror.

"I'm here."

And suddenly she was gripping him so tight he considered that he might suffocate. Words poured out of her. "I knew you'd come I just knew it so I left the corwindyl for you but maybe I left too much I don't know but then it got so hot and the lock on my cell stopped working and the guards ran away to help Ganna except one and I had to hit him on the head with my meal tray then . . ." Lula paused to suck in air, then couldn't seem to find any more words. She just sobbed once, hard, and buried her face in his robes.

Lexo thought his shoulders might burst with happiness and relief. He had found her. His Lula was all right. Now all they had to do was get away. They would leave Cantonica behind. It was the only way to be safe from Ganna. They could get passage on a freighter. If he sold every single thing he owned, if they worked off some of the fare, they might be able to scrape enough together. They'd get by. Somehow.

"We must go, my sea," Lexo said, gently extricating himself from her embrace. "The environmental controls will come back on any mom—"

And it was as though he'd summoned them with a thought, for a cool breeze suddenly coated his skin and the lights brightened to normal levels. Doors slammed closed, fountains resumed tinkling, and the overhead lights vibrated with a soft, electronic buzz.

Lula was tugging at his sleeve. "C'mon, Papa. Ganna's guards are back there, so we have to leave the way you came."

He drank in the sight of her—her big brown eyes, her smooth human skin, her hair like a charcoal cloud. Dried blood crusted her upper lip, and a smudge of dirt or grease marred her forehead. "Are you hurt, my sea?"

"I'm fine. Let's go!" She yanked him forward.

"Wait." Lexo looked around, finally absorbing the fact that there were shelves full of data storage banks and various odd items: sculptures, a purple geode, a piece of bent scrap metal mounted on a plaque. Lexo stepped closer to read the inscription on the plaque. It said: THIS PIECE OF THE DEATH STAR II IS CERTIFIED AUTHENTIC BY GARRAC & SONS, PURVEYORS OF RARE ANTIQUITIES AND FINE COLLECTIBLES.

"This is Ganna's private library," Lexo murmured.

"What? So? Papa, we have to *go.*"

"The countess told me I might find something important here. Something worth the risk."

Lula frowned. "Why would she help you?"

"It's a long story." Lexo's hands were burning in earnest now, especially his badly injured forefinger. He ignored the pain, rummaged through the shelves, picking up each item, looking underneath. Lula just stood there, gaping at him. "All this stuff is valuable, Lula," he explained. "Extraordinarily valuable. Which means now that the environmental controls are back on, the room is under lockdown again.

No one is coming in here except Ganna or his elite staff. We're safe for another minute. Quickly, help me search."

Lula followed his lead and started sorting through the shelves. "What am I looking for?"

"I'm not sure. Something valuable and portable, maybe? Or possibly just information." He picked up a dainty tiara, placed it back on its velvet pillow.

"Like a shipping manifest?" Lula said, hefting a datapad. "Blasters. A *lot* of blasters. *Sands,* Papa, this is so much money." She scrolled further. "And something about DeFancio Storsilt. Ganna had a plan . . . That's why Hard Luck has been having such a time of it! His feed was switched. Storsilt will be ruined by the end of the week."

"Let me see that." Lexo snatched it from her hands and read. Lula was right. Ganna was behind Jerdon Bly's deal. He was helping engineer the poor performance of Storsilt's stable of fathiers. He also had a plan to force Ubialla Gheal to sell her businesses, and he was pushing legislation through that would ban police speeders in favor of pursuit droids, supplied by himself of course.

He was orchestrating it to happen all at once. It would be a massive coup. Ganna was setting himself up to either flee Canto Bight one of the richest people in the galaxy, or stay and rule like a king.

"This is it," he whispered reverently. "The countess suspected. But she didn't have the resources to stop him. She *used* me. Does . . ." He didn't dare continue the thought aloud, not in front of Lula: *Does the countess own me now? Have I merely traded an unwanted arrangement with Ganna for one with her?*

He cleared his throat. "We have to take this datapad with us. It's leverage."

Lula rolled her eyes at him. "Don't be silly. All he has to do is take it from us and kill us. Haven't you watched any of the old spy vids? We need to *send* all this information somewhere."

"Can you do that?" he asked.

She grabbed the datapad from him. "Papa, you are old," she muttered under her breath as she swiped and typed. "Always so helpless with devices."

"What are you doing?"

"Compiling it into a single data burst. Security is still down from the outage, but it will come back online any moment so I have to work fast . . . there." She looked up at him. "So, where should I send it?"

Lexo had never bothered with the expense of maintaining his own data account. Maybe the countess? Zord?

"It should be someone you really trust," Lula added, "who has good encryption."

He knew exactly who. "Send it to Neepers Panpick, Private Investigator, along with a message that if we don't check in with him tomorrow, he should release the information citywide."

She programmed in the message. "All right, it's done."

"Let's go!"

"Wait," Lula said. "One more thing." She put the datapad on a massive stone slab table, grabbed the Death Star II memorial plaque, lifted it over her head, and brought it smashing down on the datapad. Bits of glass and metal and microfiber flew everywhere. She repeated it over and over, smashing the poor thing to bits.

"There. Now he'll never alter the data or track the transmission."

"Good thinking." Lexo spent a luxurious moment marveling at his clever daughter. "All right, *now* let's go!"

They reached the stairway. The trapdoor had sprung closed when the environmental controls came back on. Lexo had only a brief moment to worry that it wouldn't open from the inside before it swung wide all of its own accord. Two Gamorrean guards poked their heads into the stairwell and stared down at them. Behind them was a shiny silver protocol droid.

"Trespassers," the droid said. "How quaint. Come up here right away. My master wishes to speak with you before you die."

Lexo and Lula exchanged a glance. "We have leverage now," he assured her under his breath.

"I know."

"We'll be fine."

"Put on your 'spa face,' Papa."

Together they followed the guards and the droid up the stairs, through the vestibule, and into Ganna's receiving room.

CHAPTER 10

BIG STURG GANNA WAS HALF SUBMERGED IN A GIANT, ALGA-FILLED TANK made of a sheer, glasslike material. Only his head and shoulders and the very tip of his ticklish tail were exposed to open air. He lurked there, like a great beast waiting for his prey to chance by unawares.

"Lexo, my friend," Ganna rumbled. "I told you to behave."

Lula murmured, "I really hate that guy."

Lexo gave her shoulder a squeeze. The guards were at their backs, the protocol droid off to the side.

"Master Ganna, I found them in the library," the droid said.

"Which is a pity," Ganna said. "Now I'll have to kill them."

"That would be a big mistake," Lula spat out.

Ganna laughed, a deep, gravelly sound that vibrated Lexo's shoulders. "Your ward has spirit, I'll give her that. I must say, this is partly my fault. I should have realized, when the countess offered her gift, that she was sending a spy."

"The countess had nothing to do with this. When I learned that someone from Zord's was coming here, I made sure I was sent in his place."

Ganna frowned, considering.

"I acted alone," Lexo assured him.

"Then how did you get the environmental controls down? Took out even my emergency generators. You don't have that kind of clout."

Lexo smiled. "As you yourself have pointed out, all the richest, most important, most influential citizens of Canto Bight are my clients. Many of them owe me favors."

Ganna's frowned deepened. "That's all too plausible, I'm afraid. It's why I went to such lengths to recruit you. Doesn't matter now. You'll die. It's good timing, actually. My composting tank needs an injection of carbon-based life."

Was that why it smells so bad in here?

"You won't kill us," Lula insisted.

"She's right," Lexo agreed. "We found some very interesting information in your library." Quickly, he listed all they had discovered. "Imagine if those people—the countess, Storsilt, Gheal, the police chief—all learned about your plans at the same time and turned against you en masse? You wouldn't survive one day."

Ganna took a deep, shuddering breath, and then went silent and still. The water of his alga tank sloshed over the side, soaking the stone floor. Finally, he said, "It doesn't matter." He gestured to the guards, who stepped forward.

"We sent it away," Lula said. "All that information is someplace safe. But if we don't leave this place alive, it's going out on a citywide burst."

"You're lying," Ganna said, but he put up a hand to stop the guards.

"Master Ganna," said the protocol droid, "our system did recognize a large data transmission moments ago. Our security features weren't yet back online, and our logger failed to record it, but the size and shape of the data checks out."

Ganna sank down into his tank, submerging completely. Bubbles streamed up from his nose. More water sloshed over the side.

The protocol droid said, "Oh, dear."

Ganna resurfaced. "What do you want?" he practically yelled.

Lexo felt suddenly buoyant, like he was walking on air. This was going to work. "First, you must not buy out the countess's share of the spa."

"Done."

"You must return Storsilt's fathiers to their regular feed."

"Yes," Lula said. "No more harming fathiers."

"You must not buy out Gheal or anyone else. They are my valued clients, after all. I heard, by the way, that your intermediary Jerdon Bly met with a terrible fate tonight."

Ganna blinked. "Anything else?"

"You will never request my services again. All futures massages will be done by Maby Sagedo and Oble Rumb."

"And if I do all this, you won't release that data?"

"No one will know about it except us," Lexo assured him. "Oh, and one more thing." He looked down at Lula, his precious, precious girl.

Lula smiled, and it was like the sun rising over a perfect sea.

"You must buy my daughter's indenture debt from Bargwill Tomder. And you must sponsor her fathier riding lessons for the next five years."

Lula said, "Papa!"

Water sloshed as Ganna turned toward them. "I don't understand," he said. "All this trouble for a stupid girl. An ugly human. She's not even your real daughter!"

Lula gasped in mock disbelief. "I'm not?"

"I'm so sorry you had to find out this way," Lexo said.

"But we look so much alike!"

Ganna looked back and forth between them, utterly confused.

"Do we have a deal?" Lexo said.

In the softest voice Lexo had ever heard from Ganna, he said, "We have a deal."

"In that case, my beautiful human daughter and I are leaving now. It will be a delight to see you again at the bathhouse." This time, it wasn't a lie.

The sun was rising on the city as they exited the hotel and casino. Morning washed the walls, the fancy streets, the luxury speeders, in warmth and light. Canto Bight wasn't so bad, Lexo decided. Ostentation had its own kind of beauty.

"Lula, I have to tell you," Lexo said as they walked toward Old City. No cab for them this time; they couldn't afford it. "I did some things to find you. Some bad things."

Lula paused in the middle of the walkway. "Some things . . . like from your old life?"

"Yes."

Her eyes narrowed as she contemplated his face. "Are you sad?"

"Yes."

"Then I'm sad, too." But she reached up to take his left hand, and it was a good thing it wasn't his right because she would know at the slightest touch how badly injured he was.

They continued walking. "Also, the countess thinks she might be able to identify your biological parents. Is that something you're interested in?"

"Really? Huh." She considered for a moment. "I don't know. You're the only papa I ever want or need. But . . . it might be interesting to . . ."

"Think about it."

"I will. Hey, do you know how Hard Luck did last night? Is he okay?"

They passed a fountain, and a bench where a woman in a shimmering gown was lying, nearly passed out. "He placed sixth in his race."

"Good for him!" She extricated her hand. "I'm heading to the stables now."

"What? Why? It's been a really long night, Lula. Don't you want to go home?"

"Go on without me. I'll be there soon. I never got a chance to give him that corwindyl, remember? And I have a funny feeling . . . I just know he's going to need it tonight."

He gazed down at her. "We'll go together."

Late that afternoon, Lexo was back at work. He hadn't slept all night, his forefinger was poorly bandaged, and he'd needed more corwindyl and more injections to keep his hands going. The treatments took the edge off and gave him mobility, but he'd worked his hands too hard last night. Lexo doubted he would ever be pain-free again.

His current client was a yellow Twi'lek male with tattooed lekku. An easy client, almost as easy as a human.

Beside them, Big Sturg Ganna lay on his huge stone plinth. Maby Sagedo and Oble Rumb were climbing all over him. Apparently the councilor had had a very hard night, something to do with his regen tank losing power for several terrifying minutes, and he needed an emergency treatment at Zord's to manage the stress of it all.

"Oh, yes, I have children," Lexo was saying to his client. "A daughter."

"That's nice," the client said.

"She is the cleverest, most beautiful girl in the galaxy," Lexo added.

"Hmm," the client said.

"Thanks to the generosity of my good friend Councilor Ganna over there, she's taking fathier riding lessons. A papa ought to set up his daughter with a trade, right?"

"You are wise," the client said.

"I expect my Lula will be Canto Bight's greatest jockey in no time."

"Neat," the client said.

Lexo knew when he was being dismissed, but it didn't matter. His words were for Ganna, who snapped at poor Maby for touching his tail.

Lexo caught a movement near the balcony. He lifted his gaze and met that of the countess. His days of not getting involved were over. The countess knew what he could do. She would surely use him again, and he would do what she asked in order to keep Lula safe.

It was worth it. Though his own future was uncertain, Lula's stretched, filled with hope and possibility. "In case I haven't said it yet today, Councilor Ganna," Lexo said, loudly enough for everyone in the spa to hear, "thank you so much for your generosity. The people of Canto Bight are the real winners, to have you as our great friend and close ally."

Big Sturg Ganna seethed helplessly. The countess lifted her wineglass to Lexo and smiled.

THE
RIDE

By **JOHN JACKSON MILLER**

THE GRINDER | 1

"TERRIBLE ABOUT THAT THING."

"What thing?"

Two. Two plus seven. Down one.

"That the First Order did."

"I haven't heard. Which ones are they, again?"

Three. Two plus nine. Even.

"I'm not sure. But whatever it was, I heard it was terrible."

"Hmm. That's too bad."

Five. One plus nine. Up two.

Kaljach Sonmi did not care about the First Order, and neither did he care about the two other players at the zinbiddle table. He did care that they were ruining his count with their blather.

"Never mind," said the blue-faced one as the dealer slid her another card. "Say, have you ever been to Hosnian Prime?"

"I was treated *so* poorly by a hotelier there once," replied her pal, a skinny being that looked related to a tree. "I can assure you, I *won't* go back."

"Zinbiddle," Kal said, overturning his hole cards.

The green-clad dealer, who was suppressing yawns as the end of her shift approached, barely looked at Kal's hand. "Winner."

"So lucky!" Blue-Face said.

"Not really." Kal took the Cantocoins from the pot and stacked them neatly, leaving his next bet before him. "Let's play."

He was not lucky, of course. Zinbiddle pitted players against one another using cards dealt from multiple decks, with participants drawing additional cards from each depending on special circumstances. It was a high-class pursuit, unlike sabacc—and far too complicated for the society types he was usually stuck with. It was also extremely conducive to Kal's systems, which combined bet management with a complicated mental count of cards played and unplayed.

So Kal worked for a living, but he didn't expect the afternoon crowd at the Canto Casino to be able to tell the difference. These were the pedestrian gamers, mainly oldsters and tour-groupers just off the shuttle, still sober and waiting for the first dinner service to start. The casino didn't offer discounted meal rates for early diners, and by definition none of its patrons needed to care about money. But the afternooners were as predictable in their preferences as in their play. Not one had ever managed a hand in a way Kal hadn't expected, and that helped his math.

"You look nice," Tree Person said of Kal's ensemble. "Doesn't he look nice?"

"He must be doing well, winning all our money," her friend observed.

If that really was all your money, you won't be staying long. In fact, Kal had not been doing well for quite some time—and had the debts to prove it—but he still insisted on looking stylish. His dress jacket and slacks were as jet black as his hair, which today was combed around his crinkly gray face in a manner that spoke rakish style—even as it made reading his sky-blue eyes difficult for other players. Heptooinians were blessed with assets that made them seem born for gaming: noseless, eyebrowless faces that appeared amiable no matter what they were feeling—not to mention minds for math.

Five. One plus eight. Up three. Take a card.

"Zinbiddle," he declared again.

"Another hand to the prop," the dealer said, pushing Kal his meager winnings. A floor manager tapped the dealer on the back, ending her shift. She showed her hands to one of the many security holo-cams infesting the Canto Casino and stepped back into the pit.

Blue-Face looked at Kal's accumulated winnings and uttered what he suspected was the vilest oath she knew, only to pardon herself a second later. "He is so lucky!"

"Lucky to be at the table with you two," announced a baritone voice from behind. Ganzer, the whiskered white-and-green-clad bartender, used the break in the action to deliver a tray of drinks. "Exotic treats for our most appealing guests," he said. The tourists giggled at the old-fashioned service; no server droids for them. The manager of a popular bar just off the card room, Ganzer made a habit of making rounds on the casino floor to check on his workers—and charm the occasional patron. "There are no losers at the Canto Casino," he said with a wink.

Tree Person touched the bartender's arm. "I've never seen such luck," she said, admiring Kal's latest winnings. "What did the dealer call him just now? A perp?"

Ganzer chuckled. "Ah. You see the badge on the lapel of our good friend Kaljach here? It means he's a proposition player, employed by the casino."

Blue-Face covered her mouth. "Does that mean we're playing against the . . . the *home*?"

"House, madam. No, as you know, the dealer doesn't participate in zinbiddle hands, except to cover the bonus bets. The casino pays players like Kaljach a salary to make games in the slow hours. He bets his own money and can keep what he wins—but he receives no preferential treatment."

"That's for sure," Kal said, looking at his stacks. It had been another one of those days when he'd spent hours clawing back from a bad beat.

Ganzer passed him a drink. "Your usual, friend."

"My hero." Kal hadn't ordered anything, but Ganzer took care of him. Fizzy water in one of the tall glasses used for cocktails, to give the impression he was soused.

"Running a new system?"

"I wouldn't do *that*," Kal said.

"Of course you wouldn't." Ganzer smirked. An observant eye and excellent recall were hardly cheating, but card rooms liked their players clueless. The barkeeper looked at the digital display on the table. "Still after the progressive, I see."

"That's *all* I'm after."

The progressive bonus was funded by coins kicked in from an endless series of games; if they were left on the table, the structure would collapse under the weight. Kal had circled the progressive like a predator after its dinner—if said creature was willing to go months at a time without eating. The goal hand, the vaunted Ion Barrage, was exceedingly rare. Yet Kal was confident he would achieve one. Part of what made the hand so elusive was that there were a hundred ways to screw it up with middle-round decisions; he knew every one, and would avoid them all. The table was a battlefield. Kal would wend his way between the blaster shots on the way to his reward.

And some reward. "Eight hundred thousand," Ganzer said. "You'll get massages at Zord's for days."

"I can't think that far ahead."

"Of course you can."

Of course he could—but he knew his creditors would have to be satisfied first in any event. Kal rubbed his eyes. "What's up, Ganz? Haven't seen you all day."

"I just got here. Two late-shift staffers ran off with zillionaires. Everything's a jumble," Ganzer said. "I'm working straight through until dawn."

Not that anyone would notice the time. Casinos galaxy-wide kept the lighting steady so players remained focused on the games, but Canto Bight took it to an extreme, even washing its outdoor fathier track in light so races could run through the night. Kal hardly required a timepiece when he was already keeping track of every card dealt in every game he was in. All that mattered was his cash flow—of late, his greatest nemesis.

But not the only one. "Master Ganzer!" A towering woman approached from inside the pit, her words knives of ice. "Were you intending to play a hand?"

"My apologies, madam." After shooting Kal a sheepish look, Ganzer bowed to the floor manager and backed away, tray under his arm.

At two and a half meters—tall even for a Quermian—Vestry was well suited to life as a pit boss. She hovered over the evening shift like a ghoul, piercing yellow eyes the only obvious feature on a shrunken white face. She gestured for a new dealer to attend the table.

Kal kept his head down, hoping not to be noticed. *No such luck.* Vestry addressed the two oldsters with a charming "Welcome, honored guests," before adding *"and others,"* punctuated with a chilly glance at him. "Are you enjoying Canto Bight?"

"Oh, yes," Blue-Face gushed.

"The joy never ends," Kal said, smiling weakly.

"Fine." Vestry introduced a youth with spots on her forehead whose uniform looked as if it had just come from the manufacturer. "Minn here is a trainee on her first shift. I know she will do an exemplary job."

"How delightful," said Tree.

How wonderful, thought Kal. Now he'd have Vestry sticking her long neck into things more than usual. Bad news, as the floor manager immediately proved.

"Don't give him any more comps," she said to the rookie. "He's a prop. He buys his own meals."

"Since when?" Kal said. Catching Vestry's gaze, he amended that to, "Who has time to eat?"

Vestry stepped outside the pit and approached him on the side opposite the tourists. Extending her neck so she could speak into his ear, she said in a low voice, "I know who you're mixed up with."

Kal's eyes widened. "Come again?"

"I won't have it. The countess has her reasons for allowing . . . *a diversity of clientele.* But this room is mine."

She withdrew, leaving Kal speechless. He didn't report directly to her, and he didn't know what she thought she knew. But Vestry could cause him problems—or rather, even *more* problems. The only way out of all of them was to win, and not just an ante here and there. He needed the progressive.

Kal returned his attention to it, trying to ignore the tourists, competing now with complaints about their joints. Trying to ignore Minn the dealer, who dealt from the decks with a motion better suited to swatting insects. And trying most of all to ignore Vestry, and what she might know . . .

Eight. Two plus . . . fourteen? Kal licked his lips. *Up ten!*

He breathed quickly. After several hands, the decks had gone far into his favor. He might be able to build the legendary Ion Barrage with the right cards. And a dealer on her first day would deal them.

Kal played hand after hand. The count kept improving. And then—

"Chef Targalla has begun the first seating," announced a droid from behind. Startled, Kal looked around. At once, everyone who was an adult during the Clone Wars was up and moving, many abandoning their hands.

Including, to his horror, the Terrible Two. "Thank you, dear," Tree Person said, tipping the dealer.

Blue-Face touched his arm. "I've enjoyed your company. I'd never met a plop before!"

"But . . ." Kal gawked at the tabletop and the hands the women had abandoned. "Don't leave now!"

"Why, you make it sound like your whole life depends on it."

"It might."

"Oh. Well, we have dinner reservations. Good luck!"

THE TRIPS | 2

KAL COULDN'T FEEL HIS HEART. MINN PUSHED THE PALTRY POT TO HIM and collected the cards the tourists had forsaken. "I'm afraid I'll have to—"

"Don't close up," Kal said, reaching toward her.

"I have to." The Devaronian dealer looked around. "I can't make a game with just you. I'm sorry."

"No, wait!" Kal's eyes bulged. The decks would all be reshuffled then—and his advantage would vanish. "You can wait, can't you?"

Vestry appeared behind the dealer. "What's going on?"

"I can't make a game," Minn said.

"Then close." The floor manager glared at Kal. "Zinbiddle will be back this evening."

Kal didn't play evenings. Real money hit the room and the cost of everything went up. If he could play then, he wouldn't need to be here now. He eyed the decks again. "Just give it a minute."

Vestry clasped both her pairs of hands. "Master Sonmi, you work for the casino. We work for the casino. Exactly who profits from you sitting here alone for another ten hours?" She pointed. "Go home."

"I don't have a—"

"Then eat something. But go."

Kal's throat went dry as he saw Minn's hands move toward the undealt cards, ready to dispose of the decks. *Please, don't—*

"Oooh, it's zinbiddle!"

Kal turned to see a diminutive reptilian in a formal black coat, accentuated with a dazzling stellabora lapel bloom. The green-skinned creature flashed a smile so broad it nearly bisected his face as he dropped a fat tray of coins onto the tabletop to Kal's right. "Deal me in," he said, hopping up into the chair beside Kal.

Kal stared at the ebullient arrival, mystified, before looking to the dealer, who suspended her cleanup. He told Vestry, "I guess I'm in luck."

The pit boss stared silently at the players. Kal could swear he saw her mouth form the words, *That's what you think.*

"I was at the yacht races," the newcomer said. "Were you at the yacht races?"

"No."

"You should have been at the yacht races." He offered a chubby green hand. "Dodibin. Dodi for short—but don't call me that."

"Don't call you Dodi?"

"Don't call me short." He looked stern for a moment—and then laughed. "And you are Kaljach."

Lucky guess, he began to say, before remembering his badge. "Kal is fine." He watched as the Suerton—the species he thought Dodi was—unloaded his chips. Then Dodi pushed a large stack onto the instant-win marker, a side bet the casino covered from its rake.

"That's a long shot," Kal said.

"Excellent." Chipper, Dodi rocked back and forth in his chair as Minn started dealing.

It was no skin off Kal's nonexistent nose; the side bet was against the house, not him. Though he would have loved to cover it, because there was no greater joy than taking money off someone too stupid to—

"Zinbiddle!"

Kal gawked. "You got it?"

Dodi flipped up his cards, all in the proper suit and sequence. "Dealt pat."

Kal hadn't even looked at his cards yet. He quickly did, and took note of what Dodi had shown, before Minn recovered them all. That was the risk in riding "final station," the seat on the dealer's right; Kal saw more cards that way, but occasionally an instant winner would cut a hand short. Fortunately, the odds said that wouldn't happen very—

"Zinbiddle," Dodi chirped.

"She's still dealing the hand!" Kal spouted. Calling early was a dumb move, disqualifying if the hand wasn't as declared. *Unless the fool actually had it?*

"Well, what do you know?" Dodi said, overturning his four cards as soon as they'd landed. "I had a feeling." He'd left his winnings from before on the instant-win marker; he'd won again. Minn went to work exchanging Dodi's coins for higher-denomination ones.

And now, Kal saw, Vestry was back, keeping a discreet watch from behind Minn. She knew everything, or so she put on. What did she know about this guy?

The good news was Kal was only out two initial stakes, and the decks, if anything, had swung even more into his favor. If a hand ever lasted long enough for him to play, he could start building out his pyramid in pursuit of the progressive. But he was beginning to wonder what he was up against—

—and wondered some more when he heard a voice like Dodi's, only lower-pitched, from behind. *"There you are!"*

Kal turned to see another Suerton, looking much like Dodi apart from a few extra centimeters' height, more pronounced ears, and a necklace of silver ringlets. "Thodi!" Dodi said, hopping off his chair. "Kal, meet Thodi, my brother."

"I'm the smart one," Thodi said, and smiled. "At your service." He glanced at Dodi's stack on the table. "What are we doing?"

"Winning," Kal said.

"Well, I know *that*." Thodi pushed Dodi. "Step aside for the master, my good chump."

Dodi resisted. "I was doing fine on my own."

"I doubt that."

Minn was befuddled. "Who's playing, gentlebeings?"

"I was hatched first," Thodi said. "Ten seconds earlier. Mom said."

Dodi smirked at Kal. "He always gets me with that." The slightly younger brother withdrew, and Thodi climbed into the chair. He looked down at Dodi's winnings. "Oh, now, see, you're making these silly blind bets again." He pulled the stacks of coins back from the table and began to sort them. "What you need to do is add up the values of your cards, and bet that. If the number is even, double it. And if it's prime, you bet your age."

Wow, Kal thought. *That is completely wrong.*

"Thodi," Dodi said, "that is completely wrong."

"You're just a gambler," the elder Suerton said. "Me—I'm a *gamer.* Watch."

Thodi played the hand his way—and, in the end, was completely wrong. Kal won some coins, but not many. *He must not be that old,* Kal thought. But he could live with it. The green guys' fortunes seemed to dim as the brothers bickered—and that meant the hands lasted longer, giving Kal more data about the decks with every card. And the Ion Barrage chance was ever closer.

This is it! Kal fought to stay calm. *Forget the brothers.* This was him against fate, months and months of it. This hand, he'd be all in, buying extra draws as necessary to build his pyramid. And then all his problems would be—

"Hi ho!" shouted someone in the aisle.

"*Wodi!*" the brothers replied in unison. "Over here!"

"What now?" Kal said. He shot an anguished look at Vestry, whose steely reserve had yet to crack. Her eyes were on the aisle, where a Suerton with a bounding gait approached—and then receded, in pursuit of a droid carrying liquid refreshments.

Dodi poked Kal in the ribs. "Wodi, my kid brother. You'll like him, Kal. Dad used to call him the kind of guy who'd fly all the way to Alderaan if he heard a party was starting."

"Didn't Alderaan blow up?"

"Well, Wodi wasn't responsible." Dodi pursed his giant lips as Wodi, having scored a tray of beverages, let out a loud whoop. "At least, I don't think he was. When did it happen?"

WODI APPROACHED, SOMEONE ELSE'S DRINK IN HAND. HE RESEMBLED his brothers, or would have if they'd spent some time in a water turbine. Wodi's expensive jacket was on inside out, his tie was hanging from his neck backward, and all his clothes were dripping wet.

"I looked everywhere for you," Thodi said. He left his seat to confront Wodi. "Where have you been?"

"Incarcerated," Wodi said. "That's the word they used, but it sure looked like a jail to me." He flicked water from his forehead and downed the cocktail.

Kal looked in all directions. "There aren't any more of you, are there?"

"No," Dodi said, adding in singsong: *"Three there shall always be."*

"Except when one of us is being held for questioning," Thodi added.

"That was not my fault," Wodi said, wringing out his jacket over the floor. "When you said our yacht won, I thought we'd won the yacht."

"We only *bet* on the yachts, Wodi." Dodi looked at Kal and smirked. "At least he didn't get too far out of the harbor."

Thodi frowned. "But the race ended two hours ago. Why are you still wet?"

"That was just now," Wodi said. "The fountain outside. Somebody's child dared me."

Thodi tut-tutted. "I suppose you brought back handfuls of riches from the deep."

"No, but thanks for reminding me." Wodi fished around his coat and proudly pulled out a single coin. "Don't tell me kids aren't allowed to gamble!"

Kal looked to Vestry with bewilderment, sure she'd move to relocate these cretins immediately. But the pit boss merely spoke into her collar comlink, summoning workers who took the Suerton's coat and brought him a towel for his shiny head. Seconds later Ganzer was there with drinks for all three brothers—and a pitying glance at Kal that said he knew who these characters were. Kal longed to ask, but Wodi had other ideas.

"Hey, I want to play," Wodi said, hopping onto the seat his brothers had occupied. His wet trousers made a sickening squelch on the chair.

"This is Kal," Dodi chirped.

"Best of luck!" Wodi said, slapping Kal on the back so hard that the Heptooinian pitched forward, knocking his drink onto the table before him, sending fizzy water everywhere.

"Look what you did!" Kal said, recovering the tall glass.

"Sorry," Wodi said. "Get this guy another drink!"

Minn, overwhelmed, looked fretfully at the besotted surface. "I can't deal there."

"Wodi, you're a fool." Thodi pulled out the chair to Wodi's right. "Here, Kal. Nice spot for you."

"I don't want to move," Kal said. Of course, he did, but he didn't want to lose his last-to-play position. He looked to Wodi. "Can you scoot down?"

"And then another of our chairs will be wet," Vestry said, glowering over her dealer's shoulder. "Move to the vacant seat if you wish to play, Master Sonmi. Or I'll close this table and send you all to another."

"No, no." Kal remembered the precious cards the decks held. "I'm moving."

"Good fellow." Wodi downed the drink Ganzer had brought him and looked at the table. "What's this game, again?"

"Zinbiddle," Thodi said. "But you're not playing with our money, not after running off on us." He collected his and Dodi's funds from the table.

"That's okay," Wodi said, placing his sole coin on the bet circle before him. "I'll bet this."

Minn, mesmerized by the trio, had to be snapped to attention by Vestry. "Oh, yes. We have a game."

In his new seat, Kal leaned back over his stakes and struggled to focus as the cards fell. He'd lost position by moving, but Wodi clearly had no idea what he was doing—and, with no stake beyond his initial ante, no ability to buy extra draws to improve his hand. And the cards Kal received were a delight, everything he needed to be able to work toward an Ion Barrage. They were the cards he knew were in the decks—so good, in fact, he calculated the odds that Wodi was similarly blessed were low indeed.

"You're all in?" Kal asked the Suerton. His brothers could always supply him with late money to help him out.

"Sadly, I do not come from a generous and forgiving family." He turned and glared playfully at his relatives—who had now been joined by several curious onlookers, some no doubt surprised to find such excitement going on with the sun still up. "This coin's plenty. I'm just having fun here."

"Very well." Not having to bet the later rounds on his hand freed up Kal's finances to buy additional draw cards, replacing the less desirable ones at the higher levels of his pyramid. It cost everything he had left, but it meant that the right final card at the summit would create the mathematical piece of art he'd so long pursued.

And then that card fell. "That's it," Kal said, breathless as he exposed his bottom row of cards—the base of his pyramid. The figures and colors traced a beautiful chevron, topped off by a still more beautiful ace.

Minn looked dazzled. "Player has a natural Ion Barrage!"

"Wonderful, Kal!" Dodi said, ebullient. The green guy seemed genuinely happy for him. "You'll win the progressive!"

Vestry raised her hands, appealing for calm. "There is business left. An Ion Barrage doesn't end the game like a zinbiddle," she said. "We still have a showdown."

"Fine, whatever," Kal said, unable to stop grinning.

"Well, I do have these," Wodi said, exposing his hole cards. "Is this anything?"

The watchers gasped. "C-could be," Kal said, blood draining from his face. Wodi had somehow gotten the identical array of cards that Kal had—but *on the deal,* without having done anything to improve his hand. Kal quickly found some solace: Wodi still needed the capper, and Kal had showing the only regular card finishing an Ion Barrage. Wodi's only out was so rarely in play that Kal never bothered to account for it.

"Final card," Minn said.

When it hit the table in front of Wodi, Kal nearly fainted. Vestry looked over her dealer's shoulder, stunned—and made a pronouncement. "Gentlebeings, we have a *second* Ion Barrage—capped by the wildest of wild cards, the *Vermilion Six!*"

Cheers erupted. "The automatic shuffler puts the card near the back of the shoe," Thodi said, referring to the long container Minn had dealt from. He gawked. "It's five-hundred-to-one the card would even be in the deck!"

"Five hundred and sixty," Kal whispered, dizzy. As Dodi shook Wodi's shoulders, Kal appealed to Vestry. "Wait a second. I showed an Ion Barrage first. I should win the progressive!"

Vestry shook her head. "House rules, Master Sonmi. To take the jackpot, you must *win* with an Ion Barrage. His is ranked higher. He wins the pot *and* the jackpot."

"It's the same hand," Kal insisted, pointing to his own cards. "And mine's a natural. His uses a wild card."

"And you know very well this is Kuari zinbiddle, as developed on the *Kuari Princess.* There's one wild card and it always trumps."

Stupid cruise ship gimmicks! Kal watched as Vestry stepped aside to allow a procession of attendants to deliver to the table trays of coins worth more than eight hundred thousand units in Canto Bight currency. He'd never seen such fanfare in the afternoon. Standing, he pointed at the trays and sputtered. "I—I still hit an Ion Barrage first!"

"You know better," Vestry said, irritation evident. "It was a showdown. The hands 'happened' at the same time."

"Then we should split it!" As Dodi began piling trays onto Thodi's outstretched hands, Kal grabbed for a tray still on the table. "I paid in a lot of these coins!"

"Hands off or I call security!" Vestry circled around the table and seized the tray from him. "It's not your money," she snapped.

"I worked for this, for hours, weeks, months!" Kal turned toward Wodi and gesticulated wildly. "Then this . . . *thing* walks in and bets *one coin!*"

"A coin and a chair," Thodi said. "All it ever takes."

"Don't give me that."

Dodi touched his arm. "Relax, friend. It's all in fun."

"It's a game!" Kal yelled. "It's not *supposed* to be fun!"

Kal turned to see Minn posing for a publicity holoimage with her deal, the poor kid visibly unaware of how she should feel about having lost the house nearly a million on her first day. Kal broke the moment by swiping the Vermilion Six from the table. He eyed it. "Is this thing even real?"

"Stop!" Vestry grabbed his wrist and pulled the card from his fingers.

"Pal, there's no need to get upset," Wodi said, standing as Kal wrested away from Vestry. Wodi pulled a single coin from one of the trays and handed it to Kal. "Here, a new stake."

"A new stake?" Kal frowned at the coin in his palm. *"Thanks a lot!"*

He didn't see where the coin landed after he threw it, but he knew it went far.

THE BAD BEAT | 4

THE FIRING HAD GONE RATHER QUICKLY, KAL THOUGHT, CONSIDERING most of the administrative team had left for the day. Perhaps the gears of bureaucracy had been greased by the surveillance holorecording of his rant, which extended well after the thrown coin—and which he'd been forced to painfully watch while listening to Vestry's angry narration to the administrator. Or possibly the motivation had come from where the coin had landed: in the cocktail glass of a surprised agricultural baron of some renown.

Whatever the reason for his termination's swiftness, he wouldn't have been able to fulfill his function anyway. He'd spent all his money on the last hand, and the casino had no use for a proposition player who couldn't afford to play. And since he had "failed to comport himself in a manner consistent with Canto Bight's standards for hospitality and decorum," there wouldn't be any more money coming to him. He was out.

Just not out of the casino—not yet. Yes, he had surrendered his fine cape and jacket, which were property of the house; that had been the worst of it, in some ways. He'd loved looking suave. But there was documentation to finalize, requiring him to be back in the office in the morning—and as he had nowhere else to go, he found himself in Ganzer's Grotto, off the main card room. Music was playing, thrumming from a band famous enough to be at Canto Bight but not worthy of a larger room; Kal wished for the quiet of the daylight hours, but there was nothing to be done. He'd sat at the counter to face away from everyone else, open bottle in front of him and head in his hands—and fortunately everyone had understood that bit of interplanetary language and left him alone.

Except, of course, for the one person paid to intrude. "You were cashiered?" Ganz asked.

"That's a funny word. Sounds like they give you money." Kal tugged at his shirt. "They took my jacket."

"The cravat doesn't really work without it." Ganzer didn't look directly at him as he wiped down the bar. "You all right?"

Kal shook his head. "I don't know. It's as I told Vestry: I'm normally so disciplined. Every day, every hand. No ups, no downs. That's who I have to be."

"And you ran into something that didn't make sense."

"I don't get it," Kal said, looking up. "Who are those guys? Vestry acted like the casino knew them."

Ganz grinned. "No, I guess playing day shift you wouldn't have seen them. They're normally in later. We call them the Lucky Three."

"The Lucky Three?"

Rag in hands, Ganzer leaned against the back counter. "The way I hear it, they've turned up in casinos and at tracks across the galaxy. When they win big, they win *real* big. When they lose, they don't care—because they know they'll get it back."

"Are they cheating?"

"Not that anyone can tell," Ganzer said. "Canto keeps a close eye on them. A few winners can be good for business."

Kal concentrated. If even Vestry thought they were clean, that said something. It also explained why she'd been hanging around so much. "How are the brothers doing it, then?"

Ganzer shrugged. "I don't think even *they* know. They'll win it all and then lose it—and never stop smiling. Management's asked them to stay away from the high-limit games against the house—but they're hard to control. Minds of their own, those boys."

"I don't think they've got a brain among them. But they've got my money!"

"Not anymore. Canto Bight's won it back."

Kal's eyes went wide. "No!"

"Yep. Your big winner just threw it all away on the jubilee wheel. The one with the big ears and big ideas—"

"Thodi."

"—talked him into dividing up the money and betting every single possible outcome. The wheel stopped on Black Hole."

"The one space you can't bet." Kal was enraged anew. "That was *eight hundred thousand!*"

"They don't care. The two of them came in here and told the third—and all of them were off immediately to the hazard toss table. Winning again, my server tells me."

They only lose when they have a plan? Kal entertained the thought for a moment and dismissed it. It wasn't worth further thought. "They blew up my life. I'm busted out."

Ganzer sighed and nodded. "Only hard thing about life on Cantonica is figuring out a way to never have to leave."

It was an aphorism among those on the planet who worked—or played—for a living. So many, the two of them included, had lived in places torn by poverty, sickness, or war. Cantonica's dry air was a magic elixir, allowing one to forget—and ignore—all the sufferings of a crowded galaxy that had too much history and was making more every day.

Ganzer took Kal's empty bottle. "Where will you go? You've still got your ship, right?"

"That's—uh, complicated," Kal said.

The bartender accepted that answer.

Kal frowned. "You're *sure* they're not cheating?"

Ganzer sighed. "It's a strange galaxy. When I was young—"

"Here we go," Kal said. Ganzer had the bartender's love of tales.

"—back when I worked construction in the Core Worlds, I used to go to this diner where these two hustlers were always winning free meals off the other customers by rolling chance cubes at the counter."

"Low stakes."

"Which is why people took the bets. After I'd lost to both of them enough times, I was sure they were cheating—switching in loaded dice or something. So then one day this Jedi Knight came in. You heard of them?"

"Not much."

"They were a sort of peace officer before the Empire. People said they used some kind of magic. Anyway, this Jedi Knight offered to play both of the gamblers. The first took off and never came back; the second played him and lost."

"So he used his magic on the second guy's dice."

"No, he said he didn't do anything. He didn't have to. What was it he said?" Ganzer spoke next in a solemn voice. *"The honest person only fears losing. The cheater fears discovery, and does so long after the die is cast."*

"Pithy."

"So what did the Lucky Three fear earlier?" Ganzer asked. "Losing, or discovery?"

"I don't think they were afraid of anything."

"Then odds are they're not cheating."

Kal groaned. "Don't mention odds to me."

Ganzer snapped his fingers. "I almost forgot. I have something for you." He reached for his pocket.

"I won't take your money, Ganz."

"It's not mine, it's yours." He produced a single coin. "It's the one you threw. I fished it out of the baron's glass." He passed it to Kal. "Actually, it was the brother that was in here who suggested I give it to you. The happy one."

"Dodi, I think. I'm sorry I know." Kal studied the coin. "They must really want me to have it. Severance pay, I guess."

Seeing a group of partiers enter, Ganzer stepped out from behind the counter. He called back, "Do yourself a favor. Don't spend it here."

"In the casino or at the bar?"

"Neither!"

Kal studied the coin—and then realized he was being watched. He turned his head quickly to a table in a dark alcove on the side of the room, where a long-limbed crimson-skinned woman had stopped dead in her solitaire play to study him.

"What?" Kal blurted.

"Looking to see if you were going to throw that one." She gestured into the card room. "You'd get more elevation out there."

Kal rolled his eyes. The woman collected her cards and rose to approach him. Against the monochromatic styles of the casino, she immediately stood out. Everything about her was red: hair, dress, satchel—and eyes, narrow and watchful. He'd seen several members of her species here, all either employed as entertainers or being escorted by others. That only reminded him that company was yet another thing he could not afford to keep.

"Look, this isn't a good day," he said as she reached the bar. "And you're not my type. Or species."

"If that's how well you read people, it's no wonder that's your last coin." The woman claimed the seat next to him and started dealing a solitaire zinbiddle hand on the bar. "You're Kaljach Sonmi. We need to talk."

THE SHARP | 5

BEFORE KAL COULD ASK HOW THE WOMAN KNEW HIS NAME, IT DAWNED on him that *he* knew *her*.

"Wait a second," he said as she dealt her cards on the bar. "You're *Orisha Okum*! You won the Savareen whist tournament last month. And another before that."

"That one was pazaak."

"Yeah. I stayed up late for that." She was a star, more important in his eyes than any of the VIPs who floated through. More than a player: an artist, summoning the cards she needed when she needed them. He stared in admiration. "You're really good."

"I know," she said, never looking up at him as she played cards to her pyramid. "At Canto you have to be. And if you're not good, you'd better be rich."

"Or lucky," Kal said, sagging.

"Show me a career player who believes in luck and I'll show you a former career player. You of all people would know that."

"But how would you know me?"

She kept to her cards.

Kal decided he'd had enough of being slow-played. He slapped his hand on the bar. "Well, this has been a thrill." He rose. "It's been a long day. Nice getting to know each other."

"I told you I already knew you."

He looked at her—and she returned the glance. It was enough to make him sit back down.

"Let me tell you your story," Orisha said, continuing to play cards. "You came from one of those trade route planets—which means the planet itself got traded. Between Republic and Separatists, Empire and Alliance, First Order and New Republic . . ."

"I'm no good with names."

"But you *are* good with games, and your people learned them from the troops passing through, when your houses weren't burning down. You grew up—and when the pyrotechnics hit a lull, you got away. Freighter, probably, maybe a stowaway. Probably you made it onto a cruise liner as a domestic at some point, where you learned the games the posh crowd played in places like this. Somewhere, somebody staked you—and you made it to the table."

Kal said nothing. She was doing fine on her own.

"You've played all over, since—but you found that those wars back home followed you around, and so you've kept moving." She paused and gestured to the surroundings. "Which brings you to Canto Bight, the one place where you know they can't touch you—and where you can play against the best." She looked behind her into the card room. "There are countless pros like you here. You all think you know what you're doing. But none of you are rich enough to win against people who don't care about money. So you wind up playing earlier and earlier—and longer and longer, grinding on some system to make a third of a percent a day."

"Hey," Kal said in mock offense. "It's closer to two-fifths."

"And you have to make other concessions." She glanced at him. "Where are you sleeping?"

"In the spaceport," he said, grasping at the last chance to salvage some dignity. "My ship's parked there."

"But the ship's hocked and locked, so you can't take off—and you can't even board her. So where are you sleeping? Behind the landing gear?"

"No!" Kal said, miffed. Then, humbly: "There just happens to be a spot between the thrusters where you can swing a nice hammock."

"Because you need your sleep to run your great system."

"Some read you've got there. I didn't think I was that easy."

"My friend, you're a clone from Kamino."

Great, Kal thought. *Drinks and judgment at sunset.* "If I'm such a loser, why are you talking to me?"

"It's *because* you're such a loser. I have a request from a friend."

"A friend," Kal said, staring. "A friend of *yours* wants to offer *me* something."

"Actually, he wants you to *do* something."

Kal shook his head. "Okay, I get it. Somebody thinks I'm down and out, so you're going to ask me to do something illegal."

"And that would offend you?"

"No, I'm just trying to figure out what's going on."

"You know Big Sturg Ganna, of course?"

Kal froze. "Yeah," he said after a moment. "Councilor. Some say gangster. Big guy, big trouble."

"And you know that fur-faced fellow—the old gray-haired guy, who floated you the loans you've been playing on for the last eighteen months?"

Kal swallowed. "Yes?"

"Did you know that he's the accountant for Big Sturg Ganna?"

His blood chilled. "No." *So that's what Vestry suspected.*

"But you took his money anyway." She smirked. "You just thought there was a wealthy investor here, randomly advancing eight hundred thousand Cantocoins to every player pursuing an edge?"

Kal shrugged. "Canto's full of eccentrics. Everybody here bets on something."

"These people don't." Orisha paused in her card play. "They took you on first because your ship was worth something—then when you became a prop player they figured you could be an insider at the casino organization for them. They've got a few of those. Finally they asked me to look at a few hours of your play—"

"You saw the surveillance holos? How?"

"I mentioned insiders, Kal. Keep up. They wanted me to see whether your system might be anything."

"It is!"

"Surprising thing is I agreed, which bought you some extra time." She returned to her dealing. "But you're out of money and out of a job, so . . ."

"I'm out of time." He shook his head. "Well, my ship is the collateral." He paused. "As you know." Her prescience seemed less impressive now.

"Yeah, turns out you overstated the value of that ship, by quite a lot. Not smart. And now that the progressive's back down to zero—"

"Hey, I got the Ion Barrage. How was I to know there'd be *two*?"

"I saw the images. Impressive. Taken by a moron with a wild card is a bad beat, for sure."

"But the system works. They can put me out there and I can hit another—"

"That progressive took all year to accumulate. It's not fast enough. And these aren't patient people." She moved cards from stack to stack. "The accountant's request is that you repay the entire amount— eight hundred thousand even—by sunrise tomorrow. Failing that, he would ask that when you wake up, you find a departing starship and walk into its thruster fire."

"Do *what*?"

"Since you're already in the spaceport," Orisha shrugged, "they're hoping you'll help them out. And if not, well, they can find a way." She looked at him sternly. "Oh, and don't try to hop one of those ships. He's got people everywhere, and they won't be the ones you'll expect."

Obviously not, he thought, looking at her.

"Looks like I won," she said, admiring the final state of her card pyramid. But only for a moment. She began gathering them up.

Kal touched her wrist. "Do they really think I can make eight hundred thousand by tomorrow morning?"

"No. They don't play, but they're good with odds. And don't ask me for help." She used her other hand to remove his from her wrist. "Frankly, you grinders give gaming a bad name." She placed her cards in the pouch at her hip and rose.

Kal considered her words for several moments before his eyes narrowed. "Wait a minute," he said, hopping off his chair and calling to her. "I almost let you get away with that—playing holy. What are you doing as a go-between for Big Sturg Ganna?"

She looked back. "The councilor doesn't send muscle onto the casino floor. The countess wouldn't look highly on that. I belong."

"Yeah, but why *you*? You're a champion player."

"We've all got to get our stakes somewhere," she said. "Sunrise." With that, she exited into the card room.

Kal watched her vanish into the now teeming crowd—and calculated the challenge ahead of him. He had roughly ten and a half hours in which to earn what he'd taken a year and a half to lose.

Ganzer emerged from a gaggle of revelers, tray of empties in hand. "Still here," he said. "What did I miss?"

"Tell you later. I've got to go!"

THE BUST OUT | 6

KAL HAD NO INTENTION OF TELLING GANZER LATER, BECAUSE HE HAD NO expectation of ever seeing him again. It took just four and a half minutes for the player to traverse the quickly filling card room and lobby on his way to the front entrance.

Beautiful purple twilight bathed the entryway as Kal hit the sidewalk. Ground vehicles arriving at Canto were routed to the underground parkade, a shadowy location that Kal didn't consider safe under the circumstances. But while most patrons had their own chauffeurs, enough people spent the day shopping Cabranga Street in Old City that vehicles for hire could be found along a pullout. "Where do you want to go?" a Sullustan driver asked him.

Standing outside the open door, Kal realized he had no idea how to respond. Neither did he know how he could pay for the ride. "How far will this get me?" Kal asked, holding up the lone Cantocoin.

"You're kidding, right? I'm not a droid."

"Look, I just need to move. Can I ride up front? I can pretend to be your assistant."

"Yeah, customers will love that. If you can't pay—"

Kal had tuned the driver out. He'd seen something. The trees lining the front of the Canto Casino were Alderaanian chinar, raised from a seed bank at colossal expense. True survivors of a lost world—

but far too skinny for anyone to use for cover. This did not seem to bother the Wookiee standing behind one, arms crossed and eyes focused directly on Kal.

Kal smiled uncomfortably at the Wookiee—who, he now saw, had a comlink in her hairy hand. The titan shook her enormous head at him.

"Never mind," Kal said. "I've decided to stay for a while."

"And the countess's fortune is saved," the driver said, triggering the control to close the door.

The cab pulled away, leaving Kal on the curb. He turned to the Wookiee and shrugged innocently. The creature didn't respond—but neither did she follow Kal as he walked toward the building.

His heart sank as he scaled the steps. There was no point in trying to leave the planet, not if Ganna really did hold his debt. Kal had understood that the being he'd borrowed money from probably didn't offer it out of benevolence; he'd been around enough gambling halls to see all kinds of shenanigans. He just didn't expect Canto Bight's breed of criminal to bother with staking card players. It seemed such a low-return, slow-paying enterprise, when compared with fixing fathier races.

On the other hand, if Ganna's people could get control of someone like Orisha Okum, they could do just about anything. Including, as she'd suggested, tapping the eye-in-the-sky surveillance feeds in the casino. Ganzer had once shared a rumor that Ganna had a private suite in the building; if true, who knew what kind of operations center he had in there?

Thinking of the suite gave him sudden hope, if it could be called that. There was another way out: hiding in a place where every room wasn't under surveillance. And such a place was just off the lobby.

One of the Canto Casino's great profit centers was its resort hotel, in the business of charging exorbitant rates to guests—guests whom it then tempted into spending as little time in their rooms as possible. Empty rooms could be a boon. With so few security cams allowed to exist in a structure devoted to privacy, Kal figured he could follow a cleaning droid into a suite and hide. He'd hidden from bombing as a child; sneaking from room to room, living off the pre-stocked re-freshments, and sleeping under beds should be easy by comparison. Surely, after enough of this either Ganna's people would give up—or he'd think of a way offworld.

He just had to get up into the facility—a task, he discovered, that was more difficult than he imagined. Slipping into the large throng of guests standing before two sets of doors, waiting for the turbolifts to arrive, was easy enough. The continued wait, however, was uncharacteristic for things at Canto.

"Hey, look who's here," called out a voice in the gaggle. "The guy with the good arm."

"Wodi," Kal said, suppressing a sigh. *My luck isn't changing.* Ahead of the taller patrons, Thodi stood near his brother, his eyes scanning the numbers on the displays beside the turbolift doors. Kal scowled. They deserved a piece of his mind, for sure—but at the moment he could only afford small talk. "Waiting for a turbolift?"

"Nope," Wodi said. "Betting on them."

"Against each other?" Kal looked at the sealed doors. "Who's winning?"

"Right now, neither of us," Thodi grumbled.

"I was doing fine betting against the bellhop," Wodi said. "But when Thodi got here and started betting against me, the lifts seem to have broken."

"You were *not* doing fine," Thodi corrected. "You weren't even looking at where the cars were when you were betting."

"Which is important in turbolift races," Kal said.

"Of course." Thodi scratched his rubbery chin. "You see, most people bet on cars that are lower down in the building. My theory is the people at the highest levels have keys that put the cars into express mode. Those drop to the bottom fast."

Nothing was moving at all now. Kal looked to the doors, and then the brothers. "How long are you going to wait?"

"Until someone wins."

Or not. "I'm hungry," Wodi said. "I'll see you around."

No sooner was Wodi out of sight than the turbolift on the right began descending.

"Hey, Wodi, I win!" Thodi yelled as the car hit bottom.

A bewildered attendant stepped out, looking embarrassed. "I'm sorry, patrons," he said, as the mob piled in. "I don't know what happened. It just stopped working for a while!"

There was no way Kal was making it into that jam-packed car, he could see—but neither did he want to spend any more time around Thodi, not when the minutes of his life might be precious. At last the second car arrived—

—carrying, Kal saw as the doors opened, a Wookiee of slightly different color. But no better disposition. The brute glared at Kal and shook her head.

So much for that idea! Kal spun and made for the place most familiar to him: the casino floor. They couldn't kill him there. *Could they?*

MINUTES HAD PASSED IN THE GAMING HALL WITHOUT INCIDENT, BUT that brought Kal no cheer. His arms sagged as he walked the aisles from room to room. No low-limit action tonight; just high- and no-limit. So different from the daytime hours. So many people, so happy.

He'd been a part of it, even when he had no reason to be joyful; he had belonged. Now, without the coat and cape, he no longer looked like he was worthy of being in Canto Bight—and he no longer carried himself as if he had money. "Broke" had a stench. Sooner or later it would offend someone.

Perhaps sooner. Across the room, he saw Vestry conferring with Pemmin Brunce, the smash-faced head of security—and in his latest mistake of the day, Kal let them see him. The only casino staffer permitted to frown, Brunce would think nothing of pitching someone out for loitering. "If you want to fish around in the payout trays of the slots for spare change," Kal had once heard Vestry tell a sudden pauper, "go someplace else. Not Canto." So when Vestry pointed in Kal's direction, the Heptooinian knew he had to find a game, and fast.

He walked quickly, looking to and fro. A single Cantocoin could play afternoon zinbiddle, but after dark the minimums had all increased. At a lesser casino on another world, he might expect to find a freeroll, a tournament with no entrance fee. The idea of such a thing here was laughable. Besides, it would take far too long to play, and yield nowhere near enough for his purposes.

He glanced back to see Brunce on the move, his approach making even the most self-involved patrons—and they were plentiful—clear a path. Kal turned up an aisle only to find it a cul-de-sac, ringed by high-minimum hazard toss tables. No place he could play, not at these prices. He was trapped.

He pushed into the largest crowd. Someone there had to be on a streak. But there was no hiding in crowds from Brunce, who worked his way in until he was face-to-face with Kal, backing him up against the gaming table.

"What are you doing, sir?" Brunce asked in a voice that sounded like a thruster revving up.

"I'm enjoying my stay."

"You can't stay if you don't play." Brunce moved closer, as careful as a mountain of muscle could be not to disturb the active gamblers.

"I'm a spectator," Kal said nervously. "What's wrong with that? A lot of people are just watching."

"You can't."

Kal thought about making a scene, but couldn't imagine anyone would hear him, much less care. Instead, he did the only thing he could think of. He reached in his pocket to produce his Cantocoin. "Look! I have a bet."

Brunce snorted as he recognized the denomination. "Not enough."

Kal's face fell. *Someone taught him to count.* "I left my money in my jacket. If you'll just—"

With unexpected speed for one of his bulk, the bouncer reached forward, seizing both of Kal's wrists and cutting him off midsentence. Pinned against the table's protective railing, Kal lost hold of the coin, which fell backward onto the gaming surface. It bounced once before landing on its side, whereupon it started rolling. Its spiraling journey ended when it fell against a pile of coins on the far side.

"Bets closed," announced Thamm, the tiny quadruped who did his croupier job while standing on the table.

"Here I go," shouted the snout-faced dice roller, who hurled the polyhedrons in a return trajectory to Kal's side of the table. They bounced crazily and came to a stop.

"Three threes," Thamm declared. "Dodi wins again!"

Dodi emerged from the throng on the left side of the table, cheering loudly and banging on the railing. "Whee!" It was then that Dodi saw Kal and the counter—and he grew happier still. "Hi, Kal!"

Brunce loosened his hold on Kal slightly; his feet could at least touch the floor now.

Dodi made his way to the pair and pointed to the table, where Thamm used his croupier stick like a push broom to add nine coins for every one on the winning square. "I see you put your coin to good use, Kal." He winked. "Clever of you, adding to my bet."

The Suerton finally noticed Brunce, still gripping Kal's wrists. "Something the matter?"

"Good evening, sir," the security officer drawled grudgingly. "I'm on casino business."

"Delightful. What?"

"The minimum on the floor tonight is a hundred. This player only has one."

"Ten," Kal volunteered, eyes darting to the table.

"I'm well over the minimum, and he can certainly add to my bet," Dodi said.

All this thinking was clearly irritating Brunce, who pulled at Kal's arm some more. "He doesn't have enough to be here."

"Then just wait a moment," Dodi said.

Behind him, the snouted creature rolled the dice again—and Thamm shouted, "The Suerton has let it ride—and trip threes wins again!"

"*Now* he has a hundred," Dodi said. He placed a coin of his own in the massive bouncer's pocket and grinned pleasantly. "Thank you for taking time out of your duties to visit with us."

Brunce, speechless and smoldering, stared at Kal—then Dodi. Then he let the card player go and retreated from the area.

Dodi patted the inside of the railing table. "I'm out." Seconds later, Thamm delivered him several stacks of coins. The Suerton then handed a small pile to Kal, who was collecting himself after his rough handling. "Your winnings."

"Thank you," Kal said, catching his breath. "And, uh—thanks for helping out."

"We're all here for fun," Dodi said. "Silly rules shouldn't ruin a good time."

Kal looked at the coins in wonder. "You . . . you knew you were going to hit again."

"Uh-huh."

"How?"

That smile again, as Dodi prepared to leave. "I don't question it, Kal, so you shouldn't. Have fun." He patted Kal on the chest and disappeared into the crowd.

THE BUY-IN | 8

THE PROBLEM WITH LIFE'S MORE IMPORTANT REALIZATIONS, GANZER
had once told him, was that many came in the middle of the night
when one had little chance to do anything about them. Midnight was
still a couple of hours off, but Kal's flash of insight had hit when he
was in exactly the right place.

Unfortunately, Dodi no longer was. Kal went from table to table
searching for the Suerton, with no success. Canto was really getting
going now; Kal figured you could lose a gundark in the main hall. But
following the sounds of cheering brought him to the side of Thodi,
who had evidently given up on turbolift races in favor of the jubilee
wheel.

"Come on," Thodi declared, depositing his coins on the playing
surface. "Earn it back!"

Kal remembered the story about the brothers blowing his much-
deserved and painfully lost progressive jackpot here, and wondered
what insane theory Thodi was using to lose everything this time. But
looking at the table, Kal could see that the Suerton had placed his
bets on a single space.

Kal sidled up to Thodi. "Why Green Triangle?"

"Oh, hello again," Thodi said. His professorial tone returned. "You
see the person operating the spinner? She has three fingers. Three
fingers, triangle."

"But why green?"

"I'm green."

Kal stared at him. "That makes sense," he said. Kal put half his coins on Green Triangle, beside Thodi's, just as the operator put the wheel into motion.

"Green Triangle pays," she declared when the spinning had stopped.

Kal collected his winnings. Desperation was overcoming good sense. "What next?" he asked Thodi.

"Well, that last one was the fifth triangle in the last ten spins. Which means now we bet on Pentagon."

"I'm following you," Kal lied. "Any color?"

Thodi's face wrinkled. "You know, this table left me blue earlier."

"Blue it is." Kal and Thodi placed bets simultaneously—and rejoiced when Blue Pentagon hit on the wheel.

Okay, so Thodi isn't the jinx. He'd won the turbolift race earlier, after all. He continued to bet where Thodi did, quizzing him about his goofy reasoning each time like someone genuinely interested.

The problem was other gamblers seeing the Suerton's luck began following suit. "It's not a game if you're all copying me," Thodi said drily to the table. "Show some originality."

Kal had feared that would happen. He shifted to a different strategy, placing tangential bets that, while not exactly mimicking what Thodi was doing, still stood to benefit from his choices. On Thodi's Double Gold Star bets, Kal bet Doubles. Or Gold. Or Stars. It was less of a moneymaker, but it seemed to irritate Thodi less.

Kal couldn't believe what he was doing. He'd always avoided playing the wheel—and now this? He was even more surprised to be disappointed when Thodi stopped. "I'm moving on," Thodi announced after converting his coins to higher denominations.

"Where to now?" Kal asked.

Thodi looked unsure he wanted Kal's company. "You might not like this. I want to hit zinbiddle again, now that the stakes are raised. I never got to test my latest ideas."

"I'd love to see them. Lead the way."

And Thodi did—right into one of the high-roller rooms. Kal

gulped. He had no experience with such places, except for the times he'd watched some tournament final games—both won, he recalled, by Orisha Okum. She was there, he saw, playing Savareen whist with some mogul; on seeing Kal, she rolled her eyes before returning to her game.

Thodi claimed the only seat open at the table. "Bad luck," he said. "No space for you."

Kal scowled. Then he remembered that he wasn't out of options. He stood directly behind Thodi's chair, hanging over his shoulder. Thodi placed a pile of coins on the zinbiddle instant-win marker.

"I thought you told Dodi never to play those," Kal said.

"The sun was still up then."

Kal nodded. "I have so much to learn." Then he reached in, preparing to add a stack of his own coins to Thodi's side bet.

"Master Sonmi!"

Kal looked back to see Vestry storming toward him, looking as cross as he'd ever seen her. She rotated among all the card rooms, never seeming to sleep; it hadn't helped her disposition. "What are you doing?"

"Gambling at a casino," Kal said. "What are *you* doing?"

"Enforcing Canto's rules. This is a high-limit room, high minimums. No spectators outside tournaments—and I highly doubt you can afford to play here."

"I am playing." He pointed to Thodi, in front of him. "I'm a rider."

Vestry glanced at Thodi, and then looked back to Kal. "A rider? *You?*"

"It's legal. I can stand behind any player in the house and finish their bets, as long as they don't go over the limit."

Thodi counted out his Cantocoins on the side-bet marker for her benefit. "Nine hundred and nine. My bet counts are always numeric palindromes when the player to my right is an Ithorian," Thodi told her. "It has seldom failed me."

"See?" Kal said, as if it were the most obvious thing in the world. "Numeric palindromes." He quickly reached in and placed ninety-one of his own next to them to bring it to the limit. The dealer, a veteran Kal seldom saw during the day, ably kept the bets separate as he continued the hand.

Vestry's eyes narrowed. "This isn't Cloud City. Here, the rider must have the player's permission."

"I'm always willing to take on a learner," Thodi said. "Oh," he said, turning up his cards. "Zinbiddle."

"Zinbiddle, he says." Kal's pale face flushed as both his and Thodi's winnings were paid out. He smiled at Vestry. "I'm always willing to learn."

Vestry stared at him for several moments before stomping off without saying anything. Kal again caught a look from Orisha, who was now struck curious—but for the next hour, he had no time to worry about anything but the table. As a rider, Kal had no control whatsoever on the decisions Thodi made—and while he was free to decide whether to follow the Suerton into any bet, he wound up regretting any apprehension. Thodi was on a roll.

Or was, until Wodi showed up. "There you guys are," he said. "How are you doing, Kyle?"

"Kal."

"Don't bug me," said Thodi, in the middle of a hand.

Wodi looked at the pyramid of cards his brother was building. "You know, you can draw some cards to help that hand."

"Which you could have done earlier today, but it would have been a mistake," Thodi said. "I don't need lessons in how to play from *you,* of all—"

"Zinbiddle," called the Ithorian.

We lost? It hadn't happened in so long that Kal had almost forgotten what it felt like. He hadn't wagered all his holdings, but he'd lost ground. His brow furrowed as he tried to remember his earlier episodes with the brothers. *Something about how they got together . . .*

He followed the aggravated Thodi into the next pot, but bet much more conservatively this time. He regretted that caution when Thodi hit big—seconds after Dodi walked up.

The dealer spoke to the growing group behind Thodi. "Don't crowd the players, please."

"Forget this," Dodi said. "I've found another game. You're going to love this."

"Drinks first?" Thodi asked, rising from his chair.

"And always!" Wodi declared.

We're moving again. Kal gathered up his coins—now a nice trayful—and made for the exit, following them. On the way out, he found Orisha waiting. Keeping an eye on where the brothers went, he paused and displayed his tray with a smile.

She was unimpressed. "Big Sturg lent you eight hundred thousand. That won't cover his appetizers."

That reminded Kal that he'd forgotten to eat, but he ignored it. "There's still time. I'm onto something."

"You're on spice." Orisha shook her head. "Tagging along with those characters? I thought you were a good player."

Kal didn't defend his abandonment of everything he knew about gaming. He couldn't. But he'd heard words that caused him to look at her sideways. "You thought I was a good player?"

She pulled his shoulder to draw him closer and spoke so no one else could hear. "Don't imagine that I like you—and don't think I'm rooting for you. I made ten million last year. But Ganna is always looking for the next Orisha Okum. He funds several of you small-timers—but none of you are in my league. And you never will be."

Kal stared at her, before looking down at his tray. He wasn't so proud of it anymore.

She released him and backed away. "I'll be back before sunrise. And if you don't have the eight hundred thousand, Ganna's Wookiees are going to take you for a nice walk. And they are going to rip your arms off and beat you to death with them."

He swallowed. "Sounds lovely."

Strolling away, she said, "You can bet on it."

Kal was sure of that.

THE TELL | 9

THE SE-8 SERVER DROIDS CIRCLED THE TABLES, TRAYS IN METALLIC hands, like the Mon Calamari Ballet; zipping here, stopping there— and always having to recalibrate their destinations because of people who'd moved since ordering. And whatever safeguards Industrial Automaton had put into the servants' programming, nothing stopped four droids going in opposite directions from colliding noisily in the aisle directly outside Ganzer's bar.

"*Yes!*" Dodi shouted, clasping hands with Kal in triumph. "We did it!"

"Whoa, whoa, whoa!" Ganzer cried, drawn from his haunt by the clamor. The droids had collided at great speed, creating a tangle of limbs and sending trays and beverage containers in all directions. Maintenance droids were already on the scene, attending to the wet floor.

"That was a thing of beauty," Thodi declared, turning to the breath-mask-wearing gambler at his side. "You owe all four of us, I believe."

Disgusted, the loser paid out. "I wouldn't have thought you could make it happen."

As Thodi passed out shares of the winnings, Ganzer looked up from his cleanup. "What happened here?"

"A wager," Dodi said.

"A wager!"

Thodi faced the gaming hall and drew a picture in the air. "You see, by the four of us ordering drinks and then constantly moving, we were able to choreograph something spectacular." He glared at Wodi. "Which *you* nearly screwed up!"

Wodi shrugged. "Hey, Kal went the wrong way, too."

"Kal?" Ganzer looked at him, offended. "You were part of this?"

Kal shrank back in guilt. "Sorry."

The bartender shoved the tray of empties he'd collected into Kal's arms. "Then *you* can carry these back to the Grotto."

"Follow the leaders, boys," Dodi ordered, falling in line behind Kal and Ganzer. "There's a bar over there!"

The brothers only followed until they saw a server; then, they raced ahead. Kal turned to his friend and shook his head as they walked inside. "I'm sorry, Ganz. This hasn't been a normal night."

"I think I see why you play the day shift. What's going on?"

"What hasn't been?" Kal waited for Ganzer to go behind the counter before setting down the tray. The gambler sat in a chair and rubbed his feet. "I love these shoes, but they're killing me."

Ganzer raised an eyebrow. "Talk to me after you've waited tables all night."

"Sorry. I never dressed for running around. I've been following the Lucky Three."

"After they beat you? I wouldn't think you'd talk to them after that."

"I need to—" Kal started, before stopping. "I can't get into all that. But it's been insane. We've lost plenty, but we keep winning it back, and more. And they bet *everything*. Dice games, card games, people with their own personal uvide wheels—"

"Droid destruction," Ganzer growled, moving glasses into his sink.

"Ganz, we went out to the wharf and bet some yachtsman on whether a seabird would land on his mast. I didn't even know that was a thing."

"They're a force of nature."

"Of something. I don't know what—but I think I've got it," Kal said.

"I hope it isn't contagious," Ganzer responded.

"No, I'm serious. The brothers. Their luck. I've figured it out."

"Really." Ganzer huddled over the counter, interested. "You know what they're doing?"

"Well, no, I haven't figured out *why* they're lucky. But I have figured out *when* they're lucky." He leaned over the counter and directed Ganzer's attention to the quaffing Dodi. "When one brother is alone, he's lucky. Beating the odds most of the time."

"Okay."

He pointed at Thodi and Wodi. "But when two of them get together—*any two!*—they tank. They start bickering, and they stink. Their luck gets ticked off at them and runs off with whoever is playing solo."

"Luck has legs?"

"And limited patience. And if the two are betting the same game against each other, nobody wins, anywhere. And I don't mean they both lose. *Everybody* loses."

"Is that a fact?"

"A fact. Awhile ago nobody was able to get up into the tower because they bet on opposite turbolifts." He took Ganzer by the shoulder. "But when all three of them get together, Ganz? Lock the doors. The probability charts go into the trash compactor. They win everything that's not welded down."

Ganzer nodded tentatively. "I follow you."

"So what I have to do is make sure I'm with them when they're all together, or with whichever one is alone. And I bet their way."

The bartender took a breath. "You've developed a system—a gambling system—*based on which brothers are in the room*?"

"I know it sounds silly."

Ganzer waved his hands. "I'm a bartender. I don't judge."

"I've got to do something, or I'll lose my mind. I've gone from one to thirty-three thousand since hooking up with them." He reached into the pouch on his belt and drew forth his coins, all high denominations—but he did not know how to feel about them. "Tell me as a friend, Ganz—and someone who's been around. I'm not crazy for playing with these guys, am I? This works, doesn't it?"

Ganzer snorted—and then chuckled. "If you—as someone who's

devoted his whole life to memorizing complicated sets of numbers—can get those numbers down to three, I say more power to you."

Dodi appeared nearby. "Oh, this was for the trouble earlier," he said, passing Ganzer a handful of coins.

It was a generous gift. "Thank you, sir."

"Kal, the red-eye runs are going at the fathier track. Want to tag along?"

Kal looked at Ganzer, and his eyes widened. *Fathier races?*

"Sure," Kal said. "I'll be right there."

"Great," Dodi said. "We'll go in a minute. Wodi's hand is stuck in a mug and I have to help him get it off." He departed to find his brothers.

Kal felt sick. "Fathier races."

Ganzer stared at the brothers. "What do you know about fathier races?"

"Not a damn thing. Except to avoid them."

"Well, at least you've got your theory."

Kal looked nervously at his pouch. "Yeah."

"You're about to learn whether you're right," Ganzer said. He patted Kal on the back—and then pulled a bowl of snack food from the counter and shoved it toward the Heptooinian. "Eat something. The way you look, I'm worried you'll be dead tomorrow."

"No time," Kal said. The brothers were on the move. "Got to go!"

THE STRETCH | 10

"LOOK," KAL SAID AS HE HOBBLED BENEATH THE ARCHWAY, "MY RULE number one is, *Don't play the races.*"

"But they're fun," Dodi said, trotting ahead of him. "I can't believe you've never done it before."

"They're a bottomless pit," Kal replied.

"Falling's fun," Wodi said, pushing Kal along. "Sounds great!"

The brothers had adopted Kal as their fourth over the past hours, and their luck had combined with his desperation to drive him to do some reckless things. Most recently on the walk over from Ganzer's Grotto, the three had bet an inebriated human that he could not balance on a tall outdoor planter. He'd paid off before the medics carried him away, leaving Kal, who had joined in the bet, with holdings totaling forty thousand.

The amount wasn't remotely sufficient to solve his problems—but more than he'd had in a long time. The bulging pouch on his belt had started to weigh on him, enough that as he entered the racing grounds, fear was trumping abandon—fear that his crazy theory about the brothers would prove to be exactly that when tens of thousands were on the line. His aversion to racing only compounded it. At least at the jubilee wheel, Kal knew enough to recognize Thodi had no idea what he was doing. He'd somehow found the nerve to go along then—but could he now, when so much more money was at stake?

He needed reassurance, if only to slow his pulse. He had to find someone who knew the races, knew the track, and had some kind of system developed. Something, anything, that would provide a little guidance.

I need to find the racing "me."

He marveled as the brothers led him through another set of arches. Canto's trackside clubhouse was legendary for its opulence and splendor; even now, late at night after multiple races, it remained brightly lit, without a scrap of garbage in sight. The grandstands and remote betting locations he'd seen on other worlds always grew filthier as the card progressed and gamblers discarded losing tickets. One could still get a physical voucher of one's bet at Canto Bight as a memento, but no one would think of despoiling the spectator area by casting them away.

A warm fresh breeze greeted him as he and the Suertons stepped out to the apron, the grassy spectator area between the grandstand and the track. Canto Bight's most tireless handicappers stood on the sidewalk alongside the railing, watching each of the long but lean animals saunter out of the barn on four dexterous legs. This was the post parade for the thirteenth race of the late-night card, or so Kal understood from one of the displays. The brothers headed straight for the rail—having once again gotten someplace just in time.

Dodi craned his neck to look up at one. "They're big."

"That's observant," Thodi replied.

Wodi pointed to one whose winglike ears were pinned back. "I like that one with the spot on her snout."

"She's a he, and he's a loser," called out an eavesdropper in a gravelly voice. "Bet him and regret him."

Kal looked to see who'd spoken. Behind the Suertons, a figure sat cross-legged on a stripe of well-manicured grass. Wearing a light hood, she pored over an array of datapads as she sipped from a tumbler. Around her neck hung macrobinoculars, hardly necessary at this distance—and when she looked up at Kal and the Three, he realized she, too, was Heptooinian; one of the few others in Canto Bight.

The racing "me," he supposed. *No coincidences around the Lucky Three.*

The woman tilted her head to look at the fathier Wodi had mentioned. "That's Time for Flatcakes, out of Kreegah."

"It's always time for flatcakes," Wodi said, hypnotized by the creature.

"I want flatcakes," Kal mumbled, feeling hungry. He remembered where he was. "We shouldn't bet him?"

"No wins, no places, no shows," the woman said without looking at her notes. "Completely deaf and barely needs the blinders. You'd win more betting that the stable master could run around the track on *his* hands."

Dodi looked back. "They'll let us bet on that?"

"No, sweetheart. It's an expression."

Kal sighed, and the brothers went back to watching. It was clear they were going to bet based on something silly, and given the current stakes he wasn't sure if he could handle that. He turned back to the woman—and, no longer half blinded by the track's lights, he realized he recognized her.

"You work at the casino. Currency exchange."

"Guilty," she said, pulling back her hood to expose silver hair. Her name was Joris, he recalled; she reminded him of his grandmother, long gone. "I can only afford to play the red-eyes," she said. "I sleep a few hours and get up early before work."

"Devotion." Seeing that the post parade had stalled—Time for Flatcakes had decided that sideways was the way to go—Kal gestured to the ground beside Joris. "May I?"

"Luxury seats, no waiting."

Kal's joints cracked as he sat, happy for relief from the brothers' frenetic pace.

"Kick your shoes off," she said, noticing his expression. "This isn't the elite balcony at this hour."

He did exactly as she said. Dress shoes doffed, he sat back and let his stocking feet rub against the softest grass he'd ever touched with his hands. "Kaljach Sonmi," he said. "My friends and I need a sure bet."

"Let me guess. You need to double up by sunrise."

"Actually, closer to a factor of twenty." He smiled weakly. "Is that possible?"

"Oh, I double up three times a day." Joris rolled her eyes at him. "You work the comedy club here?"

"Look, I'm not insane. I know probabilities, and that systems only work over the long term. But I'm guessing you know nuances to this game that would take fifty years—"

"Watch it."

"—for *anyone else* to learn," he said, rescuing himself. "People like you make their money off people like me."

"Not nearly enough," she said, drinking from her tumbler.

Thodi looked back and said tartly, "If you know so much, I'd think you'd be rich."

"I make enough to keep coming back," she said. "What would I do if I hit big? I'm already in Canto Bight."

Kal nodded with recognition. He respected grinders with longevity, whatever the game. "I'm just asking—begging—you to tell me *anything.* Because my friends are likely to bet because they like the color of the jockey's hat, and at the stakes I need I'd feel a lot more comfortable knowing something."

She studied him, trying to decide what to make of him. "Hats aren't the worst system I've heard of."

At the railing, Thodi slapped Dodi's arm. "Hear that? I told you I was right!"

Kal's breath quickened. "This race, which one do you like?"

She clicked her tongue. "None of them."

"None?"

"That's why I'm keeping such a laser focus on the parade, dear." She waved dismissively. "These are claimers."

Kal had heard the term. "What's that?"

She snickered. "Sure you aren't just off the shuttle?"

"Three years in the card room and a death mark in three hours," he said with a straight face. "Claimers?"

She seemed to decide he was entertaining. "Okay," she said, passing him one of her datapads. Kal beckoned for the brothers to gather behind him.

"I don't want to get grass on my trousers," Wodi said.

"You were in the fountain earlier," Kal said. "Get over here."

"What's all that stuff?" Dodi asked, kneeling with the others to peer over Kal's shoulder.

"It's research," Thodi said, sniffing with disdain. "*Some* people trust it."

Dodi nodded vigorously. "Oh, yes. It's what the bigwigs do."

"Ah," Wodi said. "How big are our wigs?"

The screen was filled with numbers and letters Kal was familiar with—but not in any combination that looked like a rational language to him. "You were saying, Joris?"

"See that icon by the race number? This is a claiming race, which means the fathier can be bought before the race starts."

"Bought?" Kal asked. "By whom?"

"By anyone who meets the posted price. I think this one's forty thousand."

"How interesting!" Dodi said. He turned to his brothers. "Hear that?"

Kal was confused. "I don't get it. What's the idea?"

"It keeps the owners from putting really good animals in the race," Joris said. "If a fathier is truly better than the ones it's classed with, someone will recognize that and buy it out from under them."

Kal nodded. "It makes sure everything's even."

"At this hour, it makes sure everything's junk. How much faith can you have in an animal you'd be willing to lose? But forty thousand Cantocoins and you're an owner."

Kal pored over the racing form—and looked at the live odds updates. "These odds are mostly the same."

"That's a sign that nobody betting knows anything," Joris said. "The smart money doesn't know where to go. Fathier racing is parimutuel—"

Behind Kal, Thodi and Wodi rose and walked away, while Dodi yawned loudly.

"Simpler," Kal said.

"Usually I sit here trying to find the best value. A fathier that's better than its odds," Joris said. She glanced at one of her devices. "But the only consensus on this race is that your Number Three, who is currently holding up traffic out there by trying to lick the steward, is bound for life as a private citizen."

Ninety-nine to one. Kal scrolled past it. *No time for losers now.* "You don't see *anything*?"

Joris sighed and skimmed her screen. "I guess I'd play the Six."

Kal read the names beside the numbers—and couldn't believe his eyes. *"Vermilion."*

Dodi snapped awake. "Vermilion Six was our wild card!" He shook Kal's arm. "We *have* to bet it, Kal. It was lucky earlier."

"Lucky for you, not for me." He hated to even to consider it. "These odds to win don't pay much."

"I wouldn't bet it to win," Joris said. "To show, maybe. With a blaster to my head."

"Just a top-three finish?" The odds Kal saw disappointed him. "That pays even less." He returned her datapad. "Nothing better?"

"I'd be surprised if any of these things completes the oval without needing the track coroner." Joris began collecting her gear. "Now, if you'll excuse me, I need some more caf. I still have to work this morning."

This morning. The words were a punch in his empty gut. Kal had known the track was a mistake. Too long between races—and as a purely mathematical matter, there was nothing he could bet on that would give him the odds he needed.

Joris stood, and he and Dodi rose to thank her. Kal started looking for his shoes on the grass when he noticed something else.

"Wait a second," he said, feeling for his belt. "Where's my pouch?" He looked down. His shoes were there, but nothing else.

"Lose something?" Joris asked. She'd been sitting on his right; the pouch had been on his left hip.

"My money."

"Most people say that *after* they bet."

Kal stooped over and looked around on the ground. Nothing.

"*We have a change,*" blared the public address system, "*regarding the Number Three in the thirteenth.*"

"That will be them scratching your Flatcakes friend," Joris said, "on grounds of causing offense to the great sport of fathier racing."

"*Time for Flatcakes, sired by Kreegah, has just been purchased from the Blumba Stables and Genetic Research Corporation.*"

"Wait a minute," Kal said, looking one direction after another while the announcer paused. "Dodi, where are your brothers?"

The announcer paused. "*New owner: Kaljach Sonmi!*"

KAL SPRINTED ALL THE WAY INTO THE CLUBHOUSE BEFORE HE REALIZED his money wasn't the only thing he was missing.

"Sir, where are your shoes?" asked the female Ithorian behind the information desk. "I hesitate to ask, but even at this hour, there are certain expectations—"

"Do *you* wear shoes?"

The hammer-headed creature was taken aback. "Uh . . . no. I can't."

Kal spun and began pointing around the betting hall. "Look at all the people here that don't wear shoes. You're not the only one."

"I see your point, sir."

"Then skip the dress code and tell me why they just called my name over the public address system!"

"Was . . . it about lost shoes?" she asked tentatively.

"They said I bought a fathier!"

"Congratulations, sir. It's a wonderful sport. I'm sure you'll enjoy—"

He let loose an anguished wail that both silenced and unnerved the attendant.

"Kal, are you all right?" Dodi called out.

Kal looked to his left and saw that Dodi was standing at a betting window. "Can you stop for even a moment?" Kal called out. "That's not the information desk!"

Looking guilty, Dodi pocketed something and joined Kal. "No need to shout."

Now they start worrying about disrupting things? Kal looked away to hide his expression—and saw Thodi and Wodi enter from down a staircase. Wodi bubbled with glee. "Did you hear, Kal?"

"I heard. I heard!" He stepped in front of the pair. "Why did you do it?"

"What?" Wodi said.

"The fathier! You stole my money and bought the fathier with it."

Thodi and Wodi looked at each other. Both seemed baffled. "We didn't steal anything, Kal," Thodi said. He passed Kal his empty pouch—and a sheet of flimsiplast. "Here's your title and receipt, see?"

Kal stared at it, seeing but not understanding.

"We did what you wanted," Wodi said.

"What are you talking about?"

"You said 'I want Flatcakes,'" Thodi said. "That lady had said we could buy him. Wodi suggested we could help you out."

"I—" Kal went slack-jawed. "I said I wanted flatcakes, *the food*!"

Thodi looked at Wodi. "How were we to know that?" Thodi asked.

"I don't think you can get flatcakes at this hour," Wodi said. "I've tried."

"Kal," Dodi offered, "maybe you could have been more specific,"

"Specific?" Kal grabbed the sides of his head. "Why should I need to tell people I don't want to buy a fathier?" He looked at the document. ALL SALES FINAL, it read. "Did you at least get any change?"

Thodi smiled. "You had exactly the right amount. They even waived the licensing fee. They seem to do these quick transactions all the time."

Lucky me, Kal thought.

Dodi tugged at his sleeve. "Don't you see?" he said. "You don't need any money now. You don't have to bet. When Time for Flatcakes wins, his owner wins the purse." He pointed to a display. "For the thirteenth, it's *four hundred thousand*. Imagine winning that!"

For a heartbeat, Kal did—before remembering which fathier it was that he now owned. Kal put his arm around Dodi's shoulder and directed him to the other side of the display, where the betting line was.

"He's ninety-nine to one, Dodi. There is no 'when he wins.' It's just going to be me, broke, and owning a half-blind fathier!"

Dodi seemed to reach some realization—and then he looked to his brothers. "We need to fix this, fellows."

Thodi shrugged—and Wodi wore a blank expression, still not understanding he'd done anything wrong. "What do you want us to do?"

"And they're in the paddock, saddling up at last for the thirteenth," the announcer said. *"Ten minutes to post time. Place your bets."*

Kal stayed focused on the display with the line—and closed his eyes to think for a moment. When he opened them, he addressed the others. "Bet him."

Dodi looked at him puzzled. "Bet who?"

"Bet the Three. Bet Time for Flatcakes—with your own money," Kal said emphatically. "Bet the daylights out of him."

Dodi's eyes narrowed. "Right." He headed to the betting window he'd been at before.

Thodi and Wodi quickly joined him, the latter looking more confused than usual. "Kal, you just said he couldn't win."

"But he will win, because you're betting on him. You're the Lucky Three!"

Thodi's brow furrowed, and he crossed his arms. "I don't mind you betting what we bet, Kal, but we don't give loans. That's not how Mother raised us."

"I'd never argue with your mother." Amid his ongoing panic, Kal had made a calculation. He didn't need to bet so long as Time for Flatcakes won. And if the Lucky Three were fully behind the fathier, it was like rolling funny dice—with no Jedi Knight around to stare him down.

Kal stepped back and watched the big display—where he saw the Number Three's odds change rapidly, improving from ninety-nine to one to eighty, then fifty, then finally thirty-three to one.

The Suertons hurried to his side, each holding fistfuls of transparent flimsiplast bet vouchers in their hands. "We did it, Kal!" Wodi said.

Kal was still dazzled by the board. Time for Flatcakes remained a long shot, but their bets had caused the odds of the rest of the field to worsen, with no clear favorite evident. "Just how much did you put down?

"A lot," Thodi said. "Most of what we've won today."

"I bet him in every combination they let me," Wodi said. "Exacta, perfecta, superfecta, pluperfecta, hyperfecta!"

"I don't think some of those are things, Wodi," Thodi said.

"It was enough," Dodi said. "More than enough. You're behind the fathier, Kal, and we're behind you."

Kal exhaled—and breathed normally for the first time in a while. He'd struggled with his doubts, but now he was all in on the brothers' luck. He didn't know how to feel—and it was exhilarating.

"Five minutes to post."

"Let's go!"

Kal and the brothers hurried through the parlor toward the grandstand. Along the way, he saw Joris standing nearby with her freshly filled tumbler, gawking at the changes on her datapad. "What fool put all the action on the Number Three?"

"They're not fools," Kal said as he and the trio rushed by. "They're my friends." He looked back at her and winked. "And I'm the fathier's owner!"

He didn't wait to see her reaction.

THE WIRE | 12

THE SECOND KAL STEPPED OUT FROM THE CLUBHOUSE LEVEL ONTO THE grandstand, the attendant he'd spoken with earlier appeared beside him.

"If this is about the shoes, I'll find them after the race."

"Oh, no," the Ithorian said. She pointed up and to the left. "Master Sonmi, you're entitled to view the race from the owners' boxes."

Dodi looked to him. "My brothers like to watch from the bottom row. Do you want me with you?"

"No!" Kal burst out. Then, more calmly, "No, you should be with your brothers." If his theory—if you could even have a theory about luck—still held, the three of them together would be for the best. "Root for Flatcakes."

Dodi waved and followed his kin down the steps, while Kal turned and began ascending. He'd gone only a few meters when someone rose to greet him.

"Sounds like you've been busy," Orisha Okum said. She looked awake, even for this hour—and was newly dressed in a sharp red cloak and boots, with a beret over her pulled-back hair. "I heard the announcement. You *bought* a fathier?" She laughed.

"You'll laugh harder when you find out which one."

"I was sent here to escort you somewhere, but you're going that direction anyway. The box we want is all the way at the end." She looked down at his feet. "Did you lose your shoes?"

"Life's a party."

The box was at the far upper left corner of the loge, beyond which there was a break in the grandstand for vehicle and equipment entry. Scaling the steps along the wall, he saw workers over the side, toiling in a line of maintenance pits far below. Huge cables ran in and out of the chasms. When races ran nonstop, maintenance at this hour seemed the least intrusive.

Kal gulped as he reached the box and its open gate. He didn't expect that Big Sturg Ganna would be watching from any kind of seats at this deathly hour, but nothing surprised him anymore.

"Good evening, Master Sonmi," called out a voice with a refined accent. "Please join us."

Kal stepped through the aperture and saw two rows of seats in the box. At the bottom sat his two Wookiee watchers from earlier. Behind them, alone, sat a white-haired Nimbanel in a business suit. When Kal entered, the whisker-faced creature put down the datapad he was figuring on and rose. "Greetings. I am Mosep Binneed. We spoke when our association began."

"The accountant. I remember," Kal said, gulping. "I didn't know you worked for Ganna then."

"Over the last decades I have worked for many illustrious figures. Their money is as good as anyone else's. Please sit," he said, gesturing to an empty seat between the Wookiees. Kal shuddered as he complied.

The clamorous call to the post sounded—and Mosep looked to Orisha. "Thank you, my dear. It's possible we may not need you anymore today, but please remain at the Canto Casino."

She nodded. "Goodbye, Kal." She departed.

The Nimbanel spoke over Kal's shoulder. "My contact in the surveillance office tells me you've been busy trying to meet your obligations—if a little late." Mosep gestured to the field, where Kal saw the fathiers entering the gate. "And now you own a fathier." He chuckled. "Such a peculiar act. I see quite a lot of late money has come in—I suspect you're responsible for that, too. Your odd friends have some inside information, I suppose."

"It happens."

"It certainly does. But this is not the sort of gamble I was looking for in investing in your talent—and unlike the Suertons, I do not believe in luck." He nodded to the Wookiees, who frisked Kal. All he had was the contract for Time for Flatcakes's purchase. "Nothing. Tsk, tsk."

A bell clanged below, and nine fathiers responded by bursting from the gate. It took three full seconds for the tenth to emerge, in no particular hurry.

"My eyes aren't what they used to be," Mosep said, handing Kal a pair of macrobinoculars. "Would you care to identify that sad straggler for me?"

Kal knew before he brought the animal and rider into focus. "Come on, Three," he mumbled under his breath, referring to the brothers as much as to the fathier. It looked hopeless.

"Councilor Ganna does not make bad investments—nor does he invest in those who do so themselves," Mosep said. "The losses stop here."

Kal shook as he watched the fathiers go around the near turn. Training the device closer, he saw the Lucky Three, their backs to him on the bottom row of the stands, cheering wildly—and futilely—for their miserable choice. "You . . . you gave me until sunrise," Kal said, shaking as he held the macrobinoculars.

"I'm always on the lookout for opportunities," Mosep said. He rose and leaned to look over the side into the maintenance pit. "I think this might be an excellent place for a suicide, ladies, don't you think?"

The Wookiees growled in agreement.

"A gambler loses everything and ends it all," Mosep said, sitting back down. "It happens here often, as you know. Quite a few are former mistakes of mine—but the other gamers we handle know what really happened. You're an expensive example, Master Sonmi, but at least we'll get that from you."

The fathiers were on the backstretch. Kal's pulse quickened, and his hands tightened on the forward railing of the box. It was too high to vault, and there was no way past the Wookiees. His thought was to scream—but up here, and with all the attention on the track, it would have been pointless.

"Let's not introduce delay, sir," he heard Mosep say. "I'm up earlier than usual for you, and have a full schedule. Whenever you're ready, ladies."

Kal clung to the railing, his eyes darting among the pack, the far-trailing Time for Flatcakes, and the Lucky Three. The Suertons seemed more excited than ever, apparently not in the least concerned about their flagging choice.

And then, just as the Wookiees behind Kal stood, something happened. Kal released the railing and raised the macrobinoculars—

—and watched as Wodi, in a frenzy of cheering, spread his arms wide, accidentally smacking an exotic beverage from the hand of a nearby spectator. The spraying liquid struck the long smoking implement held casually by a fashionable tentacle-headed Nautolan and continued to fall, now ignited. It landed on the hem of her colossal hoop-skirted dress, setting it on fire.

The woman ran screaming up the staircase, untouched by flames herself but her trailing skirt ablaze. Upon reaching a landing, she thought long enough to step out of the skirt, which she then unwisely threw over the side of the grandstand—into, Kal saw, one of the maintenance pits. The burning garment was out of sight for only a moment when workers quickly piled out like rodents fleeing a hole. A fiery flash so bright Kal had to put down the macrobinoculars was followed by a muffled explosion, with sparking energy crackling up along the heavy wire leading from the pit. There followed a much louder symphony of bangs, as the soaring light fixtures around the near and far turns each burned brightly for an instant before exploding.

Jarred by the noise and sights, the fathiers on the far turn stopped in the near darkness, illuminated only by the lights from the clubhouse. Jockeys struggled to retain control of their animals, most of which cowered in place; some ran backward. Another jumped the infield fence. Only one creature kept moving in the right direction: the one too deaf to hear the blasts and who knew how to do only one thing, run in a circle when he couldn't see anything.

And as the Wookiees took hold of Kal's arms, the announcer's voice boomed, *"And the winner is Time for Flatcakes!"*

When the emergency lighting came up, Kal looked down to see the Nautolan woman, unharmed, being consoled by track personnel—and the Lucky Three, below, beside themselves in their cheering. Three fathiers ultimately recovered and finished; the Six, Vermilion, finished fourth out of four. *Called that one,* Kal thought.

The distracted Wookiees, finally remembering their orders, strengthened their hold on him. "Stop!" Kal shouted. "Didn't you hear? I just won!"

"A moment, ladies," Mosep ordered. The titans released Kal while their boss looked down at the stewards flooding the track. Mosep frowned. "They'll declare this race null for sure."

"They won't," Kal said, confidence returning. "I told you when we first met. You'll get your money back." His eyes focused on the still-functioning tote board display. The race had not gone final yet, locking in his win—but he had to believe it would.

"Amazing," Mosep said, reading from his device. "My contacts tell me the presiding steward who has the power to nullify races went to the medcenter earlier tonight." He raised a hairy eyebrow. "Apparently he was drinking before his shift and fell while trying to balance on a planter."

Kal's eyes widened. He had been there—with the Lucky Three.

Mosep rose. "I'm told the race will likely go final and bets will be paid. I don't believe in luck, my friend, but you seem to have found some. Will you earn back my eight hundred thousand?"

Kal hadn't bet anything, but knew the purse would get him halfway there. "I'll be close."

"Close is not enough. I want every coin—and by sunrise, as agreed. You have three hours, by my calculations." He opened the gate to the box and looked back. "If you don't think that's possible, of course, I would be happy to take what you have."

"But you'd still kill me."

"My accounts *always* balance, Master Sonmi. Farewell." The Wookiees followed him out.

THE BREAKDOWN | 13

BY THE TIME KAL REACHED THE CLUBHOUSE LEVEL, THE TRACK LIGHTING was well on its way to being fully restored—another testament to the efficiency that ruled Canto Bight. The Lucky Three were already inside, celebrating.

"Did you see him?" Wodi asked, nearly stepping on Kal's shoeless foot as he enveloped him in a warm embrace. "Our big pal did it!"

"*You* did it," Kal said.

"Did what?"

"Never mind." It didn't surprise Kal that Wodi was oblivious to his role in events. Kal was just glad to have won. Overjoyed, in fact. Enough that he shared a similar hug with Thodi, whose self-assured imagined expertise had made him the hardest for Kal to like.

"Slowest time ever for this distance," Thodi said. "If only there'd been a way to bet that!"

"You sure bet everything else."

The boys had their vouchers out and waiting, but the race displays in the clubhouse remained blank. Outside, preparations were under way for the final race of the red-eye card—yet the thirteenth remained under review.

Kal calmed their nerves for a change. "Guys, I heard back in the box from someone who knows. The race will be official."

Dodi smiled—and then his expression grew a shade more serious. "I thought I saw you up there with some strange people. Is everything all right?"

"It's fine." He didn't know what Dodi thought he'd seen, but Kal's mood was the best it had been all day. When a waiter passed with a tray of drinks, the four seized upon glasses and toasted their victory. *"Time for Flatcakes!"*

From behind, a familiar voice. "You're back!"

Kal turned to see Joris, who had just left the betting window with her voucher for the final race. "Hey," he said with delight. "My guru!"

The brothers cheered her. She shook her head, bewildered. "In all my years, I've never seen anything like that."

"You should have bet him," Thodi said. "We'll win big."

"Don't spend it until it's on the tote." Still, she chuckled. "How much did you have riding on it?"

"Them, lots," Kal said. "Me, nothing. But it doesn't matter. I win the purse." Kal grinned. He only needed to double up again—and with the brothers on his side, that seemed possible. He'd get out of debt and get his life back, with new shoes for every day of the week. "What coins do they use to pay out four hundred thousand?"

Joris looked at him with horror. She shook her head. "Oh, sweetie, you don't know, do you?"

"What?"

"Didn't you look at your contract?"

Kal barely remembered it. He put down his drink and found it, from where one of the Wookiees had shoved it into his pocket. At first glance, it was a lot of legal folderol. On second glance, too.

"You don't have to look. Everyone who plays knows," she said, putting her hand on his. "One of the basic rules of claiming races. You can buy the fathier—but the previous owner gets any earnings from the race."

Kal's mouth went dry. "What? Why?"

"Because it's not a livestock auction." She pointed outside, where the fathiers for the final race were parading. "The owners pay to train these animals for a race. They get anything the fathier earns from it. Buyers start earning on the animal's *next* race."

No. Kal's shoulders sank. "That . . . won't be before sunrise, will it?"

"No, baby."

Kal thought back. Surely Mosep must have understood he wouldn't receive the purse, which was why he'd called the purchase peculiar. But he'd assumed Kal had also bet money on the fathier, which is why he'd let the card player go, not knowing all he had was title to the animal.

"On the bright side," Joris said as she released his hand, "your friends will still make out." She folded the voucher she'd gotten and put it into her bag. "I'll have to cash this tomorrow, if I win. I'll see you sometime, maybe."

The quartet nodded to her as she departed.

For several moments, nobody said anything. Kal had faced death mere minutes earlier, only to be saved—and now his world was falling apart again. Worse—it had already collapsed. He'd never had a chance.

Fire filled his eyes as he looked at the contract. Crumpling it in his hands, he turned on the brothers. "You see? You see? You actually have to know . . . *stuff*!"

"Hey," Thodi said, "I think we did pretty well."

"*You* did well. I win nothing." Kal threw the balled-up contract at Thodi's and Wodi's feet. "Did you hear Joris? You idiots spent all my money on a fathier that won a purse for someone else!"

Wodi stepped back, a little wounded. "How were we supposed to know any of that?"

"The way anybody knows," Kal said, uncaring that he was creating a scene. "Smart people don't just plop thousands down and hope. Smart people learn the ins and the outs of the game. This is why I didn't want to come here. I'm a card player!"

"Didn't help you much yesterday," Thodi said.

"Thodi, back off." He jabbed a finger at him. "You're the worst. You think you know what you're doing, but everything you know about every game is completely wrong." Kal got in Thodi's face. "Dice do not remember what they landed on before. Slot machines do not hit better if you rub the coin in your hands before putting it in. Jubilee wheels do not favor certain colors because of the redshift effect. And there is no benefit in zinbiddle in sitting at the table in alphabetical order!"

Thodi's upper lip trembled. "Well, I'm not giving *you* a loan."

"You weren't going to before!" Kal stepped back—and saw Dodi watching him in stunned silence. He felt he could not stop, especially when he saw the winning vouchers stuffed in their hands. "I've worked my whole life learning to forget superstition, forget luck. You guys?" His hands shook in the air—and then he shook his head. "You're amazing."

He turned away and looked down, feeling drained. He was ashamed of what he'd said, but it had also been there, simmering. He shook his head. "I've actually had a good time with you guys tonight," he admitted. "But I'm broke—and that means I'm dead."

Silence for a moment, and then another announcement: "*Kaljach Sonmi to the trackside stable, please.*"

He looked around, confused. He appealed to the information clerk. "Do you know what this is about?"

"No, sir," she said. "But I can lead you there."

He looked at the brothers. "I guess I've got to go."

"Yeah," Thodi said. "Guess you do." He turned and walked away—as did Wodi, without a word. Dodi simply watched Kal go.

When Dodi found Kal again, it was twenty minutes later, in one of the stalls in the veterinary facility off the trackside stable. The Heptooinian barely noticed his arrival. His attention was on Time for Flatcakes, whose head rested on his lap as Kal sat on the straw-covered floor.

"He died as soon as he got off the track," Kal said, stroking the pale spot on the fathier's head. "He gave it all he had."

"I know," Dodi said, approaching from outside the pen.

"I suppose you heard."

"Yes, they put the report out when they took the race final," Dodi said. "The track vet said he'd been getting injections of an illegal performance enhancer by his previous owner."

"And he nearly came in last anyway," Kal said, shaking his head. The drug plus the effort had caused the fathier to expire. "Poor guy." He looked back. "Who else is poor?"

"Well, we lost everything," Dodi said. "Flatcakes was disqualified, so the other three finishers wound up one-two-three."

Kal considered the news and shook his head. "So Vermilion wound up third after all, like Joris said."

"That's true." Dodi looked over the short wall into the pen at him. "Back there in the clubhouse, Kal—that was bad."

"I know. I'm sorry."

Dodi shook his head. "That's how you were when we met you yesterday. I thought you'd relaxed since then."

"How can I relax?" Kal eased out from under the corpse's head and started brushing the straw off his clothes. "You don't understand, Dodi. That was all my money!"

"I gathered that. But you'll get more."

Kal stood and stared at Dodi. "How?"

"What do you mean, how? You'll just get more—like we will."

"When? From where?"

Dodi shook his head, befuddled. "Where everybody gets it."

"I'm not you, Dodi." He gestured to his feet, his socks now ragged and covered with debris. "I don't walk everywhere on a cushion of gold dust!"

Dodi shrugged. "You *could.*"

"I can't. I get blisters, Dodi. So does everyone else who doesn't have your luck. You don't know where it comes from—and you don't care." Kal shook his head. "I'm not sure I could accept getting everything in life handed to me like that."

Dodi took a deep breath—and turned away. He had only gotten a few steps when he returned. "I almost forgot," he said, lifting something into the pen. "On the way over here, I found your shoes."

Expressionless, Kal took them. "Lucky they were still there, I guess."

"Good night, Kal. It's been fun . . . mostly."

THE SURRENDER | 14

NOTHING IN THE CASINO EVER CLOSED, BUT FOURTEEN HOURS WITHOUT a break was, finally, enough for Ganzer. Kal sat on a couch behind a darkened table and watched as the bartender emerged from the Grotto's back room, carrying his folded vest over his arm.

"You look beat," Kal said.

"That makes you my mirror image—if you were older, uglier, and had more hair in the wrong places." Ganzer produced a protein bar from his shirt pocket. "You want half of this?"

"Keep it. You're still on for a couple of hours."

"But you're done." Ganzer watched as Kal removed his shoes and placed them on the cushion beside him. "Sure hope nothing from the track is stuck to those."

"They were never *on* at the track," Kal said. He closed his eyes and stretched.

When he opened them, he saw that Ganzer had pulled up a chair to sit across from him. "Orbital failure around Lucky Three, I take it?"

"Crash and burn." Kal shook his head. "You're looking at the wreckage."

"I'm guessing there's a reason you had to win all this money tonight."

"The usual one."

"Sorry to hear that," Ganzer said. Kal had never told Ganzer about his debts, but the bartender didn't seem surprised. "Is there anything I can do?" he asked.

"No. But thanks." Kal looked at the table. "You know, it's funny. This is where Orisha Okum was sitting this evening."

Ganzer nodded. "I served her. Thought I saw you two talking. Quite the celebrity. Usually she stays near the high-roller rooms."

"She was here to see me," Kal said. "She was the one that passed along that Ganna had called in my debts."

The news flabbergasted Ganzer. "*Orisha Okum*—working for Ganna?" He shook his head. "I've never heard anything like that."

"But you've seen her here before."

"Usually talking with players."

"And have you ever seen those players again?" Kal gestured wearily. "Maybe that's why you've never heard anything about her being mixed up in anything."

"You astound me," Ganzer said. "Surely, that knowledge could—"

"Save me? Who'd believe me?" Kal pointed up and around. "She does her meets here, away from the surveillance cams. She knows what she's doing."

Ganzer nodded in reluctant agreement. Then he opened his protein bar and chewed slowly.

Kal looked at him. "Ganz, when was the first time you went to a casino?"

Ganzer chortled, nearly choking. "Back before the Empire," he said when he recovered. "I was younger then, for sure. Governments fall, but I stick around."

"I was nineteen," Kal said, the fingers of his hand idly tracing patterns on the table. "Planet I grew up on was run by the Empire—and after they went, the Hutts came in. Name the problem, we had it. I had to get out of there."

Kal's eyes took on a faraway look. "The first time I went offworld, there was a casino in the spaceport. And I saw people there—all different species, all walks of life. People who wouldn't help one another if they were on fire. But at the tables, they were cheering one another on. Someone would hit—anyone—and *everyone* would be happy, because someone was beating the odds. And for that moment, everyone was equal. Everyone had the same chance."

"Yeah, but money buys you more chances," Ganzer said, crumpling his wrapper. "That's not equal."

"I know—now. Maybe I knew then. But in the moment, it was . . . well, *magical.*"

Ganzer nodded. "They do like you to think that." He gestured around. "The lights, the sounds, the music—it's all about the moment."

"Until it's over."

"Everything ends. What's important is that you enjoyed the ride."

"And that's the thing," Kal said. "Even with my neck on the line and time running out, I had a better time with those guys tonight than I've had in—well, I can't remember. Yet even so, there was something nagging at me the whole time. I felt guilty, because I felt like I should know better."

Ganzer pointed at him. "You've devoted your life to killing the magic."

"Statistics. Strategies. Anything that would limit risk, minimize doubt. Dissecting every moment, before it happens." He stared at Ganzer. "You know I don't even remember the games after I've played them? Sure, I remember the cards, the bets, and how they paid. But I couldn't tell you what I was feeling when I won or lost."

Ganzer chuckled. "I bet you remember losing the progressive earlier today."

"Yesterday, you mean." Kal rubbed his eyes. "Yeah, I sure do. The Three, though—they're happy even *when* they're losing. They can afford to lose—and they know they'll win again. So they enjoy the ride and don't care when they crash. I've never felt that. I've just felt . . . *desperation.*"

"I think," Ganzer said, running his fingers through his whiskers, "you don't want to win so you can be rich. You just want to be able to enjoy the game."

"I met someone like that at the track tonight."

Ganzer put his hand on the table. "That's it. Listen, why'd you take the job as a prop player?"

"So I could work on my systems—"

"So you could get *paid to play.* You've been playing with someone else's money—every gambler's dream! How is it that you've never been happy?"

"Because I've cared so much about whether or not I win."

"And instead of limiting yourself to betting what Canto paid you each week, you dug yourself a hole."

"A hole Ganna wants to put me in."

"But why? Where were you trying to get to?" Ganzer smiled. "If you were looking for paradise, pal, I've got news for you."

"I'm here," Kal said, preempting him. He'd never really thought about it—but now he nodded. "I liked it here. I liked my suit. I liked looking like I belong." He put his hands together before his chin. "I love Canto Bight."

"Then find a way to stay alive. And then find a way to stay."

Kal rubbed his tired eyes. It was the goal, all right, and always had been. But he didn't know how he would manage it with only an hour and a half until dawn. He reached for his shoes.

"Wait," Kal said, fishing around inside the left shoe. "Something's in here." He shook it—and something small fell out onto the table.

Ganzer's eyes widened with recognition as he picked up the slip. "Why, it's a fathier bet. From tonight, it looks like." He peered closely at it. "The number six in the thirteenth?"

Kal reached for it, eyes wide. "*Vermilion,*" he said. "The Six."

Ganzer looked up at him. "It's to show. Third place."

"And she came in third." Kal laughed giddily.

"What?"

"Don't you see? I lost the progressive yesterday because the Vermilion Six was in front of the shoe. And now—"

"Vermilion, the Six, is in front of your shoe!" Ganzer smiled broadly. "Who put it there?"

Kal thought. "Dodi. He mentioned the card while we were at the track, and wanting to bet her. And then I saw him placing a bet later—but Flatcakes's odds didn't go down. He must have been betting on Vermilion. And when he brought me my shoes—"

"—he left you a gift." Ganzer beamed as Kal donned his shoes and stood. "It's not a big bet," he said, handing Kal the ticket. "What did it pay?"

"Not what I need it to. But I can take it from here."

THE FREEROLL | 15

". . . PLAYING WITH SOMEONE ELSE'S MONEY—EVERY GAMBLER'S DREAM!"

Ganzer had said it—and now, after a year and a half as a proposition player, Kal was in the position of doing it again, in what might possibly be the last hour of his life.

He'd risked his poor feet on a breakneck run back to the track, where he'd cashed the Vermilion bet. Dodi hadn't bet much compared with what he'd dropped on Time for Flatcakes. The payout was just a hundred Cantocoins—exactly what Kal had gotten by betting with Dodi on hazard toss at the beginning of the evening. He didn't know if it was a wink from Dodi or not—how could he have known how much betting Vermilion would pay? Whatever, it felt like another of the mathematical curiosities that followed the Suertons.

They were nowhere about this time, though. Any magic would purely have to be his own. He hurried through the casino, looking for anything at that predawn hour that might save him. He passed up game after game. Dice, the wheel, slots: These were not the things he knew, any more than he knew fathier racing. He wouldn't go down seeking a lucky break on a game he didn't know. He'd need a lucky break on a game he *did* know, and that took him to the place he had spent so much time: the card room.

It was only a quarter full at this hour. There was no time to consider Savareen whist or his late ex-love, zinbiddle. No, only his first love would do: an easy game he'd learned as a child and savored as an adult. In the wing devoted to it, he saw several indefatigable players amid matches—and nearby, the equally tireless Vestry proctoring trainee dealers.

"This is pazaak." Her back to Kal, Vestry gestured to rows of two-person tables. "It's a classic from the days of the Old Republic. Easy to learn, hard to master. At this hour, the Canto Casino deals no cards and takes no rake in these hundred-coin minimum pickup games, but you may be asked to assist in high-stakes contests."

As Kal searched fruitlessly for any player without an opponent, Vestry brought the dealers before an active game and continued. "Each player takes turns drawing from a common table deck whose cards are numbered one through ten. The object is to reach twenty without going over."

Minn, apparently back bright and too-early after her rough first outing, pointed to the cards in each player's hand. "The cards they're holding are different. What's that about?"

"Each player may bring a side deck," Vestry said. "Specialty cards permitted by the rules and available on the open market. For every card drawn from the main deck, the player may use one of these side cards. Most alter the total: plus one, minus five, and so on. Others offer a choice of plus or minus—and there are cards still more rare."

Kal had worked on his side deck for years, and it was a marvel. Not good enough to beat an Orisha Okum, surely, but it might help him now.

How many times will I have to double up to hit eight hundred thousand? Kal did some quick calculating and swallowed hard when he figured the result: thirteen times. He was contemplating that figure when Vestry noticed him.

"Master Sonmi, I don't care for loitering now any more than I did last night."

"I agree," Kal said, finally spotting an empty seat across from a Rodian. "I'm here to play." He plopped his hundred-Cantocoin bet on the table.

"Welcome," said the snout-faced creature, more glassy-eyed than normal from drink and time of day. "No matches at this hour, just single hands to win. Side hand refreshes each time."

"I love it." He didn't have time for more. He reached for his side deck—

—only to remember it was back in his coat. The one he had surrendered to the administrative office the day before.

Oops.

His opponent chose his own hand of side cards and shuffled the table deck. "Hold on," Kal said. "I don't have my side deck."

"—and while the player *can* go without a side deck, it is *very* foolish," Vestry lectured her students. "It puts the player *entirely* at fortune's feet." She turned and flashed him a tart look; she'd overheard him.

"Are we playing or not?" the Rodian asked.

Someone else's money, someone else's money, Kal told himself. "You know what? Deal."

The Rodian peeled from the table deck. "Eight." It was a good card.

Kal's was better. "Ten," he said.

"Nine," the Rodian said, "making seventeen." He played a blue card from his hand. "I add two for nineteen and stand."

Kal whistled—and did so again when another ten dropped. "Twenty. I win."

"Lucky."

"I hope so," Kal said, moving the pot onto his betting circle. "Two hundred this time."

The second game was messier, with more cards being drawn on both sides—but Kal found himself breathing easy. He had no decisions. He could only ride. After a night of wild ups and downs, some only moments apart, it felt good to let go of the reins and just play.

"I bust," the Rodian said.

"Again. Double or nothing." *Someone else's money, someone else's money.*

Two hundred had grown to four hundred—and when it became eight hundred, the Rodian called out to his companions at another table. "You have to see this," he said, not yet upset about his losses. Nor would he have any call to be, Kal thought: Playing against an opponent with no side cards would be an easy day for anyone. Eventually, Kal had to lose.

But not yet. "Sixteen hundred's the bet," Kal said after the fourth hand.

"Too much," the Rodian said.

His buddy, somewhat better dressed, took his seat—and the challenge. "Easy money."

A fifth win. The Rodian, a spectator now, asked, "Are you sure he's not cheating?"

"This is a square house," Vestry said, having overheard again. She suspended her lecture and called her students over. "It would take *some nerve*," she said, glaring at Kal, "to cheat before an audience of dealers."

Her attitude didn't alter Kal's mood at all. In fact, by the sixth win, he couldn't describe what he was feeling. Was this what it was like to be a Suerton, he wondered? Existing purely and completely free from the game, unafraid of losing and being pleasantly surprised at winning?

"I stand at sixteen," Kal said, having landed a horrid draw.

"Twenty-one. Blast it!"

Vestry watched, spellbound. "Is . . . this a new system?" she asked.

"Shh," Kal said. "Don't disturb the players."

The eighth win exhausted his opponent, and a new, wealthier one took his seat. It had become a challenge, a sideshow in a place made for them—the rare event able to gather a crowd at less than half an hour before dawn. "You got to see this," he heard someone say. "There's an idiot drawing blind, double-or-nothing—and winning!"

Not how I wanted to be known, but . . . "Twenty," he said, after the most peculiar run of cards he'd seen. He was above fifty thousand now, more than he'd had at his peak before the fathier races.

"Tournament table," Vestry said. "I want this under the lights."

Kal knew what she really meant: at a place where the surveillance cams were more numerous, to spot any funny business. Kal dutifully lifted his tray of coins and carried them through the card room, leader of a parade of spectators and dealers.

"Minn, deal for them," Vestry said as they arrived at the table, which offered more space for spectators. "And someone send for Master Ganzer, if he's still on shift. Our players may require refreshment."

Kal needed nothing—but another opponent, after the one he'd brought with him busted. "Player wins his tenth pot of a hundred and two thousand four hundred," Minn announced.

"But who's counting?" Kal said, nearly delirious.

"Do you know what the odds against this are?" a gawker asked.

"The same every hand," declared someone from behind Kal. He turned to see Orisha Okum approaching to a rumble of murmurs of her name. She'd changed clothes yet again, now in exquisitely tailored business wear—again, in her trademark red. She had a large satchel under her arm.

"The past doesn't matter, in hands or in life," she said, approaching the vacated seat. "This is my table, you know. I've won several events here. But if you're here to play, Kal, I'm game."

THE SHOWDOWN | 16

WHEN ORISHA SAT AT THE TOURNAMENT TABLE, MANY GASPED; WHEN she opened her satchel and placed coins matching Kal's stake on the playing surface, the ruckus swelled still further.

Kal studied her. "Why are you here?"

"You have an appointment in a few minutes," she said, casting a quick eye at Vestry. Orisha wasn't going to say more about her and Kal's private business in front of the floor manager. "I came to escort you to your meeting—but it seems you're preoccupied."

"No," Kal said, pointing to the table. "I mean what are you doing *here*?"

Stacking her coins, she nodded toward his mound of cash. "You're going to play and lose that. I can't stop you from playing—but I can determine what happens to the money." She drew forth from her jacket pocket a golden container that drew ahhs of its own. Snapping it open, she pulled out a side deck legendary in pazaak circles.

Kal stared at her. No, Mosep wouldn't want to see a deadbeat he was about to kill lose a hundred thousand to a random gambler. But something about the timing of her appearance seemed fishy.

"You're not playing for *yourself*, are you?"

She smiled at him primly. "It's been nice knowing you," she said, delicately choosing four cards from her side deck to form her hand. "Are you ready to play?"

"Not without a side deck!"

It was Dodi who'd called out. A path opened in the crowd for a new procession—this one consisting of the Lucky Three, with Ganzer bringing up the rear with a tray full of cocktails.

"Here's an eye-opener," Wodi said, grabbing one.

"And so is that," Thodi said, looking at the mountain of money. "I'm impressed."

"What's going on?" Kal asked. "I thought we were quits."

"Nonsense," Dodi said. "You were just quits with us."

"We never quits," Wodi added ungrammatically.

"And this," Thodi said, reaching for his pocket, "is for you." He handed Kal a small deck of cards bound by a green ribbon. "My special side deck. It's my best ever!"

"Hey, what is this?" Orisha appealed to Vestry. "He should play his own cards. Or non-cards."

Dodi placed a single coin on the table beside Kal. "I am—as he so put it earlier—a rider. Kal's fate is mine."

"Back bettors can't supply cards," Orisha said.

"He's not just a rider," Kal said. "He staked me." He looked back to Dodi. "I found the voucher."

Dodi grinned. "Vermilion, the Six, to show."

Orisha started gathering up her coins. "I'm not staying for this."

Kal put up his hands. "Wait a minute. If I show you the side deck, will you stay?"

She paused. "Maybe."

He pitched the small deck to her—and she undid the ribbon and started riffling through the cards. Red eyes widened with surprise—and a smirk appeared. "Okay," she said, putting them down. "Let's play."

Kal looked at her—and then the deck—with suspicion. He grabbed the cards and fanned them in front of him. Every card blue—and every card, the same awful denomination.

"They're all plus-sixes!" The pazaak players in the audience laughed.

Wodi tried to shush him. "Quiet, she'll find out!"

"She just saw them!" Kal felt his hard-won calm starting to slip away. Plus-sixes were the weakest pazaak side-deck cards, only really useful at scores of fourteen and sometimes thirteen. Kal looked to Thodi. "You didn't put in anything that reduced my count? Went both ways? *Was a smaller number?*"

"Then it would look like anyone else's side deck," Thodi said with disdain.

Kal leered at him—and then looked to Dodi, who patted his shoulder reassuringly. Kal took a deep breath and peeled off the top four cards for his side deck. "I'm stocked," he announced. "Let's play."

Orisha set herself up well, using her specialty cards to turn a busted twenty-two into a respectable nineteen. Kal, meanwhile, had drawn two sevens—which his side-deck card transformed into a winning twenty.

"See?" Thodi said. "I told you."

Orisha glared. Not at him but the Suertons. "I'm not sure I want them here."

Kal shrugged innocently. "Surely you don't want all these people to think the great Orisha Okum is superstitious."

She glowered at him—and brought over two hundred thousand in Cantocoins out of her seemingly bottomless satchel. "Again," she said, sorting through her side deck for different ammunition.

The next sequence for Kal was nerve racking. She kept hitting the board with one specialty card after another, transforming positive-number cards on both sides of the table to negative ones, and vice versa; basic arithmetic had seldom been so trying. She reached nineteen and stood, only to have him draw a two from the table deck, hopping over her to victory.

The crowd roared. Orisha stared first at Kal, and then the brothers. "People around here talk about you three, but I've never believed it."

"Do they say we're charming?" Thodi asked.

Orisha smoldered.

"Don't quit now," Kal said. Timepieces were forbidden in the casino, but he didn't need one. "I'm sure it's almost sunrise. Double or nothing for the whole bill," he added. Kal didn't want to face her again—but he doubted anyone else in the room would take a four-hundred-thousand bet, not at this hour. He gestured to his mountain of coinage. "You don't need to bring anything out. If I win, your associate gets this, and you pay the other half."

"Most of that is mine," Orisha said.

"*Was* yours."

She glared at him. "No," she said. She reached around the back of her neck and undid a chain. She pulled it, and a large locket, from beneath her jacket. She snapped the locket open and placed a shining coin on the table.

"That's half a million Cantocoins," she said. The audience swooned. "My prize from the last Savareen whist tournament."

"You just carry it around?"

"The things we love," she said, sorting through her side deck looking for cards. "I'll want change."

"Surely," Minn said, nervously counting out a hundred thousand from the pot to return to Orisha.

"You keep handling these big sums, Minn, and they'll move you to the high-roller room," Kal said.

Orisha took her first card. A five, which she doubled to a ten with a special card.

Ouch, Kal thought. She was halfway home before he played a card. "Wish me luck," he said to Dodi.

"I'm right behind you."

"Me too," Thodi said.

Kal waited for a moment—and hearing nothing from Wodi, looked around. "Oh, no. Where's Wodi?"

Dodi and Thodi looked at each other. "He was here a minute ago."

Kal put down his side deck and lifted his hands. "Things don't go well when it's just the two of you."

"One of us could go looking for him," Thodi said.

"And you'll probably buy me another fathier." He shook his head. *I'll just have to do this with the brothers I've got!*

"WHAT'S THE HOLDUP?" ORISHA DEMANDED.

"Nothing." Kal gestured for Minn to deal. She gave him a three, which he made a nine with one of Thodi's ubiquitous plus-sixes. He was an underdog now, behind ten to nine.

Minn dealt a three to Orisha, for thirteen. The champion thought long and hard before passing. That led to Kal drawing a four, also bringing him to thirteen.

"A perilous number," Thodi said, and was right for a change.

"Have to do it." Kal played a plus-six from his side deck and made nineteen. "I stand."

The audience rumbled with anticipation. A coy smile developing, Orisha motioned for Minn to deal.

"Four," said Minn. The crowd roared.

Vestry called for quiet. "Player is at seventeen. Will you alter the score?"

"Thanks for the game, Kal, but there are amateurs and there are champs." She raised a card from her hand. "And I am still the—"

"I'm back!" Wodi called, bursting from the crowd, plate in hand. "And I was right. They're serving flatcakes at the buffet!" Orisha stood frozen, card still in hand, as he intruded on her moment. "Where's that waiter with the drinks?"

"Here, sir," Ganzer said, appearing with his tray on Orisha's right. He started to pass behind her—only to find Wodi heading toward him at the same time. Wodi stubbed his foot at the back of Orisha's chair, making him lurch forward toward Ganzer. The two collided loudly, causing Ganzer's tray, assorted drinks, and some of the most delicious Trandoshani flatcakes and sautéed fruit in the known galaxy to go airborne. Liquor and foodstuffs raining on her, Orisha kicked her chair backward—and over, throwing her onto Wodi.

"Oh, dear," Vestry called. "Help her!"

Wodi grabbed Orisha's sleeve, trying to help her up. She wrested away. "Let go, moron!" She was covered with stains from the breakfast food—but seemingly more concerned about something else. She started reaching around on the floor. "Where did it go?"

"What?" Wodi asked.

She didn't answer, but continued her furtive search. Nearby, Ganzer pulled something from a puddle. "I have it," he said, lifting a soaked pazaak card.

Orisha spotted it. "Give me that," she demanded, but was still tangled with Wodi.

"It's all right," Ganzer said, rubbing the card with his fingers. "I can wipe it—"

He paused. Kal, mesmerized, asked, "What is it, Ganz?"

"I think you should see this," Ganzer said, beckoning to Vestry.

She took the card from him and studied it. A long, white thumb swept against the number on the card's face. A number that changed—from plus-three to plus-two to plus-one. "It's like a sabacc card," she said.

"A trick card," Ganzer said, forgetting his fallen drinks. "She can change its value to win the game!"

Orisha reached for it. "What do *you* know? You're just a waiter."

"Bartender," Ganzer said.

"Yes," Vestry acknowledged, "and one we allow to work the card room floor because he has long experience in spotting cheats and their devices." She shook her head. "You cannot use this card, Mistress Okum."

Orisha turned back to the table. "Then something else from my side deck."

"You can't bring a new card in. The game has started." Vestry's eyes narrowed. "And I wouldn't trust any other card you brought in."

"Then I refuse to continue," Orisha said, reaching for her card case. "This is a friendly game, not one managed by the casino. You're not refereeing, just hosting." She pointed at the pot. "I'll take my half back. And Kal," she said, looking daggers at him, "we'll see you shortly."

The room buzzed loudly with cross talk. But Kal only heard one word, from over his shoulder. "Play," Dodi said.

"What?"

"Let her play the card."

"Didn't you see it? She dials up a plus-three and wins!"

"I see a card that hasn't been played yet," Dodi said. "It's just a game."

"It's my life!"

"*Ride.*"

Orisha was halfway across the table, clawing for chips, when Kal spoke up. "She can play it," he said.

She glared at him. "What?"

"She can play it," Kal called out, getting Vestry's attention.

Vestry waved the trick card. "I told you, the card is illegal."

"It's a game between us. I can choose to accept the card," he said. He looked to Orisha, who was backing up, puzzled. "If I let you play the card, will you accept the result—before everyone here?"

Orisha looked about. Money had been on the line; now her career and credibility were in question. But as Kal knew, those already were. She straightened herself and brushed her clothing. "Yes, I'll accept it. And very sporting of you to reject this silly claim."

Ganzer stared at Kal. "Don't you understand? If she plays that card, you'll lose."

"I understand. It's my risk, my decision." He looked around to the Suerton trio. "It's only a game. Right?"

"*Right!*"

"All right," Vestry said, shaking her head and reluctantly surrendering the card to Orisha.

"Thank you," Orisha said, quickly taking the soggy card in her hand and dabbing at it in the way Vestry had demonstrated the card's value could be changed. Satisfied, she loomed over the table and spoke quickly, anxious to be done. "Kal stood at nineteen. To my seventeen, I add . . ." She slapped the card down and removed her hand. The card read:

+333

"Plus three thirty-three?" Orisha gawked at her own card. *"Plus three thirty-three?"*

Ganzer gawked, astonished. "The card must have malfunctioned after the spill!"

Minn stared at it. "That's not even a value in pazaak, is it?"

"It is not," Vestry said. "Which means the card is illegal."

"It already *was* illegal," Ganzer said. Smiling broadly, he pointed to Kal. "But he allowed it—and that makes it legal."

"That's—that's not right!" Orisha sputtered.

Vestry chuckled in spite of herself. "It's absolutely right." She slapped her hand on the table. "He allowed the card, you agreed to the result. Player busts with the unreal score of *three hundred fifty*!"

Never in Kal's recollection had there been such a clamor in the card room—and certainly not at this time of the morning. Orisha grabbed her satchel but abandoned her cards, fleeing into the crowd.

"Eight hundred thousand plus," Thodi said, shaking Kal's collar. "You did it!"

"Dealers," Vestry called out to her students over the din, "I don't want you to think this is a routine morning."

There's no chance of that! Kal looked to Wodi, who smiled goofily and raised an empty glass—and then to Dodi, who asked, "Having fun yet?"

Kal grinned. "Getting there."

"WELL, HELLO! LOOK WHO'S BACK," KAL SAID, LOOKING SMART IN HIS new cape and cravat as he stood next to the zinbiddle table. "It's Tezzie and Rooth."

"Master Sonmi! So nice to see you," bubbled blue-faced Tezzie, whom he now knew to be a construction heiress and grandmother of three.

"Thank you so much for your help this afternoon," said Rooth from the adjacent chair. He'd referred the tree-like woman, whose fortune was in fertilizer, to the spa. "Those mobility treatments were just what I needed."

"Working rather well, I'd say," he said, taking her branch in his hand. Her leaves fluttered in the Yarin equivalent of a blush. He looked to their companion, at Rooth's right. "And who is this lovely person?"

Tezzie tittered. "My sister, in from Pantora. I was hoping you could teach her pazaak like you taught us."

"Of course," Kal said. "I have a class after the first dinner serving tomorrow. And don't you worry about those reservations." He put a white-gloved finger to his temple. "It's all handled."

"He's so wonderful," Rooth said. "See you around the casino!"

"Good luck," Kal said as they returned to their game. He meant it.

Cantonica hadn't changed, but it was a different world for him now, and had been since the big game ended.

Mosep Binneed had appeared soon after the win, posing as just another businessman in the congratulatory crowd. His contacts with the casino's surveillance team were such that he already knew not only about Kal's big win, but also about Orisha's decision to play, potentially taking money for herself that should have gone to Ganna. The accountant accepted his eight hundred thousand and declared their business was at an end, returning the title to Kal's starship before departing.

As it turned out, his ship was, at that moment, already gone. Orisha, exposed as a cheat and ruined as a tournament player, had fled in it, using access codes she'd gotten from Mosep's office. If she couldn't win tournaments for Ganna, she wasn't of much use to him. Kal wondered how many of her millions were actually left, if she was trying to play Kal to enrich herself. Was she looking for getaway money? Whatever, he was certain she would find herself in Kal's old line, roaming the galaxy's card rooms as an itinerant gambler. He'd kept her bogus "333" card, frozen in its malfunctioned state, as a souvenir.

That was all he'd kept from the big payday. He'd been left with nearly twenty thousand coins after paying his debt to Mosep; Dodi had suggested giving it all to Minn, topping what the brothers had given her the night before as the biggest tip a rookie dealer had ever received. Kal, past questioning Dodi, had complied—to his ultimate benefit, as he learned on reporting to the casino offices to finalize his severance. Unbeknownst to Kal, Minn's mother had just joined the staff as the new director of hospitality—and her first act was to hire the pazaak hero as a floorwalker. Anyone capable of drawing a crowd like Kal's in the deadly hour before dawn stood a good chance of being an asset for the casino.

He was making good on that chance now—and greatly enjoying roaming the place while decked out in fine clothes, sharing his knowledge. For years, Kal had made a living observing other players—only to forget everything about them after they'd left the table. But that basic skill, repurposed and combined with his mind for minutiae, had already returned rewards.

As now. "How's it going, Salesbeing of the Year?"

Kedpin Shoklop turned from his seat at the zinbiddle table. "Master Sonmi! You remembered."

"Of course." Kal studied the puny pile of coins before the tubby creature. "Low stakes this afternoon?"

"I did everything you taught me, but I must not be doing it right." Kedpin's colossal eye grew fretful. "I started with so much—and frankly, I'm worried."

"It's a game," Kal said. "It's supposed to be fun." He clapped his hand on Kedpin's shoulder. "Consider every coin you bring into this room as already spent—spent on a good time. Maybe you'll get some back, or maybe you won't. But there's no sense ruining a good time with worry, is there?"

"No." Kedpin gazed upon him gratefully. "I needed to hear that."

"My pleasure."

Eavesdropping from the pit, Vestry looked at Kal and gently nodded as he stepped away. He didn't think she liked him any better, but now they were more clearly on the same team. Dealing from the next table over, Minn shot him a wink and a hidden thumbs-up.

"Looking good, my friend," Ganzer said as he hustled past Kal with a tray.

"Same," he said, patting his pal on the back. He was staying with Ganzer until he found a place. Kal liked the fact that, years after his encounter with the Jedi, Ganzer had been functioning as sort of a secret agent against cheats. He hoped Canto Bight was paying him for it. He deserved a day at the spa.

As for Kal, he intended to continue to play—but either in tournaments or for fun, and the latter only in certain company. He was taking his gloves off when the Suertons appeared.

"You're just in time," Kal said. "My shift's over."

"Lucky you," Wodi said. "There's a huge card game tonight on a yacht."

"A yacht that will be in the middle of a race at the time," Thodi said. "Interested?"

"Lose outside and win inside at the same time," Kal mused. "Wouldn't miss it."

"We'll head out in a bit," Wodi said, craning his neck to see where Ganzer had gone. He jostled Thodi. "Let's get a couple for the road."

"What road? It's a boat race," Thodi said as the two of them loped off, leaving Kal and Dodi behind. Kal reached into his pouch and handed Dodi some coins.

"What's this?" Dodi asked.

"It's the value of the Vermilion voucher, plus eight coins for the one you placed on the tournament table. I always pay my debts."

Dodi tossed the coins in the air and caught them all. "We'll bet it on something tonight together. Enjoying the new job?"

"You bet." Turning to walk the busy aisles with Dodi, he said, "You know, I came from a rough place—and there's a lot of bad stuff going on in the galaxy." He looked to his friend. "You ever feel guilty about this life?"

"Kal, have my brothers or I ever told you what our lives were like before, or where we came from?"

"No."

"Of course not—because people come to Canto Bight so as not to have to think about all that." He gestured to the casino floor, teeming with happy people. "When there's so much bad going on, it helps to know that there's a place where none of that matters."

"Got to have a paradise or two."

"Precisely." Dodi put his hand on Kal's back as they walked and raised the other hand in a grand gesture. "The galaxy doesn't need us to blow up starships. We are good at one thing: having fun, in a place built for it. And I say it is our solemn responsibility to have as much fun as possible, every waking moment."

Kal smiled. "We'd better do it, then." He draped his arm around Dodi and turned him around. "Hey, if we've got time, let's get in a few hands as riders over here. There's this guy at the zinbiddle table you might like. Real fun. Vaporator Salesbeing of the Year."

"Fascinating! Well, lead the way," Dodi said, reaching for his coins as they wandered into the crowd. "Er—what's a vaporator?"

"No idea. Just whatever you do, don't buy me one . . ."

ABOUT THE AUTHORS

SALADIN AHMED was born in Detroit and raised in a working-class, Arab American enclave in Dearborn, Michigan. His short stories have been nominated for the Nebula and John W. Campbell awards and have appeared in *Year's Best Fantasy* and numerous magazines, anthologies, and podcasts, as well as being translated into five languages. *Throne of the Crescent Moon* is his first novel. He lives near Detroit with his wife and twin children.

RAE CARSON is the *New York Times* bestselling author of award-winning speculative fiction, including the Girl of Fire and Thorns series and The Gold Seer Trilogy. Originally from California, she now lives in Arizona with her husband.

MIRA GRANT is the pseudonym of Hugo, Campbell, and Nebula award–winning author Seanan McGuire.

JOHN JACKSON MILLER is the *New York Times* bestselling author of *Star Wars: Kenobi, Star Wars: A New Dawn, Star Wars: Lost Tribe of the Sith*, and the *Star Wars Legends: The Old Republic* graphic novel collections from Marvel, among many other novels and comics. A comics industry analyst, he lives in Wisconsin with his wife, two children, and far too many comic books.

ABOUT THE TYPE

This book was set in Minion, a 1990 Adobe Originals typeface by Robert Slimbach (b. 1956). Minion is inspired by classical, old-style typefaces of the late Renaissance, a period of elegant, beautiful, and highly readable type designs. Created primarily for text setting, Minion combines the aesthetic and functional qualities that make text type highly readable with the versatility of digital technology.